KU-782-335

CONTROL

John Macken

CORGI BOOKS

TRANSWORLD PUBLISHERS
61–63 Uxbridge Road, London W5 5SA
A Random House Group Company
www.transworldbooks.co.uk

CONTROL
A CORGI BOOK: 9780552157575

First published in Great Britain
in 2010 by Bantam Press
an imprint of Transworld Publishers
Corgi edition published 2011

Copyright © John Macken 2010

John Macken has asserted his right under the Copyright, Designs
and Patents Act 1988 to be identified as the author of this work.

This book is a work of fiction and, except in the case of historical fact,
any resemblance to actual persons, living or dead, is purely coincidental.

A CIP catalogue record for this book
is available from the British Library.

This book is sold subject to the condition that it shall not,
by way of trade or otherwise, be lent, resold, hired out,
or otherwise circulated without the publisher's prior
consent in any form of binding or cover other than that
in which it is published and without a similar condition,
including this condition, being imposed on the
subsequent purchaser.

Addresses for Random House Group Ltd companies outside the UK
can be found at: www.randomhouse.co.uk
The Random House Group Ltd Reg. No. 954009

The Random House Group Limited supports The Forest Stewardship
Council® (FSC®), the leading international forest certification organisation.
All our titles that are printed on Greenpeace approved FSC® certified
paper carry the FSC® logo. Our paper procurement policy can be found
at www.randomhouse.co.uk/environment

Typeset in 12/15¼pt Sabon by
Kestrel Data, Exeter, Devon
Printed in the UK by
CPI Cox & Wyman, Reading, RG1 8EX

2 4 6 8 10 9 7 5 3 1

CONTROL

ABERDEENSHIRE LIBRARY & INFO SERV	
3055403	
Bertrams	17/10/2011
MYS Pbk	£6.99

ONE

1

'Hacksaw – that's a great word, don't you think?'

Dr Ian Gillick stared up at the man above him, listening to every nuance, observing every movement. He watched him pick the slender implement off the table, and imagined the cold metal handle warming to the man's touch.

'Not just sawing, but hacking as well. Two for the price of one.'

Dr Gillick didn't answer. His mouth was sealed shut with thick black gaffer tape. He could taste the adhesive on his tongue, and smell the plastic in his nostrils.

'Sawing sounds nice and neat and precise. Straight lines, measured progress, a clear objective. But hacking? That's just butchery, don't you think?'

Gillick stared past the man looking down at him, past his sickening stubble, the deep black pores of his skin, the red capillaries of his eyes. He focused on the ceiling, telling himself his only hope was not to react.

'I don't know where it came from or who invented it, but I like it.' Dr Gillick watched as the man ran his eyes along the thin serrated blade. 'I like it a lot.'

The man moved the hacksaw in front of Gillick's face, allowing him to inspect it in even greater detail. Hiding in the crevices were specks of red. An attempt had been made to clean it, fibres of cloth snagging, water creeping into the teeth, particles of rust beginning to brown the surface. Dr Gillick fought a sudden nausea. He bucked against the ties clamping him firmly in place.

'Words. Where they come from, what they mean. But then, as a scientist, you should understand all that.'

Gillick focused through the blade, its sharpness becoming blurred, its jagged profile blunt.

'The first one, he couldn't see the beauty either. But that's OK. We had different aims. His aim was to survive at any cost. Mine was to make him understand.'

The man raised his eyebrows, inviting the question, which didn't come, Gillick breathing hard through his nose, flexing against the ties, fighting to stay calm.

'You do understand why I'm here, don't you?'

Gillick grunted. It was as much noise as he had made for the past five minutes. He understood all right. At first it had been unreal, a different lifetime, events he had moved on from. But now it was as real as anything had ever been in his thirty-six years of existence.

'And you do understand how much this will hurt, Dr

Gillick? How much real, actual human pain you are about to feel? Sickening levels that will make you want to pass out, to die, anything but experience any more. And I want you to also understand that I will be doing everything I can to keep you alive and awake, so you can feel every tooth of the saw, every hack of the blade. And that I need you to watch carefully what I do with your fingertips after I've removed them. Exactly where I put them, and exactly how I do it.'

Gillick began to struggle more violently. The legs of the dining table he was tied to creaked and shook. But it was too wide and too heavy to move far. He had bought it four years ago from a shop specializing in reclaimed teak. It had needed three men to lift it into his flat. A couple of books and CDs dropped to the carpeted floor. Gillick began screaming into his sealed-off mouth, flailing his restrained limbs, sensing he was utterly trapped, panic overwhelming the calm.

The man standing above Dr Ian Gillick cast his eyes around the room, pausing for a second, taking it all in. Not bad, and a hell of a lot better than the place he was used to inhabiting these days. Deep wall colours, pale flooring, leather furniture, lots of wood. Not rich or luxurious, just plain and honest good taste.

He bent down and picked the cage off the floor. The smell infested his nostrils, sharp and piercing. 'Rattus *norvegicus*,' he said. 'The common rat. Hungry little fuckers as well. But that really needn't concern you.'

Gillick had ceased his futile attempts at escape. He was sucking air in through his nose, his cheeks red, his eyes wild and staring. The message was finally getting through.

'At least not yet.'

The man gripped the metal handle of the hacksaw tight in his right hand. With his left, he clenched Gillick's down-turned wrist, and pushed it hard into the table. 'Although now I think about the word, about the whole job it has to do, I can see some sense in it,' he added. 'First the hack, then the saw. Hacking through the flesh, sawing through the bone.' He lowered the blade. 'I'd never really thought about it before, but now there's a strange sort of beauty to it.'

The blade made contact with the three middle fingers. He rested it there, judging the line. Straight across and he could take the fingertips without touching the little finger or the thumb. Then he could do the little finger separately, and finally the thumb. Same for the right hand after that. Ten fingers with six main bouts of cutting.

Gillick's legs were shaking uncontrollably. His face was so pale that a thick blue vein was bulging down the centre of his forehead. His eyes were barely blinking, just fixed open in panic and horror.

A deep cleansing breath. First the hack, then the saw.

CONTROL

The rats were frantically scratching the plastic side of their cage, gnawing into the metal bars, climbing over each other to get out. He pulled the blade back, snagging through hairs and skin. And then he began slowly and methodically to work his way down to the bone.

2

Dr Reuben Maitland ran his long thin fingers over the spikes of the cactus plant. It stood on his new desk in a shallow brown saucer, tiny white stones covering the soil. A fine dust from the stones encircled the pot, just under its rim. Judging by the cleanness of the rest of the desk, the plant had been there some time, polished around by whoever came in and tidied the office each day.

Reuben examined it in more detail. The cactus was remote, the lush fruit of its body sitting serenely behind a barbed-wire exoskeleton. Protection radiating in all directions, fending off all-comers. The body was six inches high and tubular, the spines an inch long in every direction. Reuben had no idea what it was called in English, Latin or any other language. Botany was not his thing. He had clearly inherited the plant along with the office, the only piece of greenery among the browns, whites and greys. Probably, he guessed, it had been left over from the previous occupant, too sharp to carry home or dispose of easily. He glanced around the bare room. There was of course another option: it could be a small token to say hello, to welcome him back to GeneCrime. But if it was a welcome present, he told himself, it was one hell of an unfriendly one.

Reuben wrapped his right hand round the cactus. He started to squeeze slowly, long second after long second. Multiple points of contact between human and plant. He glanced up at the two internal windows on adjacent walls which opened into separate laboratories. Through the one-way glass he watched forensic scientists chatting, leaning on benches, shrugging themselves into lab coats, ambling around, calling across to each other or staring into computer screens. Reuben gripped harder, the spikes making tiny white pricks, bloodless indentations, in his skin. The left window opened into the Gross Debris lab, the right into the DNA lab. He flashed through the hours he had spent in each, the scientists he had trained and become friends with, the ones who had died, the ones who had survived.

The phone rang. One long trill followed by silence. An internal call. He looked down at his hand. A couple of spikes had broken through, droplets of blood appearing. The phone continued to sound. One second on, one second off. He let it ring another ten times. Then he glanced at his watch and sighed. He used his left hand to lift the receiver.

'Yes,' he said.

'Reuben? It's Sarah. You ready?'

Reuben glanced down at his right hand. Slowly, he let go of the plant. 'Yeah,' he grunted.

'You sure?'

'I guess I am.'

'They're in the Command Room. Meet you in the corridor. Two minutes.'

The call ended, and Reuben replaced the receiver. He sucked the blood from his palm, sensing the sweet iron taste of haemoglobin. The Command Room. He sighed. Here we go again.

He paced towards the door, pausing to get a good look through the adjacent windows. Gross Debris handling hairs, footprints, fibres. A more casual attitude clearly visible from his vantage point. A couple of forensic technicians slowly and methodically picking hairs from sections of Sellotape, matching fibres under a dual-light microscope. The DNA lab, by contrast, looked more precise and pressured. Scientists scanning elongated lists of sequences, pipetting minute volumes of liquids into tiny tubes. Different levels of detection with the same end point. And both of them about to get busy.

Reuben had a final scope of the office. A different room in the same building. Subterranean, no daylight, cooled air pumped in on a loop. Back again, he told himself. A year and a half away, and now a jumble of feelings he hadn't experienced for a long time. Excitement. Unease. Impatience. Ambition. The possibilities and the pitfalls. The pressure, the thrill of working in a team. The long troughs of endeavour, the short peaks of success. Everything came flooding back at once.

He took a second to compose himself, examining the army of small indentations in his palm, a few of them red, the rest white. 'Here we go,' he said quietly to himself, soft words that just escaped being sighed.

And then he opened the door and stepped out into the hallway.

3

Sarah Hirst had beaten him to it. She was standing at the end of the corridor, one leg bent at the knee, her foot resting against the wall. In her arms she had a couple of A4 files which she was pressing to her chest. She looked oddly like a schoolgirl loitering in a hallway, waiting impatiently for something better to happen. Reuben shook the idea from his head. DCI Hirst as anything but the unit commander was now unimaginable.

As Reuben approached, she said, 'Dr Maitland.'

'DCI Hirst,' he answered.

Sarah began walking. 'Just like the bad old days, eh? How does it feel to be back?'

'Scary.'

'Scared? You?'

'It's been a long time.'

'It's only been a year.'

'Eighteen months.'

'So what's your point? Ten years here and only eighteen months away. Blink of an eye.'

'Blink of a slow and painful eye that still feels bruised and swollen.'

They turned into another long walkway, thin blue carpet underfoot, the walls white, neon strips lighting the way. Standard civilian police decor.

'How's the office?' Sarah asked.

'What happened to my old one?'

'It's mine now. And before you say anything, finders keepers.'

'There's some sort of cactus on the desk.'

'Count yourself lucky.'

'Whose was it originally?'

'No idea. But like I said, finders keepers.'

They reached a set of concrete stairs and climbed three flights, Sarah quickly jogging up one at a time, Reuben taking two steps per stride. A thick double door led to another of GeneCrime's long straight corridors. The building was a five-storey box. Reuben wondered whether the architect had ever drawn anything without a ruler.

Sarah slowed. 'Here,' she said, unfolding a broadsheet newspaper from a cardboard file. 'Have a listen to this.'

Reuben suspected that Sarah spent a lot of her free time running, or in the gym, or doing whatever cardiac exercise came to hand. She was slim and fit, her movements nimble and quick. As she spoke, her breathing was barely any different, despite having just jogged up three flights of stairs.

'"Police have officially linked the second death, of scientist Dr Ian Gillick, thirty-six, to the murder of a man found at his home last week in" blah blah blah.' She turned to Reuben and a mischievous grin lit up her features. 'Here's the interesting bit. "Police sources revealed that the case is being handed over to GeneCrime, the elite but controversial Forensics division based in Euston. Tellingly, Dr Reuben Maitland, thirty-nine, recently reinstated to GeneCrime, will be overseeing the investigation." New paragraph.' Sarah grinned again. 'You ready for some more?'

Reuben raised his eyebrows. 'I'm thirty-eight,' he said.

'Either way, here we go.' They pushed through another set of off-white double doors, Sarah scanning the paper. 'They've gone to town on you big time. "Dr Maitland was implicated in a previous incident of serious misconduct and dismissed from the Forensic Science Service eighteen months ago. That case involved the use of pioneering forensic techniques by Dr Maitland to profile the lover of his now former wife Lucy Maitland, and resulted in the arrest of Shaun Graves, a junior partner in the corporate law firm of Bostock and Tuson."'

Reuben noted that Sarah could barely keep the glee out of her voice. He walked on, appreciating that this was a long way from how he had imagined the start of his first day back.

'"Mr Graves, thirty-six, subsequently received a five-figure settlement from the Metropolitan Police for false imprisonment and arrest. The reinstatement of Dr Maitland is bound to be seen in some quarters of the Met as inappropriate, so soon after a charge of serious misconduct and the ensuing legal fallout."'

'I wish they'd get their facts right,' Reuben said dourly. 'It wasn't serious misconduct.'

'No?'

'No. It was *improper* conduct.'

'Shhh. It gets better. They've done a biog on you.'

'Sounds painful.'

'"Dr Maitland formerly headed the Forensics section of GeneCrime before his dismissal. He was a regular contributor to the general media, writing articles for this newspaper as well as several others, and appearing occasionally on television and radio—"'

'What paper is this?'

'The *Independent*. Will you shut up?'

Sarah was enjoying herself. Reuben walked on in silence. Ten metres ahead of them a large wood-effect door was marked Command Room. He felt his stomach tighten involuntarily.

'"Inside the force, Dr Maitland has a reputation as a maverick scientist, a fierce obsessive who has pioneered several forensic breakthroughs."' Sarah stopped in front of the Command Room door and lowered the paper. 'I could go on. Maybe I should have walked slower. So, Mr Fierce Obsessive, with the improper conduct record, are you ready to join the big time again?'

Reuben grabbed the paper and quickly scanned what was left. He saw his son Joshua's name, the term 'acute lymphocytic leukaemia', the hospital he had been treated in, the wonderful word 'remission', his wife's name and the not-so-wonderful word 'estranged'. They had been thorough. The press as detectives. Digging, enquiring, speculating. It would be an interesting experiment to get a good reporter on to a serious crime, see if they dug up the truth quicker than CID or Forensics.

'How do the press get all this?' he said, almost to himself.

'Maybe because we brief them every single bloody day.'

'There used to be a time when the force's movements were not for public consumption.'

There was a moment of silence, Reuben's words hanging in the artificial light. He examined Sarah out of the corner of his eye. As pretty and hassled as ever, blonde hair restrained, mouth slightly pursed, a frown breaking like a slow wave across her forehead.

'Shall we?' she asked.

Reuben handed back the paper. At the top, the headline proclaimed 'Police Link Deaths of Two Fingerless Men'.

A cold nervousness continued to burrow into his stomach. His mobile phone started vibrating inside his pocket. Two plainclothes CID officers hesitated, then entered the room ahead of them. Sarah passed him one of her files, and gripped the door handle.

'Let's catch some killers,' she said.

4

In her right hand Lucy Maitland held on to the training reins that kept her two-year-old son tethered within a few feet of her. The reins were a new weapon in the battle to keep Joshua from running off as fast as his short little legs would carry him. All morning Lucy had felt like the centre point of a circle, the reins a radius, Joshua orbiting around her in a tight circumference. On the bus it was different, however, his progress hampered by seats and passengers. She stared at him while she waited for Reuben to answer. He was straining against her, wanting to explore the full length of the aisle, occasionally wailing in frustration as his progress was halted. In a couple of minutes Lucy would harness him in an altogether more defeating fashion. She would strap him back in his buggy, with its double belts that crossed at the shoulder and hip, a system of binding that would require some bribery.

Lucy's call was finally answered by the single word 'yes'.

'Reuben,' she said. 'It's Lucy.'

Her ex-husband cleared his throat. 'I'm just about to enter the Command Room.'

'I'm sorry.'

'You weren't to know.'

This is what it has become, Lucy thought with a sigh, holding the weight of Joshua in check. Brief sentences, a brusque politeness, functional communication.

Reuben seemed to soften. 'Look, I was going to call you in an hour or so anyway. How did it go?'

Lucy hesitated, savouring the moment. Good news shouldn't be rushed, particularly when it had been in such short supply recently. 'He's been passed over to the long-term medical team, who have reviewed his progress.'

'And?'

'The new team are extremely happy with Joshua's progress. Blood counts good, all traces of anaemia finally gone, clean bill of health since the last check-up. Dr Khiara, he's the oncologist, and Dr Morgan, the haematologist, reckon we're very probably out of the woods.'

Lucy heard her ex-husband breathe out. It was slow and measured, an exhalation of relief.

'Fantastic,' he said. 'Where are you?'

'On the way back. Going to drop him at nursery and then head into the office.'

'I would have been there. If, you know . . .'

'I know. Anyway, I just thought I'd let you know what they had to say.'

Reuben was quiet again. Lucy heard a door open and close a couple of times in the background and tried to picture him back at work, serious, focused, reverting to his former self. She appreciated that Joshua's three-month check-up had come on a difficult day.

'You still there?' she asked. 'The reception isn't great.'

'I'm still here,' he answered. 'And that really is fantastic news. Thank you.'

From the tone of his voice, Lucy knew he was ending the conversation.

'I'll maybe talk to you later,' she said.

'Yeah. Sorry, got to get things moving here.' Above his voice, a door scraped open and banged shut again. 'But thanks, Luce. Bye.'

'Bye.'

Lucy slotted her phone into the depths of her handbag, and pulled out a yoghurt drink. She showed it to Joshua, feeling a fresh wave of relief wash through her. A clean bill of health. It didn't get much better than that. Joshua scampered towards her, unsteady on his feet as the elongated London bus took a corner, the reins that had held him back now keeping him upright. He reached for the drink with both hands, a toothy smile on his face, a dimple on his right side, just like his father, his pale cheeks rosy after his constrained efforts to explore the bus.

'Dink, dink, dink!' he squealed.

Lucy held it just out of reach. 'Not till you're in your buggy,' she said.

Bribery and coercion. The two cornerstones of parenting, Lucy told herself. It was no wonder so many people turned out so bad.

She lifted Joshua up and kissed his cheek. Then she stood and shuffled towards the doors, grabbing Joshua's buggy and unfolding it in one practised movement. She strapped her son in and finally handed him the yoghurt drink.

The bus slowed, and Lucy pushed forward, closer to the doors. She checked her son. He had managed to tip most of the yoghurt down his front. Lucy cursed silently. She had forgotten the wet-wipes. The euphoria of Joshua's remission was already fading as she left the bus. Parenting was difficult enough with two of you. With just one it was nearly impossible – something she had recently been telling Reuben with increasing frequency.

5

The Command Room was long and thin, almost an extension of one of GeneCrime's many corridors. A table ran nearly the whole length, its occupants facing one another, their legs close to touching beneath the wooden surface. Reuben shuffled to the far end of the room, while Sarah remained closest to the door. They pulled their chairs out in unison, and the background chatter of the fifteen or so staff ceased.

DCI Sarah Hirst sat forward in her chair. 'OK,' she said, 'let's get cracking. Those of you lucky enough not to have been stuck here over the weekend will doubtless have seen the papers, who seem to know more about ongoing crime than we do. Two men missing the tips of their fingers, cause of death not confirmed at the moment.' Sarah took in a sweep of the assembled CID officers, forensic scientists and support staff. 'You will be thrilled to know that GeneCrime have been tasked with investigating. The Met have asked us as a matter of urgency to identify the killer or killers. It's what we do quickly, and it's what we do well.'

Sarah smiled at Reuben, and he took a deep breath, his reservations dissipating in an instant. The hardest part had been waiting, being away, having the time to think about everything. But now, back in the fold, at the very start of a new investigation, that was the thrill which overcame all the doubts. He realized that he was born for this, the hunt for the truth, the search for people who killed and raped and maimed.

'And of course,' Sarah continued, 'today marks the return to GeneCrime of Dr Maitland, who is going to lead this investigation. Be nice to him. He might be slightly rusty after forgetting which side of the law is the right one for so long.'

There were a couple of low noises halfway between laughs and grunted acknowledgements of the truth. Three or four of the Forensics team nodded and smiled. Reuben scanned the room, naming names, reacquainting himself with faces. Bernie Harrison, bearded and scruffy. Mina Ali, bony and slightly gaunt. Simon Jankowski, pale skin, loud shirt. Paul Mackay, cropped hair, unusually smart for a scientist. A couple of CID made reassuring faces: Helen Alders, slim and boyish, and Leigh Harding, broad and fair. The support staff and IT largely ignored him. Chris Stevens from

Pathology doodled in a notebook. It was as good a welcome as he was going to get.

'Dr Maitland?' Sarah said, raising her eyebrows. 'Would you care to say a few words?'

Reuben nudged his chair back across the carpet and stood up slowly. 'OK. No speeches, but it's good to be back, and it's nice to see some familiar faces.' He opened the cardboard folder that Sarah had given him and slid its contents on to the table. 'Now, as DCI Hirst said, over the weekend CID have officially linked two shocking and unusual murders. A sales executive was killed a week or so ago. The killing on Friday of a scientist shows striking similarities. Both victims had the tips of all their fingers removed, possibly with a saw of some sort. Worse, the fingertips were left inside a cage housing a couple of rats. The symbolism of this feels a little clumsy, but there may be more to it than we think at this stage. We shall see. Either way, we are about to embark upon an intense and high-profile investigation.'

Reuben forced himself to slow down, to suppress his eagerness to get started. People have died in horrible ways, he told himself. You have to coordinate a thorough and methodical search for their killer. Don't ever make the mistake of enjoying this.

He glanced across at one of the IT support team. 'Do we have visuals?'

A thin, nervous male slid a remote control towards

him. 'Just press the left button to flick through.'

Reuben turned to face a flatscreen monitor behind him. 'Those of you who've just had breakfast might want to look away.' Whatever was on the screen was going to be nasty. Despite his impatience to get the investigation started, he knew he would feel the same mild nausea he always felt when confronted with the violent loss of a human life, the ending of one person's hopes and dreams. At least he hadn't eaten. He hadn't felt like it.

He pointed the remote and clicked the button. The image of a man lying on a kitchen floor filled the screen. It was bad, but not enough to make him pause for more than a couple of seconds.

'I'm guessing this is in situ, at the victim's house?'

Reuben began to run his eyes rapidly across the image, mining it for information. It was the first time he had seen it, but several things struck him simultaneously. Nice floor tiles. Expensive units. The rat cage. Signs of a struggle: two spoons on the floor, a broken mug in the corner of the shot. A lot of blood. Enough, in fact, to suggest the victim had still been alive when most of the blood loss took place. Small sprays of red on the fridge and a cabinet confirmed that the body hadn't been moved, and that this was where the murder had taken place. He flicked to the next picture. The same image but with evidence tags, bright yellow plastic markers with black numbers at their centre. The rat cage was number 4, the broken mug number 7. He forwarded again. A close-up of the victim's right hand. Congealed stumps lacking fingernails and final phalanges, crudely squared off, oozing thick clotted redness. He peered into the screen. A series of parallel scratches were visible close to the cage. Reuben realized suddenly that the killer wanted his victim to see the rats, to watch what they did.

'The rats were for him,' he said, 'not for us.'

'What do you mean?' Sarah asked.

'It's a fairly spooky thing to do, and a difficult one as well. Taking live animals in a cage to the house of someone you want to kill. Not the sort of thing a spontaneous killer does. This takes planning. Therefore it must be important. Now the question is, important to whom? To the victim, to the police, to the public at large, or a message to the next victim? Plenty of killers leave us things, miscellaneous stuff to throw us off the scent, bizarre items their mental illness persuades them would be a good idea.'

'But you think the rats are for the deceased?' Sarah said. She glanced down at her own cardboard folder. 'A Mr Carl Everitt?'

'Look at the position of the cage. It's close to the victim's head, eye level almost. The killer was making Mr Everitt watch what happened to his fingertips. He didn't shove them between the bars, even though he could have reached, and the bars are just wide enough. This wasn't about live rats chewing his fingers down. It was about what happened after they were removed.'

'I don't know about anyone else, but this is giving me the creeps.' Dr Bernie Harrison scratched his beard for a couple of seconds. 'It reminds me of Winston Smith in *1984*.'

'Why, what did he do?' Detective Leigh Harding asked. 'Is he still banged up?'

Reuben watched closely as Bernie's smile got lost somewhere in the thick brown hair that covered his face. Literate Forensics versus less literate CID.

'As in the book *1984*,' Bernie answered. 'Orwell's hero threatened with a cage of rats gnawing into his face.'

'I thought—'

'We all know what you thought, Detective Harding,' Sarah interjected, 'but can we get back to the current year's events, and not those of a fictionalized future now set in the past?'

Detective Harding remained silent, a pained coldness about his clean-shaven face. Reuben sensed the gulf between the two sides of the narrow table, just as wide as it had ever been. CID officers who had shown exceptional aptitude on other cases headhunted for GeneCrime. Talented forensic scientists and bio-statisticians recruited from industry and academia. All bright people with sharp minds, but very different personalities and backgrounds. An uneasy mix, but a gifted one nonetheless.

'I think there's one other significant thing here,' Reuben said, turning back to the screen. 'The patterns on the slate floor tiles near the fingers. Difficult to spot from a distance, but there are red striations on the tiles that lie almost exactly perpendicular to the sprays of blood on some of the kitchen units. The fingers have been removed here, the killer pushing downwards, through skin, flesh, bone and out again the other side, before scratching into the stone surface.' Reuben turned back to the occupants of the room. 'So what does this tell us?'

'He's strong,' Detective Helen Alders answered, her boyish face frowning. 'Or this was done in a frenzied hurry.'

'A frenzy, no,' Reuben said. 'You don't carefully place a cage of rats near the victim's head and then set about removing his fingers all in a frenzy. But strong I would agree with. There's no obvious evidence of restraint.'

'What you're saying,' Mina Ali interjected, 'is that you don't just hold a fully grown man down and saw his phalanges off.'

'Not unless you've married him first,' Reuben muttered under his breath. 'But no.'

Reuben smiled at Mina and she grinned back, a lopsided toothy grin, her eyes wrinkling behind her glasses. His new deputy, the senior forensic scientist who was going to make his life a hell of a lot more bearable than it had been before he left.

'So how did he do it?'

'This is what I want everyone to think about.' Reuben peered down at his notes to check the name. 'Carl Everitt was five eleven. Looking at him, he probably weighed in at twelve stone or so. How do you control someone like that for long enough to do what you've got to do?'

Reuben ran his eyes around the group. No one wanted to say anything. The room was silent except for the ever-present hum of the air conditioning. Somewhere in and around that lurked the buzz of the neon strip lights. The question floated unanswered in the windowless atmosphere.

'OK,' Reuben said finally, 'let's get some coffees in here. Someone grab me a tea. Let's drink and think.'

6

Reuben spent half an hour flicking through photos, reading lab reports, checking times and dates, writing lists of questions and studying inventories of crime-scene objects. From time to time he sipped at the tea in his old GeneCrime mug. It had been with him from the start. Originally it was silver in colour, but this had long since perished, leaving a mottled grey and black covering. In all his time in the unit, no one had ever asked to borrow it, and no one had attempted to steal it when they lost their own mug. It reminded him for a second of the cactus, an object that survived simply because it was unappealing to the touch. Reuben took another sip, the tea now almost cold.

In the background, Forensics and CID combed through their own notes, cross-checking with each other, exchanging ideas. The hum of conversation was getting louder and Reuben knew it was time to get the meeting going again.

His mobile vibrated, and he flicked back to the conversation he had had with Lucy, the relief in her voice, the implication that the dark days were behind them. He thought briefly of his son, and the fact that he was on the mend. He checked the screen of his phone, which registered an unknown caller. Reuben hesitated, then pressed answer.

'Yes?' he said.

'Dr Maitland?'

'Yes.'

'I have your son.'

'What?'

'Your two-year-old son Joshua. I have him here.'

Reuben got out of his chair and walked unsteadily over to the window.

'Who is this?'

'Someone I hope you will never meet.'

'Look, I don't know what you're talking about. He's with my ex-wife. I spoke to her half an hour ago.'

'A lot can happen in thirty minutes.'

The sound of a crying child in the background. A clawing resonance in the gentle sobbing. Something painfully familiar in the voice.

'Who are you?' Reuben repeated.

A second's pause. A rasping breath through the receiver.

'The man who is in the papers, the one you are hunting.'

'Which man?'

'The one who takes fingers.'

'Where's my ex-wife?'

'Looking for your child. But she won't find him because I have him.'

The ticking of the Command Room clock. The room quietening down, staff waiting for the meeting to resume. A deafening throb beginning to beat through Reuben's temples. This couldn't be right. He checked his watch. Half an hour, forty minutes at the most.

'Listen to me. I am the wrong sort of person to prank-call. Entirely the wrong sort of person.'

'This is no prank, Dr Maitland. And in a second I will prove it. I have your son, and you'd better get your head around that now.'

A coldness surged in Reuben's chest, a tightening in his stomach. Panic started to set in, implications stabbing home, a hammer blow of understanding arriving late.

'What do you want?' Reuben asked, as calmly as he could.

'That you don't try and find me.'

Reuben glanced over his shoulder. Some of the fifteen faces were monitoring him with a variety of expressions.

Boredom. Indifference. Mild curiosity. A couple of Forensics were chatting to each other. A CID officer studied one of the sheets from Reuben's file. Another had walked over to stare at the image of a mutilated hand. Two support staff were tapping into laptops. He saw Sarah glance impatiently at her watch. But time had utterly stopped for Reuben.

The voice in his ear continued. 'You can speak to him. Ten seconds, that's all.'

There was a scraping noise – the phone obviously being moved. Reuben heard the sound of his son's distress intensify.

'Joshua, this is Daddy. Are you OK, little fella? Where's Mummy?'

Joshua said the word 'Daddy' and started crying louder, unmistakable and unique sounds hardwired into Reuben's recognition centres.

'Don't cry. Mummy will be there soon. Mummy and Daddy love you very much.'

Joshua's crying became more irregular, interrupted by jagged breaths, deep intakes of air. Reuben bunched the fist of his other hand, fingernails digging hard into his palm. Any lingering disbelief had just evaporated. Joshua was with this man, crying and scared.

More scraping noises told him the phone was moving back again.

'Spell out exactly what you want,' Reuben said evenly.

'Just this, Dr Maitland. Do nothing to catch me. Say nothing to anyone. If your team makes any progress towards finding me, your son will die.'

'Why?'

'I need one more person, and then I will stop for good. This one deserves to die, just like the other two. He has committed an atrocity against society and will commit others. This is natural justice. The sort you secretly approve of. You are not to interfere, or your son will die. And you've seen what I'm capable of.'

Reuben pictured Joshua's tiny hand and its delicate fingers. He looked over at the door. He wanted to be out in the corridor shouting at this fucker, telling him that he was going to find him and make him pay. But he was stuck at the far end of the room, trying to sound as normal as he possibly could as his heart and stomach and head felt crushed and sick and horrified.

'And if I don't?' Reuben said quietly.

'I will know. I've set you a trap, Dr Maitland. A big messy horrible trap. If you track me down, or I even sense that you're trying, Joshua will die instantly.'

'And I'm supposed to believe that?'

'Believe what you want. But a life for a life, that's what I'm offering you. You let me kill one more person, someone who deserves to die, and I'll disappear for ever.'

In the background, Joshua's sobs were sounding more and more broken and uneven. Reuben closed his eyes, drawn into the distress of his son, feeling it burrow deep into his soul, tugging at his composure. The sound of your only child, scared, alone, trapped with a stranger.

'If you do anything,' Reuben said quietly, his teeth clenched together, 'anything at all, I will—'

'You'll do nothing. I'm in control, not you. And don't make the mistake of letting this get personal, Dr Maitland. This isn't about you or your family. This is about me.'

'How the fuck is it not personal?' Reuben hissed. 'You have my only son.'

'Like I say, this is just business. A trade. A swap. An agreement. A bargaining position.'

'You sick fucking—'

The line went dead. A nothingness in his ear. Joshua cut off, isolated from him, taken away.

Out of the corner of his eye, Reuben sensed Sarah giving him disapproving looks. A couple of others were raising their eyebrows, their curiosity ebbing. This had just been Daddy Talk, Reuben talking to his son at work.

He slowly placed the phone back in his pocket, his mind racing. The killer of two men holding his son. Was he telling the truth? How had he got Joshua? How had he known about his son?

He walked back to his chair and sat down, his head filling with images and questions, plans and strategies. Tell no one, the killer had said. Stop the investigation dead. I am in control. Reuben needed to buy some time, talk to Lucy, see what the real situation was. He took his phone out again.

Someone cleared their throat. The team was waiting. Fifteen bright and impatient minds looking from Reuben to the screen and back again. Legs shuffling under the narrow desk. Feet almost touching, grinding into the carpet with nervous energy, a killer to catch. A paralysing moment of indecision. The air conditioning kicking in for a few seconds, blowing its cooled and filtered air around the room and then resting again. And Sarah, staring at him.

'Dr Maitland?'

'Right,' Reuben muttered. 'Where were we?'

'How do you cut someone's fingers off without tying them up,' Mina Ali prompted.

Reuben cleared his throat. He stared into the keypad of his phone for a second, memorizing the numbers. 'Any ideas yet?' he said. As he waited for an answer, he typed the number from memory: 2255#63#669. A code, like the triplet code of DNA. Translated by predictive text into Call Me Now.

Simon Jankowski spoke first. 'He knocks the man out elsewhere, then takes him to the kitchen and kills him there.'

'And why would he do that?' Reuben asked as he entered Lucy's eleven-digit number and pressed send.

'I don't know.' Simon bit into the inside of his cheek.

'From what I've read, it doesn't look like the same MO as the other death.'

The other death. Reuben put down his phone and reached for the remote control. Two bodies so far, one more promised, and then he would stop. That was what he had said. Everything now personal, related to Joshua, small significances looming large.

'Let's have a look,' Reuben muttered. He flicked through several other slides of Carl Everitt. Then the backgrounds changed – a different house, rich interior wall colours, lots of wood. A solid dining table, looking down on it. Reuben pictured a police photographer balancing on a chair to get the angle right. A man tied to it, rope digging into one wrist, passing under the sturdy table and wrapping around the other wrist. The man on his back. Reuben scanned a piece of paper on his desk but couldn't find what he was looking for.

'Dr Ian Gillick,' Sarah prompted.

Reuben glanced quickly at her then turned back to the screen, taking it all in, mining it for fresh information, anything that might pertain to his son. Ian Gillick was on his back. His fingertips were missing. Pools of dark redness had seeped over the edge of the table, most of it dripping heavily on to the wooden floor, some of it running along the ropes that bound his wrists. A plastic cage with metal bars sat near Gillick's head. A different cage to the last one, smaller, scruffier.

Out of the corner of his eye, Reuben monitored his phone, willing it to ring, Lucy saying there's obviously been some sort of mistake, Joshua's here with me, safe and well. The phone sat silent and still, a lump of plastic and glass, inert and unmoved by human emotion.

'You're right, Simon,' Reuben said. 'This one is different. He looks to have been incapacitated and then bound.' Reuben pointed the remote control at the screen. 'Blood sprays on the CD rack there to the left. His fingertips were removed here. But again, how do you remove someone's fingers without them moving their hands? He's only tied at the wrist. Why didn't he ball his fists up?'

The phone remained lifeless. Reuben tried to slow his breathing.

'Could they pass out with the pain of having one fingertip removed?' Simon asked. 'And then the others are easy?'

Reuben shook his head, almost absently, barely hearing the response for the hundreds of thoughts and scenarios bouncing around his skull, smashing into one another. A few seconds of telephone conversation that threatened to change everything. Mere words that felt real and not real at the same time. 'I don't think so.' Joshua alone with the man who had done this. A two-year-old boy with a fully grown psychopath. 'You might black out for a bit, but surely you'd come round again.' A cold ache was beginning to burrow inwards from each temple, grinding through his frontal lobes.

Reuben looked up at the man across the table from him. 'Chris, you're the closest thing we have to a real doctor. You care to comment?'

Dr Chris Stevens stopped doodling in his pad. 'Pathologists *are* real doctors,' he said. 'It's just that our patients complain less.'

While Dr Stevens outlined the intense nervous system of the fingers, and the concentration of pain receptors near the tips, Reuben focused on the words the killer had spoken to him, and the noises his son had made. He stared at his phone again, increasingly sensing that this was no mistake, that Lucy failing to return his text was an ominous sign.

7

Reuben checked the reception on his mobile. One bar, cutting in and out, flashing as the phone signal wafted back and forth. A frail electronic waveform struggling to penetrate a solid room with thick walls and a concrete floor. Still nothing from Lucy. Nearly an hour since his text, and absolute silence. Lucy always carried her phone, always had it switched on, always had it charged and ready. It was her home, her work, her social circle. Almost everything in Lucy's life was filtered through that small chunk of plastic. She had called him earlier so she clearly had it with her. Yet she was silent now.

They had filed out of the Command Room, along the stretched corridors of GeneCrime, back down concrete stairs and into the depths of the building where the morgue lay. Reuben watched Dr Chris Stevens pull open an elongated steel drawer, which glided out in deferential silence. He dialled Lucy's number. Nothing, the phone flashing the words 'no signal'. Dr Stevens rolled back a blue plastic sheet to reveal Ian Gillick's face. An expression of horror remained, clinging to the corners of his open mouth and the glazed whites of his eyes. Reuben dialled again, picturing Dr Gillick's journey. Being untied from his dining table. Lifted on to a stretcher and straight into a body bag. Being carried out of his house. A black unmarked Ford Transit transporting him across London. Slipping through the traffic, no external indication of what was inside. Stopping at red lights and pedestrian crossings, the diesel engine idling, living people standing inches away from the dead. The phone showed a symbol that suggested it was trying to connect. After a few more seconds, it cut out. Dr Stevens walked over and pulled on the handle of another brushed-steel drawer.

Reuben cast his eyes over the forensic scientists and CID officers staring silently at the corpse. He reflected on the power he now had. It hadn't felt like power before today. If anything, it was an inconvenience, a responsibility, a set of behaviours to adopt and a book of regulations to uphold. Being in charge rarely felt like control or authority. Rather, Reuben believed that managing teams of people was like opening the door to a fuck of a lot of problems that threatened to wash you away on a daily basis. Of course there were small perks, but these were set against the huge and overwhelming fucker of having to manage a disparate group of human beings. And in GeneCrime, that meant the bright and the fragile, the gifted and the unpredictable.

He tried Lucy's number again, gritting his teeth as he dialled.

Reuben was well aware that he had stumbled into authority rather than sought it out. And here he was, back in charge of GeneCrime Forensics. But he saw now that his power had one important perk: it could keep his son alive. Delay the investigation, push things in the wrong direction, make poor strategic choices. All of these could placate the killer for a while, protect Joshua from harm, if that's what needed to be done.

The pathologist pulled back the blue plastic sheet that hid Carl Everitt from view. Reuben wondered momentarily why all GeneCrime bodies were covered in sheets, despite being buried deep in a metal racking system. Everitt looked similarly shocked, an aftertaste of horror remaining in his doughy features.

The phone had given up on dialling and was displaying its usual photographic image: Joshua on the first official day of remission, staring directly into the camera, smiling, small gaps between each tooth, gaps that spoke of future growth. The cold ache between Reuben's temples was getting sharper and more intense, pushing and squeezing his frontal lobes. He clenched his fist and opened it slowly. Several of the cactus holes were bleeding, as if the pressure in his skull was forcing the blood out of him.

Act naturally, he told himself. Don't panic. Don't do anything until you've spoken with Lucy.

He tried again. This time, from somewhere in the ether, two bars of reception appeared. Dr Chris Stevens looked like he was ready to speak. Reuben turned away, jamming the phone hard against his ear. After four rings the call went through to Lucy's messaging system. Reuben cursed. When it was finally ready for him, he whispered his message: 'Luce, it's Reuben. Ring me the second you get this. If I don't answer, keep ringing. I have to speak to you.'

He replaced the phone in his pocket, his mind still racing. Lucy not answering the text, her phone going through to messages. He thought about running out of the morgue, out of GeneCrime, into his car, speeding round to Lucy's house. But he had no idea if she was there. All he knew was that his son was missing, and now his ex-wife. Maybe they were together. Maybe they had both been snatched. He shook his head quickly, almost a twitch, and rubbed his face. Despite the cold still air of the morgue, Reuben was sweating.

'Getting squeamish in your old age, Dr Maitland?' Chris Stevens asked. 'You look awfully pale.'

Reuben managed something approaching a smile. 'I'm not that badly out of practice.' In the absence of any clear notion of what to do, he had to learn as much about the killer as possible. 'So, what can you tell us?'

'OK.' Chris was standing between the bodies, both still on their trays, staring blindly into the strip lighting, arms by their sides, feet inside the rack. Ian Gillick was to the left of Dr Stevens, Carl Everitt to the right. The pathologist grabbed Ian's left hand and Carl's right. 'First thing to note is that there are serrations on the second and third phalanges of both victims. These weren't clean cuts. The saw slipped a few times before digging into bone and getting started. This could suggest some amount of struggle on behalf of the victim, or else a fairly reckless bout of sawing.'

Reuben watched the GeneCrime pathologist pull two clear plastic tubes out of his lab coat pocket. They rattled together as he screwed their white lids open. He up-ended them one at a time. Reuben strained for a better look.

'These are a couple of fingertips we retrieved from the cages. One from each victim. As far as I have been able to see, neither of them has sustained substantial rodent damage.' Dr Stevens lined up one short stubby fingertip with a finger on Gillick's hand. Reuben noted that it was only a couple of centimetres long, half of it made up of nail, the rest a sick shade of off-white flesh. 'If you look closely, you'll notice that the tissue of the amputated phalange is also jagged. I have dissected a couple of the others, and the bone is pretty smooth. Now, this confirms that the implement used was definitely a saw.'

'As opposed to what?' Sarah asked sharply.

'Bolt cutters. A cigar chopper. A sword. Whatever else might relieve someone of the tips of their fingers. Cutting, as opposed to sawing, inevitably results in fragmentation and compression, splinters of bone detaching themselves. And another thing to note: most of the joints are intact. The killer hasn't tried to saw between the ligaments which bind the phalanges.'

'What else?' Reuben asked. 'Anybody?'

Mina Ali cleared her throat, the noise bouncing sharply off the low ceiling. 'What do you think about fingerprinting the fingertips?'

'Lifting a fingerprint off a fingerprint?'

Mina nodded slowly. 'I know it sounds weird, but the killer could have left imprints on the amputated digits.'

'Not sure that would work,' Reuben said. 'But you're right, we should swab for DNA in case the killer wasn't wearing gloves.' Immediately, a rush of other ideas came to Reuben, things they could try, unconventional approaches that might work. But he kept them to himself.

'But won't the fingers be contaminated with rat DNA?' Sarah asked.

'Probably,' Mina answered. 'We should be able to differentiate rat DNA from human, though.'

A low rumble of discussion followed, which Dr Stevens cut into. 'I think what we're really missing here is something important, something I haven't made my mind up about yet.'

'What?' Reuben asked.

'The actual cause of death. Would you lose enough blood through your fingertips to bleed to death, or is the blood supply insufficient? I mean, we're hardly talking about arteries here.'

'So what else are you proposing?'

'Death by trauma, or death by something we haven't checked for yet.'

'Like what?' Reuben scanned the torsos of Ian Gillick and Carl Everitt. A few bruises here and there, but no significant wounds. Some redness around Everitt's neck, and deep abrasions around Gillick's wrists and ankles where he had been tied. But no major fatal wounding. He thought again about his son, his delicate white flesh, his chubby arms and legs, his small frail body.

'They haven't exactly been clubbed to death,' Sarah said.

'I know,' Dr Stevens said, picking up both hands again, uniting the corpses as if they were forming a human chain. 'I've only had a cursory look while Forensics have been doing the obvious testing. I need to examine airways, internal bleeding, all sorts of things we pathologists like to do.'

There was a sudden vibration in Reuben's pocket. His phone was ringing. He snatched it out. The display said 'Lucy'. Reuben took a couple of quick paces away into the corner.

'Luce?'

'Reuben, I've got some terrible news. I'm so sorry. I don't know how to tell you. It just happened completely out of the blue, a few minutes after I rang you. I don't know . . .' Lucy was sobbing, her usually measured voice spilling out thick and fast, as torn and ragged as Joshua's. She took a deep breath. 'Reuben, Joshua is missing. I'm with the police.'

Reuben wondered how he should react. This was confirmation that the worst event in his life so far was true. But if he was going to keep his son alive, he had to be hearing this for the first time.

'What do you mean "missing"?' he asked.

'Taken. Snatched. Disappeared . . .'

'Fuck,' Reuben said, a little too loudly. 'I'll come down.'

'I'm heading back to the house.'

'Right. I'll see you there.'

He ended the call and walked over to Sarah, who was staring intently at a mark on Ian Gillick's neck. 'Sarah, I've got to run. Something extremely serious has happened to Joshua. I'll call.' And with that, Reuben paced out of the morgue and into the corridor, speeding up, starting to run, tilting forward, crashing through double doors, past security and out into the car park, his worst fears assailing him, adrenalin surging through his body.

8

The unmarked Volvo S60 was white and squat, wedged between concrete pillars. Reuben jumped in. He smelled the seductive plastic scent of a nearly new car. Then he fired the engine and screeched off, circling down the multi-storey, heading rapidly towards the exit.

The north London streets were quieter than when he had arrived at GeneCrime. The rush hour had been in full grinding swing, but now there were gaps to aim at, openings to lunge into, lanes to slew across. As he sped through the traffic, silent and focused, he let the past two hours of his life catch up with him. His first day back in charge. The start of a new case. Two bodies with horrific and unusual injuries. The killer calling him. His son's distressed voice in the background. The deal: a life for a life. Forensic immunity on one more killing for his son back safe and well.

Reuben took a roundabout at speed, barely checking

his mirrors. His heart was racing, his pupils wide, his hands tight on the steering wheel. But the headache was clearing. And it was freeing up room for intense concentration. The question at the centre, as always, was why? Why kill three people and then promise to stop? Why go to the lengths of snatching a child? Why feel the need to subvert forensic evidence? Why not just be careful, wear gloves, leave nothing behind at the scene? Why target the head of the forensics team trying to catch you? The hows could come later. For now, as Reuben hurtled through junctions and intersections, he occupied himself with the whys.

Reuben lowered his window, an icy blast of November air streaming in and slapping his face. He knew that he was under pressure from above to solve this crime quickly. Fingerless corpses made large headlines in newspapers. Sarah had fought for his reinstatement, against the wishes of powerful senior officers. Commander William Thorner had backed her up, and as usual she had got her own way. But big things were expected of him. Commander Thorner had called him over the weekend to say as much. Cases like this make and break careers, Reuben, he had said in his deep Essex drawl. Your reputation will be on the line at a time when your reappointment is already controversial. Get this killer quickly, and you will do yourself a power of good. Don't catch him and, well, Reuben, you know the score.

Reuben glanced in the rear-view. His face was ashen and haunted, reminiscent of the bodies in the morgue. His pale green eyes flicked quickly back and forth in silent agitation. Strands of silver sparked amid his light brown hair. His mouth looked suddenly tight, his lips drained of colour. 'The fucker has compromised himself,' he said out loud. 'He has left something at one of the crime scenes.' Reuben focused back on the road, screeching down a side alley barely wider than the car. The wing mirrors reached out, nearly touching the walls. 'That has to be it,' he whispered to himself. 'The killer has made a mistake.'

Reuben emerged on to a wide dual carriageway and floored it. The bonnet of the heavy car lifted in response, eager and willing to please. Two murders, and something has happened. Reuben squinted. No contact after the first death, so something had to have occurred when he killed the scientist Ian Gillick. Reuben realized his team at GeneCrime would not make the same deduction. They were a bright lot, but they didn't know what he knew.

As he changed down and took a tight left turn off the carriageway, Reuben began to see that things were going to get tricky. He couldn't risk catching the killer. Worse, he appreciated that he might have to begin actively to mislead his team, at least for the time being. He thought back to the morgue, to the ideas he had suppressed, the testing strategies he had kept silent. He realized he would now have to act consistently as if he had never received the phone call, as if there had been no communication with the man holding his son.

Reuben punched the steering wheel. This was fucked up, and things were only going to get worse.

He overtook a car on the wrong side of the road. Five or six more turns and he would be at Lucy's house, the address he used to call home, the building where he used to put his son to bed, and read him stories, and play with him in the bath, before everything went wrong eighteen months ago. A sense of dread began to eat into him. Lucy had sounded distraught, almost hysterical. If someone with Lucy's composure was panicking, then God help the rest of the world.

He dragged himself back to the case, forcing his mind to extract as much detail from the facts as he could before he reached Lucy's house. A sales executive and a scientist. Seemingly no connection between them. He pictured the killer tracking his mobile number down. The name Reuben Maitland in the weekend papers, the news that he was going to be heading the case. The incredible availability of information in the twenty-first century. Websites, databases, electronic fragments of facts, figures and personal records. Almost everything out there if you knew where to look. And the killer clearly hadn't struggled to find him. Reuben tried to build a mental picture of the man holding his son. Smart, resourceful, rational about his need to kill, unusual and brutal in his methods.

Fingertips and rats. This was no hot-blooded killer or random psychopath. This was someone with a planned mission, a strategy, a fierce and sadistic murderer who was comfortable with his ability to take on the police.

Reuben kept his foot pressed hard into the floor as he thought. Three elongated London streets to go. White terraces with lacquered doors. Georgian residences that passed in a blur. Trees every ten metres, wide pavements, cars lining both sides. He tried to summon up the killer's voice. Nasal, slightly monotonous, mid range. Over the distress of his son, he realized he had barely heard it; his ears had hunted for the high-pitched crying, searching out the alarm in Joshua's sobs. It was primeval – the anxious infant, the protective parent. Reuben wondered whether he had met the killer before, come across him as a criminal, or served him as a client. The first strand in any kidnap or extortion case: consider acquaintances of the victim, the inner circle. And that was what Reuben was, he belatedly realized. The victim. The killer was targeting him, blackmailing him, extorting him. Joshua was simply the guarantee that Reuben did as he said.

Reuben punched the steering wheel again. The horn sounded, and a couple of people glanced round before quickly returning to their business. He sped through a T-junction into Lucy's road. Smart semis, built in the thirties. Tiny front gardens that had been paved over to make room for cars. All except for Lucy's. Reuben loved the fact that they had grass between them and the street. He had reinstated it when they moved in, a defiant statement of something he had never quite been able to define in words.

Reuben pulled up quickly, the tyres complaining, the cooling fan kicking in. He parked twenty metres away, spotting two squad cars and a support vehicle as he walked towards the black front door. The sense of dread returned, burrowing into his gut. He paced across the grass, feeling its springy softness underfoot.

Reuben put the killer out of his mind. He had done as much thinking as he could for the time being. What mattered now was finding his son. He rapped hard with his knuckles, and his ex-wife pulled open the door.

9

Lucy's usually immaculate bob was out of shape, stray strands jutting sideways, refusing to be marshalled back into line. She hugged Reuben close. Reuben took in her smell, a moisturizer on her skin that seemed vaguely familiar, a perfume on top of it that he didn't recognize. Then she let him go and looked directly at him in a way she hadn't for months. Her large hazel eyes seemed to expand, a film of moisture gathering across their surface and thickening. And then she began to cry, tears spilling over the dam of her lower eyelid and diving down her cheeks. Behind her, Reuben saw a support officer loitering just inside the kitchen door. In the living room, he spotted two uniforms sharing the sofa, examining their clipboards, talking quietly. All three officers gave the impression of controlled awkwardness, as if they were practised at intruding during the critical moments of people's lives.

'Tell me exactly what happened,' Reuben said.

'Like I said on the phone, he was just snatched.'

Lucy wiped her eyes with the back of her hands. Reuben wanted to grab her and hug her, but he didn't. They had been through too much, a distance had settled between them, a physical awkwardness that hung in the gap between their bodies. He felt suddenly and acutely that this was all his fault, like he was somehow guilty, as if he had kidnapped Joshua himself.

'We've had a couple of sightings, that's all,' Lucy added.

'But how did it happen?'

'Don't blame me, Reuben. I couldn't bear it.'

'I'm not blaming you, Luce. I just want to know what happened.'

Lucy turned away and led him into the kitchen, blowing her nose as she walked. She perched herself on a stool, her elbows resting on the counter, her hands covering most of her face. When she talked, it was through her fingers, her words flat and filtered. 'As you know, we were on our way home from his three-monthly check. I caught the bus because Paddington is a nightmare for parking. After I spoke to you on the phone, Josh made a thorough mess of himself with a yoghurt drink I gave him. Spilled most of it down himself, soaked everywhere.'

Reuben glanced over at the support officer. Early twenties, female, stocky, square glasses and blonde hair.

He knew she was taking it all in. Not just Lucy's words, his own as well.

'Go on,' he said.

Lucy wiped her eyes again, but kept her hands over her face. 'I ran into a newsagent's to get some wet-wipes. One of those long, thin, cramped places that sell everything. Would have been a struggle to get the bloody buggy in. Parked it where I could see it. Only turned away for seconds.' Lucy was sobbing again, her words spilling out between broken breaths, just the way Joshua's had. 'I was in there thirty seconds at the most. I edged my way back out of the shop. And that was that. The buggy had disappeared into a packed sea of shoppers. He was gone.' She started crying more loudly, her sobs echoing around the hard surfaces of the kitchen. Almost mechanically, the support officer pulled out a small pack of tissues and brought them over. 'We've got to find him, Reuben.' Lucy looked frantic. 'We've got to get out there.'

It was as much as Reuben could do not to kick down the front door and rush into the street.

'Where was it?' he asked.

'On the high street. A mile away at the most.'

'He couldn't have got out of the buggy and just wandered off? And then someone nicked it?'

'He was strapped in. There was no way he could have freed himself.' Lucy nodded in the direction of the front room. 'I've been through all this with the police. We combed the streets for nearly an hour. Fifteen officers, more now. A couple of sightings that turned out to be false. A few seconds was all it took for our son to disappear into the bloody shoppers of St John's Wood.'

Reuben watched Lucy. He felt sick to the bone. At GeneCrime, he had got on with his job, let the mechanics of forensic procedure protect him. Now, outside the police unit, he was just as raw and exposed as Lucy. He was suddenly restless, wanting to get back in the car and join the hunt for his son. But he knew it would only be a token effort. CID would be systematically stopping cars, monitoring CCTV, taking witness statements. Reuben knew how it worked. He had to do whatever was most useful.

He stood up and walked into the living room. One of the uniforms was making a call on his mobile. He ended it as Reuben approached.

'I'm Dr Reuben Maitland,' Reuben said. 'Head of Forensics at the GeneCrime Unit in Euston.' It felt awkward using his official designation in his own living room, but if there was one thing police responded to it was rank and title.

'We know who you are, sir,' the officer said, his light blue eyes creased with concern. 'And for what it's worth, we're very sorry about what has happened.'

'So what do we know?' Reuben asked.

'Just what your ex-wife has told you.'

His partner, thin and dark, opened a standard-issue Metropolitan notebook. 'We received a call at 10.09 a.m. Three different units were on the scene within nine minutes.'

Reuben thought back. The call from the killer had come through at 10.31. He had made a mental note, glancing up at the Command Room clock. Lucy had called him just over half an hour earlier. The killer had had Joshua certainly for no more than thirty minutes before dialling Reuben's number. That meant he had to live somewhere reasonably near. Half an hour in mid-morning traffic got you four or five miles in a car, same distance on the Tube, a mile and a half on foot. He had a buggy, which made things slow. Removing a child, folding the buggy into the boot, strapping the child into the car, it all took time. Same issues with a taxi. Or negotiating the Tube, taking the lift instead of the elevators, fighting through the human tide, pushing a bulky object. So the kidnapper had travelled two or three miles at most.

'And then what?' he asked.

'We've been combing the area, knocking on doors, sealing off the pavement where the incident took place, setting up road blocks, everything we can do. Your wife, ex-wife, has provided us with photos which we've emailed to the scene and are showing around.'

Reuben checked his watch. 12.24. His son had been missing almost two and a half hours. 'And what else are you doing? Now, I mean, at this very minute?'

'No point shaking out known paedos at this stage, sir. Statistically, your son is probably on the young side. But we're working through similar cases over the last few years.' The blue-eyed officer turned his phone over in his hand to emphasize the point that he was in constant communication. 'Mostly, we're assembling a team, looking at media liaison.'

Reuben tried not to spit the words back. 'Media liaison?'

'We need to start generating publicity, see if we can get this on the six o'clocks.'

Reuben slumped down on the leather sofa opposite the two cops. His headache was returning with a vengeance. He was fighting an enormous urge to rush over to where Joshua was taken from and run around the streets screaming his name, convinced that he alone could find him. But years of police training were marshalling his thoughts in other directions. Bad directions. Statistics on snatched children. Timelines and outcomes. The kind of person who took infants from their parents. This was different, though. A whole new arena. A man had taken Joshua for a specific reason. He wasn't lost or missing, he was being used. Reuben had to find a way of telling Lucy. And he had to keep his end of the bargain. Delay the investigation, keep his son alive. Trawling the streets wouldn't help his son. The only thing that would save him was obstructing GeneCrime's investigation into the man holding him.

The officer's mobile vibrated and he answered it. From the kitchen, Reuben could just make out the sounds of Lucy crying. He stared into the carpet, rage and violence coming to the boil, needing to be released. Joshua, the tiny embodiment of everything he held dear.

The dark-haired officer stood up. 'We'll bring them over now, boss,' he said into his phone. 'I've explained the situation. We'll see you in fifteen.'

10

Reuben tagged the police Mondeo, staying a couple of car lengths behind. He glanced across at Lucy, who was staring silently out of the side window. She hadn't bothered with her seatbelt and was leaning forward in her seat, her hands in her lap. She was picking at her fingers, tearing at loose flaps of skin with small rapid movements. Reuben knew this was his one opportunity to talk to her.

'Luce,' he said.

She didn't turn away from the window.

'There are a few issues I have to talk to you about. Joshua being snatched . . . I know something I haven't told the police, something you can't tell them either.'

Lucy moved her head slowly towards him. 'What?' she asked, almost absently.

Reuben followed the Mondeo through a tight T-junction. Inside it, the support officer was sitting in the back, her two male colleagues up front. He chose his words carefully. 'I had a phone call shortly after Joshua went missing.'

'Yes?'

'From the man who has him.'

'Someone's got him?' Lucy scanned his face. Reuben knew the look. It was a desperate search for hope. 'Is he safe?'

Reuben focused on the road. 'No.'

'What do you mean?'

'I mean that the man who has him is anything but safe. He has killed twice and wants to kill again.'

'Not Joshua?' Lucy's usual self-possession was long gone. Now, her reaction to every word and implication appeared instantly across her face. 'Please, not Joshua?'

'No.' Reuben spoke softly and without emotion. 'He has Joshua, and all I have to do to get him back is to allow him to kill a third person, who he says deserves to die. This is not about us. This is about control. Joshua is a . . .' Reuben tried to recall the precise coldness of the killer's words. 'A bargaining position.'

Reuben watched something approaching relief wash across Lucy's face. 'So . . .'

'So this is a problem. He is the man I've been tasked with catching. The one currently exciting the tabloids, the one who has been removing the fingertips from his victims.'

'But, Reuben, you can do this, can't you? Fail to

apprehend him so that we get our boy back? What harm would it do?'

'An innocent person dies so that our son lives?'

'Our son, Reuben. A two-year-old boy with his whole life ahead of him, a born survivor who has already come through leukaemia against the odds. Our own flesh and blood, for Christ's sake.'

Reuben slowed for a roundabout, changing down through the Volvo's heavy gears. 'It's not that simple.'

'No? Well, explain to me how the life of your child is complicated.'

'I mean, can we trust him? GeneCrime have profiled him as a smart and resourceful sadist, and one who has killed twice already. He has snatched our boy, torn him away from us. Think about that. Is this the kind of person we can put our faith in?'

Lucy's cheeks flushed, her arms now firmly crossed in front of her. 'And what other option might we have, exactly?'

Reuben was silent for a few moments, the only noise the rise and fall of the engine. They were close to Tottenham Court Road. A couple of minutes and they would be at the station. They had to get this sorted now, before everything got complicated.

'Subverting a manhunt is not something I really want to do,' he said.

'But you have the authority?'

'The killer obviously thinks so.'

'So could you?'

'Yes,' Reuben answered slowly. 'In theory.'

'Or what's to stop you lying to him? Keep the case going, keep trying to find him, keep trying to find our son, but pretend you're not.'

'That's the obvious course of action.' Reuben scratched the back of his neck. 'I can't do that, though.'

'Why not?' Lucy demanded.

'He's set a trap. He said he will know if we're getting close to him.'

'What kind of a trap? Is that even possible?'

The police car turned sharply off the street and came to a stop in front of a set of large grey metal gates. Reuben pulled in behind, the engine idling, his brain racing. 'I don't know,' he said, 'I really don't. But, Luce, we've got about thirty seconds to decide what we're going to do.' The gates swung open and the Mondeo entered, Reuben close behind. 'Quick.'

Lucy massaged her temples with her thumb and middle finger. When she looked up at Reuben she was serious again, like she had reverted to the corporate seriousness her law firm had insidiously breathed into her over the years. Her voice was tight and focused. 'Right, we don't tell the police about the phone call. Ever. We watch our words in front of the support officer and everyone else. If the killer has set a trap for you I guess we don't gamble with our son's life. We trust nothing but our own instincts. The only option as I see it is for you to actively mislead your team in the hunt for this man. There's no guarantee you would catch him anyway before he commits another murder. We take it one day at a time. And then we get our son back safe and well.'

Reuben aimed for a parking space, taking his time over backing in. The three officers were already emerging from their car and starting to head over.

'You sure that's what you want to do, Luce?'

'No. But it's the best plan we've got. And at least we know our boy is alive. That's the thing we have to cling to, Reuben. This is about regaining control. I think the killer has made a mistake.'

Reuben straightened the wheel and killed the engine. He turned to his ex-wife, wondering when they had last sat in the front of a car together. She was right. They had no other option. She had said exactly what he had been thinking. He also wondered when that had last happened. Probably not for a couple of years. He glanced round at the support officer, who had her hand out and was reaching for the door handle.

'You ready for this?' he asked quietly.

'Of course not,' Lucy answered. 'How could you ever be ready for this?'

Reuben undid his seatbelt and began to climb out. 'Because this isn't going to be pleasant.'

11

As he walked through the rear entrance and into the operational heart of the police station in Paddington Green, Reuben saw the building in a very different light. He had visited the station a handful of times on police business and knew its layout fairly well. An unwelcoming reception area, scruffy and tired-looking, the walls festooned with crime posters to hide the poor paint job. A front desk, worn from its interaction with countless agitated pairs of hands, its lower surface scuffed through contact with shoes and trainers. A long corridor through a thick door to the right. Small cramped offices with no direct sunlight, opening out into a large communal area of tables and chairs. A canteen upstairs, along with changing rooms, the cells and the toilet block below, accessed via a different door in the main reception. But now Reuben was viewing it like a member of the public would. It had ceased to be yet another police station housing men to take DNA samples from. It was now a building that was going to make life very awkward for him.

Reuben and Lucy were led into the open-plan office, and pointed towards a couple of chairs. The sick feeling was still gnawing into Reuben's gut, refusing to abate. He checked his watch against a large metal clock on the wall. It had been three hours since Joshua was taken; it felt like days. Beside him, Lucy was silent, staring into the cheap laminate flooring.

He continued to think. The situation was changing all the time, the police taking control, discussing tactics. All three officers in the Mondeo had been on and off their mobiles. It felt weird not to be involved. Usually Reuben was the one making the strategic calls. In fact that was exactly what he should be doing now at GeneCrime, coordinating forensic approaches, visiting crime scenes, reviewing the evidence.

Reuben's phone vibrated and he pulled it out. The caller ID read 'Sarah'. 'Hello,' he said.

'I've been trying to contact you. What's going on?'

'Sorry, had my phone switched off.'

'You muttered something serious about Joshua before you ran off. Are you OK?'

Reuben scanned the empty room, listening to the background drone of activity coming from one of the offices down the corridor. 'Not really. Joshua has gone missing. We think he could have been snatched by someone.'

'Fuck.' Sarah fell silent. From the sounds, Reuben guessed she was walking along a street, maybe outside GeneCrime, taking a break to grab lunch. 'You OK?'

'Have a wild guess.'

'Look, you need any extra support? Any manpower?'

'We're fine. Haven't met the team yet but I've a feeling we're about to. Meanwhile squads of uniform are patrolling the streets.'

'Fuck,' Sarah said again. 'Look, I'm sorry to cut to the chase, but what about the investigation here?'

'No change. I'll be in later. Nothing else I can reasonably do except wait for some news. And that's killing me.'

'You sure?'

Reuben was utterly certain. If he didn't discover all he could about the killer, he might never see his son again. 'Like I said, there's not a lot else I can do.'

'Well, if anyone can help us catch the sick bastard who's removing people's fingers then I guess it's you.'

'I'll see what I can do.' Reuben glanced up as several people approached along the corridor, a dark blur of uniform in his peripheral vision. 'Look, Sarah, I'll catch up with you later, fill you in on everything. But I've got to go.' Reuben recognized one of the group and suppressed a grimace. 'Shit,' he said quietly. 'Looks like I've been assigned Paul Veno.'

'Veno? DI Charlie Baker's old mate?' Sarah snorted, a noise of derision and pity. 'You lucky boy.'

'Thanks for your support. I'll talk to you later.'

Reuben ended the call and watched the lead officer picking his way through the tables and chairs of the elongated room. He was five ten, blond-haired, with a dense beard that turned redder the closer he got. He had the sort of fat that seems to solidify, a firm round stomach as hard as a bowling ball. Above his gut he was stocky, his arms folded, his walk driven through his shoulders, making him look unnervingly robotic. Reuben sensed that if he saw him coming along the pavement, he would move the hell out of his way. But then, Reuben had other reasons for wanting to avoid Detective Paul Veno.

'So, the famous Dr Reuben Maitland,' he said, stopping just in front. 'The man who spends almost as much time investigating his fellow officers as catching the bad guys.'

'They're sometimes the same thing, Detective Veno.'

'Word is you'd shop your own team if you could. How many CID have you put behind bars now? Ten? Twenty?'

'Four. And surely you're not condoning corrupt police officers?'

'I'm not condoning anything. I'm just pointing out the rich irony of the man who arrests coppers now asking for their help.'

Reuben glanced across at Lucy, who was staring with undisguised hatred at Detective Veno. 'I can assure you this is not a situation I would wish on anybody.' He bored into the face looking down at him. 'Now, are you going to help us or not?'

Paul Veno pulled up a chair, and his team did likewise. 'I've been assigned to run the case, Dr Maitland.' He sighed and stretched, rotating his neck as if it was stiff. 'I will endeavour to put past events behind me. Bottom line is that we don't have anything. Nothing at all. A couple of vague witness statements, people who thought they might have seen a man loitering, dropping a cigarette in the street, pushing a buggy away. But no description of the man. No other sightings. A total of twenty-three officers out there meeting and greeting, and no luck at all.' The detective acknowledged Lucy for the first time, and gave her a look intended to convey sympathy. 'It's what we do from now on that matters. But I need to ask you a few questions first.'

'Go on,' Reuben said.

'Have you had any contact with anyone?'

Reuben suddenly thought about mobile phone records, how easy it was to trace numbers and conversations. It would only take seconds. They could determine that he had received a call from a number his phone hadn't recognized half an hour after Joshua was taken. 'Spell it out, Detective.'

'Have you had a ransom demand, or anything similar?'

'No, we have not,' Lucy said flatly.

The legal profession, Reuben thought. You couldn't beat it for bare-faced lying.

'Have you any reason to suspect someone would snatch your son? Any unusual communications with anyone?'

'Nothing,' Lucy said.

'OK, so no one has contacted you, and nothing unusual has happened in the last few days.'

'That's correct.'

'And where were you, Dr Maitland, when you found out that your son had been taken?'

Reuben filtered his response for a second, quickly checking for inconsistencies, as Detective Veno stared into his face, watching him closely. 'I was at GeneCrime. First day back, coordinating a manhunt into the—'

'Ah yes,' Veno said, cutting him off, 'I heard. The force reinstating you, in its wisdom.' He glanced around at the three silent members of his team for support. 'London's only serving CID officer with a criminal record. Would have loved to have been in that fucking meeting.'

'Look, are you going to help us or not, Veno?' Reuben couldn't help but shout, the anger and frustration bursting out of him. He thought briefly of calling in a few favours, getting Veno taken off the case and replaced with someone who wasn't so actively hostile. But Reuben knew he would need to save his favours for what lay ahead. And besides, distrust of Reuben was by no means confined to one Metropolitan officer. He immediately tried to calm down. 'Can't we just get on with this,' he said more quietly.

Veno turned to Lucy. 'So we can rule out kidnapping. Which leaves us with not a lot. The random abduction of a two-year-old boy. Just an opportunistic strike. The bad news is that witnesses suggest a male perpetrator. Could be sexual. Profiling would suggest probably not, given your child's age and sex, et cetera, but we can't rule it out. What we have to hope is that whoever took him is now sweating over it, and in the cold light of day realizes they've made one hell of a mistake.'

'So what do we do?'

'The only thing we can. We have to appeal to him, get the message across that there is a way out of this. And failing that, we have to jog someone's memory, make someone come forward who has seen something or knows something.' Detective Veno scratched his beard. 'And I'm afraid that means TV.'

Reuben shuddered. The press conference. Tearful parents staring bleakly out into the stroboscopic flashing of cameras. Viewers at home watching every nuance, taking it all in. The sorrow, the tragedy, but also the nagging suspicion. Are these people telling the truth about their child? Are they really what they seem? Did they actually deserve this? Are the police asking them to do the press conference just to witness their demeanour, their behaviour, their reaction? The modern age. Trial by media. The innocent never really innocent. The guilty deserving everything they get.

Reuben shuddered again. This was fucked up, and quickly getting worse.

12

'No, I don't want to do my bloody make-up,' Lucy spat, directing her wrath at the media liaison officer. 'I'm not here because I want to look good on television. My child has been taken, for Christ's sake.'

'That's great,' the media liaison officer said. 'I'm relieved.'

Reuben glared up at him. 'Why?'

'You should see what some of them want to look like before they go on air.'

'Some of who?'

'Some of the parents.'

Reuben took him in. He was well groomed, effeminate, wouldn't last ten minutes on the beat. Then he cursed himself. He recognized the first signs of turning into the sort of grizzled CID dinosaur you found in police bars, drinking hard, complaining about the state of the modern force.

'Well, let's show them the real you. The paleness, the nervousness, the desperation. The "I'm a parent and all I want is my child back" look.' The media liaison officer placed his hands on Lucy's shoulders. 'That's what we want, and that's what really captures the public imagination.'

Reuben decided suddenly that maybe the dinosaurs had a point. 'Get the hell away from my wife,' he growled.

The media liaison officer raised his eyebrows, his head tilting back. He surveyed Reuben for a second and removed his hands from Lucy's shoulders. Then, very slowly, a look of disdain on his face, he turned and walked away.

When he had gone, Lucy looked at Reuben and raised her own eyebrows. 'That would be ex-wife,' she said.

Reuben nearly mustered a smile. 'I mean, the I-want-my-child-back look. For fuck's sake.'

'He's only doing his job.'

'And I should be doing mine. You ready for this?'

'Are you trying to be serious?'

'Just a little.'

'This is going to be horrible.'

'Well, remember what we're doing it for. We're going to reassure the psycho who has our son that everything is OK. And we're also trawling for witnesses, people who know something. Any information that gets us closer to Joshua.' Reuben's left leg was shaking rapidly,

John Macken

a nervous habit he had, an involuntary tick that implied
the accumulation of pent-up energy. He stopped it and
turned to Lucy. 'Remember, as well as several million
people sitting on their sofas, the police are going to be
watching us.'

'Meaning what, exactly?'

'Classic missing child stuff. Support and suspect the
parents in equal measure. See how they perform in front
of the camera.'

'But that's what we're doing, isn't it? Performing. We
know who has our child. We are lying to the whole na-
tion. Look, Rube, are you sure about this?'

Reuben spotted Detective Veno heading their way down
the corridor. He had left them alone for the past three
hours, making calls, keeping track of the investigation,
coordinating the media liaison, briefing the corporate
communications officer, keeping the force incident
manager up to speed. Reuben and Lucy had spent the
time separately with different officers, answering, Reuben
suspected, the same questions over and over again. But
now, in the determination of Veno's walk, in the way he
leaned his body forward, pointing towards them, Reuben
sensed it was finally about to happen.

'I'm not sure about anything, Luce,' he said quietly. 'But
it's what I do for a living. React to events, adopt strategies,
keep track of the information and devise a plan.'

'And what about me?'

'You have to do what you do best for a living.'

'Which is?'

'Lying. Avoiding the truth. Hiding in the gaps and exploiting the weaknesses. Doing whatever it takes to win.'

'You're a cynical bastard,' Lucy answered. 'And you're getting worse.'

Veno stopped in front of them, his hearing obviously acute. 'Cynical?' he asked sternly. 'Does this explain why you've been upsetting my media officer, Dr Maitland?'

Reuben grunted. 'You know how it is, Detective Veno.'

Veno scanned the large room. 'This is the modern age, Maitland. It's where we are. What other option is there? Do you want ten million witnesses out there, or just the single alcoholic one we've dredged up so far?' He left it hanging, a question he wanted answering.

Reuben muttered, 'Let's get it over with.'

'Right. Follow me.'

Veno turned and headed back towards the corridor. Reuben and Lucy followed, staring at the floor, watching as it changed from laminate to vinyl to fake wooden tiles, and then into the soft blue carpet of the media room. Reuben glanced up. It was two thirds full, a crush towards the front. He shuddered. A thin desk, three plastic chairs, blue background boards. Blank and stark, the only focus the faces of two parents, with a copper to one side.

Veno pulled out the right-hand chair, Reuben took

the middle, to shield Lucy from too much attention, and she took the left. Stroboscopic flashes made their movements seem stuttering. Reuben blinked hard. He couldn't see anyone directly, but when he blinked, the impression of a human form was etched behind each individual flash.

Veno spoke first, reading from a piece of paper that Reuben noted was taped to the desk. He parroted the words, barely pausing for breath, a calm London monotone that said 'this is all just routine'. 'Ladies and gentlemen of the press, this morning at approximately ten a.m. a two-year-old boy in a light-blue three-wheeled buggy was taken from the vicinity of Grove End Road in St John's Wood.' He glanced up. 'We will be distributing maps of the precise area at the end.'

Reuben felt the squeeze of Lucy's hand under the table. He squeezed back.

Veno stared back into his sheet. 'After intensive searches of the environs, the boy, Joshua Maitland, remains missing. Given that he was strapped firmly into his buggy, we are working on the assumption that he has been taken. We now have grave concerns for his safety and whereabouts. We are therefore appealing to the public at large, particularly in the capital but also in the rest of the country, to be vigilant. All calls to the number now appearing on the screen will be treated in the strictest confidence.'

Reuben blinked in the light. The cameras seemed intent on blinding and then staring, blinding and then staring. He imagined TV stations flashing up the photos of Joshua that Lucy had provided, the phone number running beneath.

'OK, I will now pass you over to the father of Joshua, Reuben Maitland.'

Reuben sensed it. Being fed to the press. Being passed to them for their words and images to devour.

A voice from behind the barrage of flashes asked, 'Do you have a message for the person who has taken your child?'

Reuben stared bleakly into the nearest TV camera. Joshua. Defenceless and helpless. A tiny boy being held by someone who had already killed two grown men. He suddenly appreciated that the man was watching. Wherever he was, perched forward on his chair, monitoring every aspect of Reuben's behaviour, even more intently than the rest of the public. Needing to know if Reuben was going to play ball.

Reuben cleared his throat. 'I just want to reassure whoever has my child. Don't do anything rash. We can step back from this. There is no need to harm Joshua. I can reassure you, there is no need to harm Joshua.'

Reuben caught Lucy's eye. He couldn't have made it any plainer. Don't harm Joshua and I will help you.

Another question fired through the room. 'How are

you feeling at this moment, now that your only child has been taken?'

Reuben knew what they were after. They wanted tears. This wasn't a press conference for a missing infant until they had tears. But Lucy was as hard as they came, and Reuben hadn't cried since the moment in the middle of the night almost two years ago when his son was born.

'How do you think?' he asked.

'Simon Shaw, *Evening Standard*. Can you confirm that a witness has said your son was taken by a man?'

Veno intervened, barking his answer, his hard round stomach forced into the table. 'We won't be entering into any speculation at this time, Mr Shaw.'

'Do you have any words for your son?'

'Not at this time,' Reuben said.

'None at all?'

'Well, just that Mummy and Daddy love you and will see you soon.'

Another voice, this time from further back in the room. 'Is it true, Mrs Maitland, that you left Joshua's buggy un-attended outside a shop?'

'Yes,' Lucy answered quietly.

'And what would you say to him if he could hear you now?'

She didn't answer.

'How long did you leave the buggy on the street?'

Silence.

'Do you regret your actions, Mrs Maitland?'

Reuben looked at Lucy. She was silently crying, her eyes wide and open, her head tilted forward, tears dripping on to the wooden veneer of the table. The flashes intensified, individual droplets caught on their way down, trapped for ever as frozen newspaper images.

Reuben stood up and grabbed Lucy by the arm. He pushed the table back and began to stride through the crowded room. Voices shouted, a clamour of words and questions. But Reuben kept walking, pulling Lucy beside him, placing his arm around her shoulder, pacing out of the media room, out through the open-plan office, along its main corridor and towards his car.

13

'They'll be here any minute.'

'Christ. If they spent as much time hunting the man who has Joshua as they do tracking us . . .' Lucy tailed off, her elbows on the kitchen counter, her head in her hands. She wiped her eyes. She'd been crying for almost two hours, waves of grief broken by phone calls from Veno and periods of deafening silence.

Reuben had held her for much of that time, her sobs cutting right through him. He rubbed his face, his forehead tight, his skin greasy. He was suddenly and acutely aware of the other side of the crimes he investigated. The emotion, the fear, the helplessness. When you were banging on doors, speeding through databases, matching evidence and interrogating suspects, there was a momentum that prevented you from stopping to think. For every rape, for every murder, for every abduction, tens of lives ground to a halt, off balance, caught up in the static horror of the aftermath.

'You hungry?' he asked.

'No.'

'We should eat. Get some energy inside us while we can.'

'What are you thinking?'

'I'll cook us something.'

Lucy sighed. 'You don't know where anything is. It's all changed round since you last spent time in here.'

Reuben ran his eyes around the kitchen. He didn't doubt it. Eighteen months, give or take. Most of the time the house had been rented out. Now Lucy had moved back in, she had put her stamp on it again. A new shelving unit, different chairs under the soft wooden table, a couple of pictures, new utensils in a metal rack.

A month ago, she had asked him to move back in as well. Joshua needed a father, someone he saw more than once a fortnight. Reuben had accepted, but bit by bit. They had both agreed that there was nothing to gain from rushing. There were too many wounds between them simply to take up where they had left off. So Reuben had begun to visit his son more often, occasionally staying later, chatting with Lucy until they were tired or starting to argue, or orbiting around the same old issues. It was platonic, wary and damaged, but heading in the right direction. And up to now, Reuben hadn't troubled the kitchen with any cooking.

'I guess you're right,' he said. 'Though I ought to find out where you keep everything at some stage.'

'Maybe now's not the time,' Lucy said softly. She stood up and began rooting in kitchen cupboards. 'And I guess a bit of food can only help. Like you say, before the bloody police arrive and set up camp again. Which, after your antics earlier—'

'I know I shouldn't have stormed out, Luce. It's just, what were we there for?'

'To encourage witnesses to come forward.'

'But isn't it enough to show a picture of Joshua? It's not like you'd need to scrutinize the agony of the parents on TV before you finally decided to call the police. We were just the freak show. Media impact, that's all.'

'Reuben, how long do you think we have? Until the killer gets what he wants and releases Joshua?'

'It can't be long. Looking after your own two-year-old is no easy matter, let alone someone else's.'

'It's just . . . we should be doing more. I feel so bloody helpless. These are the critical hours, the first few after an abduction.'

Reuben could see his ex-wife was on the verge of tears again. Something about the moisture in her eyes tugged at his own, making them wet, forcing him to blink rapidly.

The doorbell sounded and he walked out of the kitchen

to the front door. He waited a second, composing himself, before pulling it open.

'Not smart.' Detective Veno was standing on the doorstep, his hard round belly almost intruding into the house. He was shaking his head slowly back and forth. 'Not smart at all.'

'Yeah, well. That wasn't exactly a pleasant experience.'

'Losing your child isn't a pleasant experience. And if we don't find him soon, that's what we're looking at. It doesn't matter how you feel, Dr Maitland. If we're being frank, I don't give a fuck that you might be upset. In fact, there's something about your unhappiness that would appeal to a lot of coppers I know. All that matters to me is that child. Getting him back, rescuing him from the sick bastard who has taken him.'

A cold blast of air was rushing into the house. Reuben stepped back from the door and let Veno push past. Behind, the support officer and one of his team from the police station followed him in. Reuben waited for them to sit down in the living room and asked them what they wanted to drink.

'Coffee,' Veno said. 'And plenty of it.'

In the kitchen, Lucy was boiling some pasta. Reuben filled the kettle and switched it on. It started to boil, its rumble getting louder and louder. He flicked the extractor fan on above the hob.

'I've got to head out,' he said, just loud enough so that

Lucy could hear. 'It's time to start searching for the man who has our child.'

'What about food?'

'I'll grab something later. But make sure you eat. Even if you don't feel like it.'

'There's too much now,' Lucy said.

'I'm sure Veno will help you out.'

'What should I say to them?'

'Stick to the story. We don't know any more than they do. Christ, if they knew we'd had contact, it would be all over the front pages by the morning. And Josh wouldn't stand a chance.'

'Why don't they go, call it a night?'

'They need to be here in case the killer rings. Plus, they need to look after you.'

'I don't need any looking after,' Lucy whispered. 'I just need my boy back.'

'Well, that's what I'm going to start working on.'

The kettle switched itself off and Reuben poured out three coffees.

'I'll see you later,' he said. 'Stay strong.'

He walked the hot drinks into the living room and distributed them. Then he pulled his leather jacket off the banister, grabbed his car keys and headed towards the front door.

'Where are you going, Dr Maitland?' Veno shouted, watching him from the room.

'GeneCrime. You might remember that I'm in the middle of catching a villain at the moment.'

Veno raised his eyebrows. 'And what the fuck do you think I'm doing?'

Reuben opened the front door. 'Sitting on my couch, drinking my coffee, wondering whether you're going to make the ten o'clock news reports.'

'Oh don't you worry. After your performance on the six o'clocks, the ten o'clocks are going to be all over it.'

Reuben stepped out into the freezing air and slammed the door.

14

The traffic was light. It was late and cold, a Monday night, and only the people who needed to be on the roads were. The unmarked police Volvo slowly began to warm as Reuben picked his way towards GeneCrime. It was a route he used to take every day, and the tangle of roads and junctions had obviously settled somewhere deep in his brain, there to be called upon should he ever need them again. He drove on autopilot, following the memorized directions, a fuzzy tiredness washing through him. He squinted at oncoming headlights, his eyes feeling dry. It was coming up to ten o'clock and the day was nowhere near over yet.

Reuben started to think everything through again, examining it from every conceivable angle, trying to sort the critical facts from the mess of information he had absorbed already that day. The scenes of death of Ian Gillick and Carl Everitt. The removal of their fingertips with a saw. Their pale bodies in the morgue. The rats. The phone call. The man's voice, his use of words, his accent. Who the man was likely to be, what was motivating him, why he needed to kill three people and then return to normality. That was the crux, Reuben decided, the fact that this was planned. It had taken a precise strategy to enter the homes of two men, to incapacitate them, to remove their fingertips, to obtain rats and transport them to each scene, to snatch the son of the forensics officer leading the hunt for him. Again, Reuben wondered, if this had all been so meticulously planned, why not just ensure that the scenes weren't contaminated? Gloves, mask, shoe covers – just like the forensics squad did. Why risk the abduction of a child? Or else, why not start with the abduction and then carry out the three killings? What had changed? Was the taking of Joshua an alternative strategy, a modified circumstance, a reaction to events?

Reuben approached a junction and checked his mirrors. He shook his head quickly, as if doing so could shake the thoughts of Joshua from his mind. He had to think carefully, without emotion, a cold logic unclouded by sentiment. But even as he tried, he realized he couldn't. At this exact moment in time, short-cutting through the back streets of London, driving through the cold November air, Joshua was all that mattered.

He took a mini-roundabout, flying across it at speed,

and glanced in his rear-view again. A vehicle had followed him through the last series of junctions, and it took the roundabout at a similar speed. Reuben turned left at a small intersection, then immediately right. The car behind did the same. This was not an established London route, a well-worn path from one part of the capital to another. This was Reuben's personal means of avoiding the traffic between his former house and his place of work. That fact was an important one, he decided.

He accelerated, the large Volvo engine whining and picking up speed. At the end of a long straight road of terraced housing, he turned left into a tree-lined street, one eye on his mirrors. The car behind did the same. Reuben strained to look at the vehicle. It was an Audi of some sort. An A4, or maybe an A6. A big, heavy, solid chunk of black. One bright white headlight, the other dimmer, the glass cracked. Not a classic police marque, or even an unmarked squad car. The Met used Fords, Volvos, Peugeots, the occasional BMW, but never Audis. They were expensive to buy, costly to maintain.

The road opened out and the street lighting picked up. Reuben squinted in the mirror. The car was five or six years old, judging from its condition. Too old for CID. But who else? And what did they want? No one followed you for ten minutes late at night through a mesh of intersections and crossroads for no reason. There was only one way to find out.

A set of lights ahead began to change. The green became amber. Reuben floored it. He screamed through the empty junction at nearly seventy. He took a roundabout on the wrong side. The tyres complained, the heavy momentum of the Volvo wanting to plough straight on. The road joined a carriageway. Reuben pulled on to it, hammering the gears, accelerating hard. An overpass, two lanes, concrete barrier in the middle. Eighty-five, the road spotted with other vehicles, no speed cameras in sight. He looked back. The Audi was fifty metres back and gaining. Reuben tried to make out the driver. Male. Caucasian. Thick-set.

There was a slipway ahead, just over the crest. He plunged between a bus and a white van and slammed on his brakes. The pedal juddered, the ABS kicking in. The Audi disappeared behind the bus. Reuben indicated to turn off.

Fifteen seconds.

Who the fuck was chasing him? Reuben had a sudden premonition that it could be the killer.

He started to move into the feeder lane. It was a short section quickly divided by a barriered-off section of tarmac.

Ten seconds.

He hesitated. If this was the killer, he was not to be fucked with. Then another icy thought hit him. Joshua could be in the car. His son in the back of that speeding vehicle. Whoever it was had been happy to jump red lights and drive on the wrong side of the road. They meant business.

Five seconds.

The narrow turn-off was looming. It was now or never. But if it was the killer, and if Joshua was in the back, what was the best plan? Losing him might not be the smartest idea. And if it wasn't the killer, what then?

Reuben started to move back across, calculating, theorizing, planning, implications and scenarios gnawing away at him. He slowed while he thought. The bus behind him closed up, flashing its lights at him. Reuben got a good look at it and made his mind up. He stamped hard on the brakes. The bus lurched towards him, then Reuben kicked it down a gear and pounded the throttle, screeching off the flyover at the last second. He stared over his shoulder. The empty bus was slewing sideways, momentarily out of control, blocking off the exit. The driver quickly corrected the slide, but the Audi was unable to turn off and follow. Reuben watched it go above him. He didn't get a clear look inside. It was impossible to see whether anyone else was in the back of the car.

For good or for bad he had lost his tail. He wondered whether he should try and get back on the flyover at another junction, but realized he would never catch the

Audi. So he spun the unmarked Volvo all the way round a roundabout and headed back towards GeneCrime, no longer cold and tired but sweating and alert, his mind buzzing with questions.

15

Reuben slotted the Volvo back in the space it had occupied that morning. The cooling fan stayed on after he turned the key, the engine running hot. He climbed out and signed in at the security gate, checking his watch and writing 22:13 next to his name. The guard nodded at him, then returned to his paper.

Sarah's office was on the first floor. Reuben took the stairs down from the main car park level, which was at the top of the building. He suspected that whoever designed GeneCrime had enjoyed the premise of a large concrete ramp up the side, and a car park which still managed to feel subterranean, even though it was three or four storeys off the ground. They probably also enjoyed the large windows and great views over rolling fields and meadows, and were happy to let CID and Forensics sweat it out in what was virtually a sealed box.

GeneCrime was empty. Some of the offices still had

their lights on, and Reuben flicked them off as he passed. When he reached Sarah's door he rapped on it and entered. She was sitting back in her chair, bare feet on her desk, a biro in her mouth, flicking through a thick wad of papers. Her light hair, which was usually pinned up tight, hung loose and tangled. Reuben thought her office looked like a hospice for terminal plants. All around, different varieties were slowly dying, their leaves curling or turning brown. He thought briefly of the cactus left behind in his office, tiny particles of his blood coating its spines.

'Thanks for staying,' he said.

Sarah pulled her feet off the desk and sat up, taking the biro from her mouth. 'Actually, I went home and came back.'

'Really?'

'There's something depressing about being on your own in a large building with only a bored security guard for company. Besides, I thought I'd catch the news.'

'What did you think?'

'Raw. Painful. Terrible technique you have with the media.'

'It was fucking horrible.' Reuben pointed his eyes at the file she had been reading, eager to shift the subject. 'Anything useful?'

'I guess so. But I don't know how you'll take it.'

'Take what?'

'This.'

She angled the cardboard file upwards. Reuben read the information on the front.

'How did you get that?'

'I'm sorry I didn't clear it with you, but I thought under the circumstances you wouldn't mind too much.' Sarah ran the fingers of her left hand through her tangled hair. Although her eyes were bright, she looked tired. Even her hair seemed drained of vitality. 'I used what remain of my favours to request that GeneCrime handle the forensics on Joshua's abduction.'

'Why?' Reuben asked.

'Daft not to. We are, after all, a rapid response unit. No point sending the samples up the bloody M1 all the way to Birmingham. They'd only do the same things we would here, but slower.'

Reuben tried not to appear too pleased. 'Thanks,' he said.

'A witness apparently saw someone drop a cigarette butt close to the snatch. A man. The butt is in a plastic bag in the routine samples lab, along with several others collected from the vicinity. They were couriered over half an hour ago from the unit at Paddington.'

'So what's the plan?'

'I've asked Simon Jankowski to come in before dawn. We take fingerprints and DNA, run them through the national database, see if anything comes up trumps. Unless you've got a better idea?'

Reuben was silent for a few seconds. GeneCrime hunting the killer and now also hunting the kidnapper. Not appreciating that they were looking for the same man. He continued to think it through. GeneCrime were good at catching villains. It was what they were set up to do, it was what they did. And if they closed in on the killer, Joshua would die. A standard police lab would be days behind them, pushing the samples through routine testing, sending the results off elsewhere for analysis. This suddenly raised the stakes, fast-forwarded everything. But there was another side, Reuben quickly appreciated. Possible samples from the man holding his son. If Reuben could get his hands on them, he could get closer to the truth.

'No,' he said, 'that sounds fine.'

'Look, Reuben, you're not to get involved in this yourself, OK?'

Reuben nodded.

'I'm doing this as a personal favour for, well, you know . . .' Sarah was suddenly awkward with her words in a way Reuben had seldom witnessed. She avoided his eye, staring instead into the thin dying leaves of a spider plant. For a second, she almost appeared vulnerable. 'What we've been through in the past. I haven't forgotten how close I came to losing my life . . .'

'Thanks,' Reuben said.

'But there's something else I want you to think about.'

'Yes?'

'I want you to think about standing down from the investigation into the fingertip killer.'

'Is that what you're calling him now?'

'You got anything better?'

'I haven't exactly had a chance to think about it.'

'Exactly. Your son is missing. You're caught up in the most important hours and days of your life. I don't see how you can coordinate events here.' Sarah was back to eye contact, her voice as steely as ever. She had a knack for opening the door and letting you peer in for a second or two, before slamming it shut again. 'There's no room for sentimentality, Reuben. We have a sadistic killer on the loose. Personal problems, no matter how serious or upsetting, can't be allowed to get in the way. Otherwise we put innocent people in grave danger.'

Reuben bit the inside of his cheek. She wanted him off the case. He wondered for a second whether she had only agreed to take on the forensics from Joshua's abduction to soften the blow. But even by his own low standards, Reuben was forced to concede that that was a fairly cynical thought.

'Look, Sarah, you have to understand a few things. While Joshua is missing, there's nothing else I can do. The police want us as circus freaks to keep the media hungry.'

'As I've seen.'

'It doesn't feel right, though.'

'But it's the only option, surely?'

'Is it?' Reuben rubbed his face, once again feeling the greasy tiredness in his skin. He nodded at an empty chair. 'You mind?'

Sarah shook her head.

'You know, I read a story once about a woman who was taken hostage in South America by Communist guerrillas. Missing for seven years. Then one day her husband charters a light aircraft. He gets the pilot to circle over a large area of jungle. The husband has spent weeks printing off twenty thousand photos of their children, showing what they look like now, seven years later, how they've grown, how beautiful they've become. He throws handfuls out, hour after hour, in the hope that she will find just one, and know that her family loves her and misses her.' Reuben stopped talking. His mouth was feeling strange, out of shape, achy. 'The point is, she never saw the photos. She was rescued a year later. A military police unit stormed in and took her. But that's what every bone in my body feels like doing. I want to be out there searching, dropping photos of his mum and dad for Joshua, hoping I can get something through to him, let him know that he's going to be OK.'

'So?'

'So, nearly two decades in the force have convinced me that I wouldn't make any difference. I have to sit back and let Veno's Missing Child unit do what they're trained to do. But it's killing me, Sarah. No news, no nothing. Trying to forget the statistics . . .'

Reuben hesitated, wanting to tell Sarah everything, to blurt it all out, to tell her he had spoken to the killer, to stop lying to her. He felt terrible. Like she had said, they went way back. But he couldn't just spit it out. Sarah wouldn't be able to hold back a manhunt. Reuben knew, for the time being, he couldn't do anything but trust his instincts.

'Look, the energy I'm putting into worrying could be going into catching this man. You know I can do it.'

'Usually, yes.'

'And that's what I intend to do.' Reuben stood up. 'And I'm sorry to say this,' he muttered, running his fingers through the browning tips of the dying spider plant on Sarah's desk, 'but you don't have the authority to suspend the Head of Forensics.'

Sarah regarded him coolly. 'I don't want to fall out over this, Reuben.' Her tone was hard, her words sounding more like a threat than an expression of potential regret. 'Do your job, and do it well. Catch the killer, and I hope you get your son back. But don't bite off more than you can chew.'

'Sure,' Reuben said, turning to walk away.

'One more thing, Dr Maitland. You are not to handle your son's forensics. You can't get involved in your own investigation. You understand that, don't you?'

Reuben nodded solemnly. He gave Sarah a brief smile and walked slowly out. He made his way quietly down the long GeneCrime corridors, through sets of double doors, past offices, his pace quickening the closer he got, until he was jogging, running, tipping forward at full tilt, sprinting towards the lab housing DNA samples from the man who was holding his son.

16

Reuben flicked the switches of several pieces of equipment. There was an off-white PCR machine the size of a small microwave oven, 384 wells in its metal block. Next to it, an ABI3700 sequencer, kitchen cabinet in width, a flatscreen monitor balancing on top. A metallic blue microfuge with two circular dials, one marked Time, the other Speed, squatted on the lab bench. He picked a lab coat from an identity parade of white garments hanging next to the door. The inside collar was marked Dr Bernie Harrison. Wider than Reuben, an inch or two shorter. He raised his eyebrows and tried it on for size. It would do.

Reuben chose an under-bench freezer labelled New Arrivals. Inside he quickly found a clear plastic evidence bag. On a square white section the words Joshua Maitland Abduction Prelims had been scrawled in black marker pen. From the uneven look of the letters, Reuben guessed it had been labelled after the cigarette butts had been placed inside.

He held the bag up to the bright light of the lab. Like all forensic scientists, Reuben liked smokers. Cigarette butts gave you two simultaneous pieces of information: DNA from buccal cells deposited as the smoker wrapped his lips around the filter and pulled, and greasy fingerprints as the cigarette was slid from its pack, or from restless seconds in between drags.

He pulled on a pair of blue vinyl gloves and set about assembling the things he would need. Solutions from shelves, reagents from fridges and freezers, forceps from autoclaved bags, ice from the large white ice machine, a set of Gilson pipettes from a rack, filtered tips from a pile near the main sink. For the first time in over twelve hours he felt positive. Just to be doing something, to be hunting, forensically chasing the man who had his son. The familiar mechanics of detection. Moving forward, starting the investigation.

As he rolled the cigarette butts on to a section of stretched-out clingfilm, he picked up the nearby lab phone and dialled Sarah's office. No answer. He let it ring and then replaced the receiver. She had gone.

He stared intently down at the bench in front of him. Nine butts, their identities branded just above their filters. A Benson and Hedges, a Super King, a Camel, three Marlboro Lights, two Silk Cut, a Lambert and

Butler. Two of the butts flattened, their residual tobacco hanging out like innards. One of them maybe dropped by the man who was holding Joshua and who had killed twice. The first thing was to examine for fingerprints, but Simon Jankowski would be in maybe as early as five or six a.m., if Sarah had applied enough pressure. He would want to do the same things Reuben was about to do. Reuben had trained him, and unless his procedures had deviated wildly over the last eighteen months, Simon would be taking fingerprints and then DNA swabs. But if Reuben got there first, it would be obvious to Simon. There would be white powder from the fingerprint detection, red dye from the DNA testing. Reuben paused. He would have to take forensic samples in a way that would fool a forensic scientist. And a good one at that.

Reuben glanced at the clock. It was nudging eleven, at least six hours before Simon turned up. Everything back as he had found it. Cigarette butts looking like they had been plucked fresh from a grimy London street. The lab as pristine as when he had entered. And then Reuben had an idea. He gripped the Benson and Hedges with a pair of blue plastic forceps, and dusted the filter with powder from a glass vial. Then he carried it through to the adjacent microscopy suite. The ante-room was dark, a thick ceiling-to-floor curtain and a windowless door separating it from the rest of the lab. Reuben placed the butt carefully on the stage of a 20× light microscope and focused through the viewfinder until he was happy with the image. He clicked the shutter of the attached camera and then looked across at a monitor which was showing the captured digital view. Then he flipped the roach of the cigarette round with the forceps and examined the other side. Another partial print. Probably gripped between index finger and thumb, he guessed. He took another couple of photos, checked they had been captured OK by the imaging software, then carried the butt back into the lab and dripped distilled water across its surface, slowly and delicately, for several minutes, until he couldn't see any residual powder. A soggy cigarette butt, he thought to himself. Not exactly an unusual state of affairs.

Next, Reuben returned to the lab bench. He used a small cottonwool bud – like a miniature ear bud – to dab at the paper surface, staying at the edges of where the two fingerprints had been. Not obliterating the print, just swabbing the periphery. Simon would still get useable prints, and Reuben would have sufficient DNA for Low Copy Number Analysis. Bingo. He snipped the cotton bud into a small tube, then repeated the procedure for the other eight samples.

Later, while he waited for the DNA samples to denature in a mild phenol solution, Reuben picked up the lab phone and dialled a familiar number. He pulled out his mobile and examined the Calls Received log. 'Yes,' he said as it was answered, 'a trace on a phone which made a call to a CID-registered mobile at just after ten this morning. The number was blocked on my display, but you should be able to trace it, right?' Reuben listened for a second, then recited his mobile number and the duration of the call he had received. 'Dr Reuben Maitland, Head of Forensics at GeneCrime, Euston. OK. Can you send the info to the mobile number I've given you, please? Thanks.'

Reuben put down the phone and began to set up the nine DNA profiling reactions which would run for a couple of hours on the PCR machine. He was feeling light-headed and tired, his eyes itchy, his stomach rumbling. He had forgotten to eat, despite his words of advice for Lucy. He knew he should sleep, maybe pull a few chairs together in his office and doze for an hour or so. But along with the fatigue, prowling and restless, was a hard ball of excitement. It was somewhere in his gut, a tight feeling of cold, impatient energy. He knew he wouldn't sleep, he would just fidget. In a few short hours he would have nine DNA profiles. Eight of them would be from innocent Londoners who had dropped their cigarettes outside a cramped newsagent's in Westbourne Green, maybe on their way in to buy fresh packets. But one of them, Reuben was sure, had been stamped on by a man witnessed only from a distance who, with Lucy only a few metres from him, had calmly pushed Joshua's buggy away and into the mass of people streaming along the pavement.

Reuben loaded the PCR machine and stretched. After this, he would take minute quantities of each reaction from their plastic Eppendorf tubes and run them through the 3700 sequencer. An hour or two after that and he would have all the information he needed.

Reuben was woken by his mobile phone vibrating along the hard white lab bench. He was sitting in a lab chair, his head slumped forward. Despite his eagerness, he had obviously dozed off. The phone stopped, coming to a rest right on the edge of the bench. A couple more rings and it would have plunged to the floor.

He rubbed his face and glanced over at the sequencer. The run had finished. The DNA profiles were ready. The clock on the screen read 05:41. He had slept for nearly two and a half hours.

Reuben pulled a memory stick out of his pocket and stood up. As he copied the profiles on to the stick, he listened to the message on his phone, trying to force his brain back into gear. It was a high-pitched male voice. Northern accent. Long pauses between sentences. It wasn't the killer. 'Dr Maitland, we have the trace results. The mobile number you requested was 07761622341. An unregistered phone on a pay-as-you-go tariff. From the associated PAC digits, the handset could have been one of a large batch stolen from a Customs and Excise facility last year. Fairly untraceable, and from a couple of tests

I've run, the number doesn't seem to accept incoming calls. They can be programmed that way if you know what you're doing. That's all we have I'm afraid. If you need anything else, please call us back.'

Reuben shut down the phone, deleted the entire sequencing run from the computer's memory, then walked around the lab tidying up. Maybe, just maybe, he now had the phone number of the man holding his son. And maybe as well he had a fingerprint and a tiny sample of his DNA with a matching profile that could be run through the National DNA Database. After one final check of the lab, he turned off the lights and walked back up towards the car park, gripping the memory stick tight in his hand, grateful as hell that Simon Jankowski was no early riser.

17

Reuben took a different pool car. A Ford Focus. Smaller and more agile, but equally anonymous. As he drove, he checked his rear-view, but nothing was following him. He could just about make out the beginnings of a pale winter dawn, a half-hearted effort compared with the way a summer sunrise began. The sky was virtually cloudless, the stars in the closing stages of their vigil. It was just after six; full sunrise wouldn't happen for the best part of an hour. Reuben yawned. The two hours of sleep had helped, but he needed a couple more if he was going to function.

The thought of Lucy's spare room suddenly felt appealing, and he put his foot down, carving through the sparse traffic. As he drove, he dialled the number he had been given. There was no ringing sound, no answer service, nothing. Just a full stop, a continuous tone. He was less than surprised. The killer was hardly going to give Reuben an easy means of tracking him. Still, he had felt compelled to try.

Reuben parked close to Lucy's house. Inside, he crept silently upstairs in his socks. Lucy's bedroom door was wide open. Reuben hesitated on the landing. This was the room they used to share, the room in which he had discovered the forensic evidence that had sparked everything off. He listened for a second before peering inside. The curtains were open, the bed not slept in.

A sudden thought hit him. First Joshua. And now Lucy.

She wasn't downstairs and she wasn't in bed. Reuben headed along the landing. The spare room was empty too. In a panic, he checked the bathroom. Nothing. He ran downstairs, no longer worried about being quiet, and threw the living-room door open. Cups of coffee littered the table and floor; he'd half expected Veno's team still to be there. He walked through to his old study at the back of the house. Its walls were bare now, his pictures gone, a dark square computer squatting silently on the desk. Lucy hadn't redecorated the room. In a way, he hoped she never did. He closed the study door and headed for the kitchen. The washing-up had been done, the pan she had cooked the pasta in lying upside down on the draining board.

He stopped to think, a sense of unreality flashing through his fatigued brain. No police liaison officer, no Lucy. Surely if there had been a development, someone would have called him. His mobile had been on through the night. It didn't make sense.

Reuben ran back up the stairs and switched on the light. Three bedrooms and one bathroom. A classic English semi-detached layout. Soft carpet under his socks. He checked the spare room and Lucy's room again. And then he stopped. In front of him was a sky-blue door with animal letters on it spelling out J-O-S-H-U-A. He pushed the door open. Light from the hallway seeped past him and into the room. A scaled-down wardrobe. A chest of drawers with a changing mat on top. A small cot with wooden bars that Joshua had slept in from the day he had left their bedroom. A chair that Lucy had breast-fed him in until he was six months old. The one room in the house that Reuben hadn't wanted to go into since Joshua had been taken, the literal evidence that his son was sleeping somewhere else. And there on the floor, nuzzled next to the cot, Joshua's favourite blue bunny in her arms, Lucy was fast asleep.

Reuben stood in the doorway, breathing hard. He watched his wife, her own respiration slow and deep. He realized he had almost never seen her like this when they'd been together. Peaceful and still and oblivious. Somewhere in the midst of parenting and long hours at crime scenes, the habit of observation had been lost. They had stopped watching each other and watched their son instead.

Reuben suddenly felt drained. He turned to go. Lucy stirred, rubbing her face.

'That you?' she asked drowsily.

'Yep,' Reuben answered. 'If you mean your estranged husband.'

'Hmm.' Lucy yawned, her eyes staying closed. 'Do me a favour?'

'What?'

'Come and lie down on the floor with me.'

Reuben hesitated. Being in Joshua's room felt wrong, like an intrusion or a trespass. And lying next to Lucy raised a whole different set of issues. He was suddenly awkward and unsure.

'Maybe I ought to go . . .'

'Don't get any ideas,' Lucy said through another yawn. 'I just need some company.'

'Anyone's company?'

'The father of my missing son's company.'

Reuben stayed where he was.

'Don't make me beg,' Lucy said, 'but without some platonic help I'm not sure I'm going to make it through what remains of the night.'

Reuben struggled out of his jacket. The carpet, which had felt soft through his socks, was rough against his cheek as he lay down. Lucy pulled his arm around her. Reuben lay in the half light, next to the empty cot, close to his wife. Rest, he told himself. Drift off to sleep. Recharge yourself, ready for the battle ahead. Console your ex-wife in her moment of need. Grab a couple of hours of peace before the mayhem starts.

But it was difficult to settle, to switch off. In his pocket, he knew he probably had the DNA profile of the man holding Joshua. He worked through the next step. Attempting to match the nine cigarette profiles to samples from the two fingertip murders. He would have to get access to the crime-scene specimens, somehow smuggle them out of GeneCrime, see whether anything corresponded. And then if something did, the cigarette butt was almost certainly dropped by the killer, and Reuben could—

'You always were a fidget,' Lucy muttered, interrupting his line of thought.

'Sorry.'

'Is there any chance at all of you keeping still?'

'I'm trying.'

Lucy pulled his arm tighter around her, holding it just below the line of her breasts. Reuben forced himself to remain motionless. The thought of Lucy's body so close to his started to swamp his thoughts. This was as close to her as he had been in eighteen months. He realized that despite everything they had been through, he wanted her. A pure, physical longing. Naked, on the floor, in the nursery. As crazy as it could be, the human sexual urge cutting through everything in its path, overriding logic and decorum—

'I told you not to get any ideas,' she said.

Reuben checked himself. He had been pushing against her. He scratched his scalp and clenched his teeth. Then he forced his mind to switch back to the man who had killed twice and taken his son.

18

'So, what have we got?' Reuben asked. He leaned back in his office chair, tilting it on two legs, hands flat on the desk in front of him. With six extra people in it, his subterranean office felt squashed; there was a damp claustrophobia about its low ceiling and diluted greys and browns. The cactus sat staring back at him, resolute and unyielding, refusing to lie down and die like the other plants of GeneCrime.

Bernie Harrison was the first to answer. 'Since yesterday morning in the morgue we've been analysing samples from the two crime scenes. Mainly DNA, but some fibre work, fingerprints, shoe patterns, et cetera. We sent bloods and urines to Toxicology—'

'How did you get the urines?'

'With a long needle and a patient pathologist.'

'And what are you screening for?'

'It's the question you posed from the start. How did the killer control his victims?'

'So, specifically, you're looking for drugs, sedatives, whatever?'

'Yep. We also took scrapes from under the nails of the fingertips, and we had a bash at Mina's idea of finger-printing the fingerprints.'

'And?'

Bernie rummaged around in his thick untidy beard. 'No direct matches as yet, but we've swabbed extensively, taken everything we can think of. Sarah has requested thoroughness over speed.'

'OK, well I'm requesting speed first.'

'But Sarah—'

'DCI Hirst isn't running this investigation. I am. And I want us flat out on it. We can go back and test our controls when we've got positives, not before.'

Mina Ali squinted at him through her square glasses. 'What Bernie means is that in your absence yesterday we came to the general agreement that we would play it safe, be methodical, do first things first. This is high profile. Newspapers, TV, everything. We can't afford to screw it up. Judging from the time frame of the two deaths, we've probably got a few days before the next killing, if there actually is one.'

Reuben tipped forward in his chair, all four legs digging deep into the thin carpet. 'I don't think we have.'

'Why not?' Mina asked.

Reuben wiped a sharp fragment of sleep from the corner of his eye. *Because the fucker is holding a two-year-old boy captive. Because no one would do that longer than they had to. Because he already knows who he is going to kill next. Because he wants this finished with as quickly as I do.* 'I just don't. We can't assume anything. When a man has killed successfully for the first time, there's often a gap. A period of reflection, an interval until the urge returns. Maybe it never will. When he's killed twice, though, carried out well-planned executions, all bets are off. This isn't a rampage, but it also isn't necessarily a drawn-out game of cat and mouse.'

'So what are you proposing?'

I want double shifts. I want you sleeping at your benches. I want every conceivable test running until we've nailed the fucker who has my boy. Again, Reuben restrained himself, edited his answer, watered down its meaning. 'We need to move quicker. I'd like to see the profiles run through the National DNA Database as they emerge. Cross-reference between the two scenes second. I want someone to coordinate gross forensics with the DNA.' Reuben cast his eyes around his office. Mina Ali, his deputy, dark and petite; Bernie Harrison, Paul Mackay, Helen Alders, Leigh Harding; and Chris Stevens, dogged pathologist, bald and intense. Behind them on either side, lab-coated scientists visible through the internal windows. 'Paul,' he said, 'can you do that?'

'Sure,' Paul answered, barely glancing up from his notebook.

'Right. Leigh, what about CID?'

Detective Leigh Harding cleared his throat. Reuben didn't know him well. He had been recruited just before Reuben's dismissal. He looked like he belonged in the forces, his face bony and hard. 'The sales executive, Carl Everitt, worked for a Swiss pharmaceutical company, and the scientist, Dr Ian Gillick, worked at the Royal Holloway.'

'As in the medical school?' Bernie asked.

'Yep. And the Swiss company is Roche.'

'A link?' Reuben asked.

'Nothing obvious. Pharmaceutical companies and universities sometimes have overlaps, of course, but we've found no direct personal association between Mr Everitt and UCL. He doesn't appear to have been a frequent visitor. In fact, no one at University HR, or the three research departments we visited, recognized his picture.'

'And Roche?'

'Everitt had been with them two and a half years, recruited from another drug company. Apparently he was a pharma sales exec who spent the majority of his time in the London office.'

'What about the company he came from before that?' Reuben asked.

Detective Harding chewed his lip. 'We're looking into it.'

'Right.'

Reuben rubbed his eyes, which felt heavy and tired and dry. He was having to hold himself back. Instinctively, all he wanted to do was catch the sick bastard who had sawn the fingertips off two men in a week. This was what he lived for, what he succeeded at, what GeneCrime had taken him back to do. He felt frustrated by the dearth of progress, by the lack of a connection between the two victims, by Sarah's insistence on slow, methodical progress. But he had to keep reminding himself. All of this was good. All of this kept his son alive. The more samples Forensics examined, the more people CID interviewed, the longer it took to bring everything together, the more hope he would have. Still, it didn't sit right.

Running his eyes around the members of his team patiently waiting for him to say something, Reuben wondered whether he had it in him to actively lead them astray, to subvert the investigation they were throwing themselves into. Could he mislead the very people he had helped to train? Could he lie to colleagues to whom he had taught the truth? The time, he knew, would come soon. At the beginning of an investigation, no one knows anything. It isn't until separate lines of evidence begin to snag, until small insignificant fragments start to reinforce one another, that identities and motives emerge. They weren't quite there yet, but they soon would be.

'OK. Has anyone else got anything useful?'

Reuben saw something flick between the faces in front of him.

'What?' he asked.

Mina reached her hand forward and placed it on his. He glanced down at her slender fingers, the smattering of black hairs where the hand narrowed at the wrist, the smooth region of empty pores above it, where the repeated pulling on and off of lab gloves prevented any hairs from growing. 'Boss, we're all aware that Joshua has been taken, and if there's anything we can possibly do for you . . .' Mina searched the faces of her colleagues for support. 'If there's anything you need . . .' Mina withdrew her hand, and shrugged at Reuben. 'We just thought, you know . . .'

Reuben flashed her a sad smile. At that moment, caught in Mina's dark eyes, he felt more conflicted than he could ever recall. Nine DNA profiles on the USB stick in his pocket. A total of three or four hours' sleep. Years of training and police procedures crashing into the over-whelming intensity of parental instinct. Simon Jankowski through the window extracting DNA from the cigarette butts, a few hours behind him but quickly catching up. And Mina, loyal Mina, holding his eye, making him feel like a fucking fraud.

Reuben focused intently on the spines of the cactus on his desk. 'Look, I just want to say one thing. I don't want any sympathy. I don't mean to be ungrateful about it, Mina, really I don't, but my personal life stays personal. In the meantime, we get on with the job at hand. We have an active and dangerous killer to catch. OK?'

There was a muted nod of agreement around the group. Reuben stood up to signify that the meeting was over. As his team filed out and made their way into the adjacent labs, he checked his watch and cursed. 10.13. He was late. They would be waiting for him in the café around the corner. He left the office and strode down the corridor.

19

Judith Meadows had her back to Reuben as he entered the café. On the round steel table in front of her sat a blue car seat, Fraser Meadows lying inside it, sleeping the comatose sleep of a newborn. Reuben leaned over for a better look. Fraser had a shock of black hair, puffy pink eyes, red lips, a small snub of a nose. The table was littered with nappy sacks, a pack of wet-wipes, a couple of dummies, a grey tub of Sudocrem, a bottle of milk and an upturned lid.

'So this is what maternity leave looks like,' he said.

Judith craned her neck round to him. 'It may look awful, but it feels great.'

'How is the little fella?'

'Perfect. Especially when he's asleep.'

Across the table, Moray Carnock was sitting a pace back. He looked uncomfortable, as if worried the baby might be sick over him. Judging from Moray's clothes, it would be difficult to tell. He was wearing a bulky overcoat which had faded to a nondescript grey-brown, a pair of battered shoes, and jeans which had probably never been in fashion.

'Not one for babies, I guess,' Reuben said to Moray.

'Like Judith said, great concept while they're asleep,' Moray answered in his Aberdonian drawl. 'The rest of the time a bloody nightmare. Just as long as no one asks me to change a nappy.'

'You're fairly safe,' Judith said.

Reuben pulled out a chair. He hadn't seen Judith or Moray for nearly four weeks, and it was good to be with them again. He was well aware that they had been the only constancy of his last two years.

'Missing GeneCrime?' Reuben asked Judith.

The building was only a few streets away, and Judith glanced out of the window, as if looking for it. 'Not so much. Going to pop in to show Fraser off some time this week. You missing your freedom?'

'I've only been back two days.'

'You didn't answer the question.'

Reuben smiled. His senior technician never let anything go that easily. 'We'll come to that.'

He inspected the specials board behind Moray. Ordinarily, a snack and a cup of tea would have kept his restless metabolism going until lunch. But he wasn't hungry. His stomach seemed to have shrunk over the last few hours. He wanted to sit back and catch up with his friends, but there were more pressing issues. He had asked them to meet him for a reason, knowing that if anyone could help him they could.

'Look,' he said, 'I've got a few serious things to say. I need your help. Any remaining favours I've got, I want to use up. Cash them in here and now. This is life and death.'

Moray shuffled closer to the table. Judith regarded him intently.

'You'd better just spit it out,' Moray said.

Reuben told them what had happened. The kidnapping, the killings, the phone call, the deal he had been offered. A life for a life. Judith's eyes flicked momentarily to her sleeping baby when Reuben described the abduction of Joshua. And her eyes sparkled when he mentioned the cigarette butts. Neither of them had seen him on the news, Judith absorbed in her baby, Moray stuck on a long-haul flight. Reuben was glad.

'So what do you need, big man?' Moray asked.

'Simply this,' Reuben said. 'I need to set the lab up again.'

'Where?'

'My old garage.'

'Is that where you moved all the stuff?'

'Yeah.'

Reuben pictured the equipment. A sequencer that had

seen better days. A couple of small freezers. A battered microfuge that vibrated like hell when it spun. Two storage boxes full of reagents. A PCR machine. A cardboard box full of Gilsons, Eppendorfs and plastic tips. A box full of glassware that had rattled and clanked as he carried it into the garage a month earlier. Sarah Hirst had made it a condition of his re-employment that Reuben's private lab ceased to exist. But now, Reuben could see a lot of sense in resurrecting it.

'Is there room?'

'Not much, Judith, but it'll have to do.'

'What else?'

'There's water and electrics, good lighting, and it's hidden from view. I can run an internet connection in as well. It's too risky to do anything at GeneCrime. I need to do some independent forensics, examine potential DNA left behind at the two murders, compare it with the DNA from the cigarette butts.'

'So you can isolate which DNA sample came from the killer?'

'I can't see another way of doing it.'

Most of Moray's substantial bulk was leaning forward, his thick arms propped against his equally sturdy legs. 'Putting the old team back together, eh?' he said. 'I've barely done anything illegal for weeks.'

'I don't believe that for a second.'

'I didn't say immoral, I just said illegal.'

'So?' Reuben asked.

'Count me in.'

'Judith?'

Judith was busy adjusting Fraser in his car seat, loosening the straps, sitting him up. He remained utterly unconscious. 'It's not going to be easy,' she said. 'Not with an eight-week-old baby.'

'I know. And I'm sorry.' Reuben tried not to sound impatient. 'But what do you think?'

Judith glanced from her child to Reuben and back again. 'We'll manage. We'll have to.'

Reuben clenched his fists under the table. With Judith and Moray he had half a chance.

'Look, there's one other thing.'

'Here we go,' Moray grumbled.

'The killer has set a trap.'

'What do you mean?'

'I have no idea. He simply said that if he senses Gene-Crime are closing in on him, he will kill my son. That if we are starting to get too close to him he will know.'

'Is that possible?'

'Lucy asked me the same thing.'

'You're speaking to each other?'

'More so these days.'

'What did you tell her?'

'What I'm telling you. That there's no way of knowing for sure.'

'Could be a bluff.'

'But would you gamble your child's life on a bluff?'

'I don't have a child,' Moray answered. 'Clearly.'

'Judith?'

Judith gazed deep into the sleeping perfection of her newly born son. 'Not in a million years. But is it actually possible for someone to set a trap, find out if the investigation is closing in? I don't see how they'd do it. Unless . . .'

'What?' Reuben asked.

'Unless they had someone on the inside. Someone in the force, or in the FSS, or even inside GeneCrime.'

Reuben pondered Judith's words for a second. 'An informant? It would have to be someone close to the case.'

'Maybe another member of the team has been targeted,' Moray said. 'How do you know you're the only one?'

'I don't.'

'Presumably no one in the building is aware the killer has contacted you. So it's entirely feasible he's got another member of staff doing what he wants.'

'Seems a lot of trouble to go to,' Judith said. 'I mean, what's wrong with just going out and killing a few people? Proper old-fashioned slaughter.'

'Exactly.'

Reuben picked out the Sudocrem from the crowd of baby paraphernalia on the table. It was a small grey tub with a grey plastic lid. He sniffed the contents, a rush of memories flooding in on the wave of oily antiseptic. Chaffed skin, nappy rash, the sticky ointment cooling and soothing his crying son at bedtime when he was younger. 'I can't see it. Taking a child is . . .' Reuben felt a hot tight surge of anger erupt in his temporal lobes and swell through him, making him squeeze the tub hard. He waited a second while the anger eased, loosening up and subsiding. 'Taking a child is a lot of trouble. Anything on top is even worse. If you were the killer, why would you put yourself through that?'

'Because this means something,' Judith answered. 'This is important. So important the killer can't afford it to go wrong.'

'But this has been going through my mind, over and over. What drives someone to need to kill so badly that they have to go to such lengths?'

Moray and Judith were silent. Fraser Meadows, two months old, stirred in his car seat. His eyes blinked open, dark like his mother's. The door of the café opened and closed, a shock of icy air slamming in. Reuben bit deep into a fingernail, his brain crammed tight with images and words and ideas crashing into one another. Above the background hum of activity and conversation, Fraser started to wail.

20

The garage was just like any other garage in the world. Carless, dusty, stacked full of items that didn't belong anywhere else. Reuben rooted around. Stiff useless paintbrushes, tins of paint that would never be opened again, broken items that should have been thrown away but were instead stored out of sight, a car seat that Joshua had grown out of, a few lengths of wood that would never be nailed to anything, an internal door that had been removed at some point and not rehung. Reuben paused, hands on hips, sweating. He loved the place. It was the only part of the house that escaped Lucy's regimen of immaculate orderliness.

He piled a mound of worthless junk in the corner, directed Moray towards the nearest tip, then swept up before clearing a section of racking and setting the internal door horizontally, balancing it between two sturdy kitchen stools. He covered the door in several layers of clingfilm. Then he began unpacking boxes holding the laboratory equipment. As he pulled out each piece of apparatus, he recalled where he had got it from. The sequencer was being decommissioned by a general FSS lab in Dulwich. The PCR machine, which was old-fashioned, was being junked by GeneCrime. The microfuge he got from a skip outside a hospital diagnostics department. Judith had taken the Gilsons one at a time from the lab. The freezers he had bought second-hand from an electrical shop. The reagents had been systematically begged, stolen or borrowed from former colleagues. The rudiments of a laboratory that had helped him hunt the men he hadn't been able to touch before he was sacked from the force.

Taking out a bottle marked '70% Ethanol', he began to swab the area down. He was methodical in his movements, losing himself in the repetitive action, quick but precise, sterilizing the surfaces and the equipment. He kept his brain away from the cold facts of the last twenty-four hours, and focused instead on sorting the lab out. When everything was clean, Reuben plugged the machinery in and turned it all on. It had taken an hour from start to finish, and a frantic one at that, but he was almost ready.

He walked through into the house. Female voices bounced off the kitchen surfaces and ricocheted into the hallway. Judith was holding Fraser in her arms, gazing into his face, answering Lucy's questions without looking up at her. Reuben stood and watched for a second, unnerved that there was a child in the house that Joshua lived in, and that somewhere in the city Joshua was with a complete stranger. He rocked on his feet, trying to shut out the notion of another man with his child. All that mattered now was sticking to the plan.

'Judith,' he said, walking into the kitchen, 'I think we should start. We don't have much time to get everything done.'

Judith looked up at Lucy, who was watching her intently. 'I feel horrible. Here I am with my baby while you—'

Lucy cut her off. 'Don't be silly,' she said. 'It's not your fault.'

'I know. But all the same.'

'Luce, would you mind looking after Fraser for a couple of hours while Judith gets things properly up and running in the garage?'

Lucy swung her attention from Judith to Reuben and back again.

'But if you don't feel up to it . . .'

Lucy took a step towards Judith and the child in her arms. 'No, I'd like to look after him, Judith, if that's all right.'

'You sure?'

Reuben watched his ex-wife carefully. He appreciated that she was a difficult woman to read. He imagined her battling the urge to scream. As she spoke she was composed, the corporate lawyer in her emerging and smoothing everything over.

'In a strange way it will be comforting,' she said. 'The house feels wrong without a child in it. Empty and quiet. I don't know what else to do with myself.'

Judith handed Fraser over, slowly and carefully, Lucy sliding her hands under Judith's and supporting the weight. Fraser's arms jerked upwards then stopped, falling slowly back into place. Reuben raised his eyebrows at Lucy, a brief smile twitching across his features. Then he walked Judith back towards the garage.

'Everything's plugged in, it just needs calibrating. Can you check the reference dyes on the sequencer, make sure the PCR machine is cycling OK, ensure that everything else is talking to each other?'

'I guess so. And when it is?'

'I'll be back by then.'

'To do what?'

'Ah, Judith. Having a baby hasn't changed you. Still too many questions.'

'I'm waiting.'

'My job over the next couple of hours is to snatch GeneCrime's DNA samples from the two murder scenes.'

'How the hell are you going to do that?'

'No idea.'

'Well, you'd better get thinking. It won't be easy.'

'Nope.'

'Then we'll profile them and attempt to match them against the cigarette butts?'

'Like I said, reproducing hasn't ruined you. If we get an exact match between any of the butts and the DNA samples from the houses of Everitt and Gillick, we'll know the DNA profile of our man. And if we know that, and he's ever encountered the police before, we can hunt him down.'

'If he hasn't set a trap.'

'Who else is going to find out? If we do it here in the garage, no one in the world knows anything except us. Not CID, not GeneCrime, not the killer.' He frowned, an angry ridge of skin rising up between his eyebrows as they knotted together. 'And then I intend to make him very, very sorry for what he has done to my family.'

Reuben heard the doorbell go. He waited silently. He listened to the sound of the door being pulled open. Detective Veno's voice. A pause. The Missing Child team trooping in. The door slamming shut again. Reuben checked his pockets for his car keys, then he opened the garage door and left, jogging quickly towards the white Ford Focus parked thirty metres away.

21

The midday traffic was heavier than he expected. The winter sun was struggling to warm the city. It seemed remote, too high up, not really interested. Reuben stayed in second and third, the pedal an on/off switch, darting from traffic light to traffic light, from junction to junction.

This is where the real subterfuge begins, he told himself when he pulled into the GeneCrime car park. He killed the engine, and caught himself in the rear-view mirror. His eyes stared back. Pale green irises, circled with dark green. Red capillaries searching in from the corners, looking like they were grasping for the iris. He rubbed the bags beneath, still staring deep into himself. You can do this, he said. You can lie to everyone and find out the truth about your son. He took in the parallel creases across his brow, the tightness of his mouth, the flecks of grey in his light brown hair. He needed to burn bright for every moment of the next few days, then he would be OK. Reuben opened the car door and climbed out, unconvinced by his own pep-talk.

Inside, he made straight for his office. He had no idea how he was going to take the DNA samples. They would be in a freezer somewhere, coded and hidden. Stealing from the police with no one noticing. He entered his office and stared into the DNA lab. Then he checked his watch. A quarter to one, give or take. There hadn't been another death reported yet. Joshua would still be alive. But every minute mattered.

He rested his forehead against the cold internal window. The noises of the lab made minute vibrations across the glass. The whine of a centrifuge, the buzz of a large freezer, fragments of scientists' conversations. The window was one-way and Reuben knew he couldn't be seen. He remained still, thinking, the progress of the room pressed into his forehead. Nothing constructive came to him.

There was a knock at the door. Reuben stepped away from the window, rubbing his weary face. 'Yes,' he said.

Mina Ali entered. 'You been out? I couldn't find you.'

'Sorry. Had a few things that needed sorting. What's the news?'

'Nothing much. We've done all the extractions from both crime scenes. Eighty-three priority samples, plus a couple of hundred ancillary ones. Because you've requested speed, we're already running the eighty-three through standard profiling, with the others backed up and ready to go.'

'When will we have the results?'

Mina pulled out her mobile and checked its clock. 'By two thirty, give or take. Then half an hour for quality control and manual checking. Say three o'clock.'

Reuben didn't answer. There were eighty-three DNAs that Forensics felt might be useful, plus a larger number of lower quality. Eighty-three was good. The sequencer in his garage could process ninety-six samples at a time. With Judith's help he could assess all the specimens in a single run, plus controls. If only he could get the things out of GeneCrime.

'Boss?' Mina asked.

Subterfuge. Lies. Misinformation. In the heart of the search for the truth, in the unit whose only function was to determine what was genuine and what wasn't. It starts here, Reuben reminded himself. Here and now.

He turned to his trusted deputy. 'Mina, can you show me the samples, walk me through all the analyses?'

'Sure.' She regarded him quizzically. 'If you really want to.'

'I really want to,' Reuben answered flatly. 'Let's do it.'

Mina led Reuben out of the office, around the corner and into the lab. He looked around, almost expecting to see the physical evidence of the hours he had spent at the bench through the night. Five scientists acknowledged him: Bernie, Paul, Simon, Birgit Kasper, and a technician called Alex who was covering Judith's maternity leave and whose surname he still hadn't learned.

Mina pulled on a pair of purple vinyl gloves. 'OK,' she said, leading him around the room. 'This is what we've got cooking. Those of us lucky enough to visit Ian Gillick's scene of death prioritized samples there. Because GeneCrime didn't initially handle Carl Everitt's scene, we trawled through the specimens the FSS took and prioritized retrospectively. The two scenes have been kept entirely separate to avoid cross-contamination. The Gillick DNA is in Freezer Four, and Everitt's is in Seven.'

'So the eighty-three samples currently being profiled are from both scenes?'

Mina checked with Bernie Harrison, who was overseeing the bio-informatics. 'Bernie, what's the split?'

As Bernie checked a spreadsheet, slowly running a pencil down the screen of a laptop, Reuben's mind raced. Judith would be calibrating the equipment. The sooner he got the samples to her, the quicker he could hunt down the man who had his son. He glanced at the bank of freezers against the far wall. But now the fuckers were stored separately. He would have to take them from two different locations. This was suddenly more complicated.

'OK. Thirty-eight from the salesman, forty-five from the scientist,' Bernie called over.

'Let's have a look,' Reuben instructed Mina.

Mina walked silently over to the bank of tall, white upright freezers. They loomed over her diminutive frame, impassive and broad, numbers marked in their upper right corners in black marker pen. Each displayed their internal temperature above the door. Number 4 read $-82°C$ in red digits. Mina pulled the sturdy blue handle on the side of the freezer, which unlatched it and allowed it to open. Then she opened the lower of two slim internal doors. Inside, rows of frosted metal racking held columns of white plastic boxes the size of house bricks. On the lid of each box was a number and a description. Mina pulled out the closest box to her, which read '09/#4701-4745: Ian Gillick'.

Reuben held it in his hand. He alternated his fingers. At minus eighty-two degrees his skin could easily stick. He knew from the label what was inside. Forty-five sample tubes labelled consecutively from 4701 to 4745. DNA taken from the murder scene of the scientist Ian Gillick. The box felt light and portable. Half of him wanted simply to run out of the lab with it. But no one could know. He handed it back and turned away.

Mina showed him a similar small white box in Freezer 7. Reuben then made a show of touring the lab, making sure everything was being done correctly, all the time thinking, how the hell do I get the samples out of here? He noted that Simon Jankowski was just finishing up with the cigarette butts. He checked the lab clock. GeneCrime were seven hours behind him.

Reuben stared into the clock. Lunchtime. Ordinarily, it would be quiet. But everyone was working flat out, skipping lunch, hanging around because their boss was in the vicinity. He realized belatedly that staying where he was only hindered his chances of taking the boxes unnoticed.

He left the lab. Next to it was a windowless room housing yet more slab-like minus-eighty freezers. He opened one marked Emergency Back-Up. It was half full. He checked behind it, thought for a second, then headed for the floor below. Reuben had been consulted in the original design of GeneCrime. He made his way down a set of concrete stairs and into the solitary corridor that ran through the lower floor. He passed metal storage racks housing surplus plastic ware, a locked cell, wide pipework for fume cupboards, a sturdy chemical storage cupboard, three disused offices and a reading room that was hardly ever used, finally stopping at an unmarked door which lay directly under the final strip light. Inside the room, the GeneCrime server, small banks of green flashing lights and short sections of grey cabling, squatted in the corner. This was the portal, the hub that processed the information flowing in and out of the building's computers, attached directly to the National DNA Database. A cube the size of a washing machine upon which most of GeneCrime's operations depended. But it wasn't the server that interested Reuben. Thick blue cabling led from the server into an adjacent cupboard. Reuben opened it. Inside lay exactly what he was after: rows of untouched fuse boards and trip switches, the power supply to the whole unit.

Reuben checked his mobile phone display. A much stronger signal than in the morgue, with its lining of metal racks. He ran his fingers over a panel of switches, guessing as he went. Numbers had been written in neat biro next to each switch. They could be office numbers, zones of the building, coded power sockets, anything. He took the plunge and flicked one. Nothing happened. Reuben counted a slow thirty, waited a moment longer, then reset it before trying another one.

He checked his phone. Adequate signal. No incoming call.

He tried to decipher the codes but quickly realized it was impossible. The numbers above each switch probably related to an electrical master-plan for the building. He chose another random switch, wondering where the plan might be stored. He guessed the contractors who tested the fire alarms, air conditioning and general building systems probably kept copies. Again there was no response, so he chose a different switch. After a long count to thirty, he moved it back and chose another one. He tried to picture the chaos breaking out above him but failed. He couldn't hear anything. For all he knew, he was doing nothing more than denying power momentarily to a series of empty rooms.

Impatiently, he rubbed the screen of his phone. Two bars, flashing in and out. Enough.

Reuben chose again and again but to no avail. He had just returned another small grey trip switch to its original position when his phone vibrated. He checked the display. Mina. Bingo.

Reuben answered it. 'Yes,' he said.

'Boss, you still around? We've got problems. The lab power just went out.'

'Yeah?'

'It's back on now, but it was down for what felt like the best part of a minute.'

Reuben reached for the same switch and turned it off again. 'What about the freezers?'

'Exactly,' Mina said. 'Shit. It's off again. We need access to the back-up minus-eighties in the freezer room. Where are you?'

In the background, Reuben could hear the asynchronous alarms of a whole laboratory full of freezers. Their tones were distinct, different models with different warning sounds, battery packs powering their electronic screams. Deprive a lab freezer of power and it instantly let you know about it. 'I'm on my way,' he said. He paused to turn the switch back on, then left the room and headed back to the lab.

When he got there, most of the team were stationary, staring at pieces of equipment, watching them reboot.

Mina approached him. 'The power's running, but I don't like the look of it. If it goes again we're going to start losing samples.'

Reuben didn't meet Mina's eye. 'Let's ship the precious stuff out to the back-ups,' he said.

'Right.'

A sudden thought hit him. The profiling of the eighty-three samples. If that had been ruined by the power out, they would need to start again. They would have to take the eighty-three DNAs he wanted and begin the process from scratch. He spun round to examine the sequencer. On its screen lay a multitude of brightly coloured bar codes on a black background. It was still running. And then he remembered.

'It's OK,' Mina said, reading his thoughts, 'the sequencers are on isolated power supplies. It's really just the freezers we need to worry about for now.'

Reuben followed Mina to the end of the lab. 'I'll take this one,' he said, opening Freezer 4. 'You get Three.'

As Mina opened the next freezer, the huge white door looming between them, Reuben reached for the box marked '09/#4701-4745: Ian Gillick'. He took a second identical plastic box from the shelf below it, marked '08/#1338-1383: Run Yu'. The name made him stop for a second. Although it carried memories of a previous case, he knew the samples were no longer important. Reuben switched the lids of the two containers, then pulled out six more boxes, stacking them between his straight arms.

Mina closed her freezer and carried a similar number of sample boxes out of the lab and into the adjacent freezer room. Reuben helped her insert them into the freezer marked Emergency Back-Up. They returned to the lab and repeated the process. This time Reuben targeted Freezer 7, again swapping lids with an older set of specimens marked '08/#1552-1597: Jez Heatherington Andrews'. Mina propped the Emergency Back-Up open while Reuben stacked another twelve boxes inside it. He stopped on the last two.

'No room,' he said.

'Rats,' Mina answered.

Reuben breathed in and out, the noise lost in the hum of multiple compressors. He forced himself to say the words, feeling like a bad actor, all the time cursing the fact that he was lying to someone so close and so trusted. 'How about these two?' he asked, holding out two containers for Mina to inspect. 'They look old.'

'Let's have a look. Run Yu and Jez Heatherington Andrews. That takes me back. But, yeah, they can be returned with the rest in the lab. If the power dies again, it won't be the end of the world.'

Reuben turned away from Mina and walked back towards the lab. He knew Mina would be scrawling the locations of the shifted samples into the inventory book. He kept going, past the lab and into his office, where he put on his jacket, zipping up inside it the two boxes marked Run Yu and Jez Heatherington Andrews, which contained the DNA of Carl Everitt and Dr Ian Gillick. Then he paced along corridors, through doors and up stairs to the exit of GeneCrime, no record of his deception anywhere in his wake. The cold boxes stuck to the fibres of his shirt. He signed a car out at the security desk and walked into the freezing air.

22

Reuben held the cold white boxes close to his body, a hand inside his jacket pocket keeping them in place. With his spare hand he pressed the key as he approached the row of pool cars. In fact, as he looked at it, the term 'key' was inaccurate. It was a fob. No metal, just a wedge of plastic that emitted radio waves. A large silver Volvo S60 flashed at him, one of three vehicles reserved for senior staff attending crime scenes in a hurry.

He climbed in and inspected it. The large Volvo was well specced. As Reuben reversed, the electronic tone of the parking assist became shorter and more jumpy. After a second, it flatlined, as Reuben nudged into a concrete pillar. The sound of death, a continuous tone of desolation. He pulled forward, tyres complaining, and made his way round the car park. He knew that sensors were checking road adhesion, varying the power to each wheel, modulating braking forces, finessing fuel ratios, damping the suspension, controlling temperatures and pressures and firing times. As Reuben descended the long concrete ramp which linked GeneCrime with the outside world, he wondered whether he was really in control of the car. He had run entire investigations on less computer power than the Volvo had. But all of this progress had one good thing going for it. He nudged the air conditioning to max and slotted the DNA samples into the glove box. Chilled storage area. Now that was a step forward, particularly for a forensic scientist.

He drove quickly through the early-afternoon traffic. The glove box would help, but wouldn't stop the DNAs thawing completely. He knew these specimens were as precious as any forensic samples anywhere in the world. They were his son, and they were a killer. He also knew he had to return them to GeneCrime unscathed. If they got spoiled, the unit wouldn't be able to perform corroborative testing on them. And that could ruin a conviction. He had to be quick.

He searched the dash for anything else that could help. He pressed a button and something red flashed up on the display, the letter S lit up bright. The large car hunkered down, dropping closer to the road. Bumps in the London tarmac suddenly became jarring shocks through his spine. The engine note changed, a lower growl which roared as he pressed the accelerator deep into the carpeted floor. Reuben suppressed a smile as he flew past three lanes of slower city traffic. Over-engineered, pointless, environmental lunacy. But when you needed to get somewhere in a big hurry, modern cars were fantastic machines.

A few streets from Lucy's house, Reuben flicked the sport button off again. He felt the car relax and urged his heart and stomach to calm. He was tense, off balance, operating on fast forward. He needed to think clearly, to act efficiently, to process the DNA samples in his glove box correctly. And then, if it worked, if profiles matched and police records were available, he was just hours from finding Joshua.

He turned into the long road of Georgian terraces. A grand old street lined with trees, properties out of the range of public-sector forensic scientists, even a senior one who had once been married to a successful solicitor. London money. Where it came from, how people got hold of it, how they managed to live in such opulence – these were, Reuben felt, unsolvable mysteries.

At the end of the street, Reuben checked his mirrors before turning. And that was when he saw it again. The Audi that had followed him the previous night. Turning in behind him from a side street. He stared at it, filling in the gaps. In broad daylight it was dark blue, rather than black. And it was definitely an A6, not an A4. But Reuben knew it was the same car. The driver's side headlight was cracked. It was being driven by a thick-set Caucasian man.

He strained to see. The car was ten metres back, not gaining, but not going away either. Reuben pulled across the junction. The dark Audi followed. He swerved down a side street. The car came after him. Again the thought came to Reuben, as it had done before. Is this the killer? Is he watching me, seeing where I go and what I do? Making sure I'm keeping my end of the bargain? Does he have my son in the back?

Reuben stared in the mirror, barely looking where he was going, his mind racing. And then he made a spontaneous human decision. He slammed the brakes on. The computer instantly detected that the vehicle was slewing across the road. It shot warnings to all four wheels, wrested control of the discs and callipers from Reuben, shifted the distribution towards those tyres with the greatest grip. Thousands of calculations undertaken and acted upon in the two seconds it took Reuben to screech to a halt.

Reuben pressed his seatbelt button and threw the door open in one move. He was out of the car and sprinting up the road towards the Audi, pumping his fists as he ran, his eyes fixed on the driver. The driver turned away from him, looking towards the rear seat. Reuben was five metres away. The engine note changed, a harsh revving, angry power that was about to be released. Reuben flailed forward. The Audi was spinning its wheels. He slammed both hands down on the bonnet. Tried to grip. Desperate to get at the driver. But the surface pulled away from him. The car recoiled, grinding rubber into the tarmac. Accelerating in reverse, straight between layers of parked cars. Reuben stared at the driver, but his head was still swivelled back, watching the road. Reuben changed the angle of his focus. The registration plate. Letters and numbers scanned, repeated under his breath. The Audi was now pulling a sharp turn at the junction. There was another screech of tyres and it pulled away at speed. Reuben couldn't see into the back of the car. He stood and watched it for a couple of seconds, repeating the registration number to himself.

As he walked back to his car, the smell of burning in his nose, he wondered what this meant. Being followed again, but by someone who didn't want to confront him. Was this the act of a killer? he asked himself.

When he arrived at Lucy's house, Reuben grabbed the boxes and walked quickly through the front door. Inside the garage, Judith was leaning against the sequencer, flicking through an instruction manual.

'You look bored.'

Her eyes came to rest on the two boxes. 'Not any more.'

'Can you do me a favour?'

'Another one?'

Reuben scribbled the Audi's registration number on to a piece of paper. 'Ask a friend to run this for me. I'd do it myself, but some things are best done quietly.'

Judith took the piece of paper. 'I know a man who can,' she said. 'But you'll have to give me a bit of time. Right, how many samples are there?'

Reuben tried to slow his breathing, to get back to normality. 'Eighty-three.'

'Better get cracking then.'

'Have you found everything we need?'

'Yep. Plus some of the reagents are thawing in the fridge.'

'Which one?' Reuben asked, checking out the make-shift laboratory.

'In the kitchen. The freezers in here need time to reach temperature.'

'How about Veno and his team – they still here?'

'Just gone.'

'And everyone else?'

'Fraser has been fed and is asleep. Lucy is keeping an eye on him. Moray picked up some Big Dye Terminator from your mate at the FSS.'

'Nice one.'

'Although he seemed a bit disappointed. I guess Big Dye Terminator does sound a bit more promising than what it actually is – a Small Box of Sequencing Reagent.'

'Where is our fat friend now?'

'Making a second trip to the tip. Seems to be quite enjoying himself.'

'That's men and tips for you.' Reuben paused, scanning

the area, making mental lists of what needed doing. Sequencing eighty-three samples would take an hour to set up if they worked together, and just under three hours to run. 'You ready?' he asked.

'Ready as I'll ever be,' Judith answered, raising her dark eyebrows and frowning briefly. 'Shall we?'

Reuben and Judith began the work as they had done so many times before in GeneCrime, Reuben taking the lead, Judith anticipating each step of the protocol before he got there, ready and waiting with the heat block, the labelling for the tubes, the preparation of buffers and solutions, the timing of microfuge spins. Reuben noted that Judith had improvised while he was gone. Ice cubes from the freezer in an empty tupperware box; the Big Dye Terminator kit slowly thawing in the fridge; an empty tin of paint for spent pipette tips. It felt like crude and desperate science. Tense and concentrated, making do with what came to hand; an upturned door wrapped in clingfilm for a bench, a cramped domestic garage for a laboratory. But there was no other option. This was all they had, and it had to work.

When the eighty-three DNA samples had been added to their sequencing reactions, Reuben walked the two precious GeneCrime boxes through to the kitchen and slotted them in the top section of the freezer. Lucy was in the living room, staring silently out of the window. At her feet, Fraser Meadows slept motionless in his car seat.

Reuben hesitated for a moment, wanting to say something but not knowing what to say. Then he turned and walked back to the garage. There was no time for anything else.

Judith began to load the samples into the tiny vertical wells of the sequencer, minute blue volumes falling into invisible slots, forming an elongated series of U-shapes. Reuben watched her, praying she wouldn't make a mistake or lose a sample. Every profile could be vital, the one match that would yield the killer's identity.

There was a noise outside. The unmistakably heavy footsteps of uniformed officers.

'You OK from here on in?' Reuben whispered to Judith.

'Sure,' she whispered back. 'Ready to run in about ten minutes.'

'Great.'

The doorbell rang. Reuben wondered whether Lucy would even hear it.

'Looks like Veno's team are back,' he said. The computer screen of the sequencer read 15:24. 'So the samples will be off by, what, just after seven?'

'Exactly. Once they're running, I'll take Fraser home.'

The doorbell sounded again. Reuben straightened. He was suddenly nervous. Veno could be bringing bad news. 'I'll catch you back here then.' He walked out into the corridor and down to the front door, a restless blur of black uniform visible through the spyhole.

23

Detective Paul Veno's office was even worse than Reuben's. It felt sterile, cold, brutal. Even an unwanted cactus, Reuben sensed, would have added warmth.

Lucy hadn't spoken in the car. She had simply gazed through the window, her eyes looking outwards, the rest of her retreating inwards. Reuben wondered how he would feel if he didn't have the hunt for the man holding his son. In that moment, he realized that the pursuit of evil was what kept him sane. To be doing something, to be breaking rules and tearing forward, profiling samples and gathering momentum towards the killer, all of this stopped him thinking through the awful realities of the situation. Where Joshua was, how distressed he was, how utterly petrified and alone.

Veno replaced the grubby receiver of his phone. 'That was media liaison,' he said. 'We're going with the police angle.'

Lucy reached sideways under the desk and placed her hand on top of Reuben's. 'What do you mean?' she asked.

Detective Veno made a show of sighing and rubbing his jowls. 'There have been no fresh sightings of your son, Mrs Maitland. The TV appearance yesterday generated a lot of publicity, not all of it positive. A few leads came to the fore, but they all turned out to be useless or wrong. We got decent coverage on the six o'clocks, and even better exposure on the ten o'clocks, thanks to Reuben's little fit.'

Reuben met Veno's eyes but didn't react.

'The newspapers were all over it this morning.' Detective Veno lifted a pile of papers off his desk and lowered them again. 'You seen them?'

'No,' Reuben answered. 'And I don't want to. What matters is Joshua.'

'Exactly. So we need to keep it fresh. The focus has got to shift to you now, not your child.'

'Why?' Lucy asked. Her tone was flat, as if she knew the answer already but just needed it confirming.

'Ordinarily, it would be the grieving parents, the public pain . . . you know.'

Lucy stared back, deadpan.

'But we've got the added angle of Reuben's perform-ance last night.'

'Meaning?'

Reuben answered before Veno got the chance. 'Half the population thinks I had something to do with it.'

'At a conservative estimate,' Veno muttered, pushing his arms back behind his head, his stomach protruding forward.

Reuben examined his face. Weary indifference, fatigue, a cold detachment from the actual events. He wondered whether Veno had kids. He knew that coppers hated child cases. Most were parents, and it was difficult not to feel part of the human tragedy of child murder and abduction. But Veno was different. He seemed isolated and drained, as if it was all merely an inconvenience.

'Look, like it or not, we have to use that. We have to use the public interest in you to stimulate public interest in the search. Whatever it takes.'

'So what are you proposing, Detective?'

'Like I said, the police angle. Dr Reuben Maitland as a senior forensics officer. The irony. The fact that units like yours process samples from cases like this.'

'My unit *is* processing Joshua's samples.'

'Clearly. Not that for a moment I agreed with that decision.'

Reuben shrugged, as if it didn't concern him. But without Sarah's help he would be sunk, relying solely on Veno. 'Great,' he said. 'So the public hate me already, and now you want them to find out I'm a copper.'

A thin smile flicked across Veno's thick red lips. 'More or less,' he said.

'What do I have to do?'

'A couple of TV interviews. They're already booked.' He squinted at his watch. 'Ten minutes or so. We'll run them here. Both of you, but mainly Reuben.'

'Oh fuck,' Lucy said. 'They'll take us to pieces.'

'Let them try,' Reuben answered.

Detective Veno raised his palms as an indication to stop. 'No, no, no, that's not what we want. Be nice, be humble, be cooperative for once. Christ.'

Lucy stood up and walked to the door. 'I'm going to freshen up,' she said. 'That's if you don't have anything useful to tell me about my son's disappearance?'

Detective Veno raised his eyebrows at her but didn't speak. When the door was shut, he leaned forward in his chair, pressing himself into the stark emptiness of his desk. He glared at Reuben, and Reuben waited for him to speak. It suddenly felt like an interview room, sitting on the wrong side of the desk, watching the copper insinuate without speaking, applying pressure just by staring. A voice inside Reuben's head said, 'Fucking amateur.'

While he counted the seconds, he realized that being inside a child abduction case was very different from the way he had imagined. Activity all around, but at the epicentre, a vacuum, lonely and still, just two desperate parents acutely missing their child.

Veno kept up the silent treatment. Then, finally, he said, 'I've got something to put to you.'

'Go on,' Reuben answered.

'Let me say it this way. I think you're hiding something from the police.'

Reuben didn't look him in the eye.

Veno tried again. 'I think you've got secrets from the police. Things you don't want them to know.'

'What do you mean? I am the police. You seem to have forgotten, Detective Veno, that I'm on the right side here.'

'Are you? Are you indeed. I know a lot of coppers who would disagree with that statement, Dr Maitland.'

'And who would they be?'

'The honest, hard-working ones you've sniffed around in the past.'

'Don't give me that. The only coppers I've ever been interested in are the ones who've abused forensic evidence to seal convictions. Ones like your old buddy DI Phil Kemp. That's what this is about, Veno. A grudge. A classic copper's grudge.'

Reuben stood up, a sudden anger flaring through him. Veno stood up as well, the desk screeching forward.

'While you should be out finding my son, you're wasting my time in here, trying to pretend you've got some sort of authority over me. Well, you don't. Get the hell out of my way before I move you out.'

Veno stayed where he was. 'In here, Maitland, you do what the fuck I say. Try to move out of this room and I'll have you in cuffs before you can say backstabbing bastard.'

Reuben hesitated, caught. He flicked through the idea of punching Veno in his hardened gut, grabbing Lucy and getting the hell away from the police station. But he knew that wouldn't help. He was tired and on edge, a million notions flashing through his consciousness. Thinking straight was becoming difficult. He tried to calm down by closing his eyes for a few seconds. And then he pulled his chair out and sat down again.

Veno waited a moment, then did the same. He opened a drawer and pulled out a slim cardboard file, placing it squarely on the desk in front of Reuben. The words 'Dr Reuben Maitland: Confidential' had been written on a white sticker in black biro. An ink stamp had been used to press the words 'Metropolitan Police Authority' into the cardboard in blue and red.

When he spoke, Veno's voice was calmer and quieter. 'It's time you came clean with me.'

Reuben looked over at the door. Veno's dark overcoat drooped off a hook, its shoulders sagging low. He glanced at the file, his anger fizzing inside with nowhere to go. 'Let's have it,' he said.

Veno opened the file and made a show of skimming several sheets of paper. 'Sacked for DNA-testing your wife's lover just under two years ago. Improper conduct. A very dishonourable discharge.'

'Hardly news.'

'Not to me, no. Let's see what else.' Veno licked the tip of his index finger. His tongue was pink and sharp. He flicked through the file of loose A4 sheets. 'Time in Pentonville. Two sentences, one before you joined the FSS.'

Reuben shrugged. He wondered how Veno had gained the authority to pull his file. And then he appreciated that in a child abduction case, just about everything was fair game.

'A brother who has been in more than his fair share of trouble. Oh, and a father who was an habitual pain in the arse to his local police force.'

Reuben raised his eyebrows, wondering where the hell Veno was heading. A large part of him wanted to get up and leave, but he knew the detective in front of him was building to something. 'Can't choose your family,' he said, more to himself than to Veno.

'And a child with a history of life-threatening illnesses.'

'What's that supposed to mean?'

'I'm just saying. What was it?'

'Acute lymphocytic leukaemia.'

'Ah yes. And parents with significant and ongoing relationship issues.'

Reuben took a deep breath and held it there.

'Not exactly a spotless background, is it?'

'Whose is?'

'The point I'm making, Maitland, is that we take a long hard look at the family in all child abduction cases. And what I'm seeing in yours doesn't exactly reassure me.'

Reuben dug his fingers into the flesh of his legs beneath the table. Veno poking about in his life was intensely uncomfortable. He could see now why the room was cold and brutal. It was like being inside Veno's head. Stark and pitiless, cold white walls staring back, blank and indifferent.

'Let's see what else. An illicit laboratory somewhere in Mile End, probably infringing national forensic testing laws.'

'The lab's gone.'

'Really? Where?'

'Just gone. Taken to pieces and stored.' Reuben pictured the sequencer in Lucy's garage grinding through the eighty-three samples, lighting their profiles up on its monitor, illuminating the truth against a background of black. 'It was a pre-condition of me joining GeneCrime again. Does it say that in there?'

'No. But it does say something else very interesting.'

'Go on.'

'Previous evidence of serious drug use.' Veno peered

over the top of a sheet of A4. 'You still like amphet-amines, Dr Maitland?'

'I try not to.'

'You see, you put all this lot together, it's a fucking mystery to me why the force has taken you back on.'

'That's just as well,' Reuben answered. 'Seeing as you don't know a fat lot about actually getting out there and arresting punters.'

'Maybe not,' Veno said. 'Maybe you're right. Maybe I am just a desk-bound detective, running investigations through the media. But I do know this. You have a shady past, Maitland. You have skeletons in your cupboard that are pounding on the door to get out. And that pounding is only going to get louder and louder.'

'Why don't you spell it out, Detective Veno?'

Veno smiled slyly back at him. Reuben suddenly felt outmanoeuvred. It was an uncomfortable sensation he was not used to. 'I got hold of all this information about you without breaking sweat. And what it tells me is your background is complicated.' He closed the cardboard file and laid it flat on the desk. 'You'd just better hope no one else has been digging as well. Because pretty soon, what-ever the truth about your son's disappearance, it's going to be all over the front pages.'

24

Reuben arrived at his former home in a foul mood. He had ducked out of the TV interviews, giving Veno the slip and jumping into a cab outside the station. Lucy had agreed to face the cameras, explaining only that her ex-husband had been asked to answer an urgent work call. Covering for him when he needed her to. Not lying to him any more, but to the people around him. It was sad, but Reuben appreciated that was at least progress.

It had been dark for a while by the time he opened the front door, at a shade before eight o'clock. He knew the profiling run would have ended some time ago, while Veno was toying with him, relishing his sudden power, his utter grip on Reuben's future. As he entered, he called Judith's name. There was a muffled response from the rear of the house. Reuben strode past the kitchen and into the utility room that led into the back of the garage. He threw open the door and saw Judith standing with a print-out in her hand. She looked excited.

'What?' Reuben asked.

'You're late. And I've been busy.'

'So?'

'You're going to like this.'

She was alive, her eyes wide, her mouth suppressing a smile, her brow creased. The way she had always been when a crucial strand of evidence began to snag. Quiet and demure as ever, but the animation burning out regardless, radiating through her face.

'You've got a match?'

'Here.'

She passed Reuben several sheets of paper. He noted that she had taken the printer from his office and connected it to the computer running the sequencer. Reuben wondered where her son was, whether Judith had left him at home with her husband. Clearly, she had covered a lot of ground while he had been entrenched deep inside Paddington Green police station.

'Profiles from the nine cigarette butts. And one from the home of Dr Ian Gillick.'

Reuben shuffled through the papers, just like Veno had done with his police file. But this was different. This was important. He inspected each of the ten profiles in turn. Elongated graphs with sharp spikes of blue, green, black and red. Numbers running from one hundred to four hundred along the top, from zero to fifteen hundred up the side. Pairs of peaks labelled with codes like TH01, D16, FGA and D18. A set of twin peaks in each trace marked either Male or Female. Clean profiling with very little background. One graph per sheet, printed in land-scape. Judith's blue biro in the top left corner of each, a code corresponding to sample order.

He glanced up at her, full of admiration. In between breast-feeding and changing nappies, toiling in a small garage half crammed with junk, she had worked miracles. 'Nice,' he said. He laid the profiles on the dusty concrete floor and squinted at them for a second. 'So, these are the two that match.' He picked them up and held them side by side. 'What do we do now?'

'Nothing. I've already done it.'

'You're joking.'

'Used my remote access to the work server. Trawled the matching profile through.'

Reuben pictured the server in the basement of GeneCrime, its thick blue cable leading into the junction boards he had done his best to disrupt earlier. 'And?'

He watched Judith fail to suppress a smile.

'A name.'

'Where?'

Judith slid a fresh piece of paper off the clingfilmed door. 'Here.'

Reuben scanned the information. Standard CID nomenclature, courier font, name, address, DOB, national insurance number. Judith had evidently copy/pasted the data from the National DNA Database. He scanned down to the list of previous offences. 'Fuck,' he said quietly.

'Looks like he has a bit of what CID like to call previous form.'

Reuben inspected the descriptions and dates. Theft. Driving while intoxicated. Breaking and entering. Aggravated assault. Possession of a knife. Reuben was static. His brain was racing. A knife. An existing assault. He quickly tried to dismiss the notion, checked for other explanations, but couldn't come up with any. DNA from a cigarette butt dropped where his son was taken matched DNA at the scene of Ian Gillick's murder. This was not coincidence. He peered at the name. Daniel Riefield. He had been present at both events. The taking of a scientist's life and the seizing of a two-year-old boy from his mother.

Reuben looked up at Judith. She was watching him intently. After many years of working together she didn't need to ask. Reuben patted his jacket pocket and heard the dull metallic rattle of keys.

'Reuben,' Judith said.

'What?'

'I'm not going to tell you to hold back from what you're about to do.'

'Good.'

'But don't go alone. Call it in.'

Reuben raised his eyebrows at her. He folded the piece of paper and stuffed it in the back pocket of his jeans. 'It's not that simple.' Then he stepped forward, grabbed Judith, and planted a kiss on her cheek. 'I owe you one,' he said. 'A big one.'

He turned away from her and pulled open the door, picking up speed as he ran through the house and out into the street. The Volvo he'd driven home welcomed him in with soft lighting. Reuben started the engine, put it in gear, and screeched off into the night.

As he drives, the sat nav does its best to soothe him, a calm female voice gently but firmly telling him which way to go. The roads are quiet. The car is as smooth and composed as ever. But inside it, Reuben is alight. Less than three miles. He'll be there in minutes.

He pictures the next half an hour of his life. As he does so, questions buzz through his head, vibrating in his consciousness, stinging him with the sharpness of their logic. Am I ready for this? he asks himself. If Joshua is dead . . . will I ever come to terms with that? In between junctions and traffic lights, in the glare of oncoming headlights, such notions continue to track him down and attack him. Whoever killed Carl Everitt and Ian Gillick must be strong. He overpowered two grown men and hacked off their fingertips. Will I be able to take him down alone? And if I do, will I be able to stop myself from hurting him and rehurting him? And then Joshua. His eyes when he sees me. His crying stopping, recognition spreading across his features, hope, understanding, relief. Calling out Daddy. The word that can cut straight through a grown man and tie his stomach in knots.

Reuben speeds up, pushing the large accelerator pedal hard into the floor. Among the big questions, smaller issues start to come. No car seat to take him home in. No clean clothes or nappies. The lack of a dummy or his bunny to comfort him with. No food or drink for him.

The voice in the dashboard tells him to take the first exit at the roundabout. Reuben screeches around it so quickly that he is twenty metres clear of it when the sat nav issues the instruction again as a reminder. He squints at the screen. Less than a mile. The roads aren't familiar. A residential area of once-grand housing turned into decaying modern flats. A half-built office block, a disused garage with no petrol pumps, a stretch of tarmac with a single basketball hoop. No green anywhere, just greys and blacks. A row of boarded-up shops, a pub, a betting shop with a couple of punters still inside.

He checks the screen again. The final road. Long and straight. No trees, just intermittent yellow street lights. Reuben watches the sat nav counting down the distance. Five hundred yards. Four hundred and fifty. Four hundred. He experiences a sudden urge to call Sarah, to request back-up, to do the thing properly. But he is trapped, and he knows it. He has to do this alone. He cannot give CID the full story yet. Questions would be asked, his career ending again before it started. Three hundred yards. He needs time to sort his answers out, to tidy up the pieces, to explain how he has caught the killer of two men.

But first, a desperate and terrified two-year-old boy. His own flesh and blood.

Reuben slows for the last hundred yards. No one is around. It is too cold. The city has retreated indoors, slumped in front of televisions. The sat nav voice announces that he has reached his destination.

Reuben kills the engine and climbs out. He walks to the back of the car and opens the boot. Underneath the carpet, he reaches inside the spare wheel. A jack and a tightly wrapped tool kit. Reuben pulls the heavy steel jack out of its pouch and tests its weight. It will do. He slams the boot, checks the piece of paper that Judith has given him, and opens the scruffy front door of a four-storey block of flats. Inside, the tiled floor is cracked and stained. A filthy carpet leads up the communal stairs. Reuben takes the steps two at a time. He double-checks the address. Number 41. He climbs another couple of flights. Flat 41 stands at the end of a dingy corridor. A strip of wallpaper is hanging off. Reuben stops. He smells cooking and dampness. He sniffs the air for a second longer, wondering whether the smell of rats is somewhere in the mix. A thin strip of light is escaping from under the door.

Reuben paces forward and stands directly in front of it. He places his ear against the cold wooden barrier. The noise of a TV booms through the thick surface. He grips the jack in his right hand, sensing its weight, where its balance lies. As he does so, he appreciates that whatever lies on the other side of the door will decide which way his life proceeds. A happy life or a broken one. A dead son or a living son.

Reuben takes a step back, running his eyes over the lock, guessing at the location of the hinges, estimating the best point of attack. He bows his head for a second, taking in the smell and the noises.

A child is crying somewhere.

Reuben straightens. He takes a second step back. And then he crashes into the door.

TWO

TWO

1

Daniel Riefield was slow to react. Sitting on a grubby brown sofa, staring into the TV, pulling hard on a cigarette, a can of beer held static, turning round to face the noise. A delayed response to sudden sound and movement.

Reuben smashed through the door at the second attempt, its lock buckling with the force. He regained his balance and covered the five strides to Riefield in one fluid movement. Riefield lunged upwards, an improvised rugby tackle, his arms spread out, coming for Reuben. Reuben transferred his weight and slipped free. Riefield brought his right arm round, a fist shaving Reuben's face. Reuben pulled the jack round and swung it at him. The heavy implement caught Riefield a glancing blow off his skull. There was a blunted sound, a hollow clunk above the sound of the TV, a contact between metal and bone. Riefield went down, his lunge suddenly aimless, and crashed on to the floor. Reuben aimed a kick for his torso, but stopped himself. There were more pressing issues.

He backed into a room which fed the main living area. The flat was filthy. It was damp and cold, small cracks in the walls, patches of mould. Cigarette butts were ground into the carpet. The screech of the TV echoed off bare surfaces. A music channel blaring out a screaming guitar, a pounding bass, frantic drums.

'Joshua?' he called above the noise. 'Joshua? It's Daddy!'

Reuben flicked on the light in a bedroom, tore open the wardrobe, checked under the bed. He heard Riefield moving around so he paced back to him, the jack gripped firmly in his hand. 'Sit down on the floor,' he said. 'You move an inch, and I'll knock you out cold.'

Riefield stared up at him. Reuben could see he was dangerous. An intensity in his eyes, a feral wildness in his face.

He strode into another room. A small space crammed with junk. Old newspapers, print-outs, discarded beer cans, a broken stereo. He called his son's name again. There was no reply.

He checked the bathroom. Cracked lino, broken tiles, black mould burrowing into gaps. Nothing. Only one more door.

Reuben took a good look at Riefield. He was shaking his head, colour starting to return to his cheeks. Reuben glanced at the TV. A pale skinny woman, a row of tattooed guitarists, a long-haired drummer giving it his all. He snatched the remote and pressed the mute button. The musicians continued regardless, their anger now looking faked, their efforts overwrought.

He walked over to the door, gripped the handle and pulled it hard. Utter darkness inside. He groped for a light switch and found one. An energy-saving fluorescent flickered on, gloomy at first, gradually getting brighter.

'Don't!' Riefield said.

Reuben spun round. Riefield was on his feet and coming forward.

'Sit the fuck down!' Reuben said.

'Don't go in there!' Riefield repeated.

Reuben raised the jack. 'One more step and I'll put you down.'

Riefield stopped. Reuben could tell he was weighing him up. Asking himself, can I take this stranger in front of me? Weapon or no weapon, can I get to him before he gets to me? Reuben gauged his size. Six one, give or take. Similar height but slightly leaner. A wasted, gaunt look to him, like he had previously been heavier. Reuben thought of Carl Everitt and Ian Gillick. Riefield had overpowered each of them. Reuben had caught him unawares, sitting on his sofa. Toe to toe could be a different matter. He was obviously strong. The jack, now that he looked at it, was an inadequate weapon. Something longer would have been better. A baseball bat, an iron bar. Riefield stared back at him, deadpan, silent. A trickle of blood escaped his hair, running down the side of his face, just in front of his ear. He didn't wipe it away.

'Where the fuck is my son?' Reuben asked. 'Joshua Maitland. What have you done with him?'

Riefield stared at him. A thin smile flicked across his features, the hint of a smirk. 'Your son? Your fucking son? Is that what this is about?'

'Where is he?'

Riefield took a small step forward, adjusting his weight, legs slightly splayed, ready. 'Maitland,' he spat. 'Reuben Maitland. Fucking Forensics.'

Reuben knew for certain that he had the killer in front of him. He had often looked into their eyes, wondered if he could spot what made them different. Usually he was behind a desk, the murderer restrained, CID either side. That was a very different proposition. Nothing between him and the killer now but a metre of air, the length of an arm, a void of stillness that could erupt at any second.

'Where is my boy?' he asked again.

The flat, in his peripheral vision, told him Joshua was obviously being kept somewhere else. The walls were too thin, too many people around, too many variables. But where? That was all that mattered. Surviving, and finding his son.

And then there was a movement. The scuttling of

something in the direction of the sofa. Behind Riefield, over his left shoulder. The scamper of sharp claws. Reuben couldn't see it, but knew instantly what it was. A rat.

Without waiting, he swung his right arm. Leaning forward, his arm travelling up, the metal jack heading for Riefield's face. A millisecond of instinct. Self-defence in the form of an arcing uppercut, fuelled by the knowledge that if he didn't attack, he would be attacked himself. And that if Riefield overpowered him, he would never see his son again.

Riefield didn't react in time. The jack caught him under his jaw. His head tipped back, eyes lolling. He staggered a couple of paces and collapsed on to the stained carpet. Reuben stood over him, making sure. He was breathing, but other than that there was no movement.

He took out his mobile and dialled. As it rang, he cast his eyes over the bare walls, the opened doors, the man on the floor. The man whose DNA was at the scene of a murder. The man whose DNA was at the scene of Joshua's abduction.

'Detective Paul Veno,' a voice said after five rings.

'This is Reuben. I've got some information.'

Veno sounded unimpressed. 'Really?'

'I have the kidnapper here.' Reuben gave him the address and flat number. 'He's quiet at the moment, but won't be for long.'

'And Joshua?'

'Somewhere else.' Reuben stared down at Riefield. A deep cut on his lower jaw was leaking red into the thin carpet. 'But this is the man who abducted him.'

'How do you know?'

'It's better if I don't answer that.'

Reuben took in the full length of Daniel Riefield, sprawled out beneath him. Damaged trainers, scruffy black jeans, a hooded top poking through a denim jacket. And then he noticed it. His hands. Blunted and stark. Thick stubby fingers that ended suddenly. Reuben bent down and inspected them more closely.

No fingertips.

'So what do you want me to do?' Veno asked.

'Get some people round here,' Reuben answered as he squinted at Riefield's hands in turn. The nails were gone, the digits squared off, pink scar tissue at their ends. 'Look into other addresses or aliases for one Daniel Riefield, and find my son.'

'Jesus,' Veno said. 'This is all going to have to come out, sooner or later. The truth, Reuben. That's what I need.'

'Just get some people round here. I'm going to take Riefield in for questioning.'

'And you're certain this is the man?'

Reuben inspected the fingers again. Tips removed, just like the men he had attacked. The inkling of a motive. 'Utterly. But now I guess the real search starts. We have the man but not the boy.'

Veno didn't bother to disguise a sigh. 'I'll get on to media liaison. Tell them we've got someone in custody, see if we can extract some info on your Daniel Riefield from the public consciousness.'

Reuben left Riefield and walked over to the room Riefield hadn't wanted him to go into. The bare neon energy saver struggled to illuminate the corners. 'Whatever you have to do, Detective.' He stared at the walls. Newspaper cuttings, sellotaped haphazardly everywhere. Front pages, inside features, the type of exploded diagrams that journalists use to reveal the hidden world of science. Even the windows were plastered with translucent newsprint. Immediately, Reuben tried to make the connection.

'Reuben?' Veno asked. 'You still there?'

Reuben ran his eyes around the room, almost dizzy at the sheer volume of words staring back. 'I'm still here,' he said. 'But I've got to go.'

He ended the call, thought for a second, then dialled Sarah Hirst's number. While it rang, he approached the horizontal figure on the floor and said, 'Daniel Riefield, I'm arresting you on suspicion of child abduction and murder.'

2

Sarah had beaten him to it. She was sitting in her office, surrounded by slowly dying plants, staring at the door, waiting. Reuben could tell as he entered that she had been listening for his footsteps, irritation in her eyes, consternation ruffling her brow. It was late, she didn't want to be there, and Reuben was causing her problems.

'What exactly is going on?' she asked, before Reuben had fully entered the room.

'I've got the killer,' Reuben answered, rubbing his face. He had waited at Riefield's flat for twenty minutes for Detectives Leigh Harding and Helen Alders to arrive and help transport Riefield to GeneCrime.

'And he's here?'

'Downstairs. Nursing a badly bruised jaw.'

'Does he need medical help?'

'He's refused to say anything whatsoever, so it's hard to tell.'

Reuben noticed the empty chairs in Sarah's office. He hadn't been offered a seat.

'Reuben, is there something I should know?'

'What do you mean?'

'I mean, you have single-handedly caught the man that this entire unit is hunting. How?'

Reuben shifted his weight from foot to foot. He was impatient, knowing that Sarah needed to be brought up to speed, but wanting to get into Riefield. A small interview office, the tape not running, dragging the truth out of the bastard while his son cried, frightened and desperate, in an empty room somewhere. 'It's complicated,' he said. 'I kind of put two and two together.'

'Which two? I just don't understand the leap you've made.'

'Look, Sarah, you have to trust me. We have the fingertip killer downstairs. For the moment that's more important than anything else. Can I just get on with interviewing him?'

Sarah stood up. 'Fine. But I'm sitting in with you.'

She walked out through the open door, her heels clicking against the laminate flooring, Reuben struggling to keep up. The pace of her progress told Reuben she was either angry or excited. As she thumped through a set of double doors, he guessed a bit of both.

They made their way to the row of cells and interview rooms in the basement. Leigh Harding was leaning against the metal door of a room marked with the number 3. He straightened as he saw Sarah approaching.

'Can you bring the suspect into Interview Room One?' Sarah asked him.

'Ma'am,' Harding replied.

She kept walking. The doors changed from metallic blue to light brown wood-effect. Sarah turned into Interview Room 1 without breaking stride. She pulled out a plastic chair and sat down. Reuben took the chair next to her.

'So . . .' he said.

Sarah remained quiet, sitting bolt upright, her nostrils flaring slightly from the exertion. Reuben started to frame questions in his mind, ones whose answers wouldn't compromise his position. The murders were incidental; he needed to know where Riefield was holding Joshua.

There was a scratch at the door and it swung open. Leigh Harding was gripping Riefield by his upper arm, walking him forward. Riefield's jaw was red, a cut swelling at the centre. His eyes were still wild, scanning the room and its occupants. His hands were cuffed in front of him, fingers splayed, tips missing. Out of the corner of his eye, Reuben watched Sarah absorb this information.

Detective Harding eased Riefield into a seat. 'You need me to sit in?' he asked.

'We're fine,' Sarah said absently, her focus still on

Riefield's hands. 'Dr Maitland, would you care to kick off?'

Reuben stared at Riefield. A large part of him wanted to rush the table, grab him by the throat and make him talk. But he knew he had to be patient. He had to edge Riefield round, mine him for information, snatch whatever facts he could.

'OK, Daniel. You're not being charged at this time, although you are technically under arrest. We just want to clear some facts up. If we do charge you then you have the right to representation. All right?'

Riefield stared back. His dark eyes seemed to focus through Reuben, unblinking and unmoving.

Reuben unfolded a sheet of paper from his jacket pocket. 'So, I want to ask you where you were on certain days this month. If you have a good idea of your whereabouts, just say yes.' He scanned his rough notes. 'The fifth?'

Riefield's expression didn't change.

'Mr Riefield, I'm asking you where you were on the fifth of this month. I'd like you to answer.'

'No . . . comment,' he said.

'OK, how about the twelfth?'

'No . . . comment.'

The pause between the two words was three or four seconds, long enough for Reuben to wonder each time whether he was going to finish his statement.

'Yesterday, Mr Riefield. Where were you yesterday?'

'No . . . comment.'

Reuben glanced at Sarah. 'You have no idea what you were doing or where you were yesterday?'

'No . . . comment.'

Sarah touched Reuben lightly on the shoulder. 'Let me just explain, Daniel. We want to ask you about two murders that have occurred in the last couple of weeks. If you can provide us with a general alibi, or other details we can check, that could help your case. By simply refusing to comment, you will only increase our suspicion of you. Do you understand that?'

'No . . . comment.'

'You do realize that you are not under charge at this moment, and that we are not officially recording your answers?'

'No . . . comment.'

Reuben watched Riefield. There was something disturbed about him, something outside the normal rules of human engagement. It wasn't just his refusal to answer any of the questions, but the lack of interaction, of connection. He wasn't really in the room. Reuben wondered where he was, whether he was thinking about Joshua, picturing him locked up somewhere, thriving on the fact he was scared and helpless. A hot anger flashed through him, which he battled to contain.

Sarah tried again. 'Dr Maitland and I merely want to ask you—'

'No . . . comment.'

'But it's in your interest—'

'No . . . comment.'

Reuben watched Sarah flush. She wasn't used to being cut off and interrupted. Normal detainees took a good look at her, sensed the body language of those around her, and decided it wasn't worth the trouble. Not Riefield.

Reuben leaned close to DCI Hirst, and caught a faint sweetness which he guessed was her antiperspirant fighting to keep her fresh after a long day. 'I've got an idea,' he whispered. 'Let me talk to him alone.'

Sarah turned to him, moved even closer. Amid the perfume he now detected the sour odour of recent frustration. Riefield was getting to her. 'You've been away too long, Reuben. This isn't how we do things.'

'Just give me ten minutes alone with him.'

'Where have I heard that kind of line before?'

'I don't mean it like that. There's just some sensitive details I need to ascertain, alone and unobserved. One on one maybe I can get past his barrier.'

'You're pushing it, Reuben.' Sarah glanced at her watch. 'You've got the time it takes me to drink a coffee. A small one.'

Sarah stood up and walked to the door. She used her swipe card to open it and left. When it had closed again,

Reuben sat and waited. The coffee machine was at the far end of the corridor, through a set of doors and round a corner. He began to count a slow sixty under his breath, matching Sarah's paces away from him. He locked his eyes on Riefield's, and tried to imagine Joshua shivering and dirty, unwashed and unfed, cowering in the corner of a squalid room. He dug his fingernails into his palms, feeling the burn and sting as they burrowed deep into the soft skin. All the time, he held Riefield's feral stare. And then the minute was up.

'Where's my son?' he said calmly.

Riefield smiled at him, baring his teeth. 'No . . . comment.'

'Where's my fucking son?' Reuben asked, his voice rising.

'No . . . fucking . . . comment.'

Reuben let it envelop him. The fury, the pent-up rage, the visceral need for conflict that the last two days had brought. 'I'll ask you again,' he said, starting to shout. 'Where the fuck have you got my boy?'

Riefield bore straight into him, his mouth snarling. 'No . . . fucking . . . comment.'

There was a pause. Reuben closed his eyes, took a deep breath and held it there. Then he launched himself across the table. He grabbed Riefield by the scruff and slammed his face down into the table. Before he could react, he spun round and stood behind him. Riefield straightened, and Reuben grabbed his handcuffed hands, yanking them back over his head. He rammed his knee into Riefield's back and wrenched downwards, Riefield's arms rotating in their shoulder joints, making him cry out.

'You say "no comment" one more fucking time and I'll pop your arms clean out of your shoulder joints. Right, you bastard, where is my son?'

Riefield strained against him, grunting in pain, but refusing to surrender. 'Fuck you,' he spat. 'Fuck you.'

Reuben pulled harder. Riefield was bucking against him. Reuben sensed his strength. This was a man he wouldn't want to meet on a rugby field. He knew that the pressure he was applying was enough to rip ligaments and tear rotator cuffs. But Riefield's joints held firm. He yanked harder, lost in the moment, the need for information, desperate for his only child. Riefield grunted, breathing heavily, his jaw clamped tight.

'Last chance, you piece of shit,' Reuben whispered, his mouth close to Riefield's ear. 'When I've dislocated your arms then I really will get stuck into you.'

'This isn't pain,' Riefield grunted. 'This is nothing. Do your worst, Maitland. I know what real pain is, and it's a fuck of a lot less fun than this.'

'So you lost a few fingers—'

'You know fuck all! Fuck all at all!' Riefield spat. 'Scientists. What the hell do you know about anything that matters?'

Reuben kept up the pressure. All he could see was his two-year-old boy in a cold room. Joshua freezing to death, a tiny white corpse in the morning. He was barely listening.

'Come on, do it. Pull my arms out of their sockets. It's nothing.'

Reuben felt his vision narrowing, his control ebbing. He tugged as hard as he could. Let Riefield be so brave in a few seconds.

'Where is he?' he shouted. 'Come on, where the fuck is he?'

Riefield started to yell. Reuben felt a loosening in the resistance. He had him, and he knew it.

'Tell me,' he said, 'or I'm going to hang you up by your dislocated arms.'

'No!' Riefield screamed.

'Come on!'

'No! Fucking! Comment!'

Something in Reuben snapped. He slammed his boot into Riefield's lower back, kicking him hard in the spine. And then the door flew open. Detective Harding and Sarah Hirst, their faces registering shock, bursting into the room. Harding wrestling with Reuben. Sarah shouting. Reuben starting to let go, falling away from Riefield, falling away from his son, falling away from the one chance to save him.

3

Reuben was woken up by an uncomfortable vibration in his lower back. He reached for the source of the irritation and found his mobile. Somehow he had been sleeping on it, wedged between his body and the leather of the sofa. He slid it open and it stopped vibrating.

'Yes,' he said, his eyes still closed.

'It's Sarah. Where are you?'

Reuben tried to open his lids. They felt dry and glued together. A couple of heavy blinks told him he was in Lucy's living room. He had got back so late that walking upstairs had felt an overwhelming effort. 'Lucy's,' he muttered. 'Where are you?'

'The place I virtually live these days. A charming residence with gated parking in NW1.'

'GeneCrime?'

'You guessed it.'

Reuben closed his eyes again, still lying on his back. 'How late is it?'

'It's early. But I think you should hear this.'

'Go on.'

'Last night, a man called Philip Gower was murdered in West London. Fingertips removed, lots of red fluid, rats there to watch it all.'

Reuben sat up. His eyes were no longer heavy and tired. 'Same MO?'

'Exactly.'

'What time?'

'Based on witness statements and body temp we've narrowed it down to between nine p.m. and eleven p.m.'

'Fuck.'

'You want to hear some more?'

'Not really.'

'Philip Gower was a clinical trials coordinator based at the Hammersmith Hospital. Recently divorced, lived alone. Killed, we think, on the floor of his bathroom. Fingertips look sawed rather than chopped. Little other evidence of wounding.'

'You're saying this wasn't a copycat.'

'From the initial analyses, this looks too similar.'

'And now you're worrying about Daniel Riefield launching a suit for aggravated arrest?'

'If he wasn't borderline insane, yes.'

'This doesn't make him innocent, Sarah.'

'And it's a long way from making him guilty. Reuben, I need to know what evidence you had, what led you to Riefield.'

Reuben was quiet for a second. He felt his heart resume its recent gallop. Lying to DCI Hirst was a dangerous game. 'I'll get it to you later.'

'Make sure you do. There's something else as well.'

'What?'

'Simon Jankowski is handling the forensics on your son's abduction, but he's struggling. Says the DNA from the cigarette butts is pretty degraded. He's profiled it anyway, but doesn't know if he's going to be able to use the traces. Half of them failed quality control.'

'Fuck,' Reuben said, knowing full well the reason why Simon was having difficulties. Probably, his own extractions had been more damaging than he had intended.

'I'm sorry, Reuben. It's taking time but he's going to have another crack. I know this delays things and these are critical hours, but you have my word that we're doing everything we can for your son.'

Reuben moved the subject on. 'How do you want to proceed with the case?' he asked.

'Go over to the scene when you get a chance.' Sarah gave him the address. 'And then let's meet back at GeneCrime.'

'I think Veno wants to talk first. But as soon as that's over, I'll head to the scene.'

'Mina's rounding up a crew, so no immediate rush.'

Reuben ended the call, and spent a silent minute analysing how this could be possible. Riefield had been unequivocally matched to the murder scene and the kidnap. And then another death had happened while Riefield was locked up. He pinched the loose skin between the bridge of his nose and his forehead, the pain focusing his mind. Joshua wasn't at Riefield's flat. Riefield was clearly disturbed and unstable. He had known about the abduction, but maybe, like the rest of the capital, he watched the news now and again. It wasn't exactly a secret. In fact, Veno's squad were doing all they could to ram it down everyone's throats.

Reuben stood up and stretched, his body suddenly restless, his thoughts grinding to a halt. He paced around for a few seconds before sitting down and trying again.

The killer stated that he had one more person to kill. He had taken Joshua to buy himself forensic immunity. Reuben began to mutter to himself. Let's say Riefield was entirely innocent. That his DNA appeared at one of the crime scenes incidentally, that a cigarette butt with his DNA on it was dropped outside the newsagent that Lucy visited. So . . . so if Riefield isn't the killer or the kidnapper, he must know who is. Either knowingly or unknowingly, Riefield knows this man.

Reuben blew air out of the side of his mouth. He cursed the fact that while forensics dealt only in certainty, the actions of people were universally ambiguous and difficult to define. Among the crash of ideas and images ricocheting around Reuben's brain, he appreciated that one thing was certain: Riefield didn't kill the clinical trials coordinator. The MO, as Sarah had outlined it, was exactly the same as the first two. If Riefield had been present at the first two deaths, he clearly hadn't been needed there. Whoever had killed Philip Gower had done so perfectly well without Riefield's assistance.

Reuben glanced at the TV. It stared back at him, dead, black, inert. He wondered whether the media would be running with last night's breaking story. That the suspected kidnapper had been arrested. He frowned. News that was already probably wrong. At Reuben's request, Sarah had kept the media away from the arrest of Riefield as the fingertip killer. Clearly, after the Gower murder, Riefield would soon be off the hook. But this was getting close to impossible. If anyone made the link between the kidnapping and the murders Reuben was finished and his son would be dead.

He stood up again, suddenly feeling caged. The perpendicular leather sofas, the tall bookcases, the jutting shelves, the overbearing pictures. Bars made from the angular items he and Lucy had once argued over in furniture shops. His head was closing in, tightening up. Everything he had done forensically had been correct. So why had it led him in the wrong direction? He thought again about Riefield, about his physical strength and mental weakness, his run-down flat, about the room Riefield hadn't wanted him to go in, about the three people who had been killed, about the fact that Riefield was alive, but with fingertips which looked like those of the dead.

The doorbell rang and he padded into the hallway in his socks. He glanced up the stairs. Lucy was still asleep. He wondered for a second whether she was in Joshua's room, then he turned and walked to the front door. Through the spyhole, Detective Veno was reaching for the bell again, his thick-set torso magnified and widened. Reuben swore silently and pulled open the door before he got the chance.

4

Standing toe to toe with him, Reuben appreciated that Veno liked to use his gut as a weapon. He stuck it out, emphasizing his intrusion, his forcefulness, a hard extension of him that invaded your space. Reuben took him in as he spoke. The blond hair, the orange redness of his beard, the thick arms folded across his stocky chest. He was standing close, and although Reuben was three or four inches taller, he had the impression of being surrounded, looked down upon, overwhelmed.

'We've got three tabloids running with the kidnap angle,' he said. 'Not mentioning Riefield by name, just a thirty-two-year-old man from the King's Cross area of London. Caucasian, unemployed, lives alone, that sort of thing.'

Reuben cleared his throat. Next to him, Lucy was monitoring the comings and goings in the wide communal area of desks and chairs. Reuben hadn't had a chance to talk to her on the way to the station. Veno had sat silently in the front seat of the squad car, scribbling notes, checking details. He wished to hell they'd had a couple of minutes alone. Lucy was scouring the station area for progress. It was almost as if she expected Joshua to be brought in at any moment. He needed to tell her what had transpired during the night, but all he could think as Veno continued to talk was that Sarah could soon be making the link. A slow dawning realization that the man Reuben had arrested was the same man being mooted as the kidnapper. And although Reuben had done all he could to throw her off the scent, she was bright and sharp and would not remain ignorant for much longer.

Veno was staring hard into him as if he expected Reuben to answer. 'Well?' he asked.

Reuben had a guess at what he'd been saying. 'So you're not releasing any specifics at all? Riefield's name, address, previous record?'

'Like I just said, not yet. Not till the detectives at the scene come up with tangible evidence that your son was there. If they do, then fine, it's open season. Until then, the story is simply that police have apprehended a suspect.'

Reuben breathed a silent sigh of relief. The more circumspect CID were, the longer it would take Sarah to catch up. 'Fine.'

'Look, I'm still not sure how the forensics led you to Riefield's address.' Veno jutted his belly forward, hands now folded behind him, his head angled slightly back. 'You feel like clearing that up for me?'

Reuben decided to keep it simple. 'GeneCrime are co-ordinating the forensic sweep,' he said. 'We got some info which came through that. An early association.'

'But you were driving this yourself? Surely GeneCrime don't let you get directly involved in the search for your son?'

'It's a big unit and I'm on a different case. The fingertip killer.' Reuben scanned the room. All around, coppers sat at desks, staring into screens, tapping information into databases, searching records and files. Information in and information out. 'Your media liaison team might have read you the headlines?'

Veno sidestepped the dig. 'So how does that relate to you tracking Riefield down?'

'It doesn't.'

'So?'

'It's just the same team of forensic techs, that's all. Standard police overlap.'

'Standard police overlap,' Veno repeated, the words slow and flat. He rocked back on his heels. 'Huh.'

Reuben felt his phone vibrate somewhere deep inside his jacket. 'Are you trying to make a point, Detective Veno?'

'Simply this. People who have their kids taken rarely apprehend the kidnapper themselves.'

'Surely,' Lucy interrupted, 'that's because the vast majority of them aren't leading forensic scientists?'

'That's not the point I'm making.'

'Oh? And what is? That Reuben is able to catch bad guys while you're thoroughly unable?'

Reuben fumbled for his phone. Leading forensic scientist. He would take that from Lucy any day. A dark frown descended across Veno's brow. His ex-wife was deadly. Usually it was Reuben on the receiving end. It was great to see someone else suffer the sharp end of her legal tongue.

He turned away from Veno and answered the call. 'Yes.'

'You've broken our contract.'

Reuben instantly pinpointed the voice. Forty-eight hours ago, in the GeneCrime Command Room.

'Meaning what?' Reuben asked.

'Meaning that you broke your word. That you assured me on your son's life you wouldn't come after me. But you still did. And that either makes you a liar, or someone who doesn't care about his child.'

Reuben pushed the phone hard against his ear. He needed to hear every detail, every nuance, every background sound. Veno was staring at him. In every direction, CID officers and Missing Child squad members surrounded him in a blur of desks. Veno seemed to step closer. Reuben closed his eyes. He wanted to run out of the room but he was trapped. Instead, he retreated into the sound of breathing on the other end of the line. The man was moving, maybe walking somewhere. But he was inside. There was no traffic or commotion.

'I said I needed one more person, and you said that would be OK. I said this wasn't personal, that this was simply about control. But you tried to hunt me anyway. The man you arrested was my safeguard. If you arrested him then you were trying to arrest me. I told you I was setting a trap, and you ignored that. You didn't care about the life of your only child.'

A door opened and closed. And that was when Reuben heard his son. Muffled sobs. High-pitched cries.

His eyes were suddenly wide, his jaw clenched, the phone squeezed so hard he thought he would crush it. He wanted to scream down the line, to call out to Joshua, to tell the man holding him that he was going to find him and hurt him. Instead Reuben focused on the middle distance, above Veno, over the heads of the coppers all around him.

'Joshua,' the man said. 'Come here.'

There was a cry, a piercing sound that cut straight into Reuben, crushing his lungs, cramping his stomach, pricking his heart.

'I said come here. Daddy wants to listen.'

Reuben fought for calm. Out of the corner of his eye, Veno was monitoring him closely.

There was another cry, and then silence for a moment. Reuben pictured Joshua being picked up.

'That's it, little boy. Don't struggle so much. Your daddy wants to listen.'

Joshua repeated the word 'Daddy'. Reuben heard it clearly. He looked around again, wanting to sprint out of the room, be anywhere but here. Lucy caught his eye. Reuben looked away.

'I'm listening,' he said.

There was another moment of silence, then a clear slap. Joshua began to scream. Reuben detected a second slap. His son ramped up the noise, a furious, frightened cacophony. Reuben was trembling inside his jacket, trying not to let it show. The yelling abated. The fucker was leaving Joshua, walking through into another room. He suddenly flashed to Riefield's squalid flat, wondering if this place was as filthy. The noise of a door closing, Joshua's suffering now out of earshot. Reuben wondered what was worse, hearing his son or not hearing him.

'This changes things,' the man said. 'All bets are off. From now on there are no rules.'

He cut the line, and Reuben remained standing stock still in a room full of coppers, Joshua's mother by his side, Detective Veno's stocky frame an arm's length in front, his hardened belly pushing forward, ever closer.

5

Reuben leaned close to Lucy in the station corridor, wedged between a coffee machine and a snack machine, slabs of square metal that brought relief to tired and hungry coppers. He blew across a thin plastic cup holding hot liquid. It was either strong tea or weak coffee, he couldn't be sure. Lucy picked distractedly at a packet of crisps, a layer of orange flavouring sticking to the tips of her pale white fingers.

'What does that mean, exactly, "all bets are off"?' she asked. 'This isn't some sort of wager.'

Reuben tried the liquid, the heat scalding his tongue. He had already decided not to tell her that the man had hit their son. She was upset enough. 'It means the end of our deal. A life for a life. Whatever it was he promised in the first place.'

'So, what do we do?'

'We have two options.' Reuben craned his neck past

Lucy and inspected the corridor. They were protected, the vending machines like bodyguards, shielding them from the members of Veno's team milling about. 'Option one, I ring Sarah now, tell her exactly what's been going on, what I've been doing, what the real truth is. Option two, we stick to the current plan.'

'So you tell Sarah you've been lying to her, and in fact the fingertip killer might just be the person holding Joshua?'

'Something like that. Look, let's say I'm your client. I'm in trouble with the law. What would you advise?'

Lucy gazed past him, thinking. 'All that matters is Joshua, and what gives us the best chance of getting him back. What would Sarah do if you owned up to the fact you've effectively been misleading the UK's most high-profile murder case?'

'All Sarah cares about is catching killers. She'd play it as straight as she always does.'

'Meaning?'

'She'd throw it over to her boss, Commander Thorner. He would sack me on the spot.'

'Sarah wouldn't defend you? Or even keep it quiet?'

'She'd have no choice. This would come out in the end, and her career – the thing that occupies almost all of her life – would be fucked.'

A CID officer that Reuben vaguely recognized slid a coin into the drinks machine next to them and pushed a couple of buttons. The guts of the machine whirred and clanked into life. Reuben smiled briefly, a tight contraction of his mouth. The officer raised his eyebrows, then stooped down, took his drink and walked away.

'But if you come clean, won't that help us find our son?'

'CID will be able to link the murders and the kidnap, which is what I'm currently doing. They won't know any more than I do. The gamble is whether they can work quicker than me.'

'And can they?'

'Sometimes.'

Lucy sighed. 'We've got ourselves into one hell of a mess. How would all this affect Veno, say if you told Sarah what you've been doing?'

'If Sarah knows, Veno gets to find out. He'd have to be briefed. Then the man heading the official hunt for our son finds out we've been lying to him.'

'He'd enjoy that. He's already gunning for you.'

'I'll soak up any amount of shit if it will help get Josh back safe.' Reuben tried another sip of the indeterminate drink. It was bitter and seemed to strip his mouth of moisture. 'It's just a question of whether undermining Veno is a bad thing for the manhunt.'

Lucy checked the corridor, a quick glance from behind the machines. 'So essentially you've wedged yourself in and don't know whether it will do more harm than good to pull yourself out again?'

'Something like that. But if I lose contact with the fingertip investigation, I lose contact with the man who has our son. And if I lose contact with him . . .' Joshua's screams tracked him down once more, the sound of slapping, the hysterical fear of a two-year-old boy being hit by a psychopath. 'I lose contact with everything.'

Lucy placed a hand on Reuben's shoulder, and looked into his eyes. 'We stick to the plan,' she said. 'We have to. It's not the moment for honesty with Sarah. That would do more damage than good right now. Time is what matters. Recriminations are messy and protracted. We have to dig in, hold our nerve. Meanwhile, you get the job done, and get it done fast. I don't see any other option, Reuben.'

Reuben bit into his lower lip. He blinked away the pain of Joshua's voice. Veno would be looking for them. Lucy was right. Dig in. Get the job done fast. Lie to people around them. Anything to get Joshua back home.

6

Reuben drove to the Philip Gower crime scene disorientated, numbed, still arguing it through, still hearing the killer's voice. He came close to running into a taxi, and a motorcycle had to swerve to avoid him as he changed lane suddenly. What he needed, he realized, was to compartmentalize. He had to call on his ability to store emotions, to section off the horror, to put unpleasant images in small boxes that could be opened or disposed of later. It was a skill he had learned as his job had become successively more horrific and demanding. Most of CID and Forensics had it in spades, developed over years in the force. And if they ever lost it, they would cease to be useful, unable to move from one atrocity to the next. Joshua's screams had to be internalized, closed off, buried out of reach. He had to focus on what mattered: finding the man who had called him half an hour earlier.

But as he approached the address that Sarah had

woken him with that morning, he was struggling. Joshua's shrieks, the sounds of a grown man hitting him, an adult hand smacking soft infant skin – these events continued to gnaw at him every waking second. He pulled over and glanced up at a three-storey row of red-brick terraces. The scene inside Gower's house would be much easier to deal with.

Reuben drove further down the road, looking for parking. It was busy, lots of people around, a crush of traffic. A hundred metres past, he reversed into a tight space and killed the engine. He climbed out of the car and walked back, passing a couple of CID vehicles, a Ford Focus and a BMW 3 series, unmarked and trying to blend in. Blue lights discreetly in the grille, an extra aerial in the roof, dual rear-view mirrors. Reuben checked out the rest of the street. Civilians going about their business. Pushing prams and buggies, heading for the shops, leaving work early for lunch, seeing the sights of Hammersmith. Among them, he felt an affinity for the pool cars. Unmarked, anonymous, drifting through life hoping not to draw too much attention. And now, he knew he had to turn it on again, become the one they looked to, the one who shouldered the responsibility, the one who made the breakthroughs that caught serial murderers. Visible again, the bright light at the centre of the investigation.

Reuben checked the house number and pressed its

buzzer. Almost instantly, the door was pulled open.

'There's no entry at the moment,' a young uniformed constable informed him.

Reuben pulled out his GeneCrime ID. 'Forensics,' he said.

The officer stepped aside. 'Straight up the stairs, second floor. Bit of a mess up there by all accounts.'

The words trailed after Reuben as he took the stairs quickly, two at a time. This was what he needed, he told himself. Action. The theatre of the crime scene, the crucible of the investigation.

From the landing of the second floor, Reuben could see several of his colleagues. They were in white overalls and blue shoe covers, their faces hidden by paper masks. He strode along the carpet towards them. As he did so he tried again to shut Joshua away, to force his brain to focus on the contents of the room ahead of him, a room the killer had been in just fifteen or so hours earlier. The man who had presumably murdered, then returned to Joshua, bloody and satiated.

Reuben spotted Mina and made his way over. Her diminutive figure was swollen by a shapeless contamination suit.

'How are we getting on?' he asked when he reached her.

Mina's dark brown eyes stared out of the whiteness of the hooded suit and mask. 'Fine,' she answered.

'You been here long?'

Mina glanced automatically at her wrist, which didn't yield any information. 'Ninety minutes or so, at a guess.'

'And what's the story?'

'See for yourself.'

Mina pointed with her eyes, and Reuben examined the rest of the room. Forensic technicians were combing the light green carpet with adhesive spatulas, swabbing the door frame with white powder, dabbing at surfaces with cottonwool buds, running portable UV lamps along walls, pipetting minute volumes of fluids into Eppendorf tubes. Among them he noted the camouflaged presence of Bernie Harrison, Paul Mackay, Birgit Kasper and Simon Jankowski. To the far right of the large flat, a pair of trainers protruded from the adjoining bathroom, heels down, toes pointing in the air. The deceased was lying on his back, most of him in the bathroom.

'Here we go again.'

'I heard we had someone, Reuben. One of the CID bunch said they picked a man up last night.'

'Daniel Riefield.' Reuben grimaced. 'Looks like it was a wrong call.'

Mina glanced up at him. 'How do you mean, wrong?'

'He was in custody when this happened. But that's all I should say.'

Reuben left Mina and headed over. He wondered whether she had been a bit short with him, or whether he had imagined it. Reuben pictured the two boxes of DNA still in his freezer at home and realized he needed to insert them back into the GeneCrime freezer before they were missed.

The bathroom was rental-smart. Tiled surfaces, fashionable fixtures, anonymous colours. It reminded Reuben of the many hotel rooms he had stayed in. Lying on his back, surrounded by evidence bags and sample racks, Philip Gower appeared gaunt and pale. His lips had a dry purple hue to them, his blue eyes still open. Fine sprays of red criss-crossed his grey sweatshirt. Reuben surmised that at least one of his hands must have been free after its fingertips were removed. As with the other two bodies he had examined in the GeneCrime morgue, all the tips were missing, the final phalanges sawn off. Thick, congealed blood oozed out of them. He thought again about Joshua, about the fact that the man who had just done this was now with his son, about the fact that Reuben's only bargaining tool was now gone. The killer's words, *from now on there are no rules*, crashed through his skull.

Staring bleakly down at the body, Reuben could see that his team had been thorough. He could just make out where they had swabbed and where they had taken samples for further analysis. He peered back into the living room. The investigation had obviously now shifted to the rest of the flat. A lifeless body could only tell you so much.

He watched as Sarah Hirst detached herself from the

slow-moving scientists and strode rapidly over to him. Despite everything else going on in his head, he found her as undeniably striking as ever. She also looked purposeful and focused, and Reuben knew he had to be on his guard.

'Decided to join us, Dr Maitland?' she said.

'Veno needed to brief us on progress.'

'And what is the progress?' Sarah gave the impression of softening a degree or two. 'I heard they have a suspect. Any positive news?'

'Not yet.'

'And who is he?'

The name Riefield flashed through Reuben's speeding brain. 'Just a nobody. They're busy taking his flat to pieces. Probably a false lead.'

'I'm sorry.'

Reuben watched his boss. He knew she was desperate to work the conversation round to the case, but didn't want to appear unsympathetic. She was programmed to solve crimes. Everything else was an inconvenience. Sometimes he felt that way himself. He decided to help her out. 'Anyway, this is the clinical trials coordinator,' he said, pointing with his eyes.

'Yes. Philip Gower.'

The words 'clinical trials' suddenly made a connection in Reuben's brain that hadn't been there before. Something in Riefield's flat.

'Do we have a link between the three victims?'

'As head of the investigation, I should be asking you.'

'I've just had an idea.'

'What?'

'Not yet, not till I go through the notes again. But I think there could be something.'

Sarah's eyes narrowed as she regarded him. 'As soon as you have something, I want to know. We can't afford any delays at all on this one.'

'I just want to make sure.'

'OK. Now, let me bring you up to speed. Gower was discovered when his new partner, a nurse, returned from her night-shift. Path have had a good look, and Chris reckons from core body temperature that he died some time before eleven p.m. last night. This tallies with a statement we have from a witness on the first floor who says she heard banging and shouting around that time, but just assumed a domestic.'

'Did she see anything? Anyone coming or going?'

'Apparently not.'

'And the rats?'

'A cage on the bathroom floor. The rats were going crazy when we got here. I gave Leigh Harding the unenviable task of taking it back to GeneCrime and retrieving the fingertips without getting bitten himself.'

'Nice.'

'So, as I said on the phone, same MO, a third death,

and this thing is now becoming priority number one for the Met. We've got to act quickly, or else GeneCrime will be swamped, other CID officers seconded in, forensics getting thrown out to the wider FSS so we can extend the net.' Sarah made a point of holding Reuben's eye, her alluring face cold and still. 'Basically, Reuben, you've either got to stop this man in his tracks, or . . .'

'Or what?

'Move over and let someone else do it.'

Sarah bored into him a second longer with her pale blue eyes, then walked slowly and purposefully away from him.

7

Reuben returned to Lucy's house. Nothing useful could be achieved by staying at the flat in Hammersmith. He had arrived too late to influence proceedings. His team had known what to do and had quietly got on with it. He had trained them well. When the samples were processed back at GeneCrime later in the afternoon events would hot up. He would be there to coordinate the analyses. In the meantime, Reuben decided to smuggle the DNA samples from his freezer back into GeneCrime, while most of the team were crawling around Philip Gower's residence, bagging up infinitesimally small fragments of his existence. But Reuben already suspected nothing useful would come from the sweep. So far, the only DNA profile they'd matched to anything had turned out to be Daniel Riefield's. And that hadn't exactly helped the case.

As he pulled up close to Lucy's house, Reuben checked

his rear-view. He had a good scan of the street before getting out. So far he had been followed twice, once in the day, once at night. A dark blue Audi with a broken front light. He couldn't see the car now but still couldn't shake the feeling that he was being watched, toyed with, manipulated somehow. Two phone calls from the killer, and two occasions on which he had been followed.

He walked over the small patch of grass and opened the front door. Inside, he called Lucy's name. There was a muffled answer from the upstairs bathroom. Reuben's phone vibrated and he answered the call. It was Bernie Harrison.

'I just wanted to check in with you, boss. I didn't manage to catch you at the scene.'

'Sorry, big man. I wasn't being a lot of use there. I'm heading over to GeneCrime in half an hour or so. When are you back?'

'We're wrapping up in an hour or so.'

'Great.' Reuben appreciated this would give him just enough time to replace the samples. 'I'll catch you there.'

'Is there anything you need us to do?'

'Yes. Can you call an update meeting for six tonight. We should have some prelims by then. And I want photographs from Daniel Riefield's flat at the meeting. There may be something in them. IT should be able to help if you get stuck.'

'Sure. Anything else?'

'That's it for now.' Reuben struggled out of his jacket, which didn't want to let go. 'Bernie, I'm sorry this is patchy at the moment. You know this isn't exactly how I like to do things.'

'No problem, boss. We all understand.'

'It's just . . .' Reuben swayed on his feet. 'Let's get this fucker, Bernie. Let's get everyone fired up, and let's get him.'

Bernie wrapped up the call and Reuben headed into the kitchen. He needed some food, a coffee, if he was honest with himself, something white and powdery. Three nights of fractured sleep and two long headfuck days were catching up with him. He opened a few cupboards, and checked out the fridge. As he closed it, he ran his eyes over the magnetic animals clinging to its surface. Letters spelled out by random creatures, like the ones on Joshua's door. Reuben picked out an A, a C, a G and a T. The letters of DNA. He thought about the sequencing and profiling, which had led him to the wrong man. As he thought, he ran his fingers over the surface of the fridge. It was either a metallic plastic or a plastic metal, he couldn't decide. It didn't quite seem to be either.

His stomach rumbled, bringing him round. Food. And then the doorbell rang. Swearing under his breath, Reuben headed for the front door. Fragments, half-formed thoughts, fractured patterns of activity. All he wanted was twenty minutes of peace and quiet, a warm meal, a hot drink, a chance to quietly stitch everything together, to smooth all the jagged edges.

He opened the door wearily. It was Veno, and he had come mob-handed. The three members of his team – one female, two male – and one other visitor. DCI Sarah Hirst. Reuben guessed she'd left the scene just after he had.

'Reuben,' Detective Veno began, 'we'd like to come in.'

A cold nervousness leaked instantly through Reuben's gut. Something had happened. He glanced at Sarah but she refused to meet his eye.

'What is it?'

'Can we come in?'

'You don't normally ask.'

'Well, we are today.'

'Do you have some news for me?'

Behind Reuben came the creaking of stairs, a pad of footsteps down the hallway. Lucy joined him, standing side on, squeezed in the door frame. 'What's going on?' she asked.

Veno shuffled round, feet scraping the grass. 'Can we come in?'

'Is it Joshua?' Lucy went pale, her mouth dropping. 'Tell me it's not Joshua.'

Detective Veno glanced at a member of his team, then across at Sarah. 'We are asking politely because we want you to allow us to search your home.'

'What the hell do you mean?' Reuben asked.

Veno cleared his throat. 'I mean that we want to carry out a detailed search of your residence in connection with your son's disappearance.'

'Are we suspects now?' Reuben asked, refusing to budge.

'We're asking politely,' Veno said, sidestepping the question. 'We could go and get a warrant. But of course that won't look good on you. Parents of missing child refuse to cooperate with the police. Make a nice headline in the papers, that.'

Reuben checked Sarah's body language. Veno had obviously requested her presence. After her strident performance at the murder scene in Hammersmith, she looked more guarded. This was Veno's doing, not hers. If Sarah Hirst wanted a house searched, warrants were issued and doors were kicked down with no polite requests or questions asked.

'Let me ask you again, Detective. Are we suspects?'

Veno frowned. 'Carry on any longer like this and you'll be the only suspects.'

Out of the corner of his eye, Reuben monitored Lucy. This was her house, ultimately her decision. But she was quiet, as she had been for days. Apart from the occasional outburst, his ex-wife seemed to have internalized all the hurt. She wasn't able, Reuben appreciated, to compartmentalize like he was. There was just a ball of guilt and pain, her only son gone, and it was slowly consuming her from the inside. Reuben suddenly didn't want Veno's team picking through her belongings. But there was a more important reason the police couldn't come in. A much more important reason.

'It's a risk I'm willing to take,' Reuben said.

'Meaning?'

'If you want to execute a search of these premises, I suggest you go and get a warrant. Until then, we'd prefer to be alone.'

Sarah made her presence felt. She had been standing behind Veno and to the left. Now she took a pace closer. 'That's not a smart move, Reuben,' she said. 'No matter how you feel about this, it's not a good thing to do.'

'Until Veno explains why we're officially under suspicion, no one is coming in.'

'Reuben, think about it. No one has to give you any reason. It's not the way you work in your job, or how Detective Veno works in his. We don't give reasons. If we did, criminals would destroy the evidence before we got a chance to examine it.'

'And is that what we are now? Criminals?'

Sarah stared harshly back, her cheeks rouged, her eyes wide. For a second, Reuben wanted to confess everything to her. His duplicity, his dishonesty, his crossing of the line. But he couldn't. As Lucy had suggested, he had come too far, dug himself in too deep.

His son's life was in utter danger. If CID got involved, Reuben would be sacked, Veno would go ballistic, and the police would close ranks. The chances of rescuing his son would dramatically worsen. The only option was to do what he did best. Track the killer down.

'I resent that implication,' Sarah said. 'And I don't like the way this is heading. Do yourself a favour, Reuben, let Detective Veno do his job.'

Lucy seemed to be staring at Sarah. They had met once, years ago, before Reuben was married, at the start of his relationship with Lucy. A police function, a celebration after a successful case. Lucy had turned up, stayed for a couple of drinks, gone home early. And then, two or three good years, marriage, a failing relationship, Lucy's infidelity, and one more broken home in the capital.

'Or maybe I should be asking Lucy. It's your house, Mrs Maitland. What's it to be? The nice way or the nasty way?'

Reuben studied both women. Auburn versus blonde, solicitor versus officer, former wife versus current boss.

'There is no nice way,' Lucy enunciated, still focusing on Sarah. 'And if Reuben says you aren't coming in then you're not coming in.' With that, she stepped back past Reuben and slammed the door.

Reuben stood facing Lucy in the half-light of the hall-way. He pictured the faces of the police officers outside. This was suicidal. They would be back, and they would tear the place apart. But it was the only course of action they could have taken.

'Drink?' Lucy asked.

Reuben shook his head. 'I've got one hell of a problem in the garage. A laboratory, DNA samples I shouldn't have, profiles which have been run through the National DNA Database.' Reuben started walking, past Lucy, past the kitchen and towards the garage. 'Lock the front door,' he said. 'And don't let anyone in. If they understand what I've been doing, we're absolutely fucked.'

8

In the construction of the garage twenty-four hours earlier there had been optimism. In its disassembly there was only regret. Reuben thought about calling Judith and Moray to help, but knew that Veno and his squad would be back before they arrived. So Reuben worked feverishly, unplugging equipment, boxing up solutions and reagents, tearing the clingfilm from his makeshift lab bench. He set about the computer, deleting files, profile logs, records of database searches. He knew exactly what a police search team would be looking for. Reuben hesitated for a second, then decided to format the hard drive. Better utterly paranoid than just partially so.

While the PC systematically erased its past he walked the printer back into his old study and hid the pipettes and tips in an empty can of paint. He opened the small freezer and let it thaw, removing the two boxes of DNA from Ian Gillick and Carl Everitt's crime scenes. He took them through into the kitchen where he poured the Eppendorfs into a large bag of mixed sweetcorn and peas. Lucy was sitting there in silence, both hands wrapped around a mug of something warm. She raised her eyebrows at him as he shoved the bag to the rear of the freezer. Reuben knew that even if they found the tubes, and their discovery compromised him, this was vital DNA evidence that mustn't be discarded. Getting sacked was one thing. Letting a killer off was quite another.

Reuben returned to the garage and continued to shift small pieces of lab equipment. It was desperate stuff. He was fucked, and he knew it. There was no way out that he could see. He decided at that moment his career was effectively over. His reinstatement as GeneCrime Head of Forensics, controversial as it had been anyway, had lasted a mere three days. He had compromised innocent members of the public. He had misled GeneCrime. He had subverted a missing child hunt. As he lifted the spare door that had served as his lab bench, he tried to console himself that the three deaths so far had been unrelated to his actions. All of them would have died regardless. Philip Gower was doomed, even before Reuben received the phone call.

At the time, he had quickly squared the moral black hole of the killer's blunt proposal. A life for a life. A two-year-old boy with seventy-plus years of love and happiness ahead of him against the existence of a grown man who had already experienced several decades on the planet. Not perfect, but when it was your own son, your only child, against a total stranger . . . Reuben paused, appreciating that in the cold light of day, beneath the harsh neon tubes of the garage ceiling, it didn't sit as comfortably as he might have hoped. He had been offered an impossible choice, and he had made an imperfect decision. But if the killer struck again, Reuben knew that decision would haunt him for ever.

He shuffled the heavy upright door to the back of the garage and leaned it gently against the hottest part of the central heating boiler. Any evidence clinging to it would soon be destroyed. Standing still for a moment, breathing heavily from the exertion, he dragged his brain back to the case. What linked the men who had died? A scientist, a pharmaceutical sales executive and a trials coordinator? Why had they been targeted, and why had their fingertips been systematically removed? What was the involvement of Riefield, who was clearly psychologically damaged, and was also missing his fingertips? Reuben had barely had time to think it all through. He realized belatedly that the third man held the clue. He was the final victim the killer had mentioned, the one he was going to end on, the one he said deserved to die. Three men, forensic immunity, and that was it.

Reuben cursed himself. He had been unusually slow. It hadn't been an investigation so far, just a blur of police stations, rushed conversations, endless tearing around the capital in anonymous cars. In the chaos, he had barely once sat down and tried to pull it all together. Three men, murdered one by one, no concrete links between them, just the vague notion that Philip Gower was what had really mattered.

The meeting at six at GeneCrime would start the process moving. Initial forensic analyses, background checks on Philip Gower, the story finally starting to emerge from the turmoil of three deaths in quick succession. That was how it worked. At the start, an overwhelming mass of seemingly unconnected data. And then, from amid the disorder, patterns and strands, dots joining up, loose associations becoming tightly bound certainties.

Reuben cast his eyes over the garage one last time. The sequencer was back on the floor, where it had sat until the previous day. The smaller items – the microfuge, the PCR machine, the dry block – were boxed up out of sight. The miscellaneous plastic ware – the Eppendorfs and pipette tips – were secreted in various nooks and crannies. The PC was standing silent, its screen blank. Nothing was hidden so it couldn't be found, just so that it looked like it hadn't been used recently. It was the best he could do in the time it would take Veno to rush through a warrant from the duty judge.

There was a hammering on the front door, and Reuben sighed. When he had first begun his career in CID, a warrant took twelve hours at the bare minimum. He flicked off the garage lights and walked back through the house. Veno would have phoned ahead as he drove, texted the details through, had an assistant use a pro forma, then email it to the relevant authority for clearance and an electronic signature. He checked his watch. It had taken an hour and a half, including travel time. The door shook again as it was banged. Reuben sensed anger and irritation in the fist making the noise. He waited a second, daring them to pound the wooden surface again. And then, a coldness in the pit of his stomach, he pulled it open.

Veno looked severely pissed off. He was brandishing a piece of paper which appeared to have been faxed. 'Right,' he said, 'I'm now asking you to step the hell out of my way, Maitland.'

Reuben didn't bother to read the document. He looked at Sarah, who also appeared angry. 'Fine,' he said. 'Come on in. Do your worst.'

While Veno's team took a room each, Lucy sat silently in the study at the back of the house, staring out of the window. Veno had requested they remain out of visual contact, so Reuben sat by himself in the kitchen. He finally made himself a coffee, revelling in its bitter warmth.

After a few minutes, Sarah entered and joined him. She declined the offer of a coffee, which Reuben saw as a bad sign. In the corner, the large metal-effect freezer hummed quietly, eighty-three GeneCrime Eppendorfs lurking among its bags of frozen vegetables.

'I've just been in the garage,' Sarah said, her light blue eyes fixed on Reuben.

'Really?'

'Really.'

'Some sort of point you're building up to, Sarah?'

'The equipment from your old lab seems to be in there. I saw a sequencer and a freezer, and I'll bet my backside there's a whole lot of other stuff secreted around if I could be bothered to look hard enough.'

Reuben stared back. It was only a matter of time before one of Veno's team started poking around in the kitchen. 'I'm not denying that I own some lab equipment.'

'Fine. But would you say it was usual for scientists to set up laboratories in their homes?'

'It's not my home.'

'Either way—'

'Don't you take any work back to your flat?'

'It's a bit different reading a few papers or typing some emails to sequencing genes and profiling DNA. Besides, what can you possibly do here that you can't do at GeneCrime?'

Reuben declined to answer.

Sarah stood with her hands on her hips, glaring at him. 'You know your problem, Reuben?'

'Tell me,' he said. 'We'll compare notes.'

'You're failing to see this like Detective Veno sees it. You're taking everything so bloody personally.'

'It *is* personal. My son is missing and Veno's pulling my ex-wife's house apart. How much more personal could it be?'

'Look at your recent history, Reuben, and tell me you would be any different from Veno. Infidelity, a marriage meltdown, your sacking, a child with a history of serious illness, rumours about your consumption of drugs—'

'You've seen my file as well?' he said, dismayed.

'How do you think it appears? Veno's just a blood-hound doing what he's got to do.'

'While all the time trying to fuck me over.'

Sarah peered up towards the ceiling. A heavy bang suggested the search was becoming more thorough. 'Look, Reuben, I'm not happy. It took a lot of effort to get you back. Commander Thorner and his cronies needed some serious convincing. It was not a popular appointment across the Met. I mean, Veno's not exactly the only one with a grudge.' Sarah left her words hanging. Their sharp tones ricocheted off the flat polished surfaces of the kitchen. Reuben felt sick and uncomfortable, wanting to be straight with Sarah, and knowing that he couldn't be. 'I stuck my neck out for you, Reuben.'

'I know,' Reuben answered quietly. There was another ominous thud from the floor above. 'And I can't tell you how much I owe you.'

Sarah shrugged off the sentiment. 'From now on, everything is above board, Reuben. Or else.'

'Or else what?'

Sarah fixed him squarely in the eye again. 'I shouldn't need to finish that sentence, and you shouldn't need to ask.'

9

Reuben basked in the radiated warmth of his team. They surrounded him, a human layer of protection from all the external troubles of his life. He felt truly comfortable for the first time in days. Reuben ran his eyes around the group, most of whom he had recruited and trained himself. Bernie, Mina, Simon, Paul, Birgit, Chris, Leigh, Helen. He had missed them all. He had particularly missed the sparring of bright minds, the razor-sharp insight his team of forensic scientists had developed, the intellectual leaps they made that solved cases and defeated killers.

To look at, they were nothing special. In Reuben's experience, some of the brightest minds he had ever encountered were housed in some of the dullest bodies. The popular concept of the nerd was a misleading one, he thought. Sure, some narrow avenues of academic research attracted males and females of a plainness rivalled only by young Christians. Forensics, on the other hand, which spanned biology, anatomy, chemistry and psychology, tended to reflect as much human variation as it sought to investigate. Inspecting the group crammed into his office, Reuben appreciated that there was no archetypal forensic scientist. There was instead a wealth of character, each individual bringing his or her own unique perspective.

'So,' he said, 'who'll start us off?'

No one in the arc of seats that enclosed his desk said anything.

'No one? I feel chronically out of touch with the case for obvious reasons, and I need bringing up to speed. Someone help me out here.'

Bernie ran a quick hand through his beard. 'We think this is probably the work of one man.'

'Why?'

'We're starting to get footprint analysis through. Kitchen floors, shoes treading in fine sprays of blood, partial imprints outside the environs of each murder.'

'And?'

'We don't have any consistent patterns that would indicate different pairs of footwear. When we subtract shoe patterns from the wardrobes of the deceased, we're only left with a single footwear profile at each scene.'

'Is the killer wearing the same pair of shoes to each scene?'

'No. Three different pairs.'

'And from that you're inferring just one man?'

'We've been able to match each pair via the Footwear Intelligence Agency at the FSS.'

'I love those guys over at Birmingham,' Chris Stevens muttered. 'They set up a shoe database and make it sound like they're the CI-fucking-A.'

'Either way, it works,' Bernie continued. 'They've been able to identify shoe make and model, and confirm they're all the same size. And our man has large feet. Size twelve and a half. It's extremely unlikely that there are two killers wearing the same size and type of shoes.'

'You might want to talk to my twin brother about that,' Reuben said. 'But no, you're probably correct, Bernie. Anyone else?'

Mina straightened in her chair. 'Our man in the twelve and a halfs is obviously careful.'

'Based on what?'

'The lack of useable samples we actually have. Aside from footwear, which only get used once, we don't have fingerprints, or saliva, or hairs. Someone is able to enter a residence, restrain a grown man and remove his finger-tips, all without leaving us a present. And that's not to mention the rats. That can't be easy.'

'It's the lack of forced entry on the first two that disturbs me,' Detective Leigh Harding said.

'How do you mean?'

Leigh scratched at his thinning blond hair. 'Well, why did he have to break into Philip Gower's flat but not into the residences of Ian Gillick or Carl Everitt?' He sucked in his cheeks for a second. 'What changed?'

'I'll tell you what changed,' Reuben answered. 'The news. Carl Everitt gets hit out of the blue. Nothing he could do to see it coming. Same for Ian Gillick. Even if he read somewhere that Everitt had been hacked up, he had no way of knowing he was next. Just a coincidence that he knew someone who died. But Gower, and this is why I think he is key to all this, Gower had an inkling. Maybe he saw the news, recognized the names of the two victims, wondered whether he should be careful.'

'Why didn't he go to the cops?'

'Perhaps he has something to be ashamed of.' Reuben thought back to the killer's words. *This one deserves to die.* 'Perhaps he couldn't go to the cops.'

'What makes you think he had an idea something might happen?'

Reuben edited the words in his head before he said them out loud. He had to remind himself of what he knew, and what he actually should know. 'Gower's flat was locked and chained from the inside. His new partner, a nurse, was on a night-shift, due to return in the early hours. That would mean waking Gower up when she got back, which is less than ideal. I mean, I don't know about you guys, but when a case spills into the early hours, I'm sure your significant others don't lock you out of your own house.'

'Depends how late I am,' Bernie grumbled.

'And besides, the neighbour below reported a lot of banging and crashing about. I get the feeling this wasn't as smooth as the first two, and maybe part of this is because Gower was on his guard.'

'So this implies the three victims knew one another,' Mina said. 'Can we make that assumption yet?'

Simon Jankowski, who had been silent so far, opened his notebook. 'I've got some news,' he said.

Everyone in the room turned to him.

'Don't tell me you're finally coming out,' Paul Mackay muttered.

'I think you fulfil that quota,' Simon smiled back.

'Better out and proud,' Paul answered, 'than in and ashamed.'

'Well, are you planning on sharing it with us, Simon?' Reuben asked. 'If you two don't mind too much, we've got a psychopath to catch.'

'OK,' Simon said. He ran a finger along a line in his book, silently checking his facts. Then he stood up and walked over to the whiteboard in the corner of Reuben's office. 'Do you mind, boss?' he asked.

Reuben shook his head, excited. Words were easy. If you wrote something on the whiteboard, it mattered.

'Leigh and I have been doing some background checks, ascertaining identities, making sure the samples we have match the right punters.' Simon used a red marker pen to scratch the words 'Royal' and 'Free' in large capitals. Above them, he wrote the names of the three victims in blue, the squeak of the pen the only sound in the room. 'Now, we have a scientist from the Royal Holloway, a pharmaceutical sales exec based at a couple of sites in the capital, and a clinical trials coordinator working at the Hammersmith Hospital. And what unites them all is this: the Royal Free Hospital in Hampstead.'

'Go on,' Reuben said.

Dressed in one of his trademark colourful shirts, Simon seemed to grow in confidence. 'Right. The reason we found no link between Carl Everitt, who worked for Roche, and Ian Gillick, who worked as a research scientist at the Holloway, was that we hadn't looked back far enough. Everitt worked for another pharmaceutical company, BioNovia, prior to Roche.' Simon wrote BioNovia in small blue letters. 'And, before taking a senior research position at the Holloway, Gillick worked at the medical school of University College London, which is closely affiliated with the Royal Free. The final piece of the jigsaw – and Leigh and I only found this out about forty-five minutes ago through talking to HR at the Hammersmith – is this: Philip Gower, who died last night, was previously a clinical trials coordinator at the Royal Free.'

Birgit Kasper frowned, her make-up-free face wrinkling into rows of fine lines. 'The Royal Free is a teaching hospital. I applied for a Ph.D. there. So what you're proposing is that Gillick and Gower could have encountered each other there?'

'How does Everitt fit into this?' Reuben asked.

'At BioNovia, Everitt was very active in university-led research projects, particularly in the golden triangle – Oxford, Cambridge and London.' Simon drew a series of arrows from the blue names of the three men to the red Royal Free.

'Merely coincidence,' Reuben said. 'Prove to me otherwise.'

Simon grinned back at his boss. 'Tough love. Just how I like it. For the final piece, it's over to my special friend Paul.'

Paul Mackay shuffled in his chair, upright, adjusting his Dolce and Gabbana glasses. Reuben studied him for a second, eager for the next piece of information, wondering whether Paul put up with the jokey homophobia with quite as good grace as he seemed to. Reuben took the blunt management style that if no one complained there wasn't a problem. But that had got him into a lot of trouble before.

'Leigh and Simon forwarded their info around and asked if anyone could find anything else,' Paul began. 'And I think I have.'

'What have you got?' Reuben asked, leaning forward, his elbows digging into his desk.

'A clinical trial at the Royal Free.'

Reuben felt a rush of affirmation. The cuttings in Riefield's flat. The occupation of Gower. Without knowing any more, he realized his team was fast honing in on the truth. The forensics would come; for the time being links and associations were the next best thing. But still, Reuben held back. He had to be sure.

'You've only had forty minutes at the most,' he said. 'Where's this come from?'

'Where all great discoveries are made these days. The internet.'

'Are you sure it's right?'

'Absolutely. There are hundreds of web pages about it. And there, in among them all, are the names of all three of our victims.'

'What was the trial for?' Mina asked.

'The drug was called Vasoprellin. BioNovia's new wonder compound.'

'That rings a vague bell.'

'It should do. For a short period of time nearly four years ago it was front-page news.' Paul opened a brown cardboard folder and pulled out several sheets of A4. 'I just had time to run these off,' he said.

Reuben slid his copy across the desk and spun it round. He scanned the news story, his head bowed down, his concentration absolute. Vasoprellin. A clinical trial gone wrong. And now three of the people involved in it were dead. He consumed the details, forming ideas about the man who was killing and mutilating, about the man who was holding his son. He absorbed the timelines, and also the names. Dion Morgan, Martin Randle, Syed Sanghera, Daniel Riefield, Michael Adebyo, Amanda Skeen.

His eyes flicked back to Daniel Riefield's name, and then to an accompanying photograph, of Amanda Skeen.

Just what the hell had gone so badly wrong, he wondered?

10

Amanda Skeen monitored the second hand, which jerked around the white face of the observation room clock. It was 9.59 and thirty-two seconds. A few more stutters of the bold red hand and everything would begin.

She checked out the others. The usual mix of students and members of the public, all of them skint, most of them having been here before. Her fiancé smiled at her from the far side of the room, a brief flick of the eyebrows, an acknowledgement that it was nearly time. Amanda sighed quietly to herself. His idea. Three and a half thousand pounds each for a couple of days in hospital, and they would finally have enough money to tie the knot. Crippled by student living expenses, it wasn't going to happen any other way for several years. This was their big chance, and Amanda was excited and scared in equal measure. Marrying as a student came with significant disadvantages. Quiet nights in rather than wild nights out. A shrinking social circle while everyone else's expanded. Two sets of living expenses to worry about rather than just one. But the many advantages were encapsulated in the physical form of the wonderful man grinning across the room at her.

As a third-year medical student, Amanda was well aware that the test was not inherently dangerous. The trial coordinator and the chief scientist had been through the data with each of the ten trialists. In cell work, in mouse experiments, in chimpanzee testing, Vasoprellin had exerted mild vasoconstriction effects. It was a drug to complement anti-angiogenesis treatments in cancer, to locally restrict blood flow in tumours. Amanda had read up on it in the Medical School library. Deprive tumours of their thirst for blood and you could stop them growing, even regress them. And the local action of a drug like Vasoprellin could speed the process to the point where cancers that might otherwise have invaded and metastasized into blood capillaries could be intercepted before they got the chance. Truly, this could be a small step forward in the medical treatment of cancer.

The hand finally ticked round to the vertical position, and Amanda watched the trial coordinator, Dr Philip Gower, walk over to the chief scientist, Dr Ian Gillick. She sensed for the first time that they had a lot riding on the trial. Pass this phase, and the next step would be to perform Phase Two clinical testing on cancer patients, with higher doses and direct outcomes. A poor outcome and the drug would be shelved.

Amanda knew Dr Gower vaguely. She had seen him around the university, and he had lectured her two or three times in her first and second years. He was smart, quick in his actions, neatly turned out, with an aura of cleanliness about him. He smiled at one of the nurses, and Amanda imagined for a second there was more than just friendliness in the gesture. She had only met Dr Gillick once before, when she had signed up for the trial. He was slower, more considered, an old-fashioned academic despite only being, she guessed, mid thirties at most.

She watched them confer, Gower taller than Gillick, his head angled down slightly. They were at the far end of the room, between the two rows of beds. Most of the five female and five male trialists were lying propped up on their elbows, reading magazines, enjoying the rest. Her fiancé's surgical gown made him appear older than he was, as if his casual clothes kept him young. He was a couple of years older anyway, in his final year, but not as ancient as he suddenly appeared.

Amanda wondered for a second whether she would get a placebo, or whether he might. It stood to reason that a clinical trial needed comparisons. Dr Gower had said as much. But neither he nor Dr Gillick had made any further comment. She briefly considered whether she would rather have the drug than her fiancé. This was surely a test of her love. If one of them had to have the treatment, would she rather have it herself, to spare her lover any potential danger? She thought about it, observing the nurse Dr Gower had smiled at as she prepared a series of cannulas on a blue plastic tray. And in that moment, Amanda realized that this was the right thing to do. She was ready to abandon her student freedoms and get married. She would gladly do anything for her fiancé, whatever the outcome.

Dr Gower strode towards the centre of the hospital observation room. For the Royal Free, a medical facility with a worldwide reputation, the room was less than glamorous. Its decor seemed to have been hampered by 1980s budget restrictions, and never to have recovered. Off-white walls, bare windows, cheap patterned curtains around each bed, dull green floor tiles that squeaked under Dr Gower's shoes. He stopped and addressed the room, swivelling his suited body round to direct his words at each of the ten test subjects.

'OK,' he said, 'I think we're ready to kick off. I hope you are too. If anyone has any problems, please make the nursing team aware of them as soon as I've finished talking. Now, as you've all been briefed, this is a tolerance test for the drug Vasoprellin, manufactured by BioNovia. So if you have any complaints, you should direct them to BioNovia's sales executive, Mr Everitt.'

Dr Gower nodded in the direction of a dark-haired,

tanned man standing at the far end of the suite. Everitt smiled warmly back, a corporate acknowledgement of a joke at his expense.

'Now, animal tolerance tests have been extremely well received, with no reported ill effects. Dr Gillick and I aren't expecting any issues, but there will be full medical monitoring over the whole trial period. You are, as they say, in good hands. Dr Gillick, would you care to outline the procedure?'

Amanda watched Dr Gillick's body language. Hands in pockets, less confident than Gower, thoughtful in his words.

'We're going to set off at standard five-minute intervals, so that the drug is administered for all ten of you well within the space of an hour. In a moment, the nursing team will fit you each with a cannula on the back of the hand. Then, when everyone is ready, we'll start the timed injections. Because we're nice here, we'll give you some anaesthetic gel to numb the injection.' He glanced across at Dr Gower. 'So really all we want you to do is lie back, relax and enjoy the flight.'

Amanda gave him the satisfaction of a small laugh. She was the only one to do so, and she felt bad that no one else had helped him out.

'Right, the sooner we get started, the sooner you can be paid, and the sooner the rest of us can go home.'

Dr Gillick nodded to the nursing team, and Amanda

quickly appreciated that she was going to be one of the first five. The beds were clearly set out in chronological order, a bold number in front of each, two males and two females to her right already having cannulas inserted. She felt that quick prick of adrenalin that occurs prior to an injection. The knowledge that a needle is soon going to be forced through your skin. A nurse approached and smiled, swabbing the back of Amanda's left hand with an ethanol wipe, wordlessly pulling a butterfly needle from its plastic home.

At precisely twenty-five past ten, Amanda watched a small volume of clear fluid surge through the clear plastic tubing which led into her hand. The trial had officially begun at 10.05, and as she had predicted, she was fifth in line. She glanced away from the tubing and gazed over at her fiancé, who was chatting to the man on the bed next to him. Amanda hadn't seen the man around before. She squinted at his name which was scribbled on a clipboard beside his bed. Martin Ramble or Randle, she guessed. Randle, probably. He was large and powerful, his musculature obvious even when he was lying down. Something about him spoke of military service, of a toughness that marked him out against the others. She watched for a couple more seconds. Randle would be sixth, her fiancé seventh.

The nurse removed the tube and closed the small plastic tap. Amanda sighed. The difficult bit was over.

She swung her head to the right, checking on the first four. All were relaxed, chatting with Dr Gower and Dr Gillick, sharing the odd bland platitude to cover the lack of excitement.

Amanda decided she ought to get some rest and shuffled down under her thin hospital sheets. She watched the man next to her fiancé as his treatment was administered. Five minutes later, almost metronomically with the pronounced tick of the clock, her fiancé's injection was carried out.

Amanda picked a magazine from a small stack next to her bed. It smelled of ink and perfume, and had a BioNovia sticker in the top right corner. They had all been provided with reading material – another sweetener to smooth the long hours of observation. She flicked through the pristine pages, savouring the glossy scent of promise and possibility, losing herself in a section on designer bridal outfits. She smiled across at her fiancé again. Fat chance. Most of the outfits cost more than a year's tuition fees.

And then, from the far right, there was movement. The first subject was out of bed. He was starting to pace around with a nurse at his side. Dr Gower sauntered over, a deliberate lack of haste about his upright form, hospital code for 'nothing to panic about'. Amanda sat up. The male who had received the first dose of the drug was shivering, walking quickly about, his head bowed. She checked across the room. The final patient was just being injected.

The first patient looked pale. His name was Daniel Riefield, Amanda recalled, a rugby-playing medic from the year below. Without warning he started to vomit. Thin watery fluid falling out of his mouth almost uncontrolled, dropping on to the dull green tiles. Amanda found the noise it made almost indescribably abhorrent.

She transferred her attention to the second trialist. People got sick. It happened. But if two went down . . . The second, a female in her early thirties with a dark red bob and black-framed glasses, was fine. She had barely noticed, filling in a crossword or sudoku or something similar, white headphones buried deep in her hair.

Six minutes passed. Riefield was still out of bed, unable to relax. He was scratching at his arms and face, deep red grazes appearing on his white flesh. He was freaking out. But, Amanda reminded herself, these things happened in hospitals. She had seen it herself on her ward rounds. Patients confused, disorientated or scared, medications stirring the waters. It was life.

Number two continued regardless and unconcerned. Next to her, number three, a pretty blonde she didn't recognize, was lying utterly still, the implications slowly eating into her. The blonde girl stared at her watch, seconds ticking by, barely breathing.

Another four minutes passed. If anything was wrong,

systematically wrong, they would know about it by now. Dr Gower was conferring with a nurse, and didn't look overly worried. Dr Gillick was talking to the guy from BioNovia, their bodies static, their reactions impossible to read.

Another couple of minutes. Twelve in total. Surely that was more than enough. But then a thought struck her. What if number two was a placebo? What if number three was a placebo too? It was possible.

Amanda turned to the man in the next bed, who had introduced himself in an African lilt as Michael. He shrugged back.

Fourteen minutes. This was good. Riefield had maybe reacted badly to the drug, or was a hypochondriac, or had already been ill. Amanda returned to her magazine, skimming articles for a couple of minutes. Then she turned to Michael to say something. He had gone quiet and was staring upwards. Glistening beads of sweat had appeared across his forehead. Amanda felt herself clench. 'Please be nothing,' she whispered under her breath. 'Please be nothing.'

And then Michael began as well. Groaning under his breath, moving under his sheets. 'I'm hot,' he said out loud, 'I'm hot.' A nurse dashed over to him. She held his arm and felt his pulse at the wrist. Dr Gower appeared, standing close behind her. The nurse placed a digital thermometer into Michael's ear and held it there.

After a few seconds she removed it, checked the display and showed it to Dr Gower. Amanda tried to read his reaction, but he had spun round and was walking quickly over to Dr Gillick and Everitt, the pharmaceutical guy. Michael coughed and retched, then vomited over his sheets. Amanda turned away. The smell was unbearably sharp and pungent, a stench that tugged at her own stomach, encouraging its contents to travel up her throat. She swallowed the reflex and caught her fiancé's eye. He was staring in horror.

Michael began to scratch at his skin. Amanda noted that it was almost black, long pink fingernails gouging out strips of red. In particular, he was scraping at his hands, one attacking the other, swapping almost continuously. She began to feel the first urgent heaves of panic. It was clear what was happening. The first and fourth subjects had been given the drug, the second and third hadn't. She wondered what the overall sequence was. Drug, placebo, placebo, drug . . . then what? She was next in line.

Amanda peered over at Daniel Riefield. He was being escorted back to his bed by two nurses. He was shaking uncontrollably, his head jerking from side to side as he was moved. He seemed to be losing consciousness, his legs barely supporting him. The rest of the patients were watching intently, no longer lounging around but sitting up straight. And then Amanda noticed it. Out of the corner of their eyes they were monitoring her as well. They were glancing at the clock, examining her, and looking back again. Everyone knew she was next. They lay there with the drug in their veins and waited to see if she succumbed as well. Amanda realized that Dr Gillick, too, was searching her face.

She did the maths. Nineteen minutes. If it was going to happen, it would come now. Five-minute intervals, give or take. A chain reaction passing around the room. She watched the pharmaceutical guy make a call on his mobile, saw Dr Gower pick up an internal phone. Each stutter of the clock was good, she told herself. Another second and no reaction. Several pairs of eyes tried to make it look like they weren't watching. Her fiancé was staring at her, intent and focused, no longer smiling. He seemed scared. Amanda asked herself whether he was scared for her or for himself.

And then she felt it. She tried to dismiss it, but it was there. She ripped out the cannula, knowing it was too late but doing it anyway. A sick tightness in the base of her stomach, a clamping force in her intestines. 'Please, no,' she said to herself. There was a lull, a chance for her to convince herself that she was imagining it. But as quickly as it had subsided, something grabbed her insides and crushed them again. An uncontrollable surge squeezed her pyloric sphincter, propelling a gush of fluid out of her mouth and through her nose. Her skin erupted, feeling like it was burning and freezing at the same time. She dug deep into it with her nails, instantly wanting it off her, stripped away, torn apart. Her head began to squeeze, her ears pounding, her vision narrowing. She gouged deeper into her own flesh, her fingers frostbitten and on fire, unbearable and intolerable. Her whole body started to shake, her teeth crashing into one another, chipping small fragments that she swallowed. All she could hear was a voice that sounded as if it was coming from inside her, shrieking and shrieking.

Amanda peered blindly across the room at her fiancé. She screamed his name and then her eyes closed, and she rushed headlong into a dark plunging unconsciousness.

11

'You recognize me, Martin, don't you?'

Martin Faulkner did. But he couldn't place the man standing on his front doorstep. Maybe he had met him at one of the clubs close to Soho, or maybe at a party. Either way, he was fairly good-looking. What would have been called a strapping lad a few years ago. Ten or fifteen years younger than him, but tall and wide. He didn't necessarily look part of the scene, but increasingly a lot didn't these days. Martin had read it time after time in the personals. *Straight-acting guy, non-scene, seeks similar . . .*

'I do recognize you,' Martin answered slowly. 'But I've just got off a long flight and I'm not sure where I remember you from.'

'Really?' the man asked.

There was a pause during which Martin expected the man to fill in the gaps. Instead, he appeared to be looking slightly past him and into the house. Martin wondered whether to invite him in, but quickly decided against it. Ten and a half hours from San Diego, an hour from Heathrow. He still hadn't begun to unpack after the week-long conference, and the jetlag was beginning to claw at him, making him feel tired and heavy, time alternately speeding and slowing. It was seven o'clock. Open his suit-case, throw his clothes in the washer, make some food and then, finally, get some sleep. That was his plan.

'Look,' Martin said, 'is there anything I can do to help you?'

The man stared at him. The look was empty, vacant, absent even. Martin transferred his weight from one foot to the other, then decided enough was enough.

'I'm sorry. I'm tired, and if you can't tell me—'

And then Martin felt himself reeling backwards, stumbling over, hitting the floor. The door was wide open, the man standing in it. He had something in his hand, a box of some sort. Martin shook himself round. It took a couple of seconds to appreciate that the man had shoved him abruptly in the chest, catching him off balance, leaving him sprawled on the hallway floor. He fought to get up, adrenalin kicking in. The man stepped forward and closed the front door behind him. Martin got to his feet. He experienced a sudden sense of vulnerability. The man occupied most of the narrow hallway.

'What the hell do you want?' Martin shouted, unable to stop his voice from trembling.

'You definitely don't recognize me,' the man answered, calmly putting the box down. 'Otherwise you would know already.'

Martin edged back. He flicked quickly through his options. In front of him, a man who had just pushed him to the floor without provocation. Behind him, a kitchen containing an array of extremely sharp knives. Martin peered into the eyes of the man pacing unhurriedly towards him. The vacant look had become focused and intense.

He turned and ran, sprinting past the living-room door and into the brightly lit kitchen. The knives were on the far side, around the central work-surface that was marooned in the middle like an island. He glanced at his phone, which was lying on its back on the island, grabbing it as he lunged towards the knives. Something primeval in Martin had told him that this man would not be reasoned with. A couple of images flashed through his racing brain, situations where their paths might have crossed before. Neither did anything to calm his rising panic.

He heard the slap of the man's shoes on the tiled floor and reached for the largest knife, sliding its cold aluminium handle out of a wooden block that held a row of progressively smaller ones. He started to spin round, the knife pulling clear, clenched out in front of him.

Instantly, he realized that something wasn't right. His movement was awkward and off balance. He was being pitched forward into the kitchen counter. The man had an arm around his shoulders, his full weight bearing down on him. Martin's movement stopped as quickly as it had begun. A hand slammed into the small of his back, making him cry out. An overwhelming force was pressing him against the counter, the knife held uselessly, aiming into the tiled surface of the wall. Martin tried to thrash in the opposite direction, but knew straight away that it was futile.

'What the fuck do you want?' he grunted.

'You,' the man answered calmly.

There was a second of stillness, Martin's unexercised muscles already beginning to weaken. His arms trembled, his legs suddenly frail. He was out of shape, out of time zone, out of the condition needed to fight. As a thirty-year-old man, he might have stood a chance. Now, though, forty-seven and living off a diet of caffeine and sluggish food, the vitality was draining out of him. But while his body faltered, Martin's mind remained focused and clear. He peered down at the phone. If he dropped the knife he might be able to dial three rapid nines.

And then he sensed a sharp nip in the top of each shoulder. He knew immediately that he had been injected with something. The needle jabs quickly gave way to a cold stinging sensation. A few seconds later and the man's grip loosened a little. Martin's first impulse was to raise the knife again and spin round with it. He stared down at the blade. Nine or ten inches long, extremely sharp on its lower surface, a tapered carving knife that made light work of joints of beef and ribs of lamb.

The man had taken a pace back. Out of the corner of his eye, Martin saw that he was positioning the box he had brought on the adjacent counter. Martin felt an unexpected wave of strength and energy. He could do this. Threaten the intruder, call the police, hold him at bay. If it came down to it, maybe he could use the knife as well.

He turned slowly around. And then he peered at his hands. Martin's first sensation was confusion. While the rest of his body had discovered some strength from somewhere, his fingers were weakening. It was like they belonged to someone else. The harder he clenched the knife, the weaker the grip became. He stared at his hands in disbelief. The knife tilted slowly down. He was unable to hold it up. It weighed maybe two hundred grams but it was slipping through his fingers. Martin continued to gaze at his hand in incredulity as the knife slinked out of its grip and fell to the floor, bouncing off the tiles, a sharp metal echo clattering around the surfaces. The man just watched him. Then Martin felt his arms go heavy, and fall to his side. With a rising panic he realized he couldn't lift them. It seemed to be washing through his body, a fatigue, a lack of coordination, a defeating loss of energy.

He glanced over at the box, getting his first clear look at it. It was plastic and blue, with a symmetrical series of slits. He smelled a sour damp odour. And then he sensed movement. A couple of dark forms within it, moving restlessly. The man swivelled it round. It had a caged front. Martin focused into it. Rats. Two black rats climbing over each other to look at him. Teeth gnawing at the bars, pink feet scrabbling at the plastic. At that moment, he understood.

A surge of adrenalin tried to kick him into action. But Martin felt his legs weaken and he slumped against the counter. Whatever he had been injected with was sapping him, draining him away. The man pulled a metal implement out of his coat pocket. A short hacksaw. Martin slid uselessly to the floor, more alive and frightened than he had ever been, his body refusing to cooperate, refusing to let him escape. The man smiled down at him, and Martin started to scream.

12

Reuben took the call languishing in Lucy's bath. The meeting at GeneCrime had finally ended and Detective Veno had asked him to return to the address that used to be his home. Veno was still tearing the place apart. Reuben suspected he wanted to show him the power he had over his existence. Apart from the garage, and one other item, Reuben knew he was safe. He had returned the DNA samples earlier, and no one could prove the lab equipment had been used in any ongoing case.

The mobile almost vibrated into the water with him. He caught it, noting the time on its display. It was a quarter to nine. He must have slept. The water was no longer warm, and he shivered as he found the answer button.

'Yes?' he said.

'It's Sarah.'

'Hi.' Reuben stood up, water cascading off him, and stepped out. 'Everything OK?'

'No. Not at all.'

'What is it?'

'Another one.'

Reuben stood naked, dripping water on to the floor, cold and uneasy. 'When?' he asked.

'It's just come in. Fairly fresh, so it could be any time within the last hour or two.'

'Fuck.'

'Do you have anything more constructive to offer, Dr Maitland?'

'Double fuck.'

He paced over to the radiator and grabbed a towel, catching a hazy reflection of himself in a steamed-up mirror. A few pounds of fat and maybe he would be better insulated.

'What do we know?' he asked, pulling the towel around himself.

'A neighbour heard shouting and called the police. Same outcome. Rats and fingertips. The killer got away.'

'And the deceased?'

'A man called Martin Faulkner.'

'Let me guess,' Reuben said. 'He worked in a hospital.'

'Hospital administrator. How did you know?'

'A couple of hours ago we had a breakthrough.'

'And why don't I know about this?'

'You weren't around. Veno summonsed me back to Lucy's house and I thought I'd better try and be nice. I must have fallen asleep for an hour. I was about to speak to you.'

'Well, you're speaking to me now.' Sarah sounded characteristically impatient. 'Let's have it.'

Reuben searched the bathroom for his clothes, but couldn't see them. He was freezing and needed to warm up. Lucy must have removed them while he dozed in the bath. His ex-wife seeing him naked. That was a thought that disturbed him more than it should have done. 'We're still checking it out to make sure we're right. But the first three victims all had an association with a drug trial which went seriously wrong four years ago.'

'At a hospital?'

'In a clinical research facility at the Royal Free. And I'll bet this hospital administrator was part of the trial in some way.'

'Fuck,' Sarah answered.

'Now you're at it.'

'Who else was on the trial? If you guys are right we're going to have to set up protection.'

'Simon and Bernie are hunting down a list of names and addresses. As soon as they have it they're on strict orders to pass it straight over to CID.'

'Good.'

From the crackle on the line Reuben surmised Sarah was on her mobile. It sounded as if she was moving, maybe in a car.

'Where are you?'

'Driving to the scene.'

'You want me there?'

'I don't think there's a lot of point. By the sound of it the scene looks pretty much like all the others. I guess you're better off coordinating, staying in touch, doing what you can for your son. Any news, by the way?'

'None,' Reuben said slowly, an interlinking thought striking him. *All bets are off.* That was what the killer had said as Reuben stood in front of Detective Veno at the Paddington station, after Reuben had arrested Daniel Riefield. Fuck. He banged the knuckles of his free hand into his forehead. This changed things. The three men the killer had wanted had been dispatched, and now he had killed an extra one. This was serious. He was on a rampage, and Reuben had nudged him towards it.

'Reuben,' Sarah said. 'You still there?'

Reuben voiced a quiet yes.

'You've thought about what I said earlier at your home? About everything being straight and above board from now on?'

Reuben grunted.

'Right. Well, let's work together to get this psycho before anyone else dies. I mean it, Reuben. I don't want a single other death on my hands. Otherwise this is going to go even more ballistic than it already is.'

Sarah ended the call. Reuben was glad. He had lost the inclination to speak.

He yanked open the bathroom door. His clothes were neatly folded on the landing. Reuben pulled them on, his body still damp, and took the stairs two at a time. Lucy was in the living room with two of Veno's team. They were examining a box of documents that Lucy usually kept on top of her bedroom wardrobe. Somewhere inside it, Reuben knew for a fact, lay their marriage certificate.

Reuben ignored the coppers. 'Luce, can I use your computer?'

Lucy nodded at him.

Reuben walked towards the study at the rear of the house. Inside, he booted up the computer. The rear of it felt warm, the fan working overtime. He was willing to bet Veno's team had been combing through it all afternoon, checking directories, looking for suspicious image files, picking through it like they had done with the rest of the house's contents. Then he remembered that he had formatted the hard drive. That would have severely pissed Veno off. He smiled to himself, taking out his mobile and logging on to his work email instead.

He checked his messages, squinting at the tiny screen. Forty-four. He swore again and scrolled through the important ones. Crime-scene images, further evidence of links between the victims and the drug trial, a list of names of people on the trial. While he carefully selected messages, opening and scanning their contents, a decision solidified within him. It seemed to stem from his gut, to leak out from the tense ball of apprehension and guilt lodging there, and to spread through him, tightening his muscles, clenching his sinews.

Reuben felt instinctively that his son's life was the most precious thing to him, but he also knew there was no way he could risk another innocent person getting killed. He was going to have to go full-blooded to find the killer, no matter what the consequences for Joshua, and no matter what the consequences for GeneCrime. A change of strategy, an adjustment of emphasis, an evolution of tactics. He wasn't going to rest or sleep until he had hunted the psycho and taken him down. There was no other option, no other moral judgement, no other course of action. It was time to make it very simple. He had tried to balance things, to mislead his colleagues, to do anything he could to keep his son alive. Now he was going to focus solely on the killer, and hope to God that Joshua came through it alive.

Reuben opened the top drawer of the study desk. He felt upwards, on to the solid wood of the desk top. His fingers found something. Several small packets taped to the surface. Still squinting at the evidence pro formas and data sheets of the emails, he detached the packets and stacked them beside his phone. Veno's team had been thorough, but not thorough enough. The drug would see him through the night, when the rest of the city, its good guys and bad guys, were asleep.

It was no longer time for subtlety. It was time for action.

13

The small dab of amphetamine from the desk drawer convinced his body it didn't need food. Although Reuben knew the drug could only release energy and not provide it, he felt wide awake, replenished, no longer tired and sluggish. Three awful days and two sleepless nights had been taking their toll, pulling him into a restless sleep in a cooling bath. As he looked across the table at Lucy, he could see exactly what their effect had been. Her eyes were bloodshot, her movements heavy, her posture hunched forward, like she might collapse in on herself at any moment.

Reuben tried to judge how long it had been since either of them had spoken. It was difficult to gauge time when you were speeding, but still there had been what felt like an enormous gulf of silence. He guessed maybe five minutes or so. Normally in a restaurant this would be a catastrophe. A huge void of time filled only by the clatter and conversation of other diners. But there was nothing awkward about the stillness. They knew that if they spoke it would be about their son, and that would upset them both. The information that Veno unofficially considered them as suspects in the disappearance of their own child was intensely painful. Intuitively, Reuben sensed they had both decided to stay clear of the obvious conversational issues.

Lucy cleared her throat. 'I hope you don't mind,' she said, eventually breaking the quiet, 'but I couldn't face being at home.'

'You don't need to apologize,' Reuben answered.

'Having Veno's team go through everything. The house doesn't feel ours any more.'

'It's not ours. It's yours.'

'You know what I mean.'

Reuben nodded. 'I know.'

'I feel like I'm being watched all the time. Like I'm actually guilty of something.'

The blue Audi with the cracked headlight. Reuben wondered again who had been driving it, what they had to gain.

'Are you ready to order?' he asked.

'The thought of food makes me sick. But you're right. We have to keep our energy levels up,' Lucy said joylessly. She put her menu down. Reuben suspected she had barely read it. 'I'll just have my usual.'

Reuben watched his ex-wife run a hand through her

hair, her head tilted slightly to the side. There was something about her vulnerability that Reuben found suddenly fascinating. It was a quality Lucy had never really shown throughout their marriage, but she had been showing it in spades over the last three days. He knew it was an awful and terrible thing that he should be so beguiled by it, given its root cause, but he couldn't help himself.

'Will you order for me?' she asked. 'I need to pop to the loo.'

'Of course,' he said.

They had come here, to their local Chinese restaurant, sporadically during the early phase of their relationship. And then, when Lucy was pregnant with Joshua, they had come two or three times a week. Lucy had suffered cravings for Chinese food, and Reuben had gladly come along when his caseload permitted. Over the course of several months they had worked their way through the entire menu. And the longer the pregnancy had gone on, the more Joshua had pressed on Lucy's bladder.

'An early trip to the loo. Just like the old times,' he said.

'Not at all like the old times,' Lucy answered. 'Not in any way at all.'

'I just meant, you know, ordering for you, you heading for the toilet . . .'

'I know what you meant. And they were good times, Reuben.' Lucy stood up. 'What I wouldn't do to get them back.'

'I'm sorry.'

'I'm not angry. It was a nice sentiment. It's just different.' Lucy shrugged sadly. 'Awful and terrible and different.'

Lucy set off for the rear of the restaurant and Reuben returned to the quiet contemplation of other people's noises. Clinks of metal on porcelain, scrapes and groans of chairs on the wooden floor, male and female voices duetting in quiet conversation. He felt alert to it all, sucking it in, the way that amphetamines at crime scenes had helped him absorb every detail of an investigation, hour after hour.

His phone buzzed, the vibration travelling through his fingers. He pressed the button and held it to his ear.

'Hello,' he said.

'I've got a taste for this now.'

The same voice. Deadened somehow, like the life was being flattened out of it.

Reuben sat bolt upright at the table, shielding the mouthpiece with his hand. 'A taste for what?' he asked.

'A taste for killing. You presumably know there's been another one?'

Reuben grunted. 'Another innocent person has been savagely murdered, yes.'

'Not innocent. Anything but innocent. He deserved to die.'

'That's what you said on Monday. One more person

who deserves to die. But now you've killed two more.'

'Like I said, Dr Maitland, all bets are off. You broke our agreement. This is down to you.'

'No it's not, it's down to you. And let me ask you nicely. Don't kill anyone else.'

The man laughed. And then it struck Reuben for the first time: I know this man, and he knows me. He is speaking in subdued tones. He thinks I could recognize his voice. He appreciates there is a chance I can track him down purely from the way he talks.

And then Reuben's speeding mind cut to the real issue. 'Where the fuck is my son?'

'Alive. Just.'

Another notion rushed into Reuben's brain. The timing. Lucy had been gone for a matter of seconds before his phone rang. He stared wildly around the restaurant. Couples mainly, the odd family. No one on their phone. Did he know that Lucy had just stood up and walked off? Was he watching?

'Where are you?' he demanded.

'That would be telling.'

'And where the fuck is my son?' Reuben repeated. Out of the corner of his eye, he sensed people beginning to stare. He tried to calm down. 'Give me my son and I won't hurt you,' Reuben said more quietly.

'Hollow threats are so easy to make, aren't they, Dr Maitland? But so hard to act on. The terrible thing is, you already know the stats, don't you? On what happens in child abductions, on how long the child usually stays alive, on what your chances have shrunk to already. Come on, give me a number.'

'Fuck off,' Reuben whispered.

'By now, I'd say one in fifty, maybe even one in a hundred. Once the first few hours pass, the odds narrow considerably. You ever worked any abduction cases?'

Reuben remained silent, refusing to answer.

'Seeing it from the other side now, I bet. And I'll tell you something else you are already well aware of: the parents usually split up afterwards if the child dies.'

'We're hardly together in the first place,' Reuben muttered.

The man on the end of the line was enjoying himself. Reuben let him, all the time listening acutely, gauging what he could, trying to place the voice, desperately hoping to hear the background sounds that would convince him Joshua was still alive. The longer the killer talked, the greater the chance he would compromise himself. Reuben tried to string him along. At least while he was conversing, he couldn't be hurting anyone.

'I don't get your point,' he said.

'I guess it's just that every time you see your partner you're reminded about it. The event. The loss of a child.'

'Well, we don't exactly see each other often now. And let's not talk as if this is a foregone conclusion. It's not.'

'Oh it is, Dr Maitland. It very much is.'

Reuben glanced over towards the back of the room. Lucy had just emerged from the toilets. He pushed the phone hard against his ear, still trying to wring every piece of information out of the sounds it transmitted. All he could hear was the magnified and distorted sounds of respiration, a siren in the background which quickly faded, a scrape of the receiver against skin.

'Do you want to know who's next?' the man asked.

'Surprise me,' Reuben said, peering up at Lucy.

'I will.'

The line was cut.

Reuben stared at the phone display. No caller ID. Just the length of the call – one minute and thirty-seven seconds. It had felt much longer. Every second absorbed and assessed. Reuben knew he had to catch this man. Not in days or weeks but in hours. Or other people would start dying.

'What is it?' Lucy asked, sitting down.

Reuben checked around. The speed wasn't making him paranoid, he told himself, just careful. 'The man holding Joshua.'

'And?'

'And things are about to get a hell of a lot worse.'

14

Reuben washed his face in the toilet sink. He dried himself on a roll of white towel, which hung out of a metal box bolted to the wall. The towel smelled clean and dirty at the same time, scents that had been boiled in, impregnated, unable to escape. He examined himself in the mirror. A night of no sleep and his skin looked grey, a matt of stubble beginning to poke its way through the surface, making it appear dead under the strip lights. He scratched his chin, feeling the roughness against his fingers. He wondered how women put up with kissing a man, having that sharpness pressing into them, scratching and grating. He'd pecked Lucy on the cheek after the Chinese. From his side it had been female softness. From hers, however, he wondered if all she had felt was bristly discomfort.

After he had dropped Lucy back home, he had driven straight to GeneCrime. Hour after hour hunting through evidence files, checking profiles against database entries, looking through lab books detailing the work carried out by the forensics team. He read and reread the emails from Simon, from Paul, from Bernie, from Mina. From each of their fragments of truths, a sequence of events was emerging. Always they were working backwards, trying to construct beginnings from ends, motives from outcomes. Predicting a killer's next move from his last, the knowledge of what had already happened allowing them to calculate what was going to happen next. Fractured timelines, with Reuben standing in the middle, amphetamines ebbing and flowing, time stuttering and rushing.

He rubbed his face again, frowning in the mirror. The speed had gone now, leaving nothing but fatigue and a nervous coldness in the pit of his stomach. Reuben took a small wrap of amphetamine out of his trouser pocket. Soon, the building would fill again with scientists, CID and support staff who would buzz around the place like angry wasps, desperate to catch a man who was on the rampage. He dabbed his index finger into the bitter crystal, rubbing it into his gums. Just small amounts, enough to keep him going, not enough to get him galloping. A clear head, a sharp focus, a mental energy sufficient to absorb the information from a whole team of scientists and CID, who needed strategies and lines of attack drawn up instantaneously.

After he had washed his hands, Reuben left the

GeneCrime toilets and headed back to his office. It was just before eight. As he walked, he waited for the speed to prick through the fatigue. It would take half an hour or so for the full effect to kick in, but small jabs of intent would make themselves known before then. They couldn't come soon enough. Reuben felt slightly sick, the discomfort that came from a lack of sleep and an excess of knowledge.

He reached his office and closed the door, slumping in his seat. The cactus stared back at him, remote and inaccessible. Reuben had a sudden urge to grab it again, to wrap his fingers round its spines and squeeze. But he didn't. His energy levels were too low. Instead, he turned to his computer and emailed his group. *My office when you get in.* He sat back and waited.

Within fifteen minutes, the same group of scientists and CID were seated around him, flushed from their journeys, tired from late finishes, excited about the possibilities. The amphetamine was beginning to bring Reuben round again, opening his eyes, humming through his frontal lobes. He cleared his throat and opened his hard-bound book of notes, scrawls he had made through the night, reasoning and ideas, tentative conclusions. As he inspected them now, they looked wild and unruly, black-ink scribbles written fast and gouged deep.

'So, let's get started,' he said. 'Thanks for all your correspondence last night, and thanks for visiting the scene of the fourth victim, Martin Faulkner. I know things have been moving incredibly quickly, but I think we now have enough insight to start acting. Mina, where are Forensics up to?'

Mina glanced back at him. He saw it in her magnified eyes, a look of concern and sympathy. Silently, he urged her not to mention Joshua. What he needed above everything else now was focus.

'You're sure everything's OK, boss? You know . . .'

'I'm sure. Now, same question.'

Mina flicked her eyes from Reuben to a couple of members of the team and back again. 'Well, we're running slightly behind. We have the first three scenes covered, and the fourth is churning through. But if bodies continue to come in this quickly there's a chance we'll be swamped.'

'OK, so what have we got?'

'Nothing new. On the DNA side, we have multiple samples, some matching the deceased, some not. Nothing is lighting up the NDNAD. We're cross-referencing between the four scenes, looking for matches.'

'And?'

'We think we have one. Picked up from a hair at murder scene one, and a saliva sample at murder scene two. We didn't get anything from the third scene, and we don't know if we can detect it from Martin Faulkner's residence yet.'

'So we've got the killer's DNA, but there's no match on the national database. Are you looking for sibs and parents?'

'We're just starting. But hunting through partial matches takes time. If anyone on the database is related to our killer then we need to do some serious legwork and cross-referencing.'

'How about gross forensics?'

Paul Mackay took his glasses off, folding them on to the pad of paper in front of him. 'No progress on the footprint database. Birmingham don't have any of the pairs of shoes used on record. Fibres and hairs are taking time, and are compounded by the fact that the last victim had short brown hair and a cat of similar persuasion. Differentiating between feline fur and human hair isn't always as easy as I had imagined.'

Reuben felt a pleasing twitch through the muscles of his arms. He appreciated that if it wasn't for the uneasy depression and creeping paranoia which always hunted him down afterwards, speed was one hell of a drug when you needed to get things done. 'Right, so Forensics is struggling to keep up. How about our information gathering?' Reuben raised his eyebrows at Simon Jankowski. 'Any further progress?'

Simon ran a finger along a feint line in his open notebook. 'What we've been able to confirm is that Vasoprellin was a novel vaso-inhibitor manufactured by

BioNovia, the company Carl Everitt worked for.'

'We know this already, don't we?' Reuben said.

'But what we've now got are a lot more of the details, and they make interesting reading. Ten healthy young men and women were on the drug trial. Three received a placebo, the other seven the drug treatment. Two died. Five survived, but were left with permanent damage and long-term health issues.'

'So it's classic revenge,' Bernie said. 'One of the victims hunts down the people who set the trial up. The medic, the scientist, the drug exec, and now the hospital administrator. So our job is easy. We simply protect anyone else associated with the trial. Most of them will probably come forward for help anyway. In the meantime, we churn through the forensics, chase him through family members or any other evidence that comes to light.'

Reuben stroked the hair at the base of his neck, a warm sensation travelling up from the top of his spine. The trouble with amphetamine was that it was so easy to talk without thinking. Reuben closed his eyes, thinking it through. The killer had taken a hostage. The trial had happened four years ago. Victims were being massacred, not executed. Rats were transported to each scene. Initially, the killer had only wanted three men, now he had killed four. There had to be more to it.

'Why didn't last night's victim put up a struggle?' Reuben asked.

'As you know, we've been running bloods and urines from the victims,' Mina answered. 'But toxicology takes time if you don't know what you're looking for.'

'And what do you think we might be looking for?'

'We still think some kind of sedative. That's our best guess.'

'What about the classics? Chloroform or ether?' Reuben nodded at a lab window. 'Stuff we have litres of on our own benches and shelves?'

'We're talking to the Tox people. Apparently, inhaled hydrocarbons are tricky to detect in blood, and not secreted in great quantities in the urine.'

'Well, keep trying. I agree with you – there has to be something. How long till Toxicology come up with an answer?'

'They reckon another twenty-four to forty-eight hours.'

'The other angle here,' Bernie interjected, 'is that CID found an unpacked suitcase in Faulkner's flat and were able to ascertain he had been out of the country for over a week at a conference. He mustn't have heard that three previous work colleagues had been slaughtered.'

'So his defences wouldn't have been up. OK, what about the drug trial people who are still alive? Who are they?'

Helen Alders reeled off a list of names. 'Syed Sanghera, Michael Adebyo, Daniel Riefield, Amerdeep Hughes,

Dion Morgan, Cathy Reynolds and Ann Hillyard. We're chasing them up, getting background, finding addresses.'

Reuben cut to an image of Riefield. Unhinged, living alone, the tips of his fingers missing. 'How many of the survivors have damaged fingers?' he asked.

'We don't know. CID are having a major effort this morning to contact them all. We'll find out then.'

'I think we're beginning to see where this all fits. A vaso-inhibitor which goes wrong, shutting off blood supply.' Reuben thought back to countless lectures on biology and anatomy, information he had amassed during his training and beyond. 'The peripheral vasculature are acutely sensitive to blood flow. Cold fingers and toes in winter. I'll bet you anything our man doesn't exactly need nail scissors. And I also bet he won't be leaving us any fingerprints.' The amphetamine sent a rapid flash of images through Reuben's brain: the killer, his mutilated hands, the basis of his motivations. 'And the rats. Lab rats. A classic message to the dying men he attacks. Lab rats in a cage, watching their fingers being consumed. This man has thought hard about this. He still has some mental faculty. But no women. There must have been nurses on this trial, or female medics. So far he only attacks the males. What does that mean? What does that say about the killer?'

No one answered. Reuben continued to flick through

scenarios and ideas, silent and on fire, his concentration utter and absolute.

'Can we consider them all suspects at this point?' Bernie asked after a few moments of silence. 'Get swabs, match them to the DNA we have on record?'

'Apart from Amanda Skeen, Mica Bell and Martin Randle, who died,' Simon answered.

Reuben shook himself round. 'And we can rule out the placebos. What about their families? Anything shake out from the close relations of the two deceased? Fathers or brothers with a history of violence, wanting payback?'

'Still working on it, boss,' Helen answered.

'But yes, Bernie,' Reuben continued, 'I think you're right. The killer is one of the trialists, or someone close to them. Who else would have anything to gain?' His racing brain made a small leap which he couldn't share with his team. The killer knew Reuben's team would come knocking. But with forensic immunity he was safe. One of a group of people all with the same motive. Very little chance of being singled out and prosecuted. In a crowd he was protected.

But on his own, it was a matter of time until he was tracked down and his life taken to pieces.

15

The long slender Command Room table was smothered with a white layer of papers and print-outs. Among the sheets, colour photographs of the four victims lay like islands of horror and atrocity. Full-length shots taken in the morgue, close-ups from each scene, pale anaemic flesh and vivid red damage. CID had raced through PNC checks, employment details, hospital records and personnel files from the Royal Free. The skeletal information that had only been pieced together the previous night was already being fleshed out into something tangible and solid.

Reuben had spent the hour and a half since the meeting meticulously going through all the DNA evidence with Mina and Bernie. Meanwhile, a team of seven CID officers and a handful of support staff had been gathering every scrap of information they could. Reuben peered over to the far side of the room where Sarah Hirst was sitting.

He had heard that CID were already making progress. Generally, Reuben appreciated, forensic information was much slower and harder to come by than the data that lifting a phone or tapping a keyboard could provide. He rubbed his face, forced himself to focus again. His brain had been jumping in every direction, trying to take everything in, attempting to assimilate all the facts it could. Occasionally, images of his son forced their way in, crashing him down again. He needed to get things moving, to find some comfort and consistency in the progress of the investigation.

Reuben stood up to signify a new meeting was about to begin. 'Right, everyone.' It took a few seconds, but the fifteen or so members of the room quietened down. He caught Sarah's eye, and she looked away. Reuben sensed she was still pissed off with him, unimpressed that he'd made Veno go and get a search warrant. 'It sounds like CID have been busy. Would you care to update everyone on progress?'

Reuben sat down again as Detective Leigh Harding stood up. 'We've got two operations on the go, which began late last night and resumed early this morning. The first and most urgent is to track all remaining hospital and scientific staff associated with the Vasoprellin trial. We had a strategy meeting with DCI Hirst, and decided, well . . .' Detective Harding looked over towards Sarah.

'I decided,' Sarah said, 'that we needed to prioritize potential victims ahead of searching for the murderer.'

Reuben stared at her. 'When was this agreed?' he asked.

'At the Martin Faulkner scene.'

'And why wasn't I informed?'

'Like you said to me last night, you weren't around.'

Reuben recalled using the line the previous night, while dripping water on to the bathroom floor. She had a God-given knack of being able to throw things back in your face.

'Anyway, Reuben, I'm telling you now. Look, we only have so much manpower. The Met have offered us twenty-five uniform, and they'll do the job of guarding other staff members on the clinical trial – nurses, administrators, medics, other supporting research scientists – as we identify them. And of course you and your team are still to pursue the forensics. But prevention is the goal here.'

Every cell in Reuben's body disagreed. For the moment, he could only think of his son. Protecting possible targets who had worked at a hospital four years ago wouldn't help Joshua. 'Only in the short term,' he said. 'And what makes you sure the killer won't switch tack? Target people outside the trial? Keep killing for the sake of it?'

'Impossible to know. But for now, as soon as this meeting finishes, we draw up a list of people for CID and the Met to safeguard.'

Sarah stared back at him, her blonde hair dragged tight across her scalp, her blouse stiff and ironed. Reuben knew that everything about her was held in its place, controlled and ordered. She was fierce, pulling rank, overruling him. He let it go. He was in no position to make demands or to flex his authority.

'What else have you got, Leigh?' he said quietly.

'We spoke to the Clinical Trials unit. A lot of staff changes in the meantime, particularly after what happened, with procedures being reviewed and personnel moved on. But they've got follow-up information on most of the members of the trial.'

'Let's deal with the females first. What have you learned?'

'Two of the five females were randomly assigned to the placebo treatment. One of the three who received the drug died at the time, a few hours after the trial began. Two survived, but one of them subsequently committed suicide.'

'Jesus,' Reuben muttered. 'And do we know whether any close relations to the three who suffered have any previous form?'

'Not yet.'

Reuben looked up. Sarah was edging out of the room. Doubtless more important things to do, he frowned. Reuben found that although he frequently disagreed with Sarah, and had gone through phases of wondering whether he could really trust her, the one thing he couldn't do was dislike her. She kept her motives close to her freshly ironed chest, but they were generally good. He would talk to her after the strategy meeting, smooth things out, get things back to how they had been just three days ago.

'Right,' he said. 'Let's cut to it. The men on the trial.'

Leigh Harding shuffled on his feet. Reuben nodded at him to sit down. 'Thanks, boss. So, one male was a placebo, the other four had the drug. Those four are' – Harding squinted at his own writing – 'Syed Sanghera, Daniel Riefield, Michael Adebyo and Martin Randle.'

'We've already had a good look at Mr Riefield.' Reuben turned to Simon Jankowski, three seats away, sitting upright in his chair, a bad shirt on. 'Simon, can you get as much additional info on Riefield as possible. PNC, DVLA, DSS, any acronym with a sodding database.'

Simon smiled. 'Yes, boss.'

'There's still something that doesn't ring true about Riefield.'

'Such as?'

'I can't put my finger—' Reuben stopped. In the light of what the victims had been through, it seemed right to change the wording. 'Let's just keep an eye, eh?'

Simon scribbled on one of the many sheets of paper turning the table's dark brown surface white.

Reuben returned his focus to Detective Harding. 'So, any of those four jump out at you, Leigh?'

The detective ran a hand through his receding hair. 'Well, there's Michael Adebyo, originally from Somalia, unemployed and needed the money. Fairly bad injuries, which still persist according to the Royal Free, who continue to see him on a monthly basis for treatment. But Martin Randle was the only male to die directly. He's definitely worth a look.'

'Why?' Mina asked. 'He's dead.'

'He is. But, like Adebyo, he wasn't a student. He'd been discharged from the military a few months earlier.'

'What for?'

'We've been able to do a quick bit of digging, and have come up with violent misconduct. That's all we know. And there's more. His father is ex-military as well. At the inquest eighteen months ago, Francis Randle called for the trial organizers to be punished.'

'As in what?' Bernie asked. 'Smacked on the wrists and told not to do it again?'

'We have a quote from one of the red-tops.' Leigh shuffled some sheets until he found what he was looking for. '"It's disgusting. They should have to go through what my son had to go through. Every single one of them."'

Reuben let the words sink in. Sinister and predictive, considering what had happened. Yet what would he say or feel if his own son had his life taken away? He hoped to fuck he wasn't about to find out. But that was the point, he realized. Victims on both sides, someone in the middle redressing the balance.

'So, do we have a consensus?' Reuben ran his eyes around the scientists and CID crammed along both sides of the table. 'Anyone?'

Mina was the first to react. 'Considering what information we have, and what Sarah said, I guess we divide up. CID chase down anyone associated with running the trial. Forensics steps up the batch testing from all four scenes. Meanwhile we need to investigate all the trialists and their families systematically.'

'Beginning with the four men,' Reuben added.

'Syed Sanghera, Daniel Riefield, Michael Adebyo and Francis Randle,' Leigh repeated.

'Why them specifically?' Mina asked.

'Because to my mind they're the most likely candidates to commit these atrocities.'

'Anyway,' Mina continued, 'the ultimate aim is to match the DNA which was present at two of the scenes to one of them.'

'Good,' Reuben said. 'But bear in mind we don't have enough evidence to order DNA tests on those four. For the moment we need to track them and get clearance for round-the-clock surveillance. And then, hope we get lucky. Because somewhere out there is another brutalized corpse waiting to happen.'

16

Reuben rapped his knuckles on Sarah's door. It was a door of authority, real wood, unlike the pine-effect covering on all the others. In case anyone was in any remaining doubt, a blue nameplate read 'DCI Sarah Hirst, GeneCrime Commander'.

Sarah's voice, dulled by the thickness of the oak, shouted, 'Yes.'

Reuben opened the door, then paused. Seated next to Sarah was Commander William Thorner, thick-set, advanced male pattern baldness, a prominent brow which seemed to shine. He smiled briefly. 'Hello, Reuben.'

'Hello, Commander. Good to see you.' Reuben switched to Sarah. 'I'm sorry, Sarah, I didn't realize you were busy. I'll pop back later.'

Sarah looked like she was about to answer, but Commander Thorner beat her to it. 'You may as well come in,' he said. 'Take a seat.'

Reuben found a chair, surrounded by browning plants. Thorner shuffled round Sarah's desk so they were both facing him.

Reuben had a sudden feeling of uncomfortable premonition. 'What is it?' he asked.

'Look, William's here because I didn't want to tell you myself.' Sarah stared into her desk. 'There's no easy way to say this.'

Reuben's first instinct was Joshua. GeneCrime had been overseeing the forensics on Joshua's abduction. Simon had finished processing the cigarette butts and had generated a match, or a link to something that Reuben hadn't. 'What have you found?' he asked. 'Do you have a match to Joshua?'

'As you are aware, DNA extractions from the cigarette butts didn't work well first time, and only reached partial stringency on the second and third attempts. We've drawn a blank. I guess the butts were old or completely sodden.'

'So what is it?' Reuben looked from the Commander to Sarah and back again, his heart still hammering away, amphetamines refusing to let the false alarm die down. 'There was something you were going to say.'

Sarah straightened in her seat. Commander Thorner shifted his position, turning his body to face Reuben full on.

'We're taking you off the case, Reuben,' Sarah said. 'Your position has become untenable.'

Sarah met his eye briefly, then looked across at Thorner for support.

'Sarah feels that your behaviour is becoming somewhat erratic, Reuben. And while we all understand the reasons behind it, with bodies stacking up, you are not the right person to be leading a manhunt.'

Reuben stared back. 'Define erratic,' he said. 'Half the people in this building are erratic.'

Thorner checked a piece of paper in front of him. 'Failure to attend all the scenes. Refusing CID entry to your house. A series of lab equipment in the garage. Wiped computer files. Unusual hours. Speculation in the press about your personal life. I could go on.'

'But all of this is to do with my missing son. Can't you see that? I mean, what kind of hours would you keep if your child had been taken?'

'Leave my children out of this,' Thorner answered. 'And that's the very point. I wouldn't be here. I would be with my wife, my family, not at work in charge of a manhunt.'

'I need to stay on the case,' Reuben said, his voice rising a notch. He'd needed to be from the second the killer first called him. Outside the investigation, he had no chance of finding his son. He tried to keep his words quiet. 'Please, I have to stay on it.'

'The answer is no, Reuben. Categorically no.'

'You are to have no further contact with the case,'

Sarah added. Again, she avoided his eye. 'I am really sorry, and this has been a difficult decision, but that's what the Commander and I feel.'

'Well, who's going to take it over? Who are you going to put in charge?'

'Sarah will run the investigation from now on,' Thorner said. 'Mina Ali will oversee Forensics, and Leigh Harding will collate CID.'

Reuben clenched his teeth hard. He could taste blood. Joshua was disappearing before his eyes. There had to be another way. 'OK, use me as a consultant. Take me off overall command, but continue to throw the data out to me to look at.'

Commander Thorner stood up, his chair sliding back across the carpet. His black uniform was tight around his torso. 'End of discussion, Reuben. You are to have no further input. I hope to God you find your son, and anything we can possibly do will be done. But grab your personal possessions from your office. You will be escorted from the building.'

Reuben got to his feet, slowly, disbelieving. This is so fucked up, a voice inside him said. So very fucked up. He turned and walked out of the office, the heavy door swinging slowly shut after him. He pictured Sarah picking up her phone. Dialling one of the CID officers that Reuben was in charge of, instructing him to escort Dr Maitland off the premises. He picked up speed. He needed to get to his office, grab as much of the case-load as he could.

Reuben ran down the extended corridor that led there. As he did, the amphetamine came to life again, increased blood flow carrying it to his muscles and pushing them on. He reached his office and started printing emails, output files, crime sheets, evidence inventories. He took his laptop out of its case, locked it in a drawer, and crammed the warm pieces of paper from his printer into the space the laptop had occupied.

There was a knock at the door. Reuben grabbed the last pieces of information and zipped his case shut. He stared at the cactus on his desk for a couple of seconds, wondering whether to take it with him. It was sharp and intense, defiantly standing proud. He told himself he was going to need to be every bit as resilient from now on.

The door swung open. A young officer called Callum stepped silently into the room.

'It's OK, Callum,' Reuben said. 'I'll go quietly.'

Reuben took a final glance around his office and through the windows that gave on to the labs. And then he turned and walked out, leaving GeneCrime and the hunt for his son behind.

THREE

THREE

1

'Statistically, your son is dead. You know it, I know it.'
Detective Veno arched his back, his gut pushing forward.
'No point beating round the bush.'

Reuben swayed on his feet, battling an urge to punch
Veno square in the mouth.

'You look at any child abduction over the last twenty
years, do the maths. Trafficking or murder. The age of
your son, it's not sexual. Not unless we're dealing with
someone who makes general paedos look tame and
friendly. No, you want my guess, he's not in the capital
any more. He's been smuggled out, maybe even abroad.'

Again, Reuben fought his natural inclination to smash
the man in front of him in the mouth. Veno was either
goading him or was insensitive to the point of abusive-
ness. He wondered how Veno got assigned to missing
child investigations. Did he act like this with other
parents? Reuben suspected he wasn't quite as blunt.

'So this is just to warn you,' he continued. 'The search is going to switch. We're throwing it out to the provincial agencies, the European ones as well, see what they come up with. Of course we'll still maintain a presence here, keep the publicity grinding through, but behind the scenes we're going to be spending a lot of time talking to our colleagues around the UK and overseas.'

Reuben checked the kitchen clock over the detective's shoulder. Just after eleven a.m., the minute and hour hands pointing out a wide V. The best part of a long day stretching ahead with no job, and nothing to do but think. The last thing he needed was Veno coming round and pointing out the brutal facts of the matter, misguided though they were. Joshua wasn't overseas. He was in London, probably within a radius of three miles or so, where he had been for the last seventy-two hours. And this wasn't about trafficking. This was about blackmail and coercion.

'See, you snatch a child, you suddenly feel the need to get away. You watch it on the news. Cops combing the area the child was taken from. Even if you didn't intend taking the kid somewhere, you feel compelled to. Out of sight, away from the centre of all the attention.'

Veno stared into Reuben's face, awaiting a response. Reuben grunted at him and turned away. 'Do what you've got to do,' he said. 'But just because you can't find him in London doesn't mean he's somewhere else.'

'What makes you say that?' Veno asked sharply.

'Nothing. But if I was running a manhunt, I'd concentrate more on the area someone originates from than where they might end up going.'

'But you're not running a manhunt any more, are you, Dr Maitland?'

Reuben turned back to face him. Veno's cheeks were flushed. He'd shaved at some point since he'd last seen him, the ruddiness of his stubble retreating back under the skin, ready to emerge again in a few more hours. 'News travels quick,' he said.

'When it's good news. Sacked from GeneCrime.' Veno rocked on the balls of his feet, arms behind his back. 'What was it in total? Three whole days?'

Reuben let him enjoy himself. 'Something like that.'

'I said it was a mistake for the Met to take you back, and it looks like I was right.'

'Well done.'

'Three days and then they fire you. Meanwhile a killer is still on the loose.'

'I'm not fired, Veno.' Reuben fought for calm. 'Just suspended.'

'Same thing.'

'Whatever you say.'

'So really, Dr Maitland, whether you're fired or suspended or whatever the fuck you are, you don't run manhunts any more, and you therefore don't have any right suggesting how I should run mine. Is that clear?'

Reuben stared back at him, impassive and blank. For the third time in quick succession he battled the instinct for violence. The amphetamine wasn't helping. It was lingering in his system, hardening his muscles, tensing his sinews. Attacking the officer hunting your missing child wouldn't look great, he appreciated. If the press were already on the attack, this would give them enough ammunition for a concerted war. For the moment, and through teeth that were grinding tight together, he was determined to be nice.

'So there are no fresh leads?'

'Nothing useful.'

'What about this witness? The one you described as an alcoholic.'

Veno took a pace back, leaning himself against a counter. 'We've interviewed her from drunk to sober and back again. She was close to the newsagent, just coming out of an off-licence. Said she saw a man drop his fag, then push a buggy away. We didn't have to wait till she saw your performance on the news because she came forward at the scene. Probably a good job really. Maybe she wouldn't have come.'

'What else did she see?'

'Not a fat lot. Gave us a vague description, nothing we could use. She was too pissed for the police artist to sketch anything sensible.'

'And that's it? All your hunting, all your media splash, all your detective work. You have the testimony of a single unreliable witness?'

Veno straightened again, pushing forward, invading Reuben's space. 'And what the hell do you have from your case? A morgue full of fingerless corpses, some cages full of rats, a grade A psycho on the loose. When you do something useful, Maitland, rather than tinker with forensics, then you come and criticize my work. Until then, keep the hell out.'

Veno pushed past him, striding out of the kitchen and down the hall. Reuben stayed where he was. The events of the morning were catching up with him. A list of possible suspects at GeneCrime, the investigation starting to gather momentum. And then his sudden dismissal, escorted out of the building, a civilian again, just a thirty-eight-year-old man with a missing child being shouted at in his wife's kitchen by a fractious police officer.

The amphetamine was beginning to ebb in fits and starts. Reuben could feel himself crashing. Nights of broken sleep, racing through the capital in anonymous cars, suspicions and paranoia rattling around inside his brain. He needed to get some rest, regroup, lick his wounds. But even as the thought came to him he realized he couldn't do it. While Joshua was missing, sitting still was out of the question.

Reuben patted his pockets and located his mobile. He

scrolled through its numbers until he found the name Moray, then pressed the dial button with his thumb and paced out of the kitchen. He picked up his laptop case in the hall, and as he waited for the call to be answered he opened the front door and strode out into the street.

2

Long steep escalators dragged Reuben ever deeper beneath the surface of the city. As he was lowered through the ground, he finally began to sense the degree to which he was trapped. He was the only person involved in the hunt who knew that the murder of four members of a clinical trial was inextricably linked to the kidnap of his son. Reuben tried to look at this positively, knowing that he would be able to make deductions the police couldn't, that he could act more quickly and directly than they could, that his son's life didn't hang on health and safety appraisals or the execution of warrants, or on hierarchical and procedural decision-making. But none of this cheered him. From now on, he was cut off, an outcast, and everything he did would hang or fall on his own abilities.

Reuben also knew there was little to gain from informing CID of the link. That moment had long since passed.

GeneCrime had struggled to get useable DNA profiles from the cigarette butts, and had even less information on Joshua's kidnapper than he did. At least Reuben had spoken to him, knew what he sounded like, how cold and logical he was. No, the events of the morning had served only to reinforce Reuben's conviction that he would have to do this from the outside now, surviving on his wits, without the resources of the police to call upon should it all go wrong.

Reuben reached his platform on the Central Line. He watched a rat poke through a hole in the wall and scuttle between the tracks. A woman stared at Reuben for a couple of seconds and looked away. He flashed back to the news interviews. He was public property now. The woman risked another glance. Reuben tried not to notice. A train appeared, bursting from the tunnel and out into the light. He guessed the rat would carry on beneath its wheels obliviously, hunting for scraps, gnawing at the detritus of human life, just getting on with it.

Reuben climbed on to the train and found a seat. As the Tube stuttered between stations, he opened his laptop case and began to peruse its contents. He had grabbed everything he could from his office on the way out. Items of information he knew already, and fresh reports that had come through while Sarah and Commander Thorner were busy suspending him. The carriage was half empty and he had enough room to sift through the papers in relative comfort. Give it half an hour, peak lunchtime, and there would barely be room to stand. He took out preliminary reports on the four main suspects GeneCrime had drawn up, reading each in turn, absorbing everything he could. CID had performed initial background checks, unsubstantiated profiles drawn from public and private databases. Occupations, employment history, credit ratings, education, DVLA data, hospital records, passport details. Facts and figures housed on disparate systems that together told the rough truth about each of the men.

Reuben scanned the information, barely looking up as the train alternately slowed and speeded up. He wrote the four names on the back of his left hand. Syed Sanghera. Daniel Riefield. Michael Adebyo. Francis Randle. The letters were uneven, deformed by the motion of the train. Blue biro marks, deeply etched, looking almost like a tattoo. One of them the killer. One of them holding his son. His name implanted into Reuben's epidermis. Reuben vowed to hold the names there, where he could see them, until he had Joshua back.

Out of the corner of his eye, he could see he was being watched. A different woman to the one on the platform. Maybe she recognized him, or maybe she was just wondering why he had carved four names into the back of his hand. Either way, Reuben ignored her, returning to the loose sheets of paper surrounding him, following names and dates and addresses across separate lines of corroboration. He jotted rough notes on the back of a DVLA print-out of Syed Sanghera's address, and squinted through the window every time the train slowed. Every few metres a white and red sign flashed by, slowing each time. When Reuben finally read 'Holborn' he scraped up his papers and left the carriage.

The lift back to the surface failed to raise his spirits. The data contained in each of the files was overwhelming, even at a quick glance. He had tried to extract the important stuff. Places, names, addresses, contact numbers, previous histories. Four men who needed whittling down to one. There had been photographs of all of them. Pictures from the press. Grinning photos of four young men separately caught up in a trial that went wrong. Grainy black and whites, the sort that families provided in the aftermath of a catastrophe. *This is how our son looked just months before the drug trial.* Happy, confident, smiling. Daniel Riefield's image stayed with Reuben as he left the lift and headed for the barriers. Young, fresh-faced, a smile that said 'everything is possible'.

Reuben exited Holborn station and took a second to orientate himself. The warm air of the Underground leaked from his clothing as he hesitated, a biting wind swooping down between high-rises and tearing at his jacket and jeans. It was cold, and getting colder. Shoppers all around him walked quickly, heads down, hands thrust into their pockets. He had come out at an intersection, an area he wasn't familiar with. Reuben scanned for street names, then spotted the one he was after. Up ahead he spotted the sign of the pub, swinging in the breeze, the thinness of its wood seeming to shiver along with him.

Inside, Moray Carnock was nursing a pint of beer, frowning into the screen of his phone. The mobile looked tiny in his large hands. His fleshy fingers poked heavily at the keypad, a look of grim determination on his face.

'Anything up?' Reuben asked.

'Just a client who texts me every bloody minute.'

'What's the job?'

'Corporate security. Surveillance work on a partner in an accountancy firm.'

'What have they done?'

'Developed an interesting overlap between personal and professional finance.'

Reuben glanced around the pub. Dark wood, a rough floor, dim lighting. Five or six drinkers at separate tables, looking like they'd been there for several hours already. If this is what your day starts like, Reuben wondered, where the hell does it end up? He battled the urge for a large vodka, licking his lips involuntarily. Every second was important, and he needed to stay sharp.

Moray peered up from his phone. 'You thirsty?'

Reuben scraped a chair out and sat down. 'Not really,' he lied.

'So, what's the plan?'

'We stand up and leave.'

'But we're in a pub.'

'There are more important things.'

Moray checked his watch and looked longingly towards the bar. 'They're about to start serving food.'

'And my son might be starving to death.'

'An army marches on its stomach.'

'For once in your life, Moray, I'm asking you to put that large gut of yours second. There's a child's life at stake.'

Moray straightened in his seat, his head tilted back. 'I'm sorry, big man. I just meant—'

'I know what you meant.' Reuben stood up. His mobile vibrated. A message from Judith. 'Finish your pint, my fat friend. It's time to go to war.'

3

Moray brought his old powerful Saab to an abrupt halt. 'That's the one,' he said, nodding his head in the direction of a sixties block of flats.

Reuben peered at it. Four storeys, a low-rise square of weathered brick, probably one residence per floor.

Moray pulled a piece of paper off the dash. 'Syed Sanghera. 11C Raddlebarn Gardens.'

Reuben guessed it was on the second floor. Flat 11A would be the ground level, 11B the first, 11C the second. He was quiet. Judith's text had merely said *blue audi registered keeper francis randle sorry for delay*. A second text after he'd dragged Moray out of the pub had given the address Randle had registered with the DVLA. It matched the address GeneCrime had. For a short period of time, Francis Randle had become priority number one. But Moray and Reuben had simply found a derelict block of flats. They had nosed about, kicked a few doors open, but there had been no sign of life. Nothing but mass abandonment of a building in Battersea. Reuben was still digesting the information. That the man following him in a blue Audi with a broken headlight was Francis Randle, father of one of the trialists who died. His address was false. GeneCrime didn't know any more than he did. Was it possible that Randle had Joshua?

'Let's hope we have more luck this time,' Moray said. 'Registering your vehicle to a fucked tower block is actually quite smart.'

Reuben frowned, continuing to think.

'What do you want to do?' Moray asked.

'Kill the engine. Let's just keep an eye out for a bit.'

Moray turned the key. The Saab made a series of clicking noises as its engine cooled. Reuben wound his window down. A cold blast of air streamed in and Moray fastened his overcoat tight. Reuben scanned the building, the small area of grass beside it, the people walking past the cul-de-sac, the cars parked around them, every sign of life his eyes could perceive. Moray drummed his fingers on the wheel. From time to time he shuffled through the pieces of paper Reuben had given him, muttering to himself and making notes.

After several silent minutes, Reuben said, 'There.'

He pointed below the level of the windscreen, out of sight of passers-by. Moray followed with his eyes. A white

Ford Focus, twenty metres away. One man in the driver's seat.

'The white ones are cheaper, you know,' Moray said. 'And it's an LX. No optional extras.'

'Keeps plod from feeling superior,' Reuben answered.

'Mind you, some of the cars you used to drive weren't bad.'

'The privilege of rank and the need to get to crime scenes quickly.'

'Not any more, though.'

'Thanks for the reminder.' Reuben ran his eyes back and forth between the Focus and the flat. 'Who do you reckon?'

'Can't see him well, but general plod. Average plain-clothes CID. Nothing too senior.'

Reuben flashed through the scenarios. 'You think there's an officer in the flat? Maybe carrying out a search?'

'Dunno. If you came to search you'd come mob-handed, wouldn't you?'

'And I guess you wouldn't worry about keeping a low profile.'

'I guess not,' Moray answered.

'But if GeneCrime have thrown this out to general CID, anything's possible.' The officer in the car was alert, scanning the area just like Reuben. 'The problem is, I don't think they have enough on Sanghera to order a search.'

'So what do you want to do?'

'What I want to do, Moray, is to march in, smash the front door down and see if my son is in there. But if CID are staking the place out, that's not exactly an option.' Reuben flicked his top teeth with the nails of his left hand while he thought. 'I don't want to do this,' he said, taking out his mobile, 'but I don't see another option.'

'What?'

Reuben entered a number into the keypad. 'This.' He waited for the call to be answered, then said, 'Sarah? It's Reuben.'

Sarah treated Reuben to her coldest tone of voice. 'Hello, Reuben,' she answered.

'Look, can you tell me something?'

'Probably not. But go on anyway.'

'Are you staking out the home addresses of the four suspects?'

'And which suspects are these?'

Reuben glanced down at the back of his left hand and quickly looked away. He didn't need to read the names. They were embedded in his consciousness, flashing letters that burned into every thought he had. 'Syed Sanghera, Daniel Riefield, Michael Adebyo and Francis Randle.'

'They're not all official suspects yet. Besides, we don't have an address for Randle.'

'I know.'

'Look, Reuben—'

'Sarah, I need to know whether you have warrants. Do you have enough evidence to enter their houses, or are you just keeping tabs?'

'I don't know why this concerns you any more, Reuben.'

A voice in Reuben's head screamed, *Because my fucking son could be in one of the addresses!* 'It just does.'

Sarah's voice cooled another notch. 'You're not on this case any more, Reuben. I thought I made that abundantly clear.'

'So—'

'So, no, we don't have anything that would allow us to carry out searches. We have ten people on a drug trial, most of whom are still alive. We have their family and friends, some of them doubtless harbouring grudges. We have other trials that the murdered men were associated with, as well as whole teams of researchers who worked alongside them. And other than that, no tangible evidence to put any of this coachload of people within a mile of any of the murder scenes.'

'And if I came up with some evidence?'

'Don't.' Sarah breathed out, an extended exhalation in Reuben's ear. 'I mean that. Thorner made it quite clear. Stay off the case, go home to your ex-wife, help Detective Veno, do everything you can to find your son. Please stop thinking you can do anything to help us. We're big boys and girls. We'll manage without you.'

315

Reuben smiled briefly to himself. Being told off by Sarah was becoming a daily event. 'The trouble is, Sarah, I can't leave the case alone. And it would be very difficult for you to stop me simply sitting in a car and observing things if I wanted to do that.'

'Is that what you're doing?'

'I'm just saying, what if I come up with something that gave you sufficient evidence for a search?'

'Like what?'

'Like anything. Like the scant evidence Veno had that allowed him to tear Lucy's house apart.'

'Just don't, Reuben.'

'But if I do?'

There was a long pause. An Asian male emerged from the flats and walked briskly through Raddlebarn Gardens towards the main road. The driver of the Ford Focus started his engine and pulled off slowly after him.

'If you do . . .'

Moray fired the ignition of the Saab.

'What?' Reuben asked.

'Let me know what you find.'

4

Francis Randle sat hunched in his car, staring at passers-by. Normal people going about their business, dressed in blues, greys, browns and blacks, material pulled tight against the cold wind. Civvies making lives for themselves while he rotted in combat clothes that had seen better days.

He took the pistol out of the glove box, ran the barrel under his nose. The familiar scent of violence, of promise, of the settling of scores. An oily, metallic, scorched smell. Simultaneously clean and not clean. An instrument for making people do things they wouldn't do under any other circumstance. Making them entirely willing to lie down and subject themselves to whatever you wanted of them.

He went through the drill. Flicking the safety on and off, loading and reloading the cartridge, sliding the rounds out and slotting them back in again. A mechanical process that allowed him to lose himself for a few minutes.

A well-dressed man passed the car, a couple of metres away. Randle took aim, his gun below the level of the window, tracking the man's progress. He looked like a lawyer or a City worker, something professional and well paid. Randle lifted the nose of the pistol, calculating the angle for a headshot. The man disappeared behind a parked van, then emerged again. Randle had another sight of him along the snub nose of the gun, before letting him go. 'Next time,' he said under his breath.

Randle resumed his scan of the streets. He checked his side mirrors and the rear-view. From time to time he caught his reflection. The buzz-cut hair, the cleft of his chin, the flattened-off ear.

Another male, mid-twenties, caught his eye. Broad, upright, muscular. A sense of pride about him. Randle was transfixed. 'Martin,' he whispered to himself. 'My son.' The man entered a silver phone box, made a call. Randle craned to see him. He slid the gun back in the glove box, slammed it shut, and continued to watch, fascinated, absorbed. Then the man opened the door and came out. Glanced around. Randle ducked down. He didn't want to be seen. The man turned back the way he had come, engulfed in the mass of people hurrying in all directions, trying to keep warm.

Randle stroked the top of his right ear, felt the

bluntness, flashed to the moment a piece of shrapnel could have ended his life. Instead, it took a small piece of him he didn't need anyway. Instants of life that could have changed everything. His son dying in a hospital in London, while he walked away from a roadside bomb in Ulster. Events years apart but feeling as entwined now as if they'd happened simultaneously.

Randle reached into his khaki jacket and pulled out a piece of folded paper. On it, an address, letters scrawled in blue ink. He checked his watch, glanced at the numbers on the dashboard. It was time, more or less. He opened the *A to Z* that was on his lap. Matched the road name to a page, matched a grid reference to the road. He ran his fingers across the streets, calculating the route, savouring the feel of the coarse yellowing paper his *A to Z* was printed on. He flicked to another page, following a wide road as it meandered between roundabouts and junctions. Then he placed the street atlas back on his lap and started the engine.

As he drove, Randle combed the streets for men who looked like his son. This was his constant motivation, he appreciated, the thing that kept him doing what needed to be done. Four years since his death, and not a day went by without him remembering Martin. And not a man went by of a similar age without Randle wondering what Martin would look like now, what he would be doing, how he would be getting on in the wide world.

Francis Randle drove with utter concentration, swift and efficient, anticipating problems before they happened. His mind switched to Reuben Maitland, the forensic scientist whose name he had read in the newspaper. Whose position as the lead officer in the case had kicked everything off. Maitland, whose son had been ill, but who had made a full recovery, treated with drugs that were tested on animals and then on humans. Martin Randle, twenty-one years old and never getting any older, rotting in the ground, treated with a drug that had also been tested on animals. Having it injected into him in a clinical trial to test it was safe.

Randle thumped the steering wheel hard. The horn sounded, a few people looked round. Randle's eyes flicked to the glove box and back again. This thing had started and it wasn't going to stop until the death of his son didn't make him want to scream out loud, to drive round the capital from address to address in his dark blue Audi, doing what was right, doing what needed to be done.

5

Syed Sanghera walked quickly, his breath forming small clouds in the freezing air. He was wearing a thick coat and a pair of black woollen gloves. It was impossible for Reuben to tell whether his fingers were intact.

'How close do you want to be?' Moray asked.

'As close as you can,' Reuben answered.

Moray gunned the engine, picking up speed. 'You don't want to check his flat out?'

'Not yet. Let's stick to the plan.'

Sanghera was fifty metres ahead. The white Focus passed him, then slowed. 'Get out the fucking way,' Moray muttered under his breath.

As they watched, the CID officer brought his car to a quick halt. He jumped out and approached Sanghera, pulling out his warrant card. Reuben and Moray continued forward, slowing as well, Moray cursing. The officer spoke to Sanghera and checked his ID. Moray brought the car close enough to hear Sanghera confirm his name. Then the officer said something inaudible. Reuben leaned across and fired off half a dozen quick pictures on his mobile. The quality wasn't great, but they would do. Sanghera looked a decade older than he did in the newspaper pictures Reuben had seen. The intervening few years hadn't been kind.

The officer let Sanghera go, and climbed back in his car. Reuben watched Sanghera spin round and walk off in the direction of his flat. He looked spooked, eager to return to the safety of his residence. Moray groused as the CID officer circled the block then headed back towards Raddlebarn Gardens as well.

'Fucking amateur,' he said under his breath.

'Doesn't exactly inspire hope,' Reuben answered.

'What now?'

'We cut our losses. Next one on the list. Michael Adebyo.'

Moray pulled off at speed, Reuben flicking through the images he had managed to take. He deleted most of the shots on his phone and kept the two best, examining and re-examining them. He also scanned a photo of Daniel Riefield that had been taken at GeneCrime. Riefield's eyes looked wild, the swelling on his jaw brooding and red. Reuben stared into the grainy images, the silent question playing over and over in his head. *Where the fuck is my son?*

'So what do we know about Adebyo?' Moray asked, drifting into a bus lane to overtake on the inside.

Reuben closed his phone and picked through a wad of papers, with half an eye on the road. Driving with Moray was not for the faint-hearted. 'Originally from Somalia, came here as a refugee four or five years ago. Unlike a lot of the people on the drug trial, he wasn't a student. Presumably just trying to make some cash.'

'Sound like the kind of geezer who would kill people and kidnap a child?'

'Maybe, maybe not. Today is about covering all the angles, no matter how obtuse. According to his DSS records, he's got a young family himself, so presumably there's the possibility of childcare there. Comes from atrocity-torn Somalia, so his boundaries could have been altered. Maybe, compared to a sustained machete attack, removing someone's fingertips is a piece of cake.'

Reuben kept scanning all the available information. Don't feel, just think, he told himself. No point in pausing to consider the consequences. Just do what you have to do.

'His address looks pretty kosher. Confirmed in the DVLA records, as well as from his hospital records. The Royal Free continue to see him as an outpatient, so he should be where we think he is.'

'He still has regular contact with the place where this all happened? You think that's significant?'

'It's going to stay fresh in his mind if he's there every month. He's hardly going to be able to put it behind him, forget all about it.'

'How bad were his injuries?'

'Like the others, peripheral vascular damage. From what I can see in his hospital records, he had significant finger damage, some psychological scarring, probably other long-term health issues.' Reuben squinted at a section of extremely dense and uneven handwriting. 'Looks like the doctors were monitoring the increased possibility of a stroke or seizure. That's if I've read that scrawl correctly.'

'Poor fucker,' Moray said.

'Until I have my son, Moray, there are no poor fuckers other than Joshua. Someone who kills four men is not a poor fucker.' Reuben shivered, a small spasm through the shoulders. 'These men have suffered. Daniel Riefield, the guy I arrested, he's a real mess. But there isn't one of them I wouldn't hurt severely to get my boy back.' He focused intently on the side of Moray's face. 'I want you to appreciate that, Moray.'

Moray glanced across at him and then back at the road. Reuben understood the look but tried to ignore it.

They stopped at some lights. A small convoy of traffic squeezed across the main road ahead of them. The lights changed and then they were moving again. They drove on in silence for a few minutes, Moray taking well-worn routes through back streets, skipping the worst of the traffic, Reuben focusing intently on an *A to Z*, tracking their progress. A couple of junctions, a roundabout, on to another desperate housing estate, and they would be there.

None of the four men they were hunting had prospered since the trial. Reuben thought again about Riefield's squalid flat, about the damp, the air of decay. Damaged men living in damaged houses, slowly rotting away. He turned to Moray. 'Sorry,' he said.

'For what?'

'I might have come over a bit strong just then.'

'Look, your baby boy could be in one of these houses. I think I'd be a bit strong.'

'But?'

'But take it easy, Reuben. Don't go crazy. We've got to do this calmly and logically. We have a plan. Let's stick to it, eh?'

Reuben chewed the side of his cheek. The shady security consultant was right. All eighteen stone of him. 'You're the boss,' he said. 'Now, first on the left and I'll direct from there.'

They entered a maze of high-rises. Broken windows, cracked tarmac, stained concrete. As they drove between half-empty car parks, something caught Reuben's eye in the wing mirror. A dark blue car. Moray swung right. The car behind didn't make the turn. Reuben closed his eyes for a second, mining the image for information. The same colour, large and German, one occupant. Not the sort of vehicle you often saw on an estate like this. It had been the briefest of flashes, but Reuben had just caught it.

'Did you see a car behind us?'

'What sort?'

'Dark blue Audi A6.'

Moray glanced in his rear-view. 'Not that I can recall.'

'Funny . . .' Reuben said, almost to himself. He checked around, on parallel roads, in the car parks they were skirting, in his mirror. There was nothing. He frowned, catching a glimpse of himself in the wing mirror. His skin looked pale and tired, but his light green eyes shone like they were on fire. He turned away. Maybe he had imagined the Audi. Another case of paranoia, Randle starting to haunt him. He dragged his attention back to the *A to Z*. 'Take this right,' he said. 'Then we're there.'

Moray did as he was told, and slowed to a stop. They both peered up at the block they were beneath, then took in their surroundings.

'There,' Moray said.

Reuben followed his line of sight. 'This poor sod's got an Astra. But it's white again.'

'Why don't they just announce that they're doing undercover surveillance? Big sign in the window or something.'

'It's possible CID are doing this on purpose.'

'What do you mean?'

'Letting the suspects know they're being watched. Putting them under pressure.'

'Why the hell would they do that?'

'Otherwise it's stalemate. Look what happened with Sanghera. A plainclothes stopped him, checked his ID, let him go. Maybe that wasn't as amateurish as you thought. Sarah said they don't have a warrant for entry, so there's little else to do but observe from a distance. That's one hell of a slow and labour-intensive process. Days and days of just hanging around, waiting for a potential murderer to lead them somewhere interesting. Meanwhile my son slowly starves to death. They won't be quick enough. They won't be able to save him.'

'No?'

'No. Joshua's only chance is you and me. Shortcutting all the shit CID are bogged down with on what they think is an entirely separate case.'

'I guess,' Moray answered.

From his tone of voice, Reuben suspected he wasn't entirely convinced. 'But?'

'But I still reckon this is just crap police work. Plenty of it about. Look, the fucker's even dozed off.'

Reuben looked more closely. The occupant of the car was slumped forward in his seat. 'You don't think he's . . .'

'Nah. I saw him shuffling in his seat as we pulled up. Just a lazy bastard trying to get comfortable.'

'Takes one to know one.'

'Right, shall we do this?'

Reuben ran his finger along the telephone number listed for Michael Adebyo under his DSS record. A plan. That was what they had, nothing more. No back-up, no police checks, no support. Doing the things CID couldn't, sidestepping the hoops they had to jump through if they wanted to get convictions. But Reuben was no longer interested in convictions. He wanted his son, and he wanted to stop the killer. Everything else was merely incidental.

'Yeah,' he answered, his hand tight on the door handle.

'We'd better get to him before our man wakes up.'

Reuben climbed out of the car and began to dial. He pulled open the rusting metal door at the base of the flats and walked through it. Moray followed him in, and Reuben waited for the call to be answered.

6

The detached house in St John's Wood had a faded glory to it. Once, Reuben suspected, as he slapped across the dull red floor tiles and into the high-ceilinged hallway, this place was something. Tidy it up and it would be worth money. Proper London money. But the place was a wreck. Nothing had been done to it for years. The wallpaper was brown and psychedelic, the lights dim and choked with dust, the carpet on the stairs worn to threads. And the air stank, a sour, stale smell of failure and defeat.

Laura Piddock led him through, a can of White Lightning in her right hand, a freshly lit cigarette in her left. She muttered over her shoulder as she walked. 'I told the other policeman everything I saw. Detective Veno he was called. I remembered the name. Sounded like a bloody cough medicine.' Laura Piddock laughed, a dry hacking rattle from somewhere deep in her lungs. She swigged from her can, dragged on her cigarette and laughed again.

'Maybe I could do with some of that stuff myself.'

Reuben looked away. An unreliable witness, Veno had made her out to be. He was beginning to see why. The living room was worse than the hall. Bottles and cans everywhere, cups and saucers overflowing with spent butts, newspapers and magazines covering all the remaining surfaces. There was nowhere to sit, so they both remained standing.

'I know that Detective Veno and his colleagues spoke to you at length.'

'And I'll tell you what I told them. I know what I saw. A man hanging around when I came out of the off-licence. Dropping his fag.'

'And?' Reuben prompted.

Laura Piddock was drawing deep into her cigarette, a small column of ash falling on to what remained of the carpet. She coughed, the same rattle in her chest that her laugh had disturbed. 'He hesitated, looked around. Then he pushed the buggy away, down the street, through the crowds of people.'

While she was busy with her can of White Lightning, Reuben inspected what he could see of her face. Puckered lips, dry wrinkled skin, rough and ready make-up. How did you end up like that? he asked himself. Lost, alone, dependent.

He surreptitiously checked his watch. Nearly nine o'clock. Today had been about identities. If this failed, the plan got altogether more direct. But first things first. What he was doing now, in a scruffy house with a broken inhabitant, was strictly against protocol. Reuben had to remind himself that as a suspect in the disappearance of his own son, he should not be contacting a witness in the case against him. Fuck this up, and there would be all sorts of repercussions. Veno would have the greatest field day of his entire life.

'Look,' he said, pulling out his phone, 'I've got some pictures I want to show you.'

'Holidays, is it?' Laura asked, again breaking into a long and unpleasant laugh.

'No.' Reuben smiled. 'Now, would that be OK?'

'Sure. I've got nothing else to do.'

Reuben shuffled round so he could show her the screen of his phone. The pictures of Sanghera and Riefield had been easy to get. Michael Adebyo hadn't been too difficult either. Reuben had managed to get a surreptitious shot of him as he opened his front door to Moray, who'd claimed to be a bailiff. He scrolled through the images, three of the four men who might have his son. Laura Piddock's heavy eyelids blinked slowly as she concentrated on the screen. He went through them again. Riefield, then Sanghera, then Adebyo. Current, up-to-date photos in the memory of Reuben's mobile phone, each of them looking older than his years.

'Anything?' he asked.

Veno certainly hadn't shown her these men. It was just possible, pissed as she undoubtedly was, that something would shine out in her clouded consciousness.

'One more time,' she said.

Reuben scrolled through again. Then Laura stepped back, swaying on her feet.

'And?' Reuben asked, as patiently as he could.

'Nothing,' she answered. 'I thought I recognized the coloured gentleman from my local pub. But it's not him. He's too dark.'

Reuben pulled a sheet of paper out of his jacket pocket. 'I've also got this. Have a look.' He passed her a photocopied newspaper picture of Martin Randle's father Francis, taken eighteen months earlier at the official trial inquest. Laura held her fag in her mouth while she squinted at it.

They still hadn't managed to track Francis Randle down. In the photo he looked solid, an ex-forces physique lurking under his jumper, his shoulders square, his arms broad, the top of his right ear flat where it should be round. For the hundredth time that day Reuben asked himself whether it was coincidence that Randle had disappeared at the same time that several men involved in his son's death had been killed.

Laura Piddock peered closely at the image, her cigarette almost burning it, before she jerked back again. 'No,' she said. 'Not this one either.'

'It was taken a year and a half ago. He could have changed. Do you think he could be the man who took the buggy?'

'I don't think so.' Laura Piddock turned her dull eyes to him. 'Anyway, I thought Detective Veno was the one who was leading the case.'

'He is.'

'So what's this missing boy to you?'

'I'm . . . I'm just looking for him.'

'Well, it looks like you're still looking. I don't recognize none of those men. Like I told the detective, I only saw the man from an angle. Following that lady with the buggy, then waiting, then taking the buggy.'

'But I thought you told Detective Veno—'

'What?' Laura eyed him suspiciously.

Reuben had a final look around the decay. As he looked more closely he saw burn holes everywhere, small black dots of intent, fires that nearly were. 'Nothing,' he said. 'Look, be careful, you know, with your cigarettes. Make sure you don't leave them alight.'

The cackling laugh returned with a vengeance. 'What? Now the police care for me all of a sudden?'

'I just meant . . .' Reuben didn't know what he meant. He just didn't want to read about someone who had fallen through the gaps setting her house alight. 'You've been helpful,' he said unconvincingly.

'Goodbye,' she said. 'And please don't come back again.'

7

Reuben swiped Judith's GeneCrime card through the slot and entered the building. The security desk was clear, the guard doing his rounds. Sarah's office door was open. He glanced inside the empty space. The short stubby hand of its clock pointed to eleven. Static plants crouched silently in the gloom. Reuben closed the door behind him, flicked the lights on and walked over to the desk. He opened Sarah's top drawer. Just twelve hours earlier she had sat in the seat he now lowered himself into and, together with Commander Thorner, suspended him from duty, banned him from the building.

Reuben felt a cold nervousness burrowing into the pit of his stomach. He was tired, hungry and on edge. He breathed quick shallow breaths as he pulled out a thick cardboard file marked 'Fingertip Killer'. He opened it up. The sad desperation he'd felt since talking to Laura Piddock stayed with him as he leafed through its contents.

Piddock hadn't recognized Sanghera, Riefield, Adebyo or Randle as the man who had taken Joshua. His plan to get their images to her had been the right one, he told himself. Barging into their homes, especially while they were being watched by CID, would have caused all sorts of unnecessary problems.

Aside from the spider plant, Sarah's desk was clear. Reuben quickly spread all the paper evidence of the case over its surface. Photographs, DNA profiles, background checks, crime reports, sample inventories, hospital records, press clippings, pathology descriptions, lists of names. Everything was read and absorbed. He looked up, listened intently, made sure no one was heading his way. When he looked back down, the same gritty picture of Francis Randle, photocopied from a newspaper, stared up at him. He wondered what had happened to his ear. A fight? A bullet? A roadside bomb? What? Something had damaged him. No one had been able to locate Randle yet, but Laura Piddock didn't think he was the man who'd taken the buggy. Laura failing to ID Randle was a blow. If Randle were involved, it meant he had at least one accomplice.

CID had been thorough. Since the morning, Reuben could see that they had identified a total of twenty-six people who were associated with planning, overseeing or running the trial. Reuben knew it was impossible to protect all of them all the time. From highlighted names on a printed list, he guessed they had already started to prioritize. People closest to the trial, ones the killer might still be interested in. But Reuben knew that protection was treating the symptom rather than the cause. Sooner or later, someone on the list would be exposed and vulnerable. He had to stop him before anyone else died.

Reuben clenched his fists, chewed his teeth. Images, he quickly decided, were the key. This had gone past forensics. They had a sample, but there was no database match. The killer had never had his DNA taken. Reuben knew Mina's team would be working through familial matches, trying to get close to the killer, searching for relatives on the database. But that would take days, weeks even. Low stringency tests that had to be repeated and corroborated. And then, so what? The killer's DNA is similar to an existing profile on the National DNA Database. That doesn't mean that person could or would help. They might have twenty blood relations. Narrowing it down would take time, precious police time that they simply didn't have. No, forensics wasn't going to put Reuben in a room with the killer. Forensics wasn't going to let Reuben stare into the eyes of the man holding his son. Forensics wasn't going to help Reuben reach forward and grab the son of a bitch by the neck. But lateral thinking might.

Reuben rounded up all the pictures he could find. Anyone even vaguely associated with the trial. Doctors, nurses, placebos, everyone. Twenty-six faces, the ones

CID had identified. Pictures from personnel files, from press cuttings, from civilian databases. One of these people, Reuben was certain, was the killer. This had to be someone on the inside of the trial. He glanced down at the writing on the back of his hand. Syed Sanghera. Daniel Riefield. Michael Adebyo. Francis Randle. Names were only half the battle. Faces, he appreciated, were the real answer.

Reuben left Sarah's office and walked quickly to the end of the corridor. He shoved the pieces of paper into the photocopier and pressed start. While it hummed and flashed, a warm inky smell invaded his sinuses. He thought back to Laura Piddock. Something she said that didn't ring true. A piece of information at odds with what Veno had said.

He picked up the copies and originals and returned to Sarah's office. As he walked, Reuben heard a noise. A door slamming on the floor above. He stopped and waited a second. Another door opened and shut, closer this time. Reuben dashed into Sarah's office. He stuffed all the pictures back into her file and rounded up the rest of the evidence. Then he clicked her light back off and put the file back where he had found it.

A figure passed the door, moving fast. Reuben edged forward. He heard footsteps. Another person going by. Reuben listened intently, then stepped out of the office. He checked the corridor. It was empty. Then he started towards the stairs, heading out of the building. Getting caught in GeneCrime could cause a lot of problems.

He made it to the stairs, and sprinted up the first flight. As it turned back on itself he came to a sudden halt. There, staring at him, motionless, was Mina Ali.

'Reuben, what the hell are you doing?' she asked.

'I forgot my keys,' he said, patting his pocket.

'I thought you weren't supposed to be here. I thought you'd handed your pass in to Sarah.'

'I did. Judith lent me hers. Look, Mina, don't tell anyone. Like I said, I just needed my house keys.'

Mina regarded him for a second. Reuben tried to read the look but failed. He thought he sensed curiosity and disappointment, but it was hard to tell.

'But what about your son?' she asked.

'Nothing. A vacuum of information. He's vanished into thin air. Nothing to do except sit and wait for news.'

'Which isn't exactly your style.'

'So, why the commotion?' Reuben asked, changing the subject.

'I guess you won't have heard. We've all been summonsed in. Ultra short notice, all leave cancelled.'

'Why?'

'There's been another.'

'Shit. Who?'

'Daniel Riefield.'

'Fuck.'

'The man you brought in for questioning.'

'Fuck,' Reuben repeated. He still had his picture on his phone. He'd showed it to Laura Piddock only a couple of hours ago. 'This changes things.'

'How?'

'Riefield was one of the trialists. He'd already lost his fingers. What does the killer have to gain now?'

Mina shrugged, bony collar bones arching up the neck of her blouse. 'I don't know. And I also don't know how the hell we're supposed to catch this freak. We just don't have anything useable, Reuben. And I think he knows that.'

'Wasn't Riefield under police protection?'

'No. Sarah drew up a shortlist of people for round-the-clock CID supervision. Riefield wasn't on it. Like you said, he was a victim of the trial. We didn't figure him for a victim of the killer.'

'But CID were watching him?'

'Yeah, they've staked out a number of people, ones that you initially identified. But surveillance and protection are very different things.'

'So the killer managed to evade CID on the way in and the way out.'

'He's smart,' Mina said.

There was the sound of more footsteps above. Reuben was suddenly nervous again. If Sarah caught him here . . .

'Look, Mina,' he said, 'I don't want to hold you up. But if

I were you, I would be profiling for intelligence. Look at the most able and capable people who ran the drug trial or were associated with it.'

'Thanks.'

Reuben paused, wanting for a second to wrap his arm around Mina's diminutive frame. 'Be careful, Mina,' he said. 'I think the rules have just changed.' And with that, Reuben headed up the stairs, along the main entrance corridor and out of GeneCrime, making sure no one else spotted him.

8

Reuben hammered on the door. Minute flakes of its paint fell through the cold November air in lightweight shards, lit up by the low winter sun. Reuben continued to bang hard on the surface. He had managed four hours' sleep on Lucy's sofa. Then he had left just as Veno arrived for his habitual morning update. Reuben knew there was no update, no progress, no nothing. Just potential sightings that wouldn't turn out to be true, alibi statements from intimidated paedophiles, plans to keep the disappearance in the newspapers for the fourth consecutive day.

He banged harder. He heard sounds of unhurried progress. The opening of a door somewhere, the creaking of stairs. 'Come on,' he muttered under his breath. He hadn't wanted to come back here after yesterday, but something Laura Piddock said spent the night eating away at him, festering under his skin, tunnelling into his flesh. He drove the knuckles of his right hand into the flaky surface one more time. In his left hand he held the wad of papers he had photocopied from Sarah's evidence file.

When the door finally opened, Laura Piddock looked terrible. Reuben appreciated that he probably didn't look a lot better himself, but seeing her without make-up was a sobering sight. Without quick and approximate daubs of colour, her skin was a succession of parallel wrinkles which sagged under her eyes and around her cheekbones. She stared at him for a second, until recognition crept in.

'What do you want?' she asked. 'I thought I told you not to come back.'

'I know. And I'm sorry to wake you. But I need your help.'

'Do you now?'

Reuben peered down at the floor. 'I do. And it's important.'

Laura Piddock scratched herself for a couple of seconds. 'Well, I suppose you'd better come in.'

Reuben followed her through the cluttered mess of the hall, into the stale and unpleasant living room. Once again, he looked round for somewhere to sit but didn't find anywhere. Laura pulled a half-empty pack of cigarettes out of her dressing-gown pocket and lit up. As she inhaled, her cheeks sucked inwards, leaving her face looking skeletal.

'Something you said yesterday got me thinking,' Reuben said.

'Long time since anyone said that to me.' The first fag of the day was helping to convulse her lungs, her eyes watering as she coughed.

'You said the man who abducted the child had followed the woman with the buggy.'

'Right.'

'Not, as you told Detective Veno, that he had just been standing there. But that he had actually followed behind her before she arrived at the newsagent. Are you sure that's correct?'

'Sure as I can be. Just because I drink doesn't make me blind, you know. But I don't see what difference it makes.'

Reuben didn't say anything. It made the world of difference. Lucy had been followed. 'Look, I want to show you some more pictures.'

'I won't ask about your holidays this time.'

Reuben smiled. Once, twenty or thirty years ago, Laura had been a normal person, not the withered wreck who stood in her own living room with nowhere to sit, drawing heavily on a cigarette, shaking beneath her stained dressing gown. He pulled out the pictures and started handing them to her, one by one. He kept completely quiet, silently hoping. If this was another dead end, there were no other leads. This was the only logical answer. That someone associated with the trial he hadn't come across yet had taken Joshua and was on a killing spree.

He closed his eyes for a few seconds and listened to the rustle of pieces of paper, the woman's rasping breaths, the ever-present murmur of traffic. He thought of Lucy, what she would be thinking as Veno briefed her yet again, the agonies that another day without her only child would bring. He pictured Moray, going about his business, dropping him off at GeneCrime the night before, telling him to call whenever he needed him. He pictured the forensics team spending a sleepless night in the cold, damp flat of Daniel Riefield, mopping up his samples and his fluids. He pictured Sarah Hirst, tense and under pressure, leafing through the same folder Reuben had perused the night before.

He opened his eyes. Laura Piddock was staring at one sheet of paper, the other sheets floating down to the floor, released by her spare hand. Reuben's heart felt tight in his chest.

'What?' he asked.

Laura didn't answer. He watched her intently. She squinted into the sheet, muttering to herself. Reuben couldn't see the picture, just the back of it. He didn't want to influence her decision. But keeping quiet was almost impossible.

'Do you recognize one of them?'

'Shhh,' she answered. 'I'm thinking. I didn't get a completely clear view. Mainly from behind, but as he turned his head . . . The ears are right. Out at the top, then pressed in tight, large lobes. And the nose, completely straight . . .'

Reuben's phone vibrated in his pocket. He ignored it. All he could hear were the words *Come on!* screaming inside his brain.

Laura lowered the sheet of A4 towards him. Reuben could see now that it was a picture from a newspaper article, probably at the time of the trial. He didn't recognize the face.

'I've seen him before,' she said. She took a long drag on her cigarette, burning it right down to the filter. When she spoke again, her words came hidden in puffs of smoke. 'He's the one. The one that took the buggy.'

Reuben couldn't help himself. He snatched the picture. The photo had been blown up, possibly from a group shot, maybe from an identity card or some sort of personnel record. The resolution wasn't great, but good enough. Reuben read the name scrawled in Sarah's handwriting at the bottom. Dion Morgan. He racked his brain for information.

'But he was . . .'

'What?'

Reuben glanced down at all the other pictures, faces staring up at him from Laura's littered floor, thinking hard. They might as well stay, adding to the detritus and clutter.

He folded Morgan's picture into his pocket and took

out his wallet. 'Look, please buy yourself something, Laura. Food or whatever.' He passed her four twenty-pound notes.

'I didn't think policemen were allowed to do that.'

'They're not,' Reuben answered. 'But I'm not a police-man.'

'So who are you?' Laura asked, taking the notes and folding them into her dressing-gown pocket.

Reuben started to walk out of the room. 'I'm the missing boy's father.'

'Oh, I didn't . . .'

He turned, taking out his mobile. 'And now I'm going to go and get him back.'

9

Reuben paced along the street that Laura Piddock called home. It was close to the spot where Joshua had been taken. Posters of Joshua's face stared back at him from lamp-posts and shop windows. It was a photo that Lucy had taken and then posted to Reuben a few weeks earlier. Joshua in a park somewhere, his brown coat done up tight, his cheeks red from running around, his pale hair almost translucent in the sun. It was the same coat he had been wearing on the day he was taken, the same coat he had spilled his drink down, the same coat he was probably wearing still.

Reuben had passed images of his son in other parts of the city, but nothing like this. Here, close to the scene, they were everywhere. The intensity was almost over-whelming. He stopped in front of one of them. It was in an off-licence window, presumably the one Laura had entered and left, pausing only to observe a man quickly pushing a buggy away. The words 'Missing Child' were printed above Joshua's face. Reuben couldn't help but see the picture differently now. Before, it had been about promise and potential, a photo of his eager young son that Lucy had taken on a day out. Today, seeing it through the plate-glass window of a shop, it spoke only of sadness and desperation.

He reached forward, fingertips against the freezing surface. My son, he said to himself, my beautiful son.

Reuben turned away and kept moving, tears welling in his eyes. He had managed to keep it all at bay for days, charging round the city like a man possessed, staying utterly and acutely focused. But he knew it would track him down eventually, hurting him like it hurt Lucy, tearing him apart in the same way Lucy was being ripped open. He needed to keep going.

Reuben took out his phone and checked its display. The missed call was from Judith. He pictured her at home with her son, rocking him to sleep, holding him close to her. Reuben called her back and quickly brought her up to speed. She listened quietly, taking it all in, putting it all into logical boxes, like she always did.

'If I hear anything new,' she said, 'you'll be the first to know.'

In the background, Fraser began to wail for attention. Judith ended the call with a quick 'good luck'. Reuben blocked out the sound of the child. He knew he could easily let this kill him. He could drown in the sorrow, suffocate in the grief. But that wouldn't help his son.

As he walked, Reuben tore open a wrap of amphetamine, rubbed the coarse and bitter powder into his gums. His teeth itched and his gums felt raw. It was time for action. He had to be robotic, unfeeling, numb, until he got what he wanted. Then he could let it all break loose.

Reuben dropped the empty wrap in the street and dialled with his thumb, ignoring the pictures of Joshua all around him.

It was answered almost immediately.

'I need one final favour,' he said, cutting through the preamble.

'You've had several already,' Sarah answered, equally abrupt.

'This one's the big one.'

'Look, Reuben, it's too late for that sort of thing.'

'Really? You remember what you said to me a few days ago?'

Sarah sighed. 'Remind me.'

'That considering what I once did for you, you owe me one. Well, this is the one.'

'It's not particularly gallant to keep reminding someone that once, a few months ago, you saved their life.'

'This has gone way past gallantry, Sarah.'

'Well, what is it?'

'I need whatever current details you've got on some-one.'

'Who?'

'Dion Morgan.'

'Rings a bell.'

'He was a placebo on the drug trial.'

Reuben listened intently. He heard the ruffling of papers, the tap of a computer keyboard. He clenched his fist and clamped his jaw. She was going to help him.

'Give me a couple of seconds,' she said.

Reuben stopped pacing around on the wide pavement. He caught sight of the four names etched on the back of his hand. With some saliva he began to scour off the first three. Syed Sanghera. Daniel Riefield. Michael Adebyo. Men who had direct reason to attack the trial coordinators. As he waited for Sarah, he rubbed harder, feeling the friction of skin abrading skin as he erased the letters. He left Francis Randle's name. The owner of the blue Audi couldn't be discounted yet.

'While I'm sifting through my evidence file, I can tell you there's absolutely nothing on Dion Morgan, Reuben. The placebos have been lower priority, but either way it's virtually a blank piece of paper. A good job, no previous, no nothing. The only thing that many hours of police searches have uncovered is a recent caution for drink driving.'

'Is that it?'

'Just over a week ago. And even then he hasn't been prosecuted, and probably won't be. Blood test was borderline. Just came to light in a CID background search that Leigh Harding carried out.'

Reuben started walking again. He couldn't stand still any longer. 'What else?'

'What do you want with Morgan anyway?'

'Nothing much,' Reuben answered. 'Just a hunch.'

'Your nothing muches usually turn out to be other people's something substantial.'

'Yeah, well. You found his other details yet?'

Reuben heard Sarah take a sip of something. He pictured a cardboard cup full of strong dark coffee. Sarah's legal amphetamine.

'You do realize that you're wasting your time, Reuben?'

'How?'

'We've had CID stake him out, keep tabs on him, make sure he's not going to be a victim like Daniel Riefield. And there's nothing there, Reuben. Nothing at all. Dion Morgan is a medic. Currently a house officer at St Mary's Hospital. His residence is in an apartment block leased by the trust. Because it's hospital property we've been able to have a look inside.'

'And?'

'CID found nothing at all.'

'So are you going to help me?'

'Your funeral. You got a pen?'

'Aha.'

Sarah gave Reuben Morgan's address and other details, which he etched into the bluey-white skin of his hand, below Francis Randle's name. 'Now don't go upsetting Dr Morgan. By all accounts he's a nice man. One lawsuit against your name from Lucy's boyfriend is unfortunate. Two would begin to look careless.'

Reuben crossed the road, looking for a Tube station. 'I'll see what I can do,' he answered. Then he thanked Sarah and ended the call.

He spotted a familiar red and white sign ahead, illuminated and beckoning. He quickened his pace, nervous, excited and on edge, a buzz of raw emotions and feelings colliding inside him.

10

As the Tube sped into darkness, Reuben tried to imagine Lucy's bus journey four days earlier. On the surface of the city, mired in traffic, a two-year-old ball of energy and fascination called Joshua bouncing around the lower deck. She was travelling with good news, words she would ring him with while he loitered outside the Command Room, anxious about getting stuck into the case of a man who removed fingertips for fun.

It was only three stops to Paddington from where he was. It would take minutes. Reuben glanced involuntarily at his watch. Every second Joshua was with the killer his chances of dying intensified. He checked the linear map of stations above the blackened window opposite. A line with dots on it, each marked with a familiar name. A circle that looped around the city. As the train approached his station, Reuben sensed that his own circle was rapidly returning to its origin.

Reuben took the escalator stairs two at a time, pounding ever upwards. He brushed past static passengers, his legs light, his arms strong, his breathing controlled. He checked a map at the exit and turned left. St Mary's was three streets away. Another left, a right, left again. Five minutes and he was there, looking up. Eight or nine storeys, light brown and dark brown, red window frames, like someone had tried to brighten a dismal office block. A stretch of water behind, a canal of some sort. An ambulance bay cross-hatched in yellow. Further along in his line of sight an older section of building, an archway, an elevated walkway.

He walked straight in through the automatic doors closest to him. People sitting and standing, waiting on chairs, leaning against walls. Reuben checked another map. A hospital plan in a plain metal surround, its plastic protection scratched and scuffed. Paediatrics on the sixth and seventh floors. Paediatric Haematology on the seventh.

Reuben checked for the lifts. He followed the blue vinyl floor to a lobby and pressed the up button. Another person joined him in the small lift. A man of twenty-five with a portable drip. Poor fucker, Reuben thought to himself. And then he remembered his words to Moray. Until Joshua was safe, there were no poor fuckers.

The man stayed in the lift as Reuben exited at the seventh floor. Functional NHS fixtures and fittings.

Embedded strip lighting, muted blues and greens, vinyl floor, cheap office furniture. Painted pictures of cartoon characters on the walls because it was a children's department. Reuben ignored the reception desk and stepped into a communal waiting area. He sat down on an orange plastic chair, took out his phone and dialled Lucy's number, watching medical staff come and go from the ward at the end, into consulting rooms, to the reception desk.

'It's Reuben,' he said as Lucy answered.

'Hi,' she said quietly.

'Can you talk?'

'I'm in the bathroom. Veno and his team are in the living room.'

'Any news?'

'Veno said they're following up some potential sightings.'

'So nothing, then?'

'No.'

Reuben listened to his ex-wife's breathing. Slow, shallow, broken. She was falling apart.

'You OK?' he asked.

'Not really. You?'

'Yes and no.'

'What are you up to?'

'I'm trying to get our son back.'

'Alive?'

Reuben didn't want to contemplate the alternative. 'I'm bringing him home.'

'Where are you?'

'I can't tell you.'

'Why not?'

'Because I don't want anyone else involved. You, the police, GeneCrime . . . I've got to do this by myself. I want you to understand that. A man has taken the thing I hold more precious than anything else in the world. And I want to stand face to face with him and make him give it back.'

'Where are you?' she asked.

Reuben ran his eyes around the waiting room. So far, he had seen a handful of doctors. None of them resembled Morgan. 'Like I said, it's better that I don't tell you.'

'But you know for certain who has him?'

He didn't know anything for certain. All he had was the testimony of a drunk. But it was a start. 'Let's say I'm about to narrow it down.'

More fractured breaths. 'Good luck,' Lucy whispered finally.

'I'm going to need it. Standing face to face with a psychopath is not something many people survive.'

'Just come back safe, and bring our boy with you.'

Reuben bit deep into his fingernail. 'I'll try,' he answered.

He ended the call and stood up. He couldn't sit still.

It was impossible. He was nervous and on edge, the amphetamine coming on strong, making him twitchy. There was a drinks machine at the end of the corridor. He bought some Coke. It tasted sweet and sickly, but he knew it would help him, keep his blood sugar from crashing. A couple walking through with tears in their eyes stared at him as he passed. He pictured the times he and Lucy had spent in paediatric centres, realized that his face was still in the public consciousness.

Reuben paced about, scanning around. Morgan was part of this. Reuben was sure, and getting surer. It was more than coincidence that Laura Piddock recognized him, that Joshua had been in this very hospital before he was snatched. That was all the evidence Reuben had, but it was a fuck of a lot more than he had on anyone else. Sarah had already checked Morgan, searched his house, examined his background. So that was what it came down to, Reuben realized. The word of a senior police officer against the word of a serious alcoholic.

Reuben stretched, rubbed his face, sat down for a couple of minutes and then got up again. There was no plan. He simply needed to see Morgan, get a good look at him, judge whether he was capable of being a cold-blooded killer.

Then, as he walked back to his seat a second time, he saw him. Tall, broad, light hair, ears that tapered in, as Laura Piddock had described. A white coat, a shirt and tie beneath, no stethoscope. He was heading out of a half-glass door, holding the hand of a young girl. The girl was thin with a tube taped up through her nose. Dr Morgan led her through to another room, then returned alone, scribbling notes into a pad. Reuben tried and failed to see him as the fingertip killer, the man who had taunted him on the phone, the man who could have taken his son. Finally, he was standing just metres away from him. And in the flesh, Reuben started to have serious doubts.

Reuben sat back down again on the orange chair. He had ruled out Adebyo, Sanghera and Riefield on the basis that Laura Piddock hadn't recognized them. Unless there was someone else, or more than one person working together. One to snatch Joshua, the other to carry out the killings. Another idea came to him in his speeding brain. He couldn't face talking to Sarah so he texted her.

Where is Francis Randle?

He held his mobile out in front of him, his head bowed like he was praying to it, impatient and ill at ease. He was losing focus and knew it. Just seconds of seeing Morgan had upset his reasoning. The drug wasn't helping. He had taken it for its energy and stamina, for its ability to push him onwards after days of constant activity and fatigue. But what he needed more than anything now was calm. He had to think coolly and rationally, consider all the evidence he had accumulated over the week – the cigarette butts, the rats, the death of Daniel Riefield, the motives of the people on the trial, the reasons it was resurfacing after four years, the witness statements, the abduction of Joshua, the telephone calls, the crime scenes. But his brain was misfiring, random impulses flashing through, coherent lines of logic scattering like marbles around the inside of his cranium. He pleaded for composure, willed Sarah to swallow her principles and text him back.

His phone vibrated twice. Reuben read the message: *Randle located close to Paddington. Highly dangerous. Not in custody. CID following. Stay away from case. S.*

Again, Reuben tried to reason it through. Francis Randle, the father of one of the trialists who had died, a military man with experience of active duty. Calling for justice after the inquest. Saying the trial coordinators should suffer as his son had. And now CID had tabs on him. Reuben saw the image of Randle from numerous press cuttings. Broad, strong, bony. Not to be fucked with. It was impossible. With no forensics the case was just circumstantial. Potential killers that CID were only just beginning to track down. Five murders happening so quickly that the police couldn't keep up. A man with the power to incapacitate several grown men and hack their fingertips off.

Reuben glanced over towards the ward. Morgan had swapped his white coat for a suit jacket. He shared a joke with a nurse close to reception, then made for the lift. There was no longer any time for indecision. Reuben knew he had to follow him. CID were tracking Randle. In the absence of any other option, Reuben stood up. He waited for the lift to close, then made for the steps.

11

Morgan stuck out an arm as a taxi approached. The driver slowed and stopped, lowered his window. Morgan spoke to the driver.

Reuben stared up and down the street. Amphetamine mania gripped him tight. Another desperate rush. Heart racing, muscles clenched. Scanning for a black car with a yellow light. It was cold, but Reuben was immune.

Morgan climbed into the cab. He hadn't noticed Reuben. He wasn't in any hurry. Reuben flashed through whether this was a good sign or a bad one. The door closed with an empty metallic clunk.

Reuben searched the streets with wide-open eyes as the taxi rattled off. He knew how critical these seconds were. Lose Morgan now and he would lose him for hours. And that was time he didn't have. Joshua could be anywhere, holding on, about to die. He had to know if Morgan was involved, and quick.

Reuben combed the area in both directions. Fast and busy traffic. A wide road with three lanes each way. No reservation, just a pedestrian island in the middle of the onslaught. Cars, buses, bikes, but no fucking taxis. Morgan's cab was thirty metres away and disappearing. Reuben dodged three lanes of movement and stood in the centre. Red brake lights came on in Morgan's taxi, then the indicator. Reuben watched it, still frantically trawling the streets. It was slowing, drifting into the outside lane, pulling a U-turn. And then he spied a taxi. Heading in the same direction Morgan's was about to start travelling in, on its way back past him. Reuben ran across the other three lanes towards it, his arm out, stop-stop-stop-stop grunted under his breath. The taxi slowed, its driver pulling up sharply. Reuben jumped in and slammed the door.

'There's a black cab about to pass us,' he said, pointing out of the back window. 'I want you to follow it.'

'Where to?'

'I don't know. Could be anywhere. Just follow it wherever it goes.'

The driver turned as far as his thick neck would allow, his eyebrows raised. Reuben knew he wasn't impressed. He had broken several rules of London taxi etiquette. Then the driver rotated slowly back to face the road. Morgan's taxi edged past, thick black smoke dropping heavily on to the tarmac. Reuben locked eyes with the driver in the rear-view. It was a cold look of appraisal. Then Reuben stared past him. Through the driver's cage. Through the windscreen. Deep into the mayhem of the traffic. Morgan was ten metres ahead, sitting bolt upright, staring through the window. In another few moments he would be out of sight.

'Look, I'm sorry. I just need you to help me. Please.'

The taxi driver cleared his throat. 'Now that depends.'

'On what?'

'Saw you on the telly the other night,' he said. 'Me and the missus watched it.'

'Please,' Reuben implored.

'This about your missing boy?'

'Yes.'

The driver didn't say anything. Reuben knew what he was thinking. You killed your own son and now you want me to ferry you around. He cursed the press conference that Veno had thrown them into. Unprepared and raw, loud questions hiding silent accusations.

There was a pause. Time fractured, slow and fast at the same time. Reuben's brain speeding, events crashing in slow motion. He considered jumping out and stopping another taxi. But then the engine note rose and the cab pulled off hard with a squeal of tyres. As it accelerated, Reuben saw the driver turn off the meter.

'This one's on me,' he said.

Reuben peered forward. Morgan was just in view,

slowing for a zebra crossing. Bit by bit, they were gaining, the driver putting his foot down. Reuben didn't know what to say. He was overwhelmed suddenly by the driver's act of kindness. 'Thanks,' he mumbled.

'That's the cab there,' the driver pointed. 'I'll stay close enough so we don't lose him, not so close he can see us.'

Reuben thanked him again.

They battled through the traffic, away from Paddington, heading south and then west. Reuben ticked off regions. Kensington. Shepherd's Bush. Acton. Nothing direct and straight, just the zig-zag route that taxi drivers took, avoiding jams and one-way systems.

'No news on your boy, then?' the driver asked, pulling up at a busy interchange and putting it into neutral.

Reuben stared past the two cars in front. Dion Morgan, distorted and misshapen. Refracted through the driver's cage and several sheets of rounded glass.

'Nothing,' he answered.

The driver shot him another quick look. 'How are you coping?'

The words were soft and cockney. They played through Reuben's racing mind. A gravelly murmur that felt warm and sincere. But Reuben couldn't answer. He wasn't coping. He was taking illegal drugs, hiding in the pursuit, burying his emotions under layers of investigation. Desperate lunges towards men who might have Joshua. Impulsive plans of action. Pushing on relentlessly, hour after hour. The cab suddenly felt small and cramped. The eyes in the mirror, the cage in front of him, the driver's thick neck, dark hair sprouting above his collar.

Before long, Morgan's taxi indicated and slowed. Reuben inspected the area. Standard terraced housing, probably late nineteenth century. A congested row of properties wedged tight against one another. His driver pulled up, twenty metres back. Reuben watched Morgan pay and leave the cab.

As he looked more closely, he saw there was a gap in the dense crush of terraces. A space where two or three of them had once stood. Maybe a wartime bomb had obliterated them, a tooth being punched out, leaving a gap. It had been filled with a late fifties or early sixties detached house. Newer brick, plainer design, a square box. A jarring modernist construction lurking amid Victorian elegance. Reuben watched Morgan walk up the short front path of the detached house and unlock the front door. His movements were languid, relaxed, calm. He looked about as normal as it was possible to be. Once again, the name Francis Randle came to him.

'What do you want to do?' the driver asked.

Morgan entered the house and closed the door behind him.

'I don't know,' Reuben answered.

He scratched his scalp hard and deep, as if he could get at the buzz of conflicting notions in his head. The taxi continued to vibrate, its engine rattling uneasily away. A couple of cars passed. The driver stared in his rear-view. A siren searched through the air, bouncing down the narrow street. Still Reuben waited, thinking, weighing it up, deciding.

It can't be right, he told himself. A placebo on the trial with nothing to gain or lose. A doctor in a decent hospital. No record, no skeletons in the cupboard. He tapped his knuckles against his forehead. Seconds passed. The engine continued to clatter, echoing around inside his skull. He picked through his options. GeneCrime had obviously lost interest in Dr Morgan. He scanned the street. No uniform, no CID, no unmarked squad cars. This was a false lead. A wild-goose chase based on the testimony of an unreliable witness.

'Look,' the taxi driver said, 'if it was up to me, you could stay here all day. But it's not. I'm sorry, really I am, but you got to decide what you want to do.'

Reuben thought for another few long seconds. The door of the house Morgan had entered remained closed. He considered calling for back-up. Waiting for a couple of uniform to arrive. Knocking politely on the door, a routine search of the property. Ruling it out, just for the sake of ruling it out. But Sarah had warned him off. And suspended staff didn't get to request manpower for wild hunches.

Reuben chewed his teeth. Each and every second

counted. Joshua's chances of survival were ebbing fast. Wherever he was in the capital, the quicker he got to him the greater the chance of saving him. But Morgan just didn't add up. Having seen him in the flesh, having visited his place of work, having followed him here, all fuelled by amphetamine and a need for action, Reuben suddenly wasn't sure of anything any more. He was crashing, falling apart, paying the price for so much frantic activity.

'Just give me one more minute,' he muttered to the driver.

'You want to go somewhere else?'

Reuben didn't answer. He just sat forward in his seat, head in his hands, paralysed by indecision. Outside the house of a placebo on the trial who had nothing to gain and everything to lose. A man who worked in a paediatrics department, for fuck's sake.

The engine rattled on. Reuben remained utterly static.

12

Judith parked her pram at the security desk. She unclipped the small detachable car seat from the body of the pram and carried Fraser by its handle, swinging him slightly as she walked. On her back was a compact rucksack stuffed with enough paraphernalia to survive any amount of fluid expelled from any part of her eight-week-old son. As she made her way along the brutal corridors of GeneCrime, she felt more like a beast of burden than a forensic scientist. Years of chasing along the very same hallways with vital evidence on serial killers and rapists, rushing to Reuben or Mina or Sarah, and here she was padding along with her newborn, struggling under the weight of him and his accoutrements, trying not to wake him.

Judith found her co-workers crammed into Sarah's office. Suddenly, she felt like an intruder. The way Sarah glanced up at her then quickly away made her feel it was a mistake to have come.

'Can you give us a second?' Sarah said. 'We're just wrapping up.'

'Sure,' Judith replied. 'Sorry.'

She peered around the room. Sarah seated, Mina and Bernie standing, Leigh Harding leaning against a wall, Simon on one of the two chairs that wasn't supporting a plant, Paul Mackay on the other, Birgit Kasper standing stolidly in the corner, her arms folded. Mina and Bernie smiled at her, and raised their eyebrows. Judith understood the gesture. *Sarah is giving us a pep talk*. Judith glanced down at Fraser. He was asleep, unconscious, oblivious.

'So I want people going back and checking through,' Sarah continued. 'Even though we have a DNA profile for our killer, we need to keep trawling through databases, hunting for links, cross-referencing the scenes. You know how this works. The more threads we assemble, the more difficult it becomes to unravel our case. Mina, the familial matching has to speed up. We need to know whether we can tie the killer's DNA to members of his wider family. All of this adds volume, momentum, weight, the things you need to convince juries. The sheer mass of data required to overwhelm the practised counter-arguments of those infernal defence lawyers. Although we're closing in on our man, we have to keep accumulating fragments of proof, things we can come back to, even information that doesn't seem particularly important at the time.'

Sarah ran her brilliant blue eyes around the room.

'And as well as bulking up our evidence, it goes without saying that we need to catch this sicko. Otherwise we're looking at another death any day. This man isn't going to just give it up. He's on a mission, and you people are the only people who can stop him. I want you to think about that. Out there, outside these walls, someone is going to die unless you catch the killer and tie him unequivocally to the murders. I don't care if you're tired, or out of ideas, or what. This is more important than anything else in your life at this moment. Anything.'

'But the familial matching only works if—'

'There are no buts, Mina. This is literally life, and this is literally death. The difference comes down to you. Collectively.'

No one else said anything for a few seconds. Judith considered that maybe she should leave, come back another time. She had phoned, several of Reuben's lab had been keen to meet the newborn, yet Judith appreciated her timing probably wasn't ideal. Not that there ever was a good time to visit the unit.

Sarah shuffled through some papers in silence. The clock on her wall lacked a second hand, but ticked anyway, a hidden internal mechanism counting to sixty, waiting to shuffle the minute hand forward a notch. Birgit glanced down at Fraser and looked away again.

'OK,' Sarah said, her tone softening, 'we all know what we've got to do. Look at every angle, check through every link, hope to Christ that CID and surveillance can protect all the other potential victims.' She double-clicked her mouse, focused on her screen, spoke down into her laptop. 'Now, I received something important a few minutes ago, something that I want you all to take a good look at.'

She spun the laptop round so that its screen was visible to the room. Judith caught her eye. Sarah mouthed the word 'sorry'. Judith was touched for a second. Sarah was tough and ambitious, but not immune to being human from time to time.

'This is CCTV of our main suspect, Francis Randle,' she continued. 'You will recall that he is the father of Martin Randle, who died on the trial, and that he spent several years in various military outfits. Not someone for the general public to approach under any circumstances. His whereabouts until recently haven't been known. However, what I'm about to show you is footage taken less than half a mile from the scene of Daniel Riefield's murder yesterday. We have been able to place Randle in the vicinity at the right time. And this, everybody, gives us enough probable cause to have him picked up.'

'And if we pick him up, we can swab him?' Leigh Harding asked, standing up from the wall. 'Match his profile with Riefield's crime scene?'

'With all the crime scenes,' Mina said.

'Correct.' Sarah pressed the space bar of the computer,

leaning over it. 'And it also means that if we're quick we can keep him in custody long enough to process the samples. Now, as you'll see, Randle is in a hurry. That isn't the walk of someone out for a casual evening stroll.'

Along with everyone else, Judith was watching the screen. The image was surprisingly crisp. Randle was stocky, wide, intense. He looked like he knew he was being observed, jerky in his movements, his musculature not quite relaxed. He disappeared from view. The screen was empty for a second, then it blinked back on. Black and white footage this time, taken from a lower elevation. Francis Randle pacing down a side street, time, date and camera ID number in the top right corner. Another gap in his progress, then a colour shot, even lower, almost street level. It felt to Judith like they were slowly swooping down on him. Sarah pressed the space bar again. Randle froze, a close-up of his face, lips tight, eyes narrowed, a man on a mission.

'What happened to the rest of his ear?' Bernie asked.

Sarah squinted into the screen. There was something almost sickening about the way Randle's ear had been sliced straight across, just above its aperture. 'No idea. He's ex-military, so anything's possible.'

'Why haven't we picked him up yet?'

'He's been under twenty-four-hour surveillance. But we don't have an address for him. We need him to lead us to where he lives, search for evidence of rats, a saw, gloves, all the things he's been using in his killings.'

'So why not arrest him, take DNA, then bail him? The CCTV gives us probable cause. At least then we'd have him off the streets for a few hours. In the meantime we try to get a match with one of the crime scenes, and if we do, put his identity out across the capital. We'd find his address pretty quick.'

Sarah sighed, a tight breath squeezed out through frustration. 'CID have lost him. He gave them the slip this morning. Must have known he was being followed. Apparently ducked through a shop and out of its loading bay.'

Simon Jankowski polished his glasses on the bright pattern of his shirt. 'What else do we have to put Randle as the killer?'

Judith watched Sarah turn slowly to face the junior forensic scientist. 'You mean aside from motive, hurrying away from the scene of a crime, losing CID and having been professionally trained to kill people?'

Simon held his nerve. 'Yes, ma'am.'

Sarah raised her eyebrows at Paul Mackay, who had been unusually quiet. 'Paul?'

'We managed to get our hands on Randle's military record. Shoe size matches those of the imprints left behind at Philip Gower's house. The Footwear Intelligence Agency at the FSS reckon that less than two per cent of the male population has size twelve and a half.'

Sarah stood up, her arms straight on her desk, leaning slightly forward, looking at everyone in turn. Judith watched her, sensing that Sarah revelled in the power she could convey through subtle alterations in the shape of her body. 'So this is the plan. As soon as CID locate Randle he's going to be picked up. We can only risk leaving him out there for so long. The second we take him in, I want a team of Forensics ready. We caution him, swab him and, as Bernie suggested, drag his DNA through reference samples from all five scenes. If we have an address, another team goes straight there, bags and swabs whatever it can.' Sarah glanced down at the worn grey phone on her desk. 'They are going to call it through. And then, like I said, it's action stations.' She turned her attention to Judith, and Judith felt herself blush, uncomfortable caught in the stare. 'Now, anything else, before we all tell Judith how undoubtedly beautiful her baby is?'

Leigh Harding cleared his throat. 'Just some minor bits and pieces, ma'am, that came from questioning Syed Sanghera.'

Without looking at him, Sarah said, 'Put them on the board with all the other facts that need cross-checking. The rest of you, feel free to coo away. But make it quick. We've got a killer to catch.'

The office seemed to relax as one, an exhalation of tightly held breaths, a drooping of rigid shoulders. Mina came over and kissed Judith on the cheek. Bernie stood behind her, slightly awkward, rubbing his thick beard. Mina picked Fraser's car seat up for a general inspection.

'So this is what's keeping you awake at night?' Bernie said.

Mina yawned. 'Beats trawling through endless databases,' she said, rubbing her eyes behind her glasses.

Judith smiled. 'He sleeps wonderfully during the day,' she muttered. She'd been away from GeneCrime for ten weeks, but it felt longer. She watched Leigh scrawl a few lines of text on the office whiteboard with a green pen. Simon and Paul loitered a couple of paces back, unsure of the alien object in the room. Sarah didn't come over. Judith suspected she wasn't one for babies.

'So, when are you coming back?' Simon asked.

Judith didn't answer immediately. Something that Detective Harding had written had caught her attention. Green squeaks on a white surface. Something Reuben had told her on the phone. Then her heart missed a beat, and her lungs drew in a quick breath. 'A few weeks,' she answered finally, pulling out her mobile.

Sarah seemed to hesitate, then began to walk over. At that moment the phone on her desk rang, a shrill double note. A pause, then another. Sarah swung back and picked it up. She spoke quietly, her hand cupping the receiver, her mouth invisible behind her slender fingers. Conversation in the room stopped. Everyone turned to watch Sarah.

Fraser opened his eyes and began to gripe. Judith bent down and unstrapped him. He was in a white all-in-one, and she cradled him to her with her left arm, rocking him gently.

After a couple of seconds, Sarah put down the phone. 'Right,' she said, 'they think they've spotted him. Residential area south of the river. They're going to swoop but they want us there. Go get yourselves ready. Equipment in squad cars, gloves and face masks in your pockets.' Sarah seemed to come alive, her cheeks reddening, her eyes widening, her petite frame swelling. 'No fuck-ups. Let's go and get this psycho.'

Judith stepped away from the door. A couple of CID officers almost knocked her flying. Mina winked at her on the way out. Bernie said, 'Wish us luck.'

With her right hand, and turning away from Sarah and the rest of the office, Judith used her thumb to type a rapid text message.

13

'Look, fair's fair, mate. Now, what do you want me to do?'

Reuben read the permit on the back of the driver's partition. Leonard Park. Licence number 25584. Authorized to carry up to five passengers within Greater London. He was half turned again, his thick neck creased, dark hairs trapped in the diagonal folds of his flesh.

'I've got jobs stacking up all over the place. The sat nav keeps a record of where I am. I'll be for the bloody high jump if I'm not moving soon.'

Reuben's mobile vibrated in his pocket, a faster frequency than the all-pervasive engine. But he continued to ponder, lost in contradictions and grey areas. Always grey areas. Crime was never black or white. It was opinion, circumstance, intuition, luck, guesswork. That was what had first fuelled his interest in forensics. That the science was inarguable. A positive match, a statistical value, a quantifiable absolute. What came before it, however, the tracking of criminals, the assessment of behaviour, the understanding of motives, that was all a murky grey mess. And at this frozen moment in time, he felt this more acutely than he ever had in the fifteen years of his CID career.

'I can drive you somewhere else,' the driver tried. 'Just say the word.'

Reuben straightened in his seat. He had to do something, had to fight the paralysis which had ground him to a halt. Indecision, a lack of solid information, a sense that he was on the verge of the wrong course of action. He reached his arm through the gap in the cage, squeezed the man's thick shoulder. 'You've done enough already.'

Reuben opened the door, stepped on to the street and pulled out his mobile. A text message, from Judith: *visiting genecrime with fraser. sarahs office. cant talk. have news but dont no what it means.* Reuben scrolled down. That was all.

The taxi pulled off. Leonard Park beeped his horn, and Reuben waved.

What news? He pictured Judith taking Fraser into GeneCrime to show her colleagues, that first moment, introducing the new baby, distracting the failing manhunt for half an hour. Judith in Sarah's office, overhearing something, texting him with the thumb of one hand, the other arm holding her son. He imagined Sarah, uncomfortable around the newborn, passing up the opportunity to hold him. He saw it like he was there, in the building he should still be working in, among the team he should still be commanding. Once more, he knew he had betrayed them. He had put the life of his son above everything else he held dear. He had made a series of small but critical mistakes. But under the same set of circumstances, he didn't doubt he would do it all again.

His mobile buzzed, and he opened the message almost instantly: *control engaged. amanda skeen.* He stared into the small black letters, trying them on for size. Control, Amanda Skeen. Something clicked. Scientific terminology. Judith being subtle and furtive under the nose of Sarah Hirst. Wonderful Judith, suddenly coming up with something that only she understood the relevance of.

Control.

He put the phone away. Walked down the street. Blew air into his hands, tightened his jacket against the cold. He strode slowly up to the detached house. Stopped just beside it. Silently opened the front gate. Stood outside the door for a second. Felt the squeeze of the long rows of terraces on either side. Checked again that he had understood the coded words. A deep breath. Sensing the final wrap of speed in his trouser pocket. The final burst of energy should he need it. For now, he would manage without.

A stretch of the neck. A clench of the fists. A coldness in the stomach.

Only one way to find out.

14

Reuben kicked the door in at the second try, just like he had at Riefield's flat. An unfurnished living room. Cold, unheated, his breath hanging visible in the air. The walls bare unpainted plaster. The floor unpainted wood. A shell of a space, a void, a nothingness. He spotted a letter on the floor addressed to Ms Amanda Skeen. He quickly understood. A hospital residence, and also a private one. An address CID hadn't connected him to.

Reuben strode through the room, tearing open the internal door. A second room, as cold and vacant as the first. The place had been stripped, everything laid bare. Wallpaper, carpets, curtains ripped out. A room scorched back to its bare bones. Badly painted red walls, stained wooden boards underfoot. And something in the space left behind that stopped him dead.

A wooden cot.

A small boy face down, head buried in the mattress.

Not moving.

Not moving at all.

Reuben leapt forward. A grubby strap tethered the child to one of the bars of the cot. He reached for the strap and fumbled to untie it. All the time his eyes locked on the small form in front of him. He was still wearing the brown coat, the one from the missing child posters, the one he had spilled his drink down. He touched the back of the child's head. Cold. Freezing cold. His hand recoiled from the shock. 'Joshua, Joshua, Joshua,' he said under his breath. My son. My one and only son. Nothing. No movement. Just the frozen form of a two-year-old in a stark and hostile room. Reuben shook him, repeating his name over and over again. But the child didn't budge, his face pressed into the filthy mattress.

'Oh fuck,' Reuben whispered. 'Fuck.'

As he gazed into the back of Joshua's head, he saw Lucy's face. Going over to her house, breaking the news to her. Mouthing the words.

Our child is dead.

He leaned forward to lift his son out of the cot, to pick him up, to hold him one final time. He knew this was now a crime scene, but that didn't matter any more. Human dignity was suddenly a fuck of a lot more important than preserving the evidence. Reuben hooked a hand under Joshua's cold face, and one under his legs. Again, Lucy tracked him down. The appalling and horrific descriptions he would have to give her. The ugly house in a row of terraces, the gutted rooms, the cold, the stench of shit, the sight that had greeted him. There was no way on earth that Veno was going to break this to his ex-wife. Worse even than looking into Lucy's eyes and confirming what she suspected already was the thought of an insensitive bastard like Veno knocking on her door, barging into her hallway, feeding off her reaction as he told her that Joshua was dead.

Reuben cradled his dead son in his hands, still hunched over the cot, the angle uncomfortable. His mouth suddenly bent itself into an unfamiliar shape, a tight aching in his jaw, a wetness in his eyes. Angry, desperate tears dropped on to Joshua's body. He screwed his eyes up, blinked a couple of times, and more drops tumbled down his cheeks. His breathing fragmented, just like Lucy's had been doing all along. Reuben fought it. Not here, he told himself. Not in this pit of a room.

And then he was smashed forward, his face slamming into the bars on the far side of the cot. He let go of his son, tried to regain his balance. But he was being jerked backwards, falling away, hitting the wooden floor hard. The wind was knocked out of him. Something flashed through his line of sight. Something hard and heavy crashing into his shoulder. He wiped his eyes, trying to focus. Another blow in the side. Reuben's brain fought to keep up. Three or four more seconds of rapid jolts.

Pain arrived late, in his face, his shoulder, his ribs. He had been pushed forward, pulled back, kicked on the floor. A boot stamping into his sternum. Reuben flailed his arms and legs, kicking and punching, hitting out, parrying blows. Another stamp, another kick.

He looked up, the tears drying as quick as they had come, his vision clearing. A man standing over him, lashing out, doing his best to annihilate him. This is the killer, a voice inside him screamed. Absolutely and utterly. This is the psychopath who has killed five men in the last two weeks. Held them down and hacked off their fingertips. This is the psychopath who abducted my two-year-old son and left him to die.

Reuben flipped over, jumped quickly to his feet. More brutal punches. An instant volley of attacks cutting through thoughts of Joshua. Reuben shook his head, dodged a punch, finally coming round. Dion Morgan, six two, a former rugby player, doing everything he could to overpower him. No longer a benign-looking medic. Now a beast. A livid, enraged, sadistic sociopath. A ferocious and brutal animal.

Reuben swung two punches in quick succession, the second catching Morgan hard on the jaw. He buckled for a second, took a step back. Reuben glanced round for a weapon. There was nothing. He caught sight of his son again, the air seeming to squeeze out of him. Morgan must have been upstairs, he realized. Heard the commotion and came down, catching Reuben by surprise.

Reuben forced his eyes away from Joshua. A virtually empty room. A small table cluttered with various paraphernalia. A briefcase on the floor. A portable TV on a stand in the corner. Then he turned back to face Morgan. He was breathing deep, his cheeks flushed, his teeth bared. Blood seeped out of the cut on his jaw, where Reuben had caught him. In Reuben's speeding brain all this had taken several minutes. In reality, he appreciated, it was a small number of seconds. He squeezed his fists tight, ready. And then Morgan launched himself forward.

Morgan's momentum slammed Reuben off balance. He reeled backwards, to one side of the cot. Morgan was on top of him, pushing him down. Reuben couldn't free himself. Morgan was strong, unexpectedly strong. Sixteen stones of hot-blooded psychopath. Panting hard, his body seeming to swell, pounding Reuben with punch after punch. His eyes on fire, his pupils huge, sucking it all in. Not stopping, just attacking and attacking. Reuben covered his face. A ferocious blow to the sternum. Reuben fought for air, gasping.

Then the pressure eased for a fraction. Reuben stared up. A boot, the heel slamming into his solar plexus. A huge crushing explosion in his chest. Reuben's ribcage feeling squashed. His lungs empty and useless. Gasping for breath, gulping and choking. A strangled noise in his throat.

Morgan opening his briefcase, pulling things out all over the floor. Reuben seeing the other deaths, the drawn-out sadistic ends of five men. Morgan striding quickly back to him. Reuben squinting. A slim hypodermic. A green cap protecting the fine needle. Morgan ripping it off with his teeth. Reuben understood. This was how it worked. A relaxant, a sedative, something to subdue, something GeneCrime had yet to formally identify. Something to allow him to remove all ten fingertips while the victim watched, unable to struggle but feeling every tooth of the hacksaw.

Morgan plunged the hypodermic towards Reuben's shoulder. Reuben punched at it, glancing Morgan's arm. Some of the fluid squirted out, some stabbed home, a prick just above the armpit, a cold spike. What the fuck is it? Reuben thought. What's in the syringe? Morgan ground his shoe into Reuben's neck, cutting off the air. Reuben grabbed his leg, trying to tear it off, trying to ease the pressure. He was choking, retching, still desperate for air.

As he fought, he felt himself slowly weakening. Not tiring or losing the will to struggle. Just losing his grip, his strength ebbing, his power waning. His left arm was fine. But in his right, the one that Morgan had injected, muscles were fading, sinews loosening. He concentrated with all his might, forced his fingers to grip, his arm to pull and wrench. But it was no good.

Morgan stooped down, the same crazed look in his eye. For the first time, he spoke. Reuben recognized the voice.

'That's one of them,' he said calmly. 'Let's try the other.'

And with that he stabbed the hypodermic into the top of Reuben's left arm, and emptied what remained of the fluid. Reuben knew that Morgan had injected most of it into him. Not all, but probably enough. Reuben let go of Morgan's foot. It was pointless holding on. Morgan eased the pressure and Reuben's breathing opened up again. He was panting hard, turning on his side, his left arm starting to feel limp and useless as well. Morgan walked off, out of the room.

Reuben shuffled across the floor using his feet, scraping closer to the cot, staring up. Maybe this was dignity. Dying next to the body of your only son. He realized then that no one knew where he was. No one knew about the house, otherwise CID would have checked it out. The property in the name of Amanda Skeen, the female on the trial who had committed suicide three years later. Judith's text: *control engaged. amanda skeen.* Morgan the placebo control, engaged to Amanda Skeen. And Lucy, Sarah, Mina, Moray, the people he counted on, all of them unaware of the link, and oblivious to the address.

He tried to reach for his mobile, but it was no use.

His arms had stopped cooperating. He could feel the rough wood of the floor against his knuckles, but could barely lift them. He stared around the room, desperate and afraid. He had taken on other psychopaths and won. Had faced down men who had raped and killed. And while he had been injured, shot at, stabbed, he had given as good as he had got. Reuben was not used to being overpowered, and was not used to feeling scared. He could see now that Morgan was a different breed. One of those rare people who defy normal human strength. The ones whose muscles feel like metal, whose fists feel like rocks. Powerful, frenzied, enraged. A sheer force coming at you that you couldn't defy.

His eyes flicked to the walls. At first he assumed they were just badly painted. Streaks of paint, patchy areas, an uneven flakiness. But then it hit him, and his fear stepped up a gear. Each of the four walls was covered with raw plaster. A pinky orange colour, drying out, maybe two or three weeks old. And over most of the surfaces was a layer that varied from crimson to cherry to burgundy. Daubs of red, clotted, congealed, dripping, splattered. Pushed into the corners, thin, peeling regions, darker, wetter areas. Reuben glanced up. The ceiling was the same. Five men all dead, having bled to death through amputated fingers. Men who had been involved in a clinical trial that went badly wrong. Morgan bringing a trophy home. Blood to decorate the house with. A room like a shrine. Wall to wall in the victims' blood.

The rear door swung open. Morgan was standing in the opening. In one hand he had a nail gun and two plastic bag ties. In the other, a hacksaw. Reuben's arms hung weakly by his side. He lifted them up and tried to grab the side of the cot, but they quickly fell down again. They had become fleshy appendages with no muscles or bones. No grip, no strength, no use any more.

'Oh dear,' Morgan sneered. 'Doesn't look like anyone's coming to rescue you. I guess you followed me from work, barged in all on your lonesome, couldn't help yourself. You've gone and made yourself very vulnerable, surrendered control completely.' He lifted the hacksaw, ran his eyes quickly across it. 'Right, let's get this thing finished.'

15

Reuben focused on the plastic bag ties and the nail gun. He was still fighting for air. Flattened lungs, a crushed ribcage. Coughing up blood, watching it dribble out of his mouth and on to the floor. The amphetamine in his system was doing nothing but heightening his terror. And any strength it might have given him was made irrelevant by the local effects of the muscle relaxant.

Reuben understood instantly what the nail gun was for. Morgan walked swiftly towards him. He stepped on the back of Reuben's left wrist, placed the tough plastic tie across it. Then he positioned the nail gun. With every fibre in his body Reuben tried to raise his arm and punch Morgan anywhere he could. But he couldn't. There was a little movement, but no strength. Morgan fired the gun twice in quick succession. The tie held firm. Reuben's arm was strapped tight to the floor.

Morgan reached on to the table and slid something

off it. The hacksaw. He stooped down and showed it to Reuben. The tiny razor teeth, a small row of brutal blades that would tear through almost anything. He could see now that it was a medical implement. Not the sort of tool that you kept at home, but something with cleaner lines, clinical grade steel, easy to sterilize. From the flecks of red in the crevices of each metal tooth, he suspected it still had minute fragments from previous victims on it.

'You've got to be careful with the drug,' Morgan said. 'If I inject too much, it has an anaesthetic effect. Too little and you can curl your fingers and make it difficult.' He dropped the saw on to Reuben's knuckles, bounced it up and down. Morgan stared hard into Reuben's face, watching. 'I think that's just about right though, don't you? Full sensitivity?'

Reuben grunted. He was fucked, and he knew it. Standing face to face with a psychopath was dangerous enough. But having one incapacitate you, alone, where no one could hear your life drain away, that was suicidal. The existence of his son had been everything. And that was over now too. Reuben knew that after the tips of his fingers had been removed, he would bleed slowly to death. He wondered whether there would be rats, whether his blood would make it on to one of the walls.

Although he knew there was no possibility of escape,

he had to hear the truth, had to hear Morgan tell him what he already suspected.

'I know about the drink driving,' Reuben grunted. 'That's behind this, isn't it?'

Morgan didn't answer.

'A routine DNA swab taken at the scene and the game is up. Clean record, no matching DNA, but then from out of nowhere you're no longer anonymous. There's going to be a match. What you've started, killing Carl Everitt and Ian Gillick, two of the three men you want, is now traceable. Any profile found at the scene suddenly comes back to you, where before you had no motive, no association. It's all over. So you take my son, who was treated at your hospital unit. Set Riefield up, who you still know from the trial, leave his cigarette butts at the scene. Isolate yourself again.'

Morgan stared down at him. He looked bemused. 'What, you think this matters any more? You think anything matters any more? Your last few minutes on this stinking planet and you want to get your facts straight?'

'You took my son from me. I think I deserve an explanation.'

'They took my fiancée from me. You think I got an explanation?'

'You lived here together?'

'We tried.'

392

'And then what?'

'Her family stumped up the deposit, I finished my studies, got a job. She rotted and festered. Started decorating this place, never finished it.'

'Looks like you're doing a good job yourself.'

'It's finished. Or it would have been.'

'Every one of those souls who received the Vasoprellin lost the tips of their fingers. Micro-circulatory problems. Other affected areas as well, but that was what hurt the most. That's why you've been doing this. Externalizing your hurt, inflicting what Amanda went through on the people who caused it.'

Morgan didn't say anything. He just kept staring down at Reuben, listening but not wanting to listen.

'I've been putting it all together.' Reuben flicked through everything he knew, all the evidence he had read, what Judith had said in her text. 'You must have got engaged as students. You're older. You do the trial. I bet it's your idea. You're a placebo, she gets the treatment. She doesn't die, but she has physical and mental problems. You try and make it work. You feel guilty. She's still crying in her sleep about it years later. Then she kills herself. But that's a while ago. What set you off, Dion? What put you into action?'

'Fuck you.' Morgan knelt down on the floor, one hand on the back of Reuben's hand, the other gripping the saw. He lined the blade up across Reuben's middle three

393

fingers, just below their nails. 'You think you have insight into human pain, Maitland? Well, I'm going to give you a fucking insight.'

Morgan moved the saw across, judging the line. Reuben felt the air from the blade on his finger, hairs being sliced away. Morgan met Reuben's eye. Anticipation, excitement, intent. A lust for pain staring back. Reuben was suddenly acutely scared.

'My son,' he said. 'You killed my son.'

Morgan stopped. The enormity of the words seemed to shake him.

'You fuck!' Reuben spat. It had been bottled up for days with nowhere to go. 'You fucking coward! You sad fucking bastard! You ended the life of a little boy for all this?'

Morgan smiled down at him, his face distorted into a snarl, his knee in Reuben's sternum. 'In a way that you will never understand, I suppose I did,' he said.

And then he forced the saw into Reuben's middle fingers. Pulled it back, waited a couple of seconds, ground it forward. Shredding skin, chewing flesh, snagging bone. The blade vibrated as it fought its way in, bouncing off the bone. A cold, sharp ache instantly gave way to the white light of unadulterated pain. Reuben screamed. Morgan pushed down to make a deeper cut. He was in no hurry. He gauged the next movement of the blade, lined it up, made sure he was cutting straight across all three digits. Then he yanked it back. Sharp stabs of paralysis coursed through Reuben's hand. He was shaking and sweating. His legs shook uncontrollably. He stared down. The blade was red. Morgan pushed harder still. Skin, bone, flesh, tendons and veins were all being attacked by the jagged metal teeth. There was burning in all three fingers, like Reuben was holding them in a lighter flame. Middle, index and ring fingers, just below the nail. All of them shrieking in pain. Morgan pushed the saw through, paused again, pulled it back. Slow, careful cuts. The saw was eating into the bone, gaining purchase, burying in. Reuben ground his teeth, focused on the ceiling. Another forward stroke. Reuben stared into the source of the agony. The blade covered in more red. Thick droplets of blood coating its surface. Finer sprays shooting out above and below. A back stroke that made him scream again. Nerves screeching and yelling. Pain receptors mainlining straight to his brain. Feeling sick. Choking it down, trying not to vomit. Realizing he was heading into shock. His brain wanting to shut down, isolate itself from the horror. But the speed keeping it wired, keeping the power on. Another violent and cold spark of pain. Morgan forcing the saw back. A long stroke. Each one of the army of teeth snatching more flesh, snagging at the skin. Reuben saw tiny chips of bone torn out and scattered through the surrounding flesh. He grunted, clamped his teeth even harder, tried not to cry out.

Morgan locked eyes. Reuben knew this was just the start. This would take hours. The thumb. The little finger. The same for his other hand. Bleeding slowly to death. His essence leaking and spraying from ten holes, five on either side of him.

'How's that?' Morgan asked. 'Starting to understand human pain?'

Reuben didn't respond. His gut was cramping, his stomach squeezing like it wanted to let loose.

'Daniel already understood. He lost his fingertips a long time ago. No need to show him. But just like you, Dr Maitland, he outlived the help he could give me.'

Morgan drew the saw back. Quick and hard. The movement travelled right through Reuben, through his legs, his groin, his stomach, his chest, his head. Every piece of him felt it. Raw and acute, intense, burning, crippling pain. He wondered how long he could hold on.

'You see, when you come across the same people who fucked your future over, who destroyed the one person in the world that you loved and who loved you, find they're still in the medical community, still running trials, still selling new untested drugs, just in different hospitals, what are you going to do?'

Reuben only half heard. He wondered whether Morgan had spoken to the other men he had killed. Incapacitated them and then explained in calm and rational tones exactly what he was doing to them and why. The doctor and his patient.

He thrust the saw through again. Reuben screamed. The pain just got worse. Shapes exploding behind his eyes. A roar in his chest trying to escape. Reuben counted under his breath. Telling himself if he could make it to a hundred without screaming again he would be coping. He didn't get past seven. Morgan pushed all his weight down on the blade, ripped it back through the bone. As he paused, let go of the blade, examined his handiwork, Reuben noticed that the saw was now embedded. It didn't fall over. It was inside him, a part of him, entrenched in his skeleton.

He flexed his right arm. There was some movement. Maybe more than before, but not enough. He clenched his fist as hard as he could, willing it back to life.

Morgan grinned down at him. Reuben could see it now. The face was what had confused him at the hospital. Benign, light-haired, slightly tapered ears. It wasn't a psychopath's face. But now Reuben realized it was all in the eyes. Dark green irises. The colour of bile. Small pricks of black for pupils. Sickening yellow streaks radiating out. Flecks of brown hiding in the green and yellow. Eyes that had absorbed an intensity of horror that was almost unimaginable.

'A third of the way through your first three finger-tips,' Morgan said. His voice was slow and even, barely altering in tone as he spoke. 'Soon be halfway through. But we're just beginning. How you feel now is a pleasure compared with what's to come when we hit the marrow.'

16

Reuben knew it was over. He was lost. He pictured Lucy. At some point she would be told that her ex-husband and her son were both dead. In the same room, at the hands of the same man. The physical pain was bearable for a second. The mental agony began to take over. He let his mind drift. The people he hoped would miss him. Judith. Sarah. Mina. Bernie. His old forensics team. His brother Aaron, whom he rarely saw. His ex-wife, with whom he could still only barely communicate.

And then Morgan bent closer. Ripped the saw back, tore into the bone again, attacked a fresh cluster of nerve endings. Reuben's legs shook again, uncontrollable, his heels slamming into the floor, echoing around the gutted room. More feeling returned to his right arm. He beat it into the wooden boards. Morgan grabbed the hacksaw tight. Breathed deep, let the air spill out over Reuben. A sour smell of exertion and mania. Up close, surrounding him, consuming him. A deep growl in his throat. Something primal, something animal.

And then there was another noise. Something lurking in the banging of Reuben's feet, the guttural noises Morgan was making.

Morgan hadn't heard it. He continued to move the saw, and Reuben screamed, louder than before. So loud that his lungs, which had been useless and flattened, now felt they were going to explode. Morgan fed off the screams, enjoying the sound. His tiny pupils widened, swallowing up the dull green and the sickly yellow.

'Now we're really hitting some nerves,' he said. 'This is much more like it.'

'Fuck you,' Reuben managed.

'As a paediatric haematologist, the marrow at the centre of human bones has always fascinated me. Blood cell production, what goes wrong in children with leukaemia like your son. But what I've learned recently is just how exquisitely painful it is.'

'Do your worst, Morgan,' Reuben grunted.

'Oh I will. I really will.'

Suddenly, there was another voice in the room. 'That's enough.'

Reuben couldn't see. It was not a voice he recognized. It was brutal and authoritative, not to be fucked with. Morgan froze. His knee pressed harder into Reuben's ribcage. Reuben ground his teeth, blotting out the agony of his fingers, desperate to know who was in the room.

'Get out of my house,' Morgan answered. 'Get out now.'

'I'm staying the fuck where I am.'

All Reuben wanted to know was who was standing behind Morgan. But he couldn't see. It wasn't the police. The man hadn't announced himself. The voice was calm, powerful, a frank statement of intent. Blunt words which promised action.

Morgan remained still. The other man didn't say anything. Morgan silently pressed the blade into Reuben's fingertips.

'How did you find Amanda's house?' Morgan eventually asked.

'Followed Maitland here.'

Reuben started at the mention of his name. So Morgan knew the man who was standing behind him, and the man knew Reuben. This was dangerous. Two people in the same room who could hurt him.

'Now what, Francis?' Morgan asked. He dragged the name out, pronounced it through a sneer.

Francis. Francis Randle. Reuben's mind raced. Did Francis Randle know Dion Morgan? Could they have met at the inquiry, spent time together at the court case? Morgan and Riefield had obviously known each other, so why not Morgan and Randle? Either way, Francis Randle was dangerous. The man CID had been hunting for days. Ex-services, some sort of breakdown after his son's death, now armed and highly unstable. Did Randle have something to do with Joshua's death? Had he helped? Had he carried out some of the murders? Reuben's brain sped through scenarios, trying to put it all together. Not one killer but two. Both with ample motive. An uneasy alliance. Maybe Randle supplying the rats. Morgan the paediatrician snatching Joshua.

'Stand up, nice and slowly, and let's sort this thing out between us.'

Morgan didn't budge. He just maintained the pressure on Reuben's chest, pushing his knee down, crushing Reuben into the floor.

'Why don't you just go, leave me to do what you know needs to be done. Walk away, forget the whole thing.'

'I can't forget, Dion. I can't forget at all. Now, I'm in charge, and I take things from here.'

'Don't make me fucking laugh. This isn't the army. You're not in charge of anything. You're in my house, now get the fuck out.'

Randle's voice remained calm. 'I'm going to ask you one more time.'

Reuben watched Morgan rotate his head and keep it there, staring up at Randle. 'OK,' he said, sighing so deeply that Reuben felt it through the knee that was pressing down on him. 'We'll do it your way.'

Morgan began to straighten. Reuben suddenly got a

clear view of the other man in the room. Close-cropped hair, bony cheekbones, damaged ear, broad chin with a deep cleft, the stub of a nose, dark brown eyes, irises like holes. Francis Randle. He looked wild. He gripped a pistol in front of him, arms rigid, straight at Morgan, who was now standing over Reuben.

'I still don't see what this has to do with you,' Morgan said, flexing his neck, loosening his shoulders.

Randle made no attempt to acknowledge Reuben. Reuben worked his right arm, feeling more strength return. His left continued to bleed into the floorboards, pulsing over the saw.

'This has everything to do with me,' Randle answered.

'How?'

'You know why. Enough is enough.'

There was a lull for a couple of seconds. Morgan's bulk rocked slowly back and forth. Randle remained motionless, arms out front, clenching the gun so hard his knuckles were like bones.

And then Morgan launched himself at Randle. An instant charge, letting loose his momentum, taking off through the air, like he had done to Reuben.

The amphetamine fractured time into tiny chunks. Flashes of movement. Enormous volumes of detail. Separate packets of information. Morgan tipping forward. Headlong motion. Feet leaving the floor. A neck-breaking rugby tackle. Randle barely moving.

Intense and unblinking. One of Morgan's feet brushing Reuben's head. Cold air following it. Echoes crashing off the bloody walls. Morgan slamming into Randle. Loud cracks in quick succession. Both bodies hitting the ground. Two well-built men thumping into the floor a couple of metres away. Feeling the impact through the floorboards. A hollow pop as Randle's head hit hard. A scrape of clothing. Splinters embedding. The gun flying loose. Metal skidding across wood. A moment of stillness. Reuben reaching his right arm out. Stretching for the object. Arcing his body. Walking his numb fingertips across the rough surface. Touching. Clumsily sliding the pistol closer. Grabbing it by the metal handle. Feeling the warmth. Feeling the weight. Aiming it along the floor. Trying to focus. Not knowing who to aim at. A cough, a hollow breath. The men moving. A tangle of arms and legs. A man crouching, getting to his feet. The other up. Staggering across the room. Towards Reuben. Swaying but focused. Reuben lifting the pistol. His fingers barely gripping it. Roughly aiming. Brain scrambling about. Trying to work out the last two seconds. Knowing suddenly that the man is Morgan. Feeling him get close. Intent in his eyes. The pain in Reuben's other hand. The loss of blood. The death of his son. Behind Morgan, Randle holding his head. Still crouching. Winded, concussed. Reuben knowing he only has one option. Squeezing against the trigger. The pistol feeling heavy. His arm weak and flaccid. Aiming up at Morgan. Morgan almost on top of him. Squeezing harder. The trigger tough. Made of stone. Inert and unyielding. Every ounce of concentration into his sedated arm. Useless fingers refusing to cooperate. Morgan looming. A look of intense purpose in his face. Reddened cheeks, his mouth set wide, a scream that hasn't arrived, teeth bared, pink gums showing. Reuben squeezing and squeezing. Trying to shift the aim. His arm dropping. Lifting and aiming again. Fighting the weight, fighting the drug. Years spent on ranges coming down to this. Firing a pistol with dead fingers. Forcing the trigger. Crying out. A loud crack. An instant recoil. The gun jolting. Slipping out of his fingers. Morgan still moving. Stepping over Reuben. Past him. Reaching forward. A desperate lunge for the only piece of furniture in the room. The table. Grabbing at a vase on it with both hands. Knocking packets of drugs and syringes and needles on to the floor. Time still fractured into tiny pieces. Morgan falling down. The container spilling open. Dark black powder cascading out. A fine spray of ash hanging in the air. Reuben finally understanding what the room is. A shrine, a monument to a dead fiancée. Morgan on his back. Groaning, saying something Reuben doesn't catch. Blood thickening and pooling through his shirt. Rasping for breath, a sick wheeze. Punctured lung, Reuben guesses, the hole gaping open. Randle shaking himself round. Coming over. Picking the gun up. Looking down at Reuben for the first time. An intense look. An assessment, a judgement. Staring over at Morgan, at the gun, back at Reuben. The adrenalin still spilling out. Rushing through Reuben's veins, making his breathing fast. Blood seeping out of his fingertips, quick pulses around the blade, running along, dripping off the end. Not knowing about Randle. Suddenly feeling vulnerable again. Nail-gunned to the floor, incapacitated. Morgan getting quieter, the rasps empty and thin. Randle glancing at the cot. Back at Reuben. At his fingertips, at the blood. Bending down. Placing the gun near Reuben's head. Dark eyes with black pupils. Peering into Reuben's face. A bony hardness to him. Unreadable, somewhere else, lost in something. Reuben twitching. Adrenalin and amphetamine overload. Randle taking the pistol and running it across Reuben's face, along his arm. Jabbing it against his left wrist. Pushing it hard. Reuben's understanding coming late. Forcing the barrel into the floor. Lifting it back. Popping the plastic bag tie. Freeing Reuben's arm. Helping him up.

17

Reuben held on to Francis Randle, sensing a muscular stiffness, a harsh solidity. He stared into the cot at Joshua. Still no movement. Nothing. Reuben stepped forward, yanked the saw from his fingers, blood starting to come fast. He touched his son's face. It was as cold as the room, maybe even colder.

And then there was a twitch. A flicker, an eyelid making an almost imperceptible movement. He shook his son gently. No response.

Reuben glanced down at the floor. Packets of drugs and hypodermics. He looked more closely. Pentobarbital. A barbiturate.

Reuben fumbled for his phone. He pulled it out and passed it to Randle. 'Dial nine nine nine,' he said. 'Then press the middle button at the top.' Randle silently did as he was told, then passed the mobile back. Reuben asked for an ambulance and gave them the address. He confirmed his name and the name of the patient. Morgan convulsed on the floor, a silent spasm shuddering through him. 'Better make it two ambulances,' Reuben said.

He dropped his phone into the cot and turned back to Randle. 'Help me lift my son up. I can't do it with one useless arm and one half butchered.' Reuben no longer cared about his fingertips. The pain was acute, but something stronger was washing through him. Hope.

Randle tucked the pistol into the belt of his trousers. He helped Reuben lift Joshua up out of the cot. Joshua was rigid in Reuben's arms, not moving. His lips were blue, his skin so pale the veins showed through. His tiny fingers were curled up, his fingernails transparent, the flesh below purple. Reuben just had enough strength in his right arm to cradle him close.

The room was freezing. He started to shiver, shock catching up with him. Being attacked, and shooting a man. He willed the ambulances to come, for medics to take his son and try to pull him back from the brink. He felt like running into the road and waving his arms, stopping cars, speeding things up. But he couldn't. He was in danger of sliding into shock. He needed to talk, needed to stay conscious, needed to be there for Joshua.

'Did you know Morgan, then?' Reuben asked.

'Only by name, from the trial that killed my son.'

'How did you find him?'

'I've been hunting you. Following you. Keeping an eye on you.'

Reuben suddenly remembered. The Audi A6 with the broken headlight. 'Why?'

'As soon as I read that Ian Gillick and Carl Everitt had been killed, I twigged. Something is going on here. Then I see you in the paper, the man in charge of finding the killer. I rang the police, but they weren't interested. Told them this was all about drugs, about testing, about justice. Snotty little copper cut me off.'

'So you tracked me down?'

'Easy.' Randle stroked the butt of the gun. 'Knew you'd lead me to whoever was killing the people from the trial.'

Reuben hugged Joshua tight, scared he would drop him. He leaned against the cot, waiting, yearning for the sweet sound of sirens, still not sure about Randle.

'But your son died. The men that Morgan killed were the ones responsible, the ones who instigated the trial.'

'My son died. Yours might still be alive.'

'I still don't—'

'Enough is enough. Like I said to Morgan before I shot him. I did a lot of thinking after the trial. Then the drug company finally made an offer a few months ago. Compensation. Eight grand for the life of a twenty-one-year-old boy. Eight grand. I turned it down flat. Fucking insult.'

'So why did you come after me?'

'I didn't come after you. I was keeping an eye on you. A drug trial went wrong. But that's what happens. I can see that now. I got my head around it. Accepted it. Told myself that Martin didn't die in vain. He was a hero. Taking on an enemy he could never see. And then some sick fuck starts killing. Just as I've learned to forgive, someone begins to inflict more misery.' Randle pulled the sleeve of his coat up. Reuben tried to focus on his arm, but couldn't. A bluey green shield of some sort. 'My old regiment had a motto. One in, all in. So I went out there to hunt the man who was defiling the life of my son, who was murdering in his name.'

Reuben saw another twitch in Joshua's eyelid. An overdose of pentobarbital. He slid down the bars of the cot, picked one of the packets off the floor, struggled to put it into his pocket. Something to show the medics.

'What now?' he asked Randle.

'My mission is over. I phone the cops.'

'So you just wait for them to turn up?'

'I don't really care any more. Now that sick fuck is out of the way.'

Reuben scanned the room, tried to see it like a copper would coming in for the first time. A dead doctor on the floor. An uninjured man with a gun, forensics all over the place. 'But you'll be charged.'

'Prison, whatever. It's all the same to me. Different set of rules, different enemy.'

'Pass me your gun,' Reuben said.

'What?'

'Place it in my hand.'

'Why?'

'You said you shot Morgan.'

'A couple of times, maybe, when he jumped me.'

'Well, I shot him as well.'

'So?'

'There's a big difference between you and me.'

'What?'

Reuben picked up the faint prick of a siren. 'I'm licensed to carry a firearm. I was being attacked. My son was in mortal danger.'

Randle hesitated.

'Go on, get the fuck out. Wait a few weeks, then find me. We'll talk about your son, sort out what everything means. But unless you want the next twenty years in jail, give me the gun and walk the fuck away.'

Slowly, reluctantly, Randle walked forward. He glanced at the blood on the walls, the dying man on the floor, the unconscious boy being held by his father. He stared long and hard into Reuben's eyes. As he did so, he slid the pistol into Reuben's jacket pocket. The noise of the siren was getting louder. Randle stared a second longer, taking it all in through his black irises. Then he turned and walked out.

Reuben counted to ten, propped himself upright, then

stumbled out of the freezing shrine to Amanda Skeen, with its blood-coated walls and its floor spattered with ashes. He made it through the living room and through the open front door. Outside, there was a sudden scream of rubber on tarmac. A car screeching to a halt in the middle of the street. A silver Mondeo, two aerials, extended wing mirrors. Reuben spun round. Detective Veno was jumping out, the car still moving. He sprinted forward, tearing his pepper spray from its holder.

'Put your child on the floor and step away from him!' he shouted.

'Stay away from me, Veno,' Reuben answered.

Veno levelled the pepper spray. Head height, aiming for the eyes. 'This is Child Protection protocol, Maitland. Do what the fuck I say or you're going to get hurt.'

Reuben met his eye. 'I'm armed. You come anywhere near my child and I promise I will shoot you.'

Veno stopped, unsure. Reuben watched as he noticed the blood pouring from his fingers. Veno seemed to shrink back. 'What the fuck?' he asked.

'Call for a major incident squad. Get Sarah Hirst over to the scene. You got here quick enough. Hopefully they can do the same.'

Veno didn't lower his aim. He seemed to be trying to take it all in. The unmoving child, the threat from a senior officer, the lacerated fingers. Reuben strained his eyes. Behind Veno, a long way down the street, a dark-coloured Audi was making rapid progress. And beyond that, an ambulance on a blue light was pounding towards them.

Veno finally lowered the spray. 'This is career suicide, Maitland,' he hissed.

'We're a long way past that,' Reuben said.

His arm ached from holding his son so tightly, but he wouldn't have let go for anything. 'Hang on in there, little buddy,' he said, nuzzling into Joshua's hair.

The ambulance scraped past Veno's car and pulled up. Reuben stepped towards it. Veno took out his mobile and dialled. As paramedics finally laid hands on Joshua, Reuben watched Veno, his face red, his brow knotted, his silent words angry and enraged.

18

'No, no, no, no, no, no,' Lucy said, hands in her hair, pulling hard, her mouth open. She was breathless from the stairs, her cheeks red, the rest of her face pale.

One of Veno's team, a small sympathetic female, stepped out of her way.

Lucy stopped dead in front of the tiny hospital bed. Joshua was lying on his back. Two tubes entered his body, one in the crook of his elbow, the other on the back of his hand. A plastic thimble was taped to the tip of a finger. From it, a black wire led into a small machine with the flashing digits 98 lit up in red. His body was covered in an all-in-one that Lucy didn't recognize. It was hospital blue with white bunnies on it. His face was pallid, his expression composed and still.

'No,' she whispered. 'I don't believe it.'

She hesitated for a second, then reached forward and touched his skin, kissed his face. He smelled different.

Disinfectant. Soap. Antiseptic. He didn't move, didn't respond. There were no tears. Lucy was in shock. Her son. Alive. Lying motionless in a hospital bed.

She became aware of a movement, another figure in the curtained-off section of the ward. An Asian doctor with receding hair and a shiny forehead stepped closer to her.

'We think he should be OK,' he said.

'I can't . . . I just can't . . . He looks so ill. So peaceful and so ill, almost like he's not alive.'

'He's been through a lot.' The doctor flicked through some notes, then bent down and listened to Joshua's chest with a stethoscope. 'You should have seen the man who brought him in.'

'My husband. My ex. Well, you know, my husband.'

The doctor was quiet, undoing a button, sliding the end of the stethoscope over Joshua's anaemic skin.

'Look, how sure are you that my son will be all right?' There was still panic in her voice, a sense that Joshua was not out of danger yet. 'What are the odds?'

The doctor straightened, pulled the twin arms of his stethoscope out of his ears, let the device droop around his neck like a short scarf. 'He's had an overdose of barbiturates. Probably several days of heavy sedation from what we've been able to put together since he came in. He might sleep for another day or so. But the preliminary blood tests are OK. Slightly low red cell count—'

'He's in remission,' Lucy interrupted, her hands wrapped around each other, not knowing what to do with them. 'Acute lymphocytic leukaemia.'

'So that's to be expected. His core body temperature was low when he was admitted but it's in the normal range now.'

'Thank Christ,' Lucy whispered. 'I still can't believe it.' She glanced at the Missing Child officer, who smiled back. 'I really can't. This is the best thing. The worst thing and the best thing.' And then Lucy began to cry. Holding on to the side of the bed and weeping. Large fat tears falling from her eyes. Quiet beads of desperate relief.

The officer placed her arm around Lucy's shoulders. 'It's OK,' she whispered. 'It's OK.'

Lucy didn't fight the tears. She just let them seep out of her, taking with them the agony of the last five days. It had started with a children's hospital and ended with one. Through the wet blur of her vision she focused on her son. In Joshua's features she could see Reuben. His eyes, his ears, his nose, his mouth, budding through in small fragments. Joshua was nearly two, his facial characteristics starting to set. She had never really seen herself in him, only her ex-husband. She realized in that moment that every single day she looked at her son from now on she would think of Reuben.

She wondered how he was. He had phoned some time after he arrived. He'd sounded weak, drifting in and out.

He hadn't said much. Just the small number of words that Lucy would remember for ever: 'I have our boy. I think he's going to be OK.'

Detective Veno had called her a few minutes later. He had filled her in, given her the details of the hospital, which ward, which room, what to expect. Veno had been gruff, disappointed even, put out that he hadn't found Joshua himself. Police envy. Lucy had raced over, screeching through the traffic, no seatbelt, leaning forward into the wheel, willing herself closer. From what she could gather, Reuben had brought Joshua in, then collapsed. He'd come round again, then phoned her.

Lucy ran an index finger under her eyes, feeling the cold wetness on her cheeks. She imagined her make-up had run along with her tears, streaking her skin. But she didn't care. In front of her was everything that mattered.

The doctor patted her on the shoulder. 'There's nothing you can do for him at the moment,' he said. 'But when he wakes up, he's going to want to see your face.'

Lucy dabbed at her eyes with the sleeve of her top. Black smudges stained the white cotton. 'Not like this, he isn't,' she answered.

'Either way, in this instance I think it's vitally important.'

'Will you stay here?' the officer asked, her arm still round Lucy's shoulder.

'Try getting me to leave him again,' Lucy said.

The doctor left, and Lucy sat down in a chair next to Joshua's bed, gazing into his unmoving face. It was hypnotic, the peaceful sight of her son finally lying next to her. She wondered again how Reuben was, whether he would be strong enough to come up to the children's section. He was in a ward in the general admissions unit, a separate building she would have to walk to. She'd heard he had lost a lot of blood, injured his hand badly. He was scheduled for surgery as soon as they could fit him in. Whatever the extent of his injuries, however, Lucy suspected that nothing would keep him away. For the time being, though, she wasn't leaving Joshua.

19

Reuben sat in his office chair, his desk empty, his computer missing, sheets of paper lying at various angles on the floor. Everything was exactly as he had left it before he was escorted from the building four days earlier. In the middle of his desk, the cactus acted as if nothing had ever happened. Impervious, unmoved, unwavering in its existence. Standing upright and proud, doing nothing more than simply living.

Reuben studied it for a moment. For reasons he couldn't immediately understand, he was still drawn to it. He reached forward and gripped the body of the cactus with his heavily bandaged left hand. As he squeezed, he sensed the tightness of the stitches, the restraint of the dressing beneath the bandage. This time there was no pain from the plant, the padding too thick for its spines to reach his flesh. Reuben pressed harder, then released his grip. A few spikes detached, embedding themselves in the gauze, hanging limp and useless. Reuben suddenly felt immune from pain, his son safe, the killer taken care of.

The square grey phone on Reuben's desk rang, long shrill notes, an internal call. He picked it up with his right.

'I'm ready now,' Sarah Hirst said. 'My office, straight away.'

Reuben dropped the receiver. He stood up and stretched, a yawn washing through him as he extended his arms. He had done nothing but sleep for the best part of two days. Reuben checked the adjacent windows that cut into Gross Forensics and the DNA lab. In each room, scientists and technicians silently went about their business. He watched Mina for a second, handing a memory stick to Bernie, saying something inaudible. He wondered whether they were still tying up all the DNA samples from the fingertip killer. Matching Dion Morgan to the scenes, seeing how many hits they could get. Everyone seemed more relaxed. Paul Mackay was whistling, Simon Jankowski tapping something into his mobile phone. At this stage it was all about corroboration. There was no panic any more. Just building and building, layer upon layer, constructing the forensic case against Morgan until it was impregnable. Unseen behind the one-way glass, Reuben smiled at his team. He had betrayed them for reasons he couldn't change, but still they had come through and nailed the forensics, tied one man to the deaths of five others.

As Reuben sauntered slowly towards Sarah's office, he wondered whether he would ever see his team again. He was in no rush. Bollockings weren't something he believed in hurrying. Let Sarah rehearse her words, try them on for size, practise her counter-arguments. Make sure she was prepared, already in charge of the proceedings before he even entered the room. It was the way Sarah ticked, the way she had always ticked.

Reuben used his right hand to knock on Sarah's door. As he walked in, he saw the office afresh, different to the way it had been a few nights back when he had rifled through her evidence file. A clock, no second hand. Five chairs, only two free from plant pots, a terminal rest home for dying foliage. And Sarah, upright behind her desk, a white blouse, pinned-back hair, arms resting in front of her, a thick brown folder between them. She smiled briefly at him, pointed with her eyes to a seat.

'So,' she said. 'Thank you for coming in.'

'I haven't got a lot else to do,' Reuben answered.

'How are the fingers?'

'Sore.'

'They going to be OK?'

'I don't think I'll be playing the piano for a while.'

Reuben watched Sarah shuffle in her chair, drum her fingers on the file. He could almost read the words in her mind. *Enough of the small talk.*

'Look, I might as well tell you straight away. You have really fucked up this time, Reuben.'

'Tell me something I don't know.'

She stared at him, her eyebrows slightly raised, the rest of her expression unreadable. 'But there's also no escaping the fact that you found Morgan. Other people could have died by now. No one else had made the link. Then again, no one else possibly could. You never mentioned the small fact that the killer we were chasing was also the man who had taken your son.'

'I know. And I'm genuinely sorry.' Reuben didn't meet her eye. 'That's something I think I will always regret.'

'So why did you do it? Why didn't you tell us?'

'When a psychopath is holding your only child, maybe you don't think as rationally as you might otherwise do. And when he's asking you simply to divert the case temporarily, well, I did the only thing that felt right at the time.'

'You've always preached total honesty, Reuben. What happened to that?'

'The screams of my son happened to that.'

Sarah sighed, running a fine finger along the line of her eyebrow. It was something she often did when she was caught for something to say.

A few long moments of silence. The minute hand of the clock jerked on to its next resting place.

'OK,' Reuben said, 'I've been a bad boy and I'll happily

take my punishment. But while I've been asleep for the last couple of days, what have you learned about the case? Is it sorted? Do we know everything we need to know?'

Sarah opened the thick brown folder. 'We never know everything, Reuben. We might think we do, but until we find a way of stepping inside the killer's body, I'm afraid most of it is guesswork and supposition. And when the killer is himself killed, well . . .'

Reuben was suddenly impatient, wanting to know. 'So?'

'This is what we've been able to put together. Dion Morgan and Amanda Skeen were promising medical students. He was a couple of years older, and infatuated. They got engaged but couldn't afford to marry. The university hospital had a clinical trials unit, and Morgan spotted an easy way to get some cash for them to be married. He persuaded Amanda to sign up for the trial of . . .' Sarah flicked through a couple of pieces of paper. 'Vasoprellin. But the drug trial, as we know, went wrong. Amanda was left with physical and patho-psychological problems, it says here. Morgan was one of the placebos, so he got off scot-free.'

'The control treatment,' Reuben said quietly to himself, remembering Judith's text message.

'They don't marry but eventually buy a house together in Amanda's name. Hence we didn't trace it as a property associated with Morgan. Meanwhile Amanda becomes bitter and ill, and the relationship flounders. Even if she hadn't killed herself, she would have had a highly increased chance of future vascular illnesses – a life sentence, like the other trialists. However, we still don't understand precisely what kick-started Morgan's attacks, what set them off.'

Reuben rubbed his eyes. He was still tired, an amphetamine hangover of epic proportions. But he needed to put everything together. 'Morgan said something to me about coming across the people who had run the trial. Medics, administrators, drug reps still in the clinical trials business, who had just moved on with their lives, swapping one institution for another, still testing new drugs out on hard-up patients.'

Sarah nodded. 'And there's this as well,' she said, sliding a photocopied newspaper article across her desk.

Reuben scanned it. A quarter-page article from a broadsheet. Something in it resonated with what Francis Randle had told him. The victims and families had been offered just £8,000 in compensation after the manufacturer of Vasoprellin went bust, its investors dumping their shares, scared of huge lawsuits.

'So as far as we can surmise, Morgan's fiancée commits suicide, her family get offered a paltry eight grand, and in his medical capacity Morgan starts bumping into the men who have effectively killed his fiancée.'

'I guess he must have started planning,' Reuben said.

'But then after two of the three people he really wants to kill – Ian Gillick and Carl Everitt – it all goes wrong. He gets stopped for probable drink driving, automatically gets a swab taken, one which is rapidly heading for the National DNA Database. He can't just go ahead and kill Philip Gower, and he can't just stop. He knows the power of forensics. Even being careful he will have contaminated the scenes of Everitt and Gillick.'

'And then he has the good fortune to see you in the papers, to read that your son is being treated in the hospital he works in. From there it's easy. Follows Lucy, snatches Joshua, leaves Riefield's DNA at the scene. He knows you have the forensic authority to erase any evidence of the murders, given that you're in charge of the case. Even has your contact numbers from Joshua's hospital records.'

Reuben sat perfectly still, thinking it all through. He blinked rapidly, flashbacks of the last week of his life, trying to blot out the image of Morgan crouching over him, gripping the hacksaw tight, ripping it through his fingertips.

Sarah interrupted his line of thought. 'You OK?'

'Fine,' he said.

'You know, Commander Thorner and I have had three very long and very intense meetings about you over the weekend. To be frank, Reuben, I'm sick of hearing your name. Especially when I should be relaxing and putting my feet up.'

'I can't imagine you ever relax, Sarah.'

'The outcome is, we've decided we're not going to officially reprimand you. Yet.'

'No?' Reuben was genuinely surprised.

'But we are going to suspend you from duty. Sick leave. Injured in the line of duty.'

'How long?'

'Until further notice. Or . . .' Sarah looked at him and smiled.

'Or what?'

'Until we need you again.'

Reuben stood up. He stretched, the fingertips of his left hand throbbing once more. 'Thanks,' he said.

'And let me give you some advice. Think long and hard about what happened a few days ago in that house. About who shot who. About who was in the room. About where the gun came from. Guys here in Gross Forensics are going to be examining the bullet fragments retrieved from Dion Morgan. They're going to want to match them to a weapon. They're going to want to find out where that weapon came from.'

'Are you asking me to destroy evidence related to an official inquiry, DCI Hirst?'

Sarah flashed him a second quick smile. Reuben felt privileged. 'Take some time off, Reuben. You're going to need it for what's heading your way.'

20

Reuben closed the front door behind him. Two press photographers had taken his picture as he crossed the small strip of grass in front of Lucy's house. He blinked in the hallway, the flashes staying with him.

He called Lucy's name. There was an echo, the house sounding empty. No Veno, none of his squad lounging around, soaking up the noise. He heard a shout from upstairs. He stood quietly for a second, his eyes still adjusting. He saw the small mirror he had mounted, the radiator cover he had screwed to the wall, the floor tiles he had fixed and polished. His superficial stamps on a house he no longer lived in.

There was movement above, Lucy coming into view as she thumped down the stairs. She squeezed past Reuben, pulled out a bunch of keys, rattled them in the door, rotating the keys twice, double-locking it.

'We're upstairs,' she said, turning and heading back the way she had come.

Reuben waited a moment, then followed her up. They were in Lucy's bedroom, the room that Reuben used to call his own. The room where he had once found evidence that Lucy was sleeping with another man. He glanced at the bed, then quickly away. The taking of their son had momentarily brought them closer together, finding solace and support in each other, sticking together while the world went mad around them. Now, Reuben wasn't so sure. A crisis changes things. But when the crisis is over, what then?

Lucy was in the middle of folding clothes. She had obviously been busy, catching up with household chores that had come to a grinding halt for a week. She no longer looked tired. There was a swiftness about her movements that spoke of freedom and relief. Joshua was standing against the bed, running a pair of plastic cars over the duvet, crashing them repeatedly into each other. He had been quiet since his release from hospital. Not his usual frantic, dizzying self, dashing around full of energy, alive with every new sensation and experience available to him.

Reuben walked over and kissed the top of his head. 'How are you doing, little fella?'

Joshua didn't say anything. He was absorbed in his game, quietly getting on with it.

'They're amazing,' Reuben said to Lucy. 'Children. To see him standing up, playing . . .' He stopped. He hadn't fully got over the feeling that his son was dead. Reuben still felt that at any moment he would wake from the surgery on his fingers, come round from the anaesthetic, with a sick feeling in the pit of his stomach, and be told that his son hadn't made it. Seeing him face down on the filthy mattress, paralysed by barbiturates, his breathing so shallow Reuben couldn't feel it, his skin so cold that Reuben had assumed the worst. He needed to compartmentalize it all, store it away out of sight, like he did with all the atrocity and depravity he came across. But he knew it wasn't going to be so easy this time. Morgan's shrine to his dead fiancée tracked him down again, tugging at him, infecting him with images that he was struggling to repress.

'So what did Sarah have to say?' Lucy asked, cutting into the hours he had spent in that horrific room with its blood-painted walls.

Reuben looked over at her. She was perched on the edge of the bed, a few crumpled clothes on her left, a pile of folded ones on her right. 'Not much,' he answered.

'Come on, she must have said something.'

'Mild bollocking. Suspended until further notice.'

'Could have been worse.'

'I'm surprised it isn't.'

'Why the leniency? It's not like her.'

'The sad thing is, I think it comes down to PR. I catch the man who has killed five people in the capital, and who has snatched my son. CID don't want to be seen to publicly sack me.'

'The hero saves the day.'

'I'm no hero, Lucy. Most of what I did was wrong.'

'Well, you are to me. And you are to that little boy there.'

'Just as long as you never tell him that. I don't want him ever to know what happened to him.' Reuben bent down and picked his son up. Joshua continued to crash the plastic cars into each other. To have him moving, alive, fidgeting in his arms was the best feeling he could imagine. 'And I don't want him to look up to his dad. I just want him to live his own life.' Reuben kissed him again, nuzzling himself against his son's soft and warm skin.

Lucy folded the last item, a tiny red T-shirt with the words I Do My Own Stunts printed on the front. 'While Joshua was missing I couldn't bear to wash clothes that smelled of him and might never be worn again.' She stood up, placed the pile of folded items into a plastic basket and carried it over to Reuben. 'So what now, Dr Maitland?'

'I wish I could tell you.'

Lucy stepped past him and opened the top drawer of an Ikea set that Reuben remembered battling to construct two years earlier. She pulled out a thick white A4 envelope, the crest of her law firm embossed in the top right corner. 'I finally had some divorce papers drawn up.'

She handed the package to him. He juggled Joshua round, took the envelope with his good hand. He didn't open it, just felt the weight, the mass of paper inside, the gravity of the clauses and sub-clauses, the implications for his life and for his son's.

'You don't have to read them now,' Lucy said. 'But I want you to sign them.'

Reuben felt a kick high in the stomach, like he was winded. He gripped Joshua tight, afraid that if he let him go he would disappear for ever. A Sunday dad, a part-time father, sliding gradually and inexorably out of view. 'Really?' he asked.

'I've been thinking all the time Joshua was missing.'

'And?'

'I want us to get divorced.'

'Right.'

Lucy fixed her brown eyes on him. There was light in them, a radiance that had edged further and further back inside her over the last seven days. 'And then I want us to start again. From scratch. Two individuals, the future ahead of us, nothing in our past that can ever hurt us or keep us.'

Reuben leaned forward and kissed her.

'Stop interrupting me,' Lucy said, pulling back. 'I'm trying to tell you something important.'

Reuben kissed her again, hard on the mouth. Joshua placed a chubby arm around his mother, a car still gripped tight in his hand.

'And so am I,' Reuben whispered.